FOOL ME TWICE

COURT OF PAIN
BOOK TWO

ARIANA NASH

Fool Me Twice, Court of Pain #2

Ariana Nash - *Dark Fantasy Author*

Subscribe to Ariana's mailing list & get the exclusive story 'Sealed with a Kiss' free.

Join the Ariana Nash Facebook group for all the news, as it happens.

Copyright © June 2023 Ariana Nash

Edited by No Stone Unturned / Proofreader Jennifer Griffin

Cover design by Ariana Nash

Version 1 - June 2023

www.ariananashbooks.com

Court of Pain is a dual point of view, dark MM fantasy duology brimming with courtly spice, morally ambiguous characters, and the fool who plays them all.

This is a dark world with adult content. For content warnings, please see the author's website.

COURT OF PAIN #2

FOOL ME TWICE

ARIANA NASH

BLURB

Fool Me Twice
Court of Pain #2

They say in the darkest of times, the brightest star has no
choice but to shine.

I'm no star, nor am I a hero. But I could be the villain. To
protect Arin from Razak's scheming, I'll have to be.

He's my shaft of sunlight through the storm, my hope in the
darkest of times, but Prince Arin is also my weakness. And
Razak knows it.

The shatterlands are under threat, the crowns are missing,
and as the pieces of Razak's puzzle begin to fall into place, its
picture becomes clear.

It was never about the crowns, or the courts.

It was never about vengeance, or spite.

It was always about love.

And Razak will not stop until he's destroyed mine, and all the shatterlands with it.

The Court of Pain is a dual point of view, dark MM fantasy duology brimming with courtly spice, morally ambiguous characters, and the fool who plays them all.
This is a dark world with adult content. For content warnings, please see the author's website.

CHAPTER 1

*A*rin

THE SANDSTORM RAGED. Sand spilled into my every gasp, clogging my nose and burning my throat. Draven's broad arms crushed me to Lark. "Hold on!" he yelled, but even with his face pressed close, the vicious wind tore his shout away.

Lark's breaths rasped my cheek, his lips rough with sand.

My whole world, my every thought, every muscle, became an anchor. *Hold on. Just hold on.* If I let go, I'd lose them both, and this storm could not have them. I clung to Lark, fearful should I weaken, he'd be torn from me.

Louder, the storm churned. Its fury tried to split the world asunder. I screamed too, screamed back at it and clung to the two most important people left in my life.

"Nothing lasts forever," Lark hissed into my ear, like a prayer or a dream. My Prince of Storms.

All we had to do was fight and breathe and live.

And then, breath by breath, the buffeting eased and the storm's fury ebbed away.

"Arin." Draven pulled on my arm, hefting me from the sand. I coughed and heaved, shaking dust from my hair. My eyes burned, streaming. All around, great banks of sand rose up, turning the world red.

Against the odds, I was alive. "Lark?" I scanned the desolate view. "Where's Lark?"

"Here." He waded over a dune, coughing. His dark hair had turned auburn and his face dusty, but his eyes shone, even with caked lashes.

"Are you all right?"

Lark nodded and gave his shirt a shake. "I have sand where sand has no right to be. You?"

"We must move." Draven turned his head toward the mighty walls surrounding the Court of War. "They'll come."

Ogden would send his warriors for us. The King of War believed we'd conspired *with* Razak. We couldn't stay here and couldn't go back there.

The wind still howled nearby, and the desert still churned, but the worst of the storm had passed, leaving the night skies clear. Where those stars sparkled had to be our destination.

"Where's the road?" I asked.

"Buried." Draven started forward. His boots sank, but he waded on, pushing through the sand as though pushing through water. "We'll head to Palmyra."

Palmyra? "Which way is that?"

"Follow the stars," he said, stomping on.

Lark's wan smile tucked into his cheek. He ruffled his hair, shaking sand free, turning his careless locks back to black. "As certain death awaits behind War's doors, it would appear we have no choice."

The representatives of Justice had only made it a few

steps outside of War's gates before Ogden had turned on us. And all we'd tried to do was stop Justice taking Razak back to their court—where he'd planned to be. But nobody had cared to listen.

I worked grit from around my tongue and spat, already hating the desert.

"Hurry," Draven barked. "If we don't find shelter by sunup, the heat will kill us."

Lark frowned after him. "Doesn't mince his words, does he?" He followed the divots left by Draven's boots, but I hung back a few moments and watched them move off. Under starlight, the dunes looked like frozen waves. We walked into a land of nothingness. And we *had* nothing. No aides, no supplies, no water.

Draven had saved me when my court had burned, and here he was, saving me again, always moving forward. He knew what to do, where to go, how to survive out here. We would be all right.

I pushed on. Sand shifted and washed away underfoot, making the going slow. Every step dragged. We walked until my thighs ached and sweat burned my skin. The storm had long passed, but a glance behind revealed War's enormous pyramid jutting toward the starlit horizon, still too close.

The breeze had turned cold now too. I hugged myself and jogged up alongside Lark.

His and Draven's long-legged strides outpaced mine. Draven, though, was some distance ahead, clearly accustomed to the climate.

Lark stumbled, and I caught his arm. "Are you sure you're all right?"

"Yes," he grumbled. "This sand—it's like walking in syrup."

He *was* struggling. We both were. But Lark had recently

recovered from poisoning. He shouldn't be out here; he should have been resting. "Shall I ask Draven to slow?"

"And have us die once the sun comes up? I don't need your death on my conscience too." Lark shook my hand free and stumbled on. "He said they'd do this—said War would turn on me. He told me to leave. He knew. He knew all of it."

"Who did?"

Lark's sharp, sideways glance said enough. *Razak.* "He's always right," he snarled.

I wasn't sure what to say, or where to begin. I knew so little of his past, and the small amount I did know was terrible. Razak, the Prince of Pain, was Lark's brother. I had no siblings, didn't know how brothers behaved, but he and Razak had seemed close at the joining celebration, even smiling and leaning toward each other, enjoying their private conversation. Having *fun* while Razak believed Lark had poisoned all the people around them. Clearly, Razak enjoyed watching other's squirm for him. Lark had been his prisoner for years.

Razak was... I didn't have the words to describe the kind of man he was. Had I not met him, not witnessed everything he was capable of, not been his victim, I couldn't imagine the monster he was. But I had met him. He'd murdered a friend in front of me, he'd threatened my life, and then he'd burned my court to ash, almost killing me in the process. But Lark had suffered worse. His whole life, he'd been trapped under Razak's affections.

Anything I could say to Lark seemed trivial in the face of all that. Words wouldn't fix any of it. So I waded on, shivering, aching, hurting for the both of us.

Draven stopped at a rocky outcrop, staring off into the distance. The wind teased his shoulder-length hair back, and the rising moon painted his dark face milky white. The desert warlord belonged among these dunes. This was his land, his people. I'd only just begun to understand what that meant.

Lark slumped on a rock behind Draven, buried his face in his hands, and sighed.

"He all right?" Draven grumbled, noting Lark's earlier stumbling.

Lark huffed a laugh and swept his hair back from his face. "Just fine, thank you."

I conveyed my concern to Draven in a frown, without Lark seeing. "Is it much farther?"

"Don't know."

Panic flipped my heart. "Don't you know where we're going?"

"I do, but I don't walk it. Nobody *walks* it."

I joined Draven near the edge of the outcrop. The land spreading toward the horizon might as well have been a dreamscape. Rocks pierced the sand in places, like enormous swords. The winds were visible where they brushed waves over dunes. But there was *nothing* out there. No sign of life at all. "If you don't walk it, how do you move around?"

"Kareels, mostly."

"What's a kareel?"

"Like a horse," Lark said from his rocky seat behind us. "But dumber."

Draven frowned. "They're desert creatures, perfect for crossing the sand." He spread his hands. "Wide feet, so they don't sink."

"Maybe we should ride you." Lark snickered.

I smiled at the joke, then caught Draven's scowl and coughed the grin away. Obviously, this was not the time for jesting.

Impatience and a withering tiredness made Draven's gaze cool. "If we don't find shelter, we'll die."

"Yes, you said that already." Lark pushed to his feet. "Come along then," he said in a sing-song voice. He sauntered from the outcrop and skidded down a dune, then stumbled at the bottom of the sand bowl.

Draven folded his arms, unimpressed. "We should walk along the tops of the dunes. Conserves energy."

Lark took a few more lumbering steps up the dune and fell onto his hands and knees. He pushed up. "I'm fine!" He didn't sound fine; he sounded furious.

"You could have mentioned walking the tops of the dunes earlier," I said.

"Yeah, but then I wouldn't get to see him stumble about like a drunk." He smirked, watching Lark try and climb the opposite dune.

"It's not amusing. He's still weak."

Draven's mood darkened. "His actions led to hundreds of deaths and the destruction of your home. He can suffer a little sand."

Lark *had* suffered. Scars mottled his body, but most of his scars were deeper, hidden in his eyes, visible only when he thought nobody was watching. "Draven, he's paid, many times over."

"He lost a finger," he grunted. "How does that in any way make up for it?"

"He's lost more than that." I wasn't going to be drawn into an argument and started down the dune after Lark, hearing Draven skidding behind me.

Draven didn't know Lark like I did—I was beginning to suspect nobody did—and I only knew Lark because he'd shown me tiny pieces of himself, the smallest hints of his truth, hidden under all the lies, the acts, the drama. I'd slowly, carefully, put all those pieces together. He cared. I knew his heart, despite him guarding it so fiercely it sometimes appeared as though he didn't have one.

"Are we going to survive this?" I asked Draven, lowering my voice so Lark, several paces ahead, didn't hear.

Draven caught my hand and drew me to a halt. "Arin, I won't let anything happen to you. We'll survive, or I wouldn't have brought you this way. We could have done with some water, and supplies, and—"

"—a kareel, apparently."

His smile cracked dried sand from his cheek. "Trust me?"

"I do." But I was afraid and didn't want him or Lark seeing it. I was supposed to be the one who never gave up on hope, the Prince of Love! All I'd been lately was the Prince of Failure.

I'd planned to assassinate Razak and had failed, making everything *worse*. Before that, I'd plotted for years to weed Razak's influence out of my court and failed there too.

Draven squeezed my fingers, trying to convey how he'd keep me safe, but if it hadn't been for me, he'd still have a home, a court. He'd lost everything too, because I'd dragged him into my pursuit of vengeance on Razak.

The soft understanding on his face turned my insides. He was a good man, and I'd ruined him, like I'd ruined my court.

I tugged my hand from Draven's and marched up the dune to Lark, already waiting at the top, breathing hard. "Take a moment," I told him.

"You don't need to slow for me. Draven's right, we must keep moving." Lark heaved himself onward, deliberately outpacing me again until I marched alone, stranded between him and Draven.

Although, Draven soon caught up. "He's angry," he muttered, with Lark far ahead of us.

"He's angry Razak won."

"But he didn't win," Draven replied, expression muddled. "Razak didn't get the crown. And he's still behind bars. He's still a prisoner."

"Exactly where he wants to be," I said, echoing Lark's words.

I knew Lark was furious, because that fury lived in me too. Razak had slipped through our fingers. But it was more than that. It was personal, because I'd vowed to save Lark, and Razak had taken him, hurt him, cut another finger off, choked him, and worse, considering the pale scar on his wrist. I should have stopped it. I hadn't then, but I would now. I'd keep Lark safe. We were together now, and I'd keep him at my side. Razak couldn't have him back, ever.

"Is he going in the right direction?" I nodded toward Lark striding across the top of a dune.

Draven's hand settled on my shoulder, stopping my progress, and he pointed ahead of Lark, at the stars in the sky. "You see those three stars there, just above Lark?"

I saw a whole lot of stars above Lark. "There's many."

He leaned closer, and his warmth chased the desert cold away. "The three making up a pyramid?"

I rested against his arm, shivers subsiding. Three stars in a row winked above Lark. "Oh, I see them."

"If we track under them, before they dip below the horizon, we should arrive by morning."

"Arrive where exactly?"

"A trading camp, you'll see."

"And then what? What do we do then?" I turned my head and found his face intimately close. His dark eyes widened, pupils filling, absorbing starlight. We were as close now as we'd been in his bed—how many nights had it been since we'd lain together? It felt like days, months even. So much had changed. I'd been angry at Lark, afraid, and hurt by the news he was Razak's brother. Draven had been there and willing, and... It had been right at the time, but now I wasn't sure.

Draven reached for my face.

I stepped away and cleared sand from my throat. "We should keep moving."

Lark's silhouette took a chunk out of the night sky atop a dune ahead. He stood still, but I couldn't tell if he faced away, or if he'd just seen me with Draven. Not that it should matter if Draven and I stood too close.

I waded on; I didn't dare glance back to see the hurt on Draven's face. This was difficult. He and I were joined, and that meant something, although it had been a ruse to begin with. We'd both said the words, tied the ribbon around our wrists. I'd told Draven we had a future, and at the time, I'd meant it. Now? Everything was a muddle.

Lark had agreed what we'd had was nothing, so at most, Lark and I were friends. And that would have to be enough. I couldn't stop caring about him. I'd always cared, even when I'd spent years behind a door pretending not to. But if he wanted a friend, and nothing more, I'd be that friend. Considering everything Razak had inflicted upon him and the things Razak had demanded he do to undermine the courts, if Lark never wanted to be touched again, I'd understand that too.

"Lark, we must follow those three stars," I said, coming up behind him.

"Shh." He waved me back. "Something's out there."

I peered into the gloom, searching for something out of place, but saw only sand dunes swept between jagged rocks. It was the same landscape we'd been traipsing through all night. The wind hissed, but nothing moved.

"There." Lark pointed and it took a little while to focus on a patch of sand at the bottom of the dunes. It appeared to be moving, as though stirred from below. "You see it? What is that?"

It didn't appear to be much. A dust devil? "Probably the wind."

The stirring motion swelled, and sand spiraled like water down a drain. The hair on the back of my neck prickled and the chill that had wrapped around me for hours tightened its hold. The spiraling widened, and the ground beneath our boots trembled, then shifted, slipping forward.

Lark reached for me, the dune shifted, and we both dropped.

"Draven!" I twisted, Lark's hand in mine, and grabbed hold of Draven's already-reaching fingers. He heaved, dragging us against a sudden river of earth gushing below our feet, until finding solid rock underfoot.

All around the sand flowed like water, pouring downward, into a widening vortex.

Draven grabbed me around the waist and shoved me away. "Go!" He shoved Lark toward me. But behind Draven—rising up like one of the rocky monuments come to life—a vast beast towered. Sand waterfalled off its bulk, obscuring whatever features it had. Maybe it was the desert itself, come alive to devour us.

"By Dallin." It was huge, the size of a house, or bigger.

A pair of jaws opened, revealing rows of triangular teeth and a gullet that would swallow all three of us whole. "Draven! Look out!"

Draven spun with his daggers out, as though he meant to attack, but when he saw it, he froze. He didn't lunge, or flee. Just... *looked*.

"Go!" Lark grabbed me, spun me around, and pushed. "Go, go!"

I dug my heels in. "But Draven—"

"If he wants to dance with it, let him!"

"He'll die!"

Draven still wasn't moving. He stood with his back to us, and the beast kept on rising out of the sand, growing larger and larger with every passing moment.

"Draven!?" I took a step closer.

"Don't," Lark warned. "You'll die with him."

"We can't leave!"

Lark's pained expression fell. In a single, swift turn, he bolted back toward Draven, toward the beast.

They were both idiots. They'd die, and for what?

Draven stared and the sand spun around him, like it had in the storm. But now there truly was a beast at its heart. The creature reached its full height and tilted forward, about to dive and consume them both. "Hurry!"

Lark skidded to Draven's side, grabbed his arm, and attempted to pull him out of whatever madness had gripped him. But Draven didn't move. Had he lost his mind?

Lark grabbed Draven by the neck, but instead of hauling him out of there, he said something into his ear while the raging wind and sand whipped their clothes and hair about them.

Draven broke from his statuesque state and they bolted toward me. We ran—all three of us together. The beast slammed down so close the ground lifted. Lark stumbled, Draven grabbed his arm, and we ran on. Sand burned my throat and eyes. I glanced back, and there it was, a mountain of heaving muscle and hideous reaching appendages.

"It's coming!"

"The rocks, go!" Draven yelled.

A huge, jagged spur of rocks jutted ahead.

The ground trembled and the mountainous creature thundered closer. I didn't dare look again—could only run. Lark reached the rocks first and vanished inside a cave's mouth. I skidded in after him and spun. The beast surged toward Draven, its vast mouth open, gulping sand, dwarfing him. Fear iced my skin. He wasn't going to make it.

"Draven!"

He sprinted, daggers flashing in his hands, face locked in desperation.

It was gaining on him. Growing larger with his every stride.

Dunes collapsed around Draven. Wind gusted from behind us, dragging more sand with it, obscuring Draven. And then, for a horrible moment, there was nothing to see, just the red storm and nothing of Draven. My heart seized. I couldn't lose him too. Not like this.

Draven lurched from the maelstrom and plunged toward the back of the cave. Lark and I retreated too, and the beast slammed down, shaking the rocks, the ground, the air, everything. But as quickly as it had come, the rumbling ceased, the winds dropped, and sand rained back down, settling in moments.

I blinked grit from my eyes.

All was still, outside the cave and in.

Lark lay on the cave floor to my left, Draven my right, both panting, painted red with sand, but safe.

"What by Dallin were you thinking?!" I snapped, unsure who I was mad at more: Draven for thinking he could stop an angry mountain or Lark for going back for him.

Lark caught my eye, and mischief sparkled in his. He threw his head back and laughed. His laugh echoed around the cave and out into a now eerily still night.

Nothing about any of this was amusing. We'd almost been *consumed*.

My lips twitched, and my own laughter tickled my chest.

Even Draven's haggard face broke into a smile. "Fuck me," he panted.

I hated both of them, the pair of fools. We'd almost died. Again. Yet, here we were, alive, trapped in a cave, three men from three courts lost in the middle of the desert, hunted by kings, and sandworms, apparently.

"Should have brought a kareel." Draven snorted.

By Dallin. I laughed and dropped to the cave floor between them. I didn't even know why I laughed. As our hilarity died, the quiet flowed back in, dragging reality with it.

Draven arched an eyebrow at Lark. "You came back for me?"

He shrugged, his grin sharp and bright. "I promised I'd get my mouth on your cock again."

Draven flung a handful of sand at him. "Fool."

We'd lost everything, except each other. We were probably doomed. My laughter had faded, but my smile remained. There was no one else I'd rather be doomed with than Lark and Draven.

CHAPTER 2

ark

DRAVEN THREW a rock out of the cave. It thumped onto the ground, sinking several inches. Nothing else moved. It appeared as though the worm had gone, but I wasn't convinced. A creature that big didn't vanish, as it had appeared to do after we'd narrowly escaped its gullet. It was out there, probably waiting for someone stupid enough to walk on the sand and trigger it. "You should go take a look," I told Draven.

The warlord narrowed his eyes, then tossed another rock, a little farther from the rest. Still no movement.

"It's out there," Draven grumbled. "This is what they do. They wait."

"For how long?" Arin's voice sailed from the rear of the cave.

"Longer than we've got."

What I didn't say was how I'd read about sandworms in

15

Razak's library. They might lie in wait for years and were often mistaken for rocks. Sometimes they waited so long, grass grew up around them. We did not have that long.

I retreated to the shadows deep within the cave and studied our surroundings. Rocks, dried grass, dust, sand, and more rocks.

"I should be able to start a fire. Collect any grass you can find," Draven said, scooping up old brush.

I picked up twigs, grateful for something to keep my thoughts from straying into what came next. If the worm didn't kill us, the heat would. Arin must have been thinking the same. He stayed seated and stared out of the cave mouth at the red stars. *Everything* in this land burned red.

Earlier, after our laughter had died, he'd smiled for a while but soon turned somber. When he smiled, it lit up a whole room, but that smile was a distant memory now. He'd be blaming himself for all of our misfortune. My Prince of Hope was losing his.

Draven rubbed rocks and sticks together in such a way to spark a fire, then muttered something about learning to survive among the sands. We sat huddled at the campfire's edges, the three of us wrapped in a heavy, pensive silence.

It would have been easier for them had I not been a third wheel to their wagon, unwanted and awkwardly placed between them. I'd seen them earlier, standing close, Draven's touch on Arin's cheek, the two of them so perfect even I could see they were fated for each other. If Draven was who Arin wanted, so be it. They were joined, after all.

It may have been better for me to march off into the sand and leave them alone together. Which would have been all well and good, but Draven had tried to get himself killed by the worm, and if Draven died, Arin would never survive out here.

I *would* leave them, but only *when* we found help. After we survived this grating furnace, I'd go back to Pain, to Razak, and stop him. It had to be me. There was no other way to end this madness. Love had fallen, and the remaining courts had no idea how to handle my brother. Soon, he'd leave Justice with their crown. And with all four crowns in his possession, he'd make himself a god. I didn't know how, but everything he'd predicted so far had come to pass. Razak was always right.

He'd extend the Court of Pain throughout all the shatterlands. The entire world would be one long, endless storm, with its people all working to feed Razak's greed.

"Someone in War was working with Razak," Arin said, his voice rough from sand or tiredness.

I blinked dry eyes and dragged myself from dreams of a dire future.

"I don't see how," Draven said. He lay back, propped on his elbow, as though comfortable in a desert cave. "He didn't get the crown."

"He did," I said, remembering the satisfaction in my brother's eyes. "It wasn't on him, but he knows it's safe. Arin's right, he had help."

"He has people inside all the courts," Arin added, careful not to meet my gaze. "People he's manipulated, bribed, threatened. He plants them close to those he wants to destroy, and they wait for when he makes his move. I'd call it brilliant if I didn't despise him."

My right hand ached, its two digits missing. I tucked it out of sight between my thighs and stared at the flames. I'd been that traitor in Arin's court, Razak's tool. It was a wonder Arin could look at me without hate in his eyes.

Draven tossed more sticks onto the fire. "We can't do

anything about it out there. And we can't get back inside my court. That bridge has burned."

"You could," Arin added, glancing at Draven. In the fire-light, Arin's face gathered moving shadows, sharpening his features. His freckles had darkened too. "They'd let you back in."

Draven shook his head and almost laughed, but the sound never got past his thin smile. "I'm joined with a traitor. The only reason Ogden will open those gates is to hang my head from them."

"I'm not a traitor. I didn't betray anyone." Arin kept his voice level, which was how I knew his thoughts were far from calm. He didn't just despise my brother, he despised all of this. He'd only ever tried to do the right thing, perhaps using the wrong means, but he'd used the tools he'd had available. And it hadn't been enough.

"I know that." Draven tried to smile, but it didn't stick. "But you sided with Lark, and—"

"Yes, thank you," I snapped. "We all know I'm a traitor." I'd ruined their lives by association. The traitor's son. It had been baked into me since birth.

"Draven is saying—" Arin began.

"I know what he's saying. And he's not wrong. I shouldn't be here. In fact, I may as well save us all the effort of waiting out that worm and walk onto those sands. I'll be gone, and you'll be without me, as you'd both prefer."

"That's not—" Arin straightened. "It's not like that."

"Isn't it?" I caught Draven's sultry-eyed gaze over the flickering flames. He didn't deny it. "Regardless, my brother has won."

With that revelation, we fell silent again.

"We'll get out of here," Draven said.

"With what? Wings?" I rose, needing to move, to get away

from them and the blame eating me up like that wretched worm waiting to devour us. Guilt writhed inside my chest, around my heart. My veins itched.

I paced to the cave opening, picked up a few stones, and flung them onto the sand. The creature, if it was there, didn't respond. The stars twinkled and the wind hissed. The moon had dipped lower now, making way for dawn's blush across the horizon. The air smelled of baked rock, but the view, for all its savagery, was breathtaking.

War was a land of harsh delights, until its wildlife tried to eat you.

I dropped my gaze to the suspicious plateau of sand in front of our cave. If I walked out there, would the creature swallow me?

It might come to that. In three days, thirsty and starving, we'd have no other option. One of us would have to bait the beast, while the others escaped. One of us would die.

It would obviously have to be me.

CHAPTER 3

ark

WITH DAYBREAK CAME THE HEAT. It crept into the cave like hot molasses, driving us to the cooler back wall. And there, we waited. The world outside rippled through a haze. Arin dozed against Draven's shoulder while Draven stared into the daylight, as though the weight of his glare might be enough to hold the heat at bay.

Azure skies stretched to the horizon.

I'd never missed the rain before. But I craved it now.

"Why did you try and make a stand in front of the worm?" I whispered, careful not to rouse Arin.

Draven's cheek gave a flicker. He dropped his gaze to Arin, probably checking he remained asleep. "I had hoped to distract it, giving you more time to escape."

A plausible explanation, but also a lie. I'd seen his face when I'd grabbed him. He hadn't been thinking about saving us. He'd stared up at that creature with no intention of saving anyone. He'd known it would crush him, and still he'd stayed.

"Why did you come back for me?" he asked, switching my focus off him.

"I told you why." I smiled.

"My cock is not so great a member that you'd risk your life to sample it again."

"You undervalue yourself. It is a mighty cock. One of the most impressive crotchschlongs I've ever seen, and I've seen more than two. When you die, they should display it in a museum for all to witness, such is its magnificence. Women will swoon at its wonder, men will instantly harden—if they did not do so before. Truly, the most amazing of wangs, a glorious sight to behold."

He huffed a soft laugh. "Does nothing escape your wit?"

I lowered my gaze to the prince asleep against Draven's arm, then flicked it back to Draven's face. I'd gone back to save Draven *for* Arin. Losing Draven would have broken Arin's heart. I'd told him as much as he'd stood there, staring down a beast fifty times his size. *"If you die here, so does Arin."* On hearing those words, he'd woken from whatever nightmare he'd been trapped in.

"Thank you for helping me see sense," the warlord said, glancing away.

"You're welcome."

I'd seen Draven's gaze in those almost-final moments, and he'd had the look of someone without hope. I'd seen the same gaze in my own reflection countless times. It was that of a man coveting death—one who had nothing left to live for, or one who despised himself so much that death was the final punishment.

But why was Draven so lost as to seek an end to it all? There was much about the warlord I didn't know, but he hadn't seemed the sort to take his own life. Was it an old pain driving him to consider it, or something new? Some future he did not wish to face?

My thoughts drifted unanchored around the warlord as the sun made its leisurely arc across the sky. I dozed a while too, drenched in sweat and caked in sand, until the sun dipped out of sight and the shadows grew long again.

At dusk, Arin shifted awake, muttered about relieving himself, and staggered to the corner of the cave.

"We need to do something," I rasped, finding my tongue parched. "If we stay any longer, we won't have the energy to save ourselves."

Draven nodded. He knew another day like the last would be our end.

Then we only had one option left...

I approached the cave mouth. Outside, several strides away, lay all the stones we'd thrown onto the sand. The beast was either out there, or it wasn't. The standoff ended now.

I took a step, and Draven grabbed my wrist. Hot grit cut into my skin. "What are you doing?"

"Testing it."

"It *will* swallow you."

"It didn't swallow those." I gestured at the stones. "Maybe if we step lightly, we can sneak by it."

"Those are rocks. You're a living, breathing meal. It *will* notice, Lark."

"Do you have a better idea, besides glowering for several more hours until the thirst does what you could not?"

His eyes went wide with shock. Yes, I knew he'd been contemplating his own end. Did he think me a true fool that I wouldn't recognize his pain for what it was?

"Lark's not going out there." Arin emerged from the shadows. The sparkle in his silvery eyes had dulled. His cracked lips bled a little. "If one goes, we all go."

Draven finally freed my wrist. "If the sandworm is out there, we'll never make it."

"I'll distract it," I offered. "I'll run left first. When it comes for me, you both run right."

"No." Now it was Arin's turn to glower.

"If I can lure it far enough away it won't notice you both escaping."

"Lark, no." Arin's expression further darkened, but Draven's contemplated expression suggested he was warming to the idea.

"Lark is the fastest runner," Draven agreed. "Circle back around to the cave," he said to me. "When we find the caravan, I'll send someone back for you."

Arin's beautiful silver-blue eyes narrowed to razor slits. "No, Draven. I won't use Lark as bait."

"It's all right, I'm well acquainted with being used," I quipped.

Arin's face crumpled with worry, concern, and maybe even guilt. I shouldn't have said it. I hadn't meant *him*, although, he had used me as bait with the ultimate goal of slitting my throat in front of my brother. I was right, though. Used as a tool or bait, it all came down to the same thing.

"Lark—"

No, I couldn't face the pity on his face again. I took four steps out of the cave, onto the sand, and stopped. "Oops, here I am, outside the cave."

Nothing happened.

The wind hissed sand around my boots and teased my matted hair, but there were no rumblings, no shifting sands. Maybe the worm had gone? I strode to where our pebbles had landed. Still nothing. Spreading my arms, I turned on the spot. "We've been holed up in a cave for no reason."

"Damn it." Arin took a single step before Draven's arm shot out, blocking him.

"It's fine, see? Lark is—"

The ground trembled.

"Run!" Draven dragged Arin against his chest.

The sand underfoot shifted, suddenly lifting, then dropping with a jolt. I bolted; glancing over my shoulder, I saw sand rise and spill off the heaving mass of the worm erupting with a great wave. Its vast head swung around—it was coming for me.

Draven would make sure Arin ran, and ran now.

Whether they sent someone back or not, it didn't matter. All that mattered was that Arin got free, and Draven made sure he was safe.

I ducked my head and ran, knowing Arin's life depended on it.

CHAPTER 4

rin

LARK'S RETREATING figure vanished behind the sandworm's quivering form. The ground trembled like thunder. My heart leaped into my throat, trying to choke me. This wasn't supposed to happen. Draven had already said we couldn't outrun it. I'd told them no, and Lark had lured it anyway.

"Come on, run!" Draven grabbed my arm and hauled me out of the cave.

What they'd both failed to understand was how I wasn't leaving Lark. Not to that worm, and not alone in the desert.

I yanked my arm free of Draven's grip and planted my feet. "Let go."

"Arin?!" Draven lunged, attempting to grab me again.

I danced back. "Go, Draven! Send someone back for us!"

For a moment, fury turned his face into a stranger's, but that fury quickly gave way to defeat.

"You stay here—*right fucking here*!" he yelled, and then he was gone, disappearing into a cloud of settling sand. He'd return for us, I knew he would—he'd come back for *me*.

Lark? I couldn't see him, or much of anything, just a red storm churned up by the worm. I stepped out of the cave. Lark was light on his feet, but he was also weak from his ordeal. One wrong step, one trip, and he'd be gone.

"Damn you!" This shouldn't have been happening. I'd told them both no.

I had to do something. Slow the worm somehow. Get it off his scent, or whatever it used to track us.

Perhaps I could draw the creature away, giving Lark time to circle around? I strode from the cave mouth, planted my boots on the loose ground, and breathed in. "Hey! Hey worm!" It was too far away; it didn't hear me. Did it even *have* ears? I waved my arms, shouted, and stamped my feet again.

I couldn't see Lark or Draven.

Just sand.

I started forward, leaving the cave mouth behind. "Hey!" How did it know to find us? The ground? It didn't have eyes, or ears. Only a mouth. If it didn't hear and it couldn't see, then it had to feel its way...

"Hey! Come on, you hideous beast!" I stamped my boots harder. "Get your hairless hide back here!"

Was it slowing?

Perhaps.

It was difficult to tell among the clouds of dust.

What if it was slowing because it had already consumed Lark?

"Come on you fuckin' monster." I kicked the ground. "If you've hurt him, Dallin help me I will rip you to pieces with my bare fucking hands."

It reared up in a great horseshoe of quivering skin and muscle and slammed back down, pushing up red waves, and hurtled toward me, coming *fast*. I backed up. I had to time it right, giving Lark enough space to escape it, and me enough time to get back to the cave.

I stared long and hard at its eyeless front end, willing it to come closer. The ground trembled, and the whole world shook, rattling through my bones.

It grew so big, came so close, that when its jaws opened, I saw down its vast gullet.

I spun and bolted, legs pumping, running like the endless winds, boots thumping—until I hit a soft spot and tumbled to my knees. I rolled, spilled back to my feet, and sprinted forward again. Heat beat against my back, the sand hissed. I sensed its mouth opening, ready to inhale me inside.

I shot into the cave, hit the back wall, and spun in time to see it plunge back into the ground, burying itself a second time.

Sand settled, hiding it, and I was back in the cave. Alone.

Lark and Draven had to be all right. Draven would go for help, and Lark...

Lark was close. He'd circled back around, like Draven had suggested.

But what if he hadn't?

What if he was gone?

I paced the cave.

I couldn't be alone. I'd spent four years alone, hiding behind a door. Lark had to be here. Why wasn't he back? Panic clutched my heart.

Lark hadn't survived everything—the poisoning, defying his brother—to die for me here. He couldn't have. He was made for more. I knew it, I'd dreamed it. He was my Prince of Storms, playing his fiddle on the clifftop, defying the odds, defying worlds. *He could not die here.*

I stopped at the cave mouth and glowered at the ground

where the beast now hid. Why had it chosen us? I flung a rock at it, then another.

"Lark?" I called into the night, then listened for his reply. A single call back, that was all I needed. Something to tell me he was safe.

No reply came. What if he'd died for me? Why did he have to be like this? So brilliantly infuriating? Running off to save us, like he'd swallowed the poison to save us, like he'd risked his life to tell Noemi the truth of Razak's crowns. Why did he have to be the gods be damned hero?

Grit rained from the cave's overhang. I gasped and stumbled back, expecting the worm or some other horrible beast to fall inside and finish me off.

Lark swung from the ledge and dropped to his feet in one lithe, slinky movement, then straightened, swept his knotted hair back, and grinned. "Did you miss me?"

I almost struck him—wanted to, clenched my hand to do it. He arched an eyebrow, still smiling. Damn him, damn them both! I shoved him in the chest, rocking him backwards. "Don't ever do something so foolish again. Luring that thing away like that. You're insane."

He gave me an odd look, as though puzzled by my anger. "I am your fool, am I not?"

I turned away. This man... He drove *me* insane. I'd feared him dead, and he'd dropped back in without a care, making a joke?! Didn't he know how much I— Didn't he damn well know that if I lost him, all of this would be for nothing? He and Draven were the only things left in the shatterlands I cared about.

"Arin?"

I whirled and gasped. We stood face-to-face. He blinked, slow and lazy, like a cat. Caked in sand, with his hair messy and his eyes glassy, he was so wickedly handsome he stole my breath. I couldn't do this; I couldn't stand by and watch him throw his life away. "Stop being so careless! First the poison, the cut up your forearm, trying to do Dallin knows what, and now this? It's almost as though you *want* to die."

His smile cracked and fell, and all his silly acts of bravado fell away with it, leaving just the man. "You're right. I'm sorry." He turned away. "What *was* I thinking, saving you? You don't need me, you never did—"

"No, I'm sorry. Gods! It's the desert, the heat, it's everything. I'm sorry. Lark, I—" I reached for him, but he brushed me off.

"You're right," he repeated, waving a hand. "But please continue to yell some more. I'm sure it's helping you vent your frustration. Why not strike me too? If you think it'll help. Go on, you obviously want to."

"No, god, no." I shrank back, unable to trust myself not to say or do something to make this worse.

He dropped to the floor, drew his knees up, and rested his head back against the cave wall. "Draven escaped, I assume?"

"Yes, he'll send someone for us."

"'*Us*'? Of course he will." His odd smirk suggested sarcasm, but I couldn't imagine why.

Lark terrified me, for reasons I didn't understand. Anger was better than fear. But if I told him that, I'd have to explain why. He'd think me a fool for caring when he didn't. He'd probably laugh at his weak Prince of Flowers. And he'd be right. I was weak. This was my fault. We were trapped in this forsaken cave in the middle of the desert because of *me*.

He closed his eyes, so calm. I still wanted to grab him, rattle a reaction out of him, make him fight. When we argued, I knew where I stood.

"There is nothing we can do but wait," he said, eyes still closed.

I couldn't go to him, couldn't speak. I'd say something terrible to spark a fire. So I stared at the desert, watched dusk's early stars crawl across the sky, and waited until the heat in my veins fizzled out, leaving me shivering and guilt ridden.

Lark still had his eyes closed, but the occasional shift in his position suggested he struggled to sleep.

I dropped beside him and thought of another tunnel we'd shared, on a beach, far away, in the Court of Love. So much had changed since then. "You're brave, you know."

He snorted and kept his eyes closed. "How so?"

"You must be, to survive and still smile as though all of this is easy, when we both know it's far from it."

"Perhaps I smile because I like the pain?" His eyes fluttered open. "And if I like it, does that make me brave, or does it make me like my brother?"

I couldn't pretend to understand any of what he'd been through. But I knew he was brave. The same way I knew he wasn't like his brother at all.

"What drives him, what does he want?" I asked.

Lark opened his eyes. He stretched out a dusty leg and stared at the stars beyond the cave. He stayed quiet, clearly not wanting to talk about Razak.

"You don't have to tell me—"

"He hungers," Lark blurted. "Nothing is ever enough. He always wants more—more power, more pain, more knowledge, more wealth. Even if he gets his wish and becomes a god—if such a thing is possible—it will never be enough. He's never satisfied." Lark bowed his head and the remaining fingers of his right hand twitched in his lap. He curled them into his palm.

"Has he always been that way?"

"I think so. I only really began to know him after our

father made me watch as they hung my mother. I was due to hang alongside her. Razak saved me from the noose." Lark huffed a humorless laugh. "You claim I want to end my life, and there have been many times I've wished I'd died that day beside her. Whatever comes after death, at least it would be better than my life here."

A swell of emotion cinched my heart and clogged my throat. I had no words, nothing to say that would lessen his pain. Was his life truly so terrible that he'd rather die than live it?

He cast me a sad smile, and a little of my heart broke away. "I suppose you know I sang for coins?"

"I'd heard," I croaked. To be so alone, to have nothing and nobody, and have to plead with strangers for charity. I'd lost much, but I'd never had to beg strangers for aid.

"It wasn't what you think." He rippled his two remaining fingers. "You come from your palace of white and gold, and you see my life as one long string of torture. It wasn't like that. I'm not saying it was an afternoon tea party either, but please don't waste your pity on me. I escaped Razak, for a while. I made a life for myself on the streets, before Razak's court found me again. There were times I enjoyed it. I was capable enough to protect myself. For all its pain, I was free. Briefly."

"If I still had a court to call my home, I'd set you free there," I said, in a moment of carelessness. It was a silly dream, but I wanted that for him. A home, where he didn't have to sell himself for coin, where he wasn't used, where he could sing and dance because he wanted to, not because he had no choice. "If you wanted that."

Lark's smile turned sly and brightened his whole face. "Tell me, Prince Arin, was I your first?"

"My first what?"

33

"Don't play coy. You're not as innocent as you pretend."

I swallowed, cheeks reddening. "We were talking about you."

"Hm, let's talk about you." He drew his knees to his chest and rested his forearms over them, getting comfortable. His face was all large, dark eyes and pouting, soft lips. Gods, he could seduce the knickers off a nurse with that face. "If we're to die here, what harm is there in telling me all your secrets?"

"You've been dying to have them."

"I have, genuinely. The fact you kept yourself hidden behind that door vexed me in terrible ways. I couldn't understand it, or you."

"That was rather the point." I chuckled. "Was that why you wrote me all those poems and jokes?"

"Ah." He laughed. "I look back now, from where we are, and it's like a dream."

I'd loved those notes. Every single one. I'd kept them in a box beneath my bed. They were probably gone now, buried among the rubble. I'd savored every little piece of paper—the way the paper smelled of amber and jasmine, later learning that was Lark's scent. His silly jokes and lashing poems. Sometimes, I'd seen them swoosh under the door and almost invited him in. If I had, would it have changed anything?

"So was I?" he asked, not letting his question go. "Your first?"

I sighed and teased a few pebbles between my fingers and thumb. "Why does it matter?"

"I don't know," he admitted, looking away.

"Well, we didn't technically do... the act." Had I really just said that?

"No, you're quite right, we did not have penetrative sex," he teased. "Then I wasn't your first? I wondered, was all. You were... different. Sex was different with you, is what I'm saying in a terribly-unlike-me way. It seems all of the fancy words have flown away. It must be the heat. I know it's the lack of water. I'm quite delirious."

I laughed softly. "How was I different?"

He snorted and shrugged. "You cared. Usually I have a cock in my mouth and whoever it is doesn't care who I am. They're only interested in the pleasure, not me."

"How do you know I cared when you had a knife at my throat?"

"Your eyes." He circled a finger at my face. "You have honest eyes, when I know what to look for."

He looked now, looked deep inside me. "You were," I admitted. "I suppose you're glad of it? The first to tup the Prince of Love?"

"You must admit, it's quite an accomplishment."

Laughing harder, I knocked my knee into his and he snorted a laugh back. Our chuckling faded and the soft quiet returned. I opened my mouth to say something like I was glad I wasn't alone, when he said, "If you didn't want to die without having experienced the delights of penetrative coital engagement, I'd usually offer to help, but as we're in a desert and my every inch is covered in sand, I fear we lack the necessary lubricant to facilitate such a thing."

"Gods." I buried my face in my hands. "Will you say *anything*?"

"Unless, of course, Draven has already given you that pleasure?"

Eyeing him sideways revealed an edge to his inquiring face. He really didn't like the thought of Draven and I. He watched me curiously, waiting for my reply, but this wasn't a game. He wanted to know if Draven had fucked me. Why did it matter, if he didn't care, if we were *nothing*? "No," I said. "Draven and I didn't fuck like *that*." I rolled my hand, trying to grasp the right words. "I was angry at *you*, actually. I'd just heard who you were, *Zayan,* and I felt betrayed. Honestly, I was furious. I felt used, and Draven was there, kind, and willing—"

"So you fucked him as revenge?"

Had I done that? It sounded like an awful thing, and I perhaps had. Draven had wanted to, and he'd been convenient, as my soon-to-be husband.

"Not everything is about you, Lark."

He inhaled, held the breath and sighed hard. "Draven knows."

"Knows what?"

"He knows you care for me. It is a good thing you stayed. If he'd taken you, he would not have sent help back otherwise."

No, Draven wasn't spiteful, not like that. "You're wrong. You don't know him. He wouldn't leave anyone here to die, and certainly not you. He's kind."

"Hm, yes, very kind. He's also painfully handsome and hung like a horse. His cock must have been quite the widening experience for you."

The laugh shot free. "Why do you care when you've done worse with him?"

Lark gasped dramatically and pressed a hand to his chest. "Are you implying I'm promiscuous?"

My heart swelled. "Oh no, you're the epitome of virtue. It's not as though you've dipped your cock in more ink wells than a writer's quill."

The sound of his genuine laugh was a cooling salve on the wounds of everything we'd endured. He was about to say something more when the warmth in my chest surged through my veins, and without thinking, I touched his dusty

36

cheek, turned his face, and pressed my lips to his, silencing whatever sharp quip he'd been about to unleash.

The kiss wasn't as soft as I'd hoped—our cracked lips grated—but my heart was in it. I tried to ease my hand into his hair but my fingers snagged in a nest of knots.

"Gah," he mumbled against my mouth.

"Sorry." I tried again, fumbled it, and surrendered as Lark snorted a laugh. I buried my nose against his neck instead. "I'm sure you've had much better than this."

He eased back, slipped his fingers into my hair, and pressed his forehead to mine. All the good things crackled in his eyes: humor, mischief, delight. "Nothing is better than this. If we survive, we'll come back to this moment, and I'm going to make sure you are worshipped in all the ways you deserve, Prince of Hearts." He blinked, and it was all I could do not to fall into his promise, my beautiful lie.

If we survive. What if we didn't? What if these were our final hours? I had to tell him, he had to know he was loved, he had to know *I* loved him. Hated him too, but mostly loved him. "I—"

He pressed a finger to my lips. "Save it for a better day."

Save it? I sighed and slumped against his side. The mood in our cave cooled and all our earlier humor waned with the passing of the stars.

I shuffled closer, tucked against his side, and watched the moon descend behind distant dunes. "What do you think happens after we die?" I asked, my mind half asleep and wandering.

"Justice believe the pieces inside of us that make our souls whole must return to a great well that harbors all our passion and fervor. Inside the well, our souls are weighed on a set of scales with four pans. If we're found to be lacking or missing pieces due to indiscretions, we're cast out, never to be remade. But if the weighing scales are balanced, we're remade anew. Balance is all."

I hadn't known that and should have. I'd been so consumed by my own court's decline that I'd rarely looked beyond our borders. Razak's arrival four years ago had changed that, but it also meant I'd hidden from view, losing four years of my life and time I could have used to better familiarize myself with our courtly neighbors.

"Must be difficult to balance four pans on a scale."

"I think that's the point. Life is not meant to be easy." He caught my glance and explained, "Razak has an extensive library. Sometimes, after too long in his care, I... grew quiet. He'd take me to the library. It's where I learned about the outside world. Although, he soon put a stop to the visits after my first escape."

His mood began to darken at the memories, so I hastened the conversation on. "The Court of Love believes we're returned to ashes, and our fertile remains are scattered in the meadows. From there, we help feed new life."

"We're flower food?"

It did sound rather trite, but also beautiful. I tucked myself a little closer and welcomed his warm arm draped over my shoulders. "I think I prefer Justice's version."

Lark's small, quiet laugh touched my heart. "Pain believes there is only one life, and after that, nothing's embrace."

"Cheery." I yawned into my hand. "And War?"

"There's an enormous sandworm sent to devour our souls. We're consumed and spent from its backside, born anew from its waste."

"Worm food. Wonderful," I drawled. One outcome was more likely for us than the others. "Draven is going to come back for us."

Lark's chin brushed the top of my head, then wedged there. "At least one of us is worth saving," he said quietly.

He was wrong. We were both worth saving.

I had to believe in hope. If Lark didn't, then I'd believe it for him. I'd be his light in the darkness, his pleasure in his pain. His hope that together, we'd make it through this —somehow.

CHAPTER 5

rin

A RELENTLESS THUMPING in my head grew hotter and heavier with every heartbeat. The heat of the day had returned, but I couldn't find it in me to care. Lark shifted against my side and muttered about never missing the rain before.

Hunger was a constant barb in my gut. The heat, the thirst, the lack of food—it was too much.

I considered throwing the stones again to see if the beast was out there, but even if it had gone, Lark and I had no idea which way to walk. Caught in the sun, without shelter, we'd die. Perhaps that would have been better than the slow, agonizing march toward death we endured now.

Wakefulness and dreams intermingled. In some dreams, Lark stroked my hair and hummed a tune. In others, Draven was telling me he'd kill a prince, then Lark and I would lie on our backs in the flower meadows. The sun was too bright; strange, how it made Lark shine but held no heat. That light had a hunger to it, as though, if he let it, it would swallow him, and me.

In one dream, Draven had hold of me, trying to shake me back to life. I laughed at him. The fool, there was no going back. And then the ground moved, flowing beneath me like a river of sand. The stars moved too, sailing overhead with the moon watching over us all. Those dreams clung on, and time lost all meaning. Somewhere deep inside, I knew I was delirious and that I was dying.

Death wasn't as I'd expected. I hadn't expected its embrace to be comforting.

In other dreams, Lark played his violin on the clifftop, and I stood beside him. Side by side. It felt right, it felt as though I didn't need to fight anymore. Fate had brought us here, and there was no other place in the shatterlands for us.

Voices droned.

Cool, fresh water touched my lips, and a voice I didn't know told me to drink. They were all strangers, in a strange place. Children laughed somewhere far off. People chattered. But this wasn't a dream.

"Arin... you hear me?"

I blinked at Draven, then peered down at my hand in his, unsure if he was real.

"I'm sorry," he said. His face betrayed his guilt. I knew that feeling.

I reached out and he smiled, leaning closer. My fingers skimmed his rough, whiskered jaw. Yes, he was real. *This* was all real. If he was real, then where was—"Lark?"

Draven took my hand from his face and cupped it under his. "No, it's Draven."

I knew who he was. But where was Lark? Was he alive, was he here too? I tried to push up, off the pillow, but the world spun. Draven grumbled, telling me to go slow. Dropping back, I forced my thoughts to slow and my eyes to see. I was under a canopy, in the shade, with chairs, a table, water. A bed—I laid on a bed, stripped almost naked but for my undergarments.

I clutched Draven's shoulder. "Lark? Where's Lark?" He'd been with me, right beside me. I'd dreamed of him. I'd dreamed of dying.

Draven again pried my hand free and cupped it under his against the bed, holding it there. "He's resting, as you should."

If Draven said Lark was resting, then he was, and I'd see him soon. I braced against the bed. "Water?"

He handed over a cup and I guzzled it down.

"Slowly, or it'll come back up."

Nausea churned. I pressed the back of my hand to my mouth and tried to breathe around it. Angry sores on my legs and chest caught my eye, raw and throbbing like burns. "How long?" I croaked.

"It took a few days to find the caravan, and then another to get back to you." Draven swallowed hard. "The sand-worm fled when we approached. They don't like the kareel herd."

Lark and I had been in that cave for days. We should have died. We almost had. That was why Draven had paled, and why guilt wracked his face. If I was this bad, then Lark might have been worse? "I need to see him."

"Arin, wait." His big hand pushed on my shoulder.

"Help me up. Where's my clothes?"

"Please, stay here." He held me down, and weak as I was, I couldn't fight him. "If you do too much too soon—"

"If you don't help me, Draven, I will fight you, and perhaps I won't win, but if I do, I will go out there naked if I must. Where is he?"

He sighed, then reluctantly let me up. "All right. But please, take it slowly."

"Thank you."

"Stay here, I'll find some clothes." He headed for the tent flap, then glared back. "Stay."

"Yes. I'm staying. See?"

I stayed on the edge of the bed, waiting, listening to the sounds of men and women talking outside. They had the same accents as Draven's court, but more guttural and thick. Older children squealed, playing some kind of game. Wherever we were, it bustled with life. I could only hope news of our survival wouldn't get back to Ogden anytime soon.

Draven returned with a tunic, belt, pants, and boots, then left while I dressed. He wouldn't go far. I struggled to dress myself, stopping several times to keep from passing out. It was too much, and I *should* have stayed resting. As soon as I see Lark, I'll rest. I had to know he was all right. I believed Draven, but it wasn't the same. The dreams, perhaps they were nothing, but I'd dreamed he was in danger before, and I'd been right. I couldn't rest without having seen him.

I pushed through the tent flap into piercing sunlight.

Shielding my eyes, I scanned the camp. Substantial tents were slung over multiple poles. Barefooted children ran about, kicking balls and playing chase-touch. Men and women gathered around market stalls, trading all manner of goods.

"This way." Draven offered his hand.

"I've got it, thank you." I could walk unaided. I didn't need to be propped up like a weak outsider. Which I was, but I didn't need to broadcast it.

We walked under stretched canopies, avoiding the sun, and took a branch off the main thoroughfare into a quieter area. Children kicked a ball here too.

I rounded a tent pole and there was Lark, dressed in similar clothes to me, his black hair bundled and pinned back from his face. He leaned against a tent pole, as though that pole might have been the only thing holding him up, and where his face wasn't scorched by the sun, his skin was sickly pale. He watched a group of boys playing, smiling at their antics, and didn't notice my approach until we were almost on him.

His soft smile vanished as our eyes met. "Arin, you're all right." He moved to reach out and immediately slumped. Draven swooped in, holding him up, and grumbled about how both of us were stubborn.

Lark braced against the pole again. "I er... I have the will, but my body is less eager."

"It's all right." I caught his hand and squeezed, trying to convey the surge of relief at seeing him. "We made it out."

"Thanks to your husband." Lark abruptly freed my hand. "Draven came through."

"Did you have a doubt?" Draven grumbled, eyeing us both as though we'd conspired against him. "I said I'd come back for you."

"Yes, you did," I agreed. "I didn't doubt you."

"I did," Lark said, grinning. "You continue to surprise, Draven. And you have my thanks for that."

"You both need to rest, properly—in your beds," the warlord said, using his no-argument tone. "I know neither of you will stay in a bed long, but just give me one day and night of rest, and after that, we'll discuss where we go from here. Agreed?"

"Agreed," I said, relieved, and a little light-headed.

Lark nodded and turned toward the playing boys. I accepted Draven's hand on the return to my tent.

"Stay," Draven ordered, as I planted my ass on the bed.

"When you're up to it, I'll bring you some food. If I see you out of this tent before our agreed upon time, my wrath will be so legendary Lark will write a song about it."

I was about to deny I needed his help, when he gave me the narrow-eyed warlord glare that made it clear there was no room for argument. "I almost lost you out there," he said, then softened. "Allow me to do this for you." He tipped my chin up, flicked my bangs aside, and smiled. The moment stretched, and it seemed he might say something heartfelt and poignant, like *I love you*.

"I'm glad you're all right, Arin."

"The desert cannot claim me," I said, flippantly, relieved we weren't mentioning love. All I wanted to do was flop back on the bed and close my eyes again to stop the tent from spinning.

"No," he agreed. "Because you're mine."

It wasn't until he'd left, and I'd planted my head on the pillow, that the impact of his words landed. What had he meant by *mine*?

I couldn't think on it, not with the throbbing in my head. I'd rest, and tomorrow, Lark, Draven, and I would work everything out. Until then, I was at sleep's mercy, and I surrendered the moment my head touched the pillow.

CHAPTER 6

*L*ark

THE PLAYING BOYS kicked the ball around, jostled, wrestled, threw insults, argued, made up, and seemed so carefree, so bright, and joyous. Had I not been as weak as a kitten, I'd have juggled for them, taught them a few tricks to summon their smiles, made some magic in trickery. But Draven was right, I needed rest.

It grew cold after the boys drifted away. The woman who had been tasked with nursing me back to health demanded I return to my tent. I didn't dare disobey her. She'd snapped earlier when I'd neglected to drink a cup of water she'd left, then rattled off something derogatory in trader speak. I'd downed so much water at her behest, it was a wonder I didn't slosh when I walked. And then there were the little spicy nibbles she left. Delicious, but after being poisoned and then thrown into the desert, I'd had trouble keeping anything solid down. Not that my nurse cared.

"You watch the boys today. Too long." Her voice was a guttural desert rasp. The traders here spoke their own language, but they knew the language of the courts too.

"Yes, I'm aware." The stiffness in my legs when I lowered myself to the edge of the cot bed was proof I should have heeded Draven's advice.

She handed me a cup and gestured for me to drink. I'd already finished two. She glared. She'd have done well in one of Pain's pleasure-houses, for those who enjoyed being belittled and barked at. If I didn't drink, she'd likely get her kareel whip out.

"Good boys." She clucked her tongue. "Better here."

"Meaning?"

She nodded at my right hand, and I assumed my missing fingers. Although I had no idea what that had to do with the boys.

"Scarred," she said. "Less than good."

What was she implying? She'd seen me naked, having nursed me back from oblivion. She knew I was scarred all over. *Less than good.* I opted for silence in reply.

"Drink."

"I'm drinking." I glugged the water. "See, woman?"

She tutted, then stole my cup and rattled off something in her language that was most certainly rude.

"What do you mean, 'less than good'?" I asked, struggling to come up with my own translation.

"No weak children in court. Only perfect child." She thrust a bowl at me. The dried fruit and nuts might as well have been rocks for all it did for my appetite.

I tried to think around her words and make sense of them. I hadn't seen any children in the Court of War, but I also hadn't been there long enough to notice much besides the pyramid and the guest quarters. I'd been too busy trying not to kill everyone, and then trying to kill my brother. But there must have been children there. Perhaps they had been housed elsewhere.

She grabbed my mangled hand. "Weak, given to sands."

I snatched my hand back and she frowned at my lack of understanding. "Broken, weak, damaged, not perfect, given to sands." She gestured, as though scooping something up.

"The court give *children* to the sands?"

She nodded. "Yar. Boys and girls from War. Too small, broken, different." She made the same motion again, *giving the children over to the sands.*

Different. Scarred, physically or emotionally, or different, such as loving the same sex? And the Court of War gave them up?

"The children out there are from the Court of War?" I asked again. I needed this to be clear, because it sounded unbelievable. "You take them in?"

"Yar. Too weak to be warrior." She motioned for me to eat. "Eat. Be strong. Not weak."

I plucked at the nuts and nibbled, grateful when she left so I could shove the bowl under the rear tent flap for the three children who giggled and ran off with it. They'd bring the empty bowl back once they were done so I could please my angry nurse with evidence I'd eaten.

Ogden had not looked kindly on anyone who couldn't swing their bodyweight in forged metal. The nurse implied that any child deemed useless would be cast out—given to the sands. But did they truly toss them out like trash? Not even Pain were as cruel.

The more I knew of the courts, the more warped and twisted they all revealed themselves to be. Was Justice as broken? If it was, then Razak would have no trouble manipulating them. He knew where to find weaknesses and how to make them work for him.

I tried to sleep, but the camp grew loud and jubilant as the temperature dropped. I almost wished Draven would drop by, then grouse about my lack of sleep.

But he'd be at Arin's bedside, as was proper for a joined couple.

I tossed and turned, wondering about Draven, about Arin's kiss in the cave. It had been a mere flutter. And as kisses went, it had been clumsy, and dry, both of us dehydrated and near delirious. It probably hadn't meant anything, only that Arin had been losing his mind to the heat, and he'd felt the need for company while facing our final days. Still, as much as I tried to deny it, I couldn't shake the feeling there was more there than my grasping at straws and his need for companionship. When I'd distracted the sandworm, he'd stayed. He could—*should*—have fled with Draven.

I shifted on my cot bed some more, then stared at my tent's canopy.

I'd been Arin's first sexual encounter. Had I known, I'd have made it more of an event, although we had started out attempting to cut each other's throats, so candles and silk would have been unlikely. There hadn't been time to discuss his experience or preferences. Did he *know* his preferences? Of course, the fact he'd hidden himself away for years meant he hadn't had much choice, but as the Prince of Love, he could have invited anyone into his bed, man or woman, both together.

I touched my neck, where his blade had kissed me in front of my brother. Arin had impressed Razak with that move and surprised me. He'd never stopped surprising me.

There was some way to go before trusting him. The

Prince of Flowers was a gifted liar. Yet, I sensed he'd changed —*we'd* changed.

Thoughts tumbled around my head, each one vying to be the truth. Whatever the outcome, sleep remained elusive.

Venturing from the tent, I stepped into the camp's cooler nighttime world. People sat around crackling fires, drinking, eating, and with the traders all gone, only the nomadic desert dwellers remained. I drifted on their peripheral, following the sounds of music to a crowd around a large fire. People gathered in groups, some danced, together and alone, and the music played on. The instruments were different to those I knew, unlike anything I'd seen, making music that was upbeat and fast-paced, urging me to dance.

I wandered, smiled at strangers, nodded greetings, drawing less attention than Arin might have with his golden locks and freckles.

Someone planted a drink in my hand and beamed at me. The wine was sweet, slightly warming, certainly better than the gritty water I'd been forced to consume. I finished that cup, found another, and wandered some more, losing myself to the sultry atmosphere. This was better; my mind wandered pleasantly as I drifted among these people. No bad dreams, or stalking memories. Just wine and merriment.

Arin's voice drew me up short. A woman left a nearby tent —probably a caregiver—and before I could consider talking myself out of visiting him, I ducked through the flap, plunging inside.

"Lark!" Arin sat shirtless on his bed. He flung a sheet over his lap. "Don't you knock?"

"It's a tent. There's little to knock on." I stumbled and lurched across the dirt floor. "Did I interrupt something?"

He frowned. "Are you drunk?"

"No?" I eyed my cup. I hadn't eaten, so there was a chance

the wine had gone to my head. "Perhaps." It was rather strong. I handed him the cup. "Try it."

He eyed the contents suspiciously. "Where did you get it?"

"Someone handed it to me." I waved his concern away and dropped onto the edge of the bed beside him, dislodging a small pot of what appeared to be a clear gel. "Do not worry; nobody here wishes us harm. Drink. If it's poisoned, I'd be dead."

"That's not encouraging." He drank anyway, and his blond featherlight lashes fluttered. "Hm, that really *is* good."

I picked up the pot I'd disturbed when sitting and dipped a finger into the gel. Smooth, cool, *lubricating*.

Arin spluttered a laugh. "Stop."

"Stop what?"

"Your face." He snorted.

"I clearly cannot stop my face."

Sipping more of the wine, he grinned. "I can see the thoughts in your eyes. They're very emotive. The salve is for *the sores*. The nurse was applying it." He gestured at his chest. "Where the sand rubbed, it relieves it. It's from a plant, the name of which I forgot."

"Hm, she offered to apply it, did she?" Arin was shirtless, and although he'd caught too much sun and was scorched in places, his blue eyes were as startling as ever and his body quite the handsome picture of solid masculinity. The ripple of muscles down his chest, currently bunched as he sat, provided an enticing display. One I was sure the nurse had admired. "Here's a thought. I can apply the rest of it, as I'm here. As a friendly gesture."

He smirked, sipped the wine, and glanced toward the tent's doorway. He hadn't said no, so I was left to assume he didn't hate the idea.

"What if Draven arrives?" he asked, face warming.

His blush was a beautiful thing. "What if he does? I'm applying a salve. It's not as though I have my fingers plunged anywhere else."

He snorted again and narrowed his eyes. "Just the chest?"

"Anyone would think you do not trust me."

"Hm, why ever would anyone think that?"

I stood, giving him room to stretch his legs down the bed, then perched on the edge again so I could reach all of him. He leaned back but stayed propped up on his elbows, half suspicious, half amused. He certainly did not trust me.

I fought a smile from my lips. "This may surprise you, but I am capable of touching a man without wanting to fuck him," I assured, although, that may have been something of a lie when it came to Arin.

I dipped my fingers into the pot, scooped some cool, smooth gel, and dabbed at his chest. He hissed, and I raised my eyebrows, careful to ignore the dart of lust that shot down my spine. "Does it hurt?"

"It's cold." He writhed.

I clenched my jaw, willing my body to calm. Perhaps this hadn't been such a good idea, because in a few moments, I would not be able to hide my physical response to his reaction.

"Lie back."

He dropped his head onto his pillow. So obedient.

"Close your eyes."

Frowning, he peered down his nose.

"All right, don't close your eyes." I dabbed the gel onto his sores and gently stroked it in, warming it to help with absorption. There may not have been many sores at his hip, but there was no harm in applying a little salve there. He jolted at the touch but didn't demand I stop. He had smooth, fine hips, perfect for gripping.

When I looked up, he'd closed his eyes. At least now I didn't have to hide how hard I'd become. We may have only shared a single night together in his palace bed of white and gold, but it had been enough to brand his body into my memory. That night had been a tease, and nothing like enough.

I flicked the sheet aside, exposing his naked thigh and his proud erection, lying thick against his navel. He hadn't opened his eyes, but he must have felt the kiss of cool air on his cock.

If Draven happened to walk in now, I'd replace the sheet, and the warlord never had to know I'd had my gaze on his husband's dick. A fine dick. I hadn't had it between my lips enough. How was I supposed to resist, when it lay there, so well-behaved and quietly demanding?

"I dreamed of us, when I was near death," Arin said, eyes still closed. "We were in the meadows. I've dreamed it before. And there was a light."

Scooping some gel into my right hand, I worked it between my two fingers and thumb, warming it, then slid my grip down his length in one smooth, quick action. His hips tilted, his back arched, and Arin's soft mouth opened in a perfect *O*.

We might have had trouble explaining this to Draven if he happened upon us. Still, pleasuring Arin was worth inciting the warlord's wrath.

"Did you dream?" he asked, eyes still closed.

"I rarely dream." I had dreamed, but I wasn't dragging my nightmares into this blissful moment.

His eyes fluttered open. "You don't dream?"

"Close your eyes." Instantly, he obeyed. "I craft dreams for others, not myself."

"Magic in the not knowing," he whispered, remembering my words to him. He believed in hope and light and all things righteous. He wouldn't if he'd seen my dreams.

I set the pot aside, gripped his dick, and stroked, alternating between massaging and pumping. He trembled and gasped, and it wasn't long before his breaths came in spluttered moans. His body was a symphony, and I tweaked its every note. The gel was the perfect viscosity to allow my hand to glide, but not too slick that I couldn't tighten my grip. I pumped, then let go, pumped, summoning racing gasps, and let go, pumped, watched him twitch and buck, and let go, bringing him to the edge before letting him fall back down again. He responded so beautifully, his body now slick with beads of sweat.

Arin clutched hard at the edge of the bed, his fingers turning white.

My Prince of Flowers was trying to resist the approaching wave, and his efforts were admirable, but I controlled him now. I leaned forward and whispered, "You come when I allow it."

He let out a long, agonized moan. And with his eyes still squeezed closed, he panted and writhed, bucked and shuddered. Every moan and guttural growl told me all I needed to bring him to the edge again. When he was close, I let go, let him cool, and then wrapped him in my hand, encircling just his top two inches—that extra sensitive head. The gel turned creamy with pre-cum, and his cock blushed, hot and pulsing. I'd have had him in my mouth long ago if I could have been certain the gel wasn't toxic.

"Lark—" His blue eyes fluttered open and his glare pierced my soul.

"Hm?"

"Please?"

My own dick pulsed at his whine. I could have slicked my cock, flipped him over, and hammered him into the bed, wrecking him and making him scream for more. But this moment wasn't for me. "Please what, my prince?"

His lashes fluttered down and his blunt teeth dug into his bottom lip. "Finish me?"

There was no resisting him. I hadn't been able to resist him since we'd met, and the years he'd hidden had only heightened my need. I'd make him come, make him scream, make it so every time he came in the future, he'd think of me.

I smothered his mouth with my left hand and pumped viciously with my right. The whole camp didn't need to know Arin was about to spill for me. His eyes flew open, as though in panic, but when he fixed his glare on me, his golden eyebrows narrowed with murderous intent. Some part of him hated me for this, for making him beg, but I loved that too.

He held my gaze, held it like a drowning man clings to life. But then his overwhelming pleasure broke. His eyes rolled, he thrust his head back into his pillow, his back arched up off the bed, and he moaned into my hand while his cock spurted its load over his quivering abs.

Those vicious but delightful little sparks on the edge of pain wracked him.

I'd been with many men, and none had been such a delight to admire in their pleasure throes as Arin. Gods, the color of his face and chest, how his freckles darkened, his lips plumped, and his chest flushed. I wanted him under me, or in me, whatever he wished, just so long as we were as close as two souls could get.

I freed his mouth, found a cloth, and cleaned him up while he still reeled from the aftershocks. Once he was dry, I propped myself innocently on the edge of the bed, as though nothing had happened. Draven would never know. Although, there was no hiding how Arin's nipples were as hard as tiny pebbles and his eyes were sex-drunk.

"Pleased with yourself?" His voice had gained a gravelly edge too. Delicious.

"I have no idea what you're referring to. I merely applied the salve to the desired locations, as requested."

He laughed a dirty chuckle, but when his gaze roamed me, stopping at my lap, he reached out, probably thinking to return the favor and pump me to climax. I steered his hand away and pressed it down onto the bed.

Concern stole all the warmth from his face. "Sorry, I... Do you not want to?"

I smiled, leaned over, and planted a soft, chaste kiss on his damp forehead. "Another time." I straightened and stood to leave.

He snatched my hand, jolting me to a stop. "Lark, talk to me."

How to tell him that what I needed was likely outside his experience? "It's not you. I require a little more stimulation, that's all. Please, don't take offense."

Now he was puzzled *and* hurt, which was what I'd been trying to avoid. He'd noticed how I hadn't reached climax when we'd lain together in his palace bed, and now this... He'd need an explanation, but I wasn't sure it was one he'd understand. He might even find the revelation too much, especially as the Prince of Love was new to seduction.

"We have dallied too long. I'm sure your warlord will return soon."

He dropped his hand and pulled the sheet over his lower half. "Yes, of course."

"You should rest."

"And you?"

"I'm fine."

"Lark, listen..." He twisted onto an elbow. "I'll speak with Draven. About us, you and I—"

Us? There was no us. "It's probably best you don't."

"What?"

"He won't appreciate a third in your marriage."

"I agree, and I need to explain to him that the joining was a mis—"

The tent flap rustled. "Lark." Draven's deep growl rumbled, shrinking the air inside the tent. The warlord barely spared me a glance and strode for Arin's bedside.

"I was just checking on your husband here," I explained. "He seems to be in fine health." I hurried from the tent, having no interest in making the situation uncomfortable for Arin.

My escape didn't last. Draven caught up and strode alongside me. "Now you're both recovered, it seems right that we should decide how best to proceed. Let's meet for breakfast—"

"Proceed with what?" I stopped and peered into his intense eyes.

All around people bustled and drank and sang and danced by the firesides.

"Retrieving War's crown," Draven said, firelight warming his face. But the fire didn't soften his features. It hardened them, as it had Arin's. "Stopping Razak."

"At this point, we don't know if the crown is even lost. You said you thought it was safe. And I'm not entirely sure what we can do to stop Razak, now he's already in Justice's hands."

"You can't be suggesting we simply give up?"

I wasn't, was I? The desert had almost killed Arin, and

since Arin had surprised my brother, Razak would kill him at his next opportunity. Draven was an exiled warlord who could swing a sword but not with political clout, and me... What was I, if not a fool? In what feasible way could we stand against Razak? No. Only I could stop him, and I alone. Razak would kill Draven and Arin. But not me. Not yet.

"We'll talk in the morning." I set off in no discernible direction, escaping questions I could not answer.

If I'd done more, I could have stopped Razak. Noemi, Justice Ines's aide, was the only one who had come close to killing the Prince of Pain, and she was locked up somewhere within Justice's icy castle, likely awaiting trial for helping us. We were fugitives. It would be better for us all if we went our separate ways. Arin and Draven could live their happily ever after in a corner of War's lands, and I'd return to Pain, where I belonged. If I failed, Razak would steal his crowns and make himself a god, whatever that meant. Perhaps all the courts deserved such a fate after losing their way.

I wandered the camp, found more potent wine, and sat at the fireside with strangers until the hollow pain inside no longer consumed my heart and soul, and the sun bled along the desert horizon.

I couldn't risk Arin's life again.

He and Draven must live their happily ever after. Without me.

CHAPTER 7

rin

LARK SAT ACROSS THE BENCH, arms folded, his perpetual smile on his lips. That smile was the most shallow, empty mask he wore. He was hurting—we all were—but when Lark was in pain, he built walls, keeping everyone out. His smile was that wall's locked door.

His eyes, always so elegant and bright, had dulled some since last night. He likely hadn't gotten much sleep.

He'd been at his happiest in my court, juggling balls, singing songs, and making a fool of himself. Ever since then, his spark had faded, and I missed it, missed his scathing poems, his quick wit, missed him. He was here, with us, yet so far away too. I feared that smile, and that look. It meant something, something I didn't understand about him, something he wouldn't tell me.

"Arin?" Draven said from beside me.

"Hm?"

"Would you like me to collect you some breakfast from the spread?"

"Oh, yes... Thank you."

Draven asked Lark the same, but he declined, and Draven left to collect food at the camp's long feasting table. We'd soon outstay our welcome, and the caravan would move on without us, or we'd have to bring something of value to the people in order to stay. I wasn't sure yet what tomorrow would bring or where we'd be. But that was why we'd gathered here, for breakfast, to discuss our future and stopping Razak.

"I haven't spoken with him," I said, noticing how Lark watched Draven in line at the feasting table. "But I will."

"What is there to say, Arin?" He faced me again, his smile as sharp as ever. "You make a fine pair."

Whenever I thought I understood him, he pirouetted and flung my facts back in my face. I'd thought everything that had happened this past week—the sandworm, the kiss in the cave, last night—and all we'd previously endured, though those events had been terrible in many ways, had brought us closer. Or so I'd believed. I knew we had something, a connection, something that was heart-deep, but then he'd look at me as though nothing mattered. Certainly not me, or *us*.

If I told him I loved him now, would he throw that back in my face and laugh? But it didn't feel like the right time. And last night, when he'd pushed my hand away after torturing me in the most wonderful way? He'd been hard in his trousers, I'd seen that much, and I knew he preferred men, but not me. Not since that night in my bed, when he'd clutched both our cocks in his hands. Had I done something wrong? If he didn't want to be touched, I'd understand. Or was I too *inexperienced?*

"You should smile," Lark said. "This is as close to freedom as we're going to get."

I glared. "I smile when I mean it."

His right eyebrow twitched. "You're spicy this morning."

"I wouldn't be if you'd stayed last night."

He shrugged. "Three's a crowd."

"There wouldn't have been three."

"You were leaving, were you? Because Draven stayed all night."

My glare hardened. How did he know? "He... did stay, yes," I admitted.

"In your bed?"

"What if he did?" He hadn't, but Lark's attitude was grating.

"Then that might account for your hideous mood. He's well-endowed, but rather unimaginative between the sheets."

I snorted without humor. "You'd know."

"Hm, yes, because you assume I've ridden every cock in your Court of Flowers."

"Haven't you?"

He bowed his head and laughed at the tabletop. When he looked up, the smile was so like Razak's that the heat from whatever this was turned to ice in my veins.

"Even the virgin cock belonging to the prince who cuts throats," he said, delighting in every word.

He hadn't actually *ridden* me. Still, this didn't seem the right time to split hairs on the matter. He hated me for using him as bait and revenge against Razak. And I loved him. I was a fucking idiot.

"Breakfast," Draven announced, sliding several plates between us and scooting onto the bench beside me.

"Thank you." Lark took a piece of peach-like fruit and set it down in a bowl in front of him. "Last night, while you two lovebirds slept, I wandered the camp, trying to think of a means by which we can stop Razak, and frankly, we cannot."

"Oh, well, that's settled then. We'll just give up," I snapped, then heard the whine in my voice and winced. Draven frowned, more confused than anything else. "My apologies, I'm tired. But still... This can't be the end. There's more we can do. We've been knocked down, but we're here, we survived, and that means we're strong."

"It means we got lucky," Draven said. He plucked a piece of dried bread from the plate along with some fruit and began to eat. "I've been thinking about what Lark said last night too—"

"What did he say?" I asked.

"Just that we've lost. And if we keep trying, eventually Razak will kill you, Arin."

"Lark said that?"

"Not in those words." Draven set his food back down and straightened. "But he's right."

"So you're both giving up?" I asked. "Because of me?"

"We can't get into Justice," Lark said. "They'll arrest us. There's a slim chance Draven could talk his way back into Ogden's court, at least gain an audience with him. But not with you at his side, Arin. After you argued for me, Ogden believes you're a traitor."

"He didn't need much evidence. He already believed me weak." I grabbed some of the dried, spiced bread and ate absently, thoughts swirling around what came next for us.

"And War discard their weak," Lark said.

"What did you say?" Draven turned to Lark, his tone dead-flat.

"I said, they—your court—discard their weak. They give them to the sands." There was no humor in Lark's eyes now. Only sincerity, and perhaps a hint of sadness.

"Who told you that?" Draven demanded.

"My vicious nurse. The boys here..." Lark nodded toward a few gathered near the end of another table. "They're the Court of War's rejects, thrown out like trash. Surely, you know this, Draven."

"I know." He glanced at me, then away, fearful of meeting my gaze. "It's never discussed, that's all."

"I had no idea," I whispered. "How awful."

"Excuse me." Draven stood and strode toward the food table, then veered around it, disappearing behind a tent.

"It appears I struck a nerve," Lark said.

As Draven's husband, I should have gone after him, and I would, after I'd given him some time. "You don't think *his* child was given to the sands, do you?" I whispered. I'd known he'd had a son, but little else. Nobody had been willing to discuss Draven's past, and this would explain why.

Lark slowed his chewing and winced. "I hadn't considered that. It's possible."

"And his wife? I mean, he must have had one, to have a child."

"Something happened, in childbirth maybe?" He glanced down at his assaulted hand. "I didn't think. I won't mention it again."

I sighed. If that had happened to Draven, and his family had been cast out, then our exile into the desert must have been painful for him, more so than I'd realized. I'd planned to tell him how I had strong feelings for Lark, different feelings than those I had for Draven, but that might have to wait. Although, Lark was doing his damndest for me *not* to love him.

Regardless of our personal issues, I wasn't giving up on stopping Razak. If anything, I was more determined than ever to stop that vicious prick. We couldn't get to Justice, and even if we did, we'd be on Razak's tail, following in his footsteps. Always one step behind. "There has to be another way."

"Not leaving children in the desert would be a start."

"What? No, I mean, yes, true, but ever since Razak entered my court all those years ago and killed my previous fool, I've been behind his every step, trying to keep up."

"Trying to dance with Razak is impossible; none of us know his moves." Lark reached for a nearby pitcher of water and poured himself a cup.

"Exactly. He clearly has a plan, and so far, he's won. Because we've been behind him at every step. What if we somehow maneuvered in front of him?"

Lark considered it. "We know he has his sights set on Justice's crown."

"We can't go near Justice and if we did, we'd be behind him again. He'll expect us to go there. So we don't. We do the opposite..." Yes, the more I considered this, the more it felt right.

"Then... where do we go? Justice is the final crown." Lark sipped his water.

I had an idea. An insane idea. It would mean we'd step out in front of Razak and surprise him. But as Razak had my court's crown, would soon likely have Justice's, and with War's crown's location still unknown, such a plan might be the only way. He'd never see our move coming. "Pain."

"What?" Lark hovered the cup at his lips.

"We go to the Court of Pain." Razak would *never* expect it.

Lark's dark eyebrows pinched. "What for?"

"The crown, of course. Do you know where it is?"

He slowly lowered the cup and licked his lips, careful to

school his expression. "The sun must have roasted your mind. We aren't going to Pain. Ever."

"Razak isn't there. We know that for certain. Pain is unguarded and unsuspecting. And you know the court, Lark. It's your home, you must know it."

"My 'home'?" He laughed. "I can tell you precisely what Razak's bedchamber looks like from the end of a leash, and the council chamber, from every corner to every crack in the floorboards, but as for the court or the city itself, I've only seen its slums. Do not mistake me for anything more than a pet. I'm certainly not the prince he's tried to proclaim me to be."

But Lark knew more about his court than Draven or I did. There had to be a way to use that. "Then you don't know where Pain's crown is?"

He tapped his cup. "Actually, I may know."

In truth, Lark was our only hope. He was the closest person alive to Razak. He'd spent years with the Prince of Pain. "What if *we* stole it?" I suggested.

"Take Pain's crown?" Lark mused aloud. "It's possible, I suppose. Razak won't expect it. Nobody will expect it, because it's insane."

"Exactly." I grinned. "It's perfectly mad."

He leaned forward. All around, the hubbub in the feasting tent continued, almost drowning out his hushed voice. "I have no power there, Arin. Worse, I'm nothing there. Even if we were to get inside, I'd be thrown into Razak's chamber, and you? If they find out who you are, I suspect they'd hang you, at the very least. I'd prefer not to think on it."

"Then we go as other people, in disguise." I was grasping at straws some, but it felt like something. Like an idea we could build upon. We had to get out in front of Razak, and this was the only way.

"The council are too close-knit to let strangers inside their circle, and if the crown is where I think it is, then no outsider will be permitted access. Disguises won't help."

"There must be a way. We'd only need access for a short while. Any longer and Razak would learn of it. A few days, at most—"

"Arin, it's too dangerous."

"No, it's not. We can do this. We just need to think on it some more. There's a way."

He smiled, and now the smile was soft and genuine, and so wholly Lark that the love I sometimes wished I didn't have for him made my heart both swell and flutter at once.

"I wish I had your abundance of hope and optimism," he said. "Two things the Court of Pain do not foster."

"You said it wasn't so bad there."

"No." He laughed bitterly. "I said, it looks bad from the outside looking in, because I've lived it. It's my life. For you— no. This is ludicrous. It's impossible. Pain will chew you up and spit you out."

"I'm not the fragile Prince of Flowers everyone believes me to be."

"Oh, I know. I've felt your blade at my throat." His expression changed, turning intrigued and locking on to me without blinking. Heat simmering. What was I missing? Why was he staring with the same heavy-lidded intensity he'd worn last night when I'd begged him to finish me?

"What?"

"I'm imagining you in purple and black, and it's decidedly arousing."

I leaned closer now too and the camp in my peripheral vision blurred into an indifferent haze behind Lark's beautiful eyes. "Then put me in purple and black. We will steal Pain's crown. How do we do this? How do we make it happen?"

He wet his lips with the tip of his tongue. I'd already seen him in purple and black, as a prince, standing beside his brother, the two of them so alike—

The idea struck so hard, I dropped back. "Oh."

"Oh?" Lark smirked. "I know that look. We're all doomed."

I knew how we could do this, and I knew it would work. But it all hinged on Lark pretending to be the one thing he hated more than anything else in this world.

"I apologize," Draven said, returning to our table. "There was something I had to attend to. You've barely eaten, both of you." He sat next to me and stilled, picking up on our tension. "What did I miss?"

"We have a plan." I smirked.

"We do?" They asked together.

"And you're both going to hate it."

CHAPTER 8

ark

WHEN ARIN LOOKED as he did now, all satisfied and bullish, he was scheming and thoroughly enjoying himself. Had Draven not returned, I might have suggested we leave the breakfast and hurry back to my tent to continue what we'd begun last night. Because the idea of seeing him in purple and black, and how fucking arousing that was, had taken me by surprise.

I shifted on the bench, adjusting how my trousers pinched my filling cock.

"We have a plan," he said. But with images of him coming undone beneath me playing in my head, I was only half listening.

"We do?" Draven and I said together.

I could bend Arin over my bed, lift that tunic, and bury my cock deep. He wanted it, he'd wanted it since our first night together, maybe before that, without even realizing his own desires. If Draven wasn't meeting his needs, I would.

"And you're both going to hate it," he continued.

Whatever it was, if he was there, I wouldn't hate it. I hated the knots he tied me up in, and I'd make him feel that, but he wanted my hate too. He'd had a taste when I'd made him strip with a knife at his throat. Gods, I needed to get him away from this table and Draven to make this fantasy real—

"Lark pretends to be Razak."

"What?" I blinked, and my sexual fantasy shattered.

"You look just like him," Arin added. "We'd need to cut and shape your hair."

Pretend to be Razak? The idea was ludicrous, not least because I couldn't do it. "No."

"What?" Draven said, two beats behind me. "And how does Lark dressing as Razak help?"

"Lark goes into the Court of Pain, pretending to be Razak, steals Pain's crown while Razak is locked up in Justice, Razak loses," Arin explained to Draven, leaving the warlord with his mouth open. I shared Draven's stunned sentiment.

"No," I repeated, and swallowed my fluttering heart. "I can't *be* Razak. It's not only his appearance I must mimic. He's—"

"A dick, yes. I'm sure you can pull it off," Arin said, casually throwing the barbed insult, then smiling as though he were still all sunshine and honey, when we both knew his light could be sharp and his honey poisoned.

I blinked, then laughed aloud. "Oh my dearest prince—" I cleared my throat of the words that weren't mine to say. Words like: I love you, you're a brilliant bastard, but I still love you. "You're quite something, Prince Arin. You're just going to sit there and ask me to be my butcher of a brother and you assume I'll do it for you?"

Arin shrugged and popped a piece of fruit into his mouth. He grinned, chewed, and swallowed. "More than that, you *want* to do it."

"I'm not sure what's happening here," Draven admitted. "I leave for a few moments and you've both come up with a plan to steal Pain's crown?"

"You have to admit, it's perfect." Arin beamed. "With Razak away, his court is exposed."

"It's not perfect," I said. "Because I cannot do it."

"Afraid you might like it?" Arin teased, gliding close to the truth.

His words stopped my heart, wedged it in my throat, and choked me all at once. What was it I'd said in the cave? Something about enjoying the pain, making me insane, like my brother. It was true, we did look similar. And if I cut my long hair, cropping it short, and donned some silver jewelry, few would be able to tell us apart. But what did I know of my brother's life? He attended council meetings, and if they angered him enough, or if he was particularly pleased with himself, he either fucked me hard or soft. I knew his laugh, I knew his mannerisms, I knew his quick wit and vicious rage. I knew him intimately. But I knew nothing of his life, his routine.

"A few days?" Arin urged, losing his smile while trying to pin me under his stare. "That's all we'd need."

"It's a big ask," Draven said, finally noticing my discomfort. "They'll kill Lark, if he's discovered."

Arin's eyes widened. His shoulders slumped. "Perhaps it's too much to ask—"

I sighed. "Nobody will touch me. They're afraid to." Arin's damn idea had merit. "Only Razak has that right. He's killed others for defying that rule in the past." Razak was fiercely jealous, as his obsession with Arin proved. Nobody in his court dared hurt me.

Unfortunately, Arin's plan might work. I knew my brother well enough to act like him, but not his routines. We looked alike, and if the worst happened and I was caught, I wouldn't be killed. Not until Razak returned. And if he did return, as free as a bird, then it wouldn't matter anyway because he'd have all four crowns, and Razak with power that stretched beyond his court would be the end of all of us.

"What's a few days, when you lied to me for four years?" Arin asked, both sly, vicious, and playful. I wanted to kiss him, as well as make him hurt and moan, for being right and brilliant and for knowing how, deep inside, I wanted this.

I narrowed my eyes on the prince. "Perhaps I'll take you along as a distraction so nobody notices I'm not my brother."

Arin grinned and tilted his head, considering it. He opened his mouth to speak.

"No." Draven cut him off, scowl deepening.

"It will add a layer of believability," Arin argued.

"No," Draven said. "You're not walking into the Court of Pain alone."

"I won't be alone. Lark will be beside me."

Draven snorted, scowl turning sharp. "All of this is happening *because* of Lark."

"Thank you for the accusations," I said. "But I'm not my brother yet. All of this is his doing, not mine."

Draven twisted on the bench and glowered, his dark eyes full of accusations. "How much of this could he have accomplished if he hadn't had you maneuvering people for him?"

"Draven," Arin warned.

Draven's hand had dropped to his hip, where he'd typically be carrying a blade. Interesting. There was that anger again, the same anger that had always simmered below his surface, the anger of past hurt. "Let him speak. I want to hear the warlord's insightful words."

"I don't have *insightful* words, as you well know. But I see you for what you are. Someone who uses others to get what they want. You don't care about anyone but yourself. Arin is not going with you on this insane plan, but if you want to go home, where you belong, I won't stop you."

A silence fell over our table. Draven's outburst had been brewing for days and he wasn't wholly wrong. I did use people, but so did his blond-haired, bubbly husband who currently stared at Draven as though determining where to shove a dagger.

"I'll do what I like," Arin said, his voice steady and thin, pulled tight with restraint. He'd sounded like that moments before backhanding his father. "And if you think to stop me, Draven, then this is the end of our relationship, or friendship, or whatever it is we have."

My surge of satisfaction faded at the sight of Draven's pained face. Arin had Draven's heart in his hands, and I knew exactly how that felt.

Draven swallowed hard, frowned at this food, then picked up his fruit and began to eat. "Do as you wish. While Lark takes you on what is clearly a fool's mission, I'll attempt to talk my way back into War and determine if the crown is missing. To get back inside, I'll have to denounce our joining." His voice hitched. "Claim you're a traitor and I was... duped."

"That's probably for the best," Arin agreed and laid his hand over Draven's on the table. "The joining was convenient, at the time."

"'Convenient'?" Draven grunted, taking his hand back. "I guess I was."

Perhaps I should have been more sympathetic. But Draven knew Arin had only joined with him for political power, and any connection they had forged was tenuous. Or perhaps that was my own wishful thinking? Because if Draven stepped back, that made Arin free for my taking.

WE TRAVELED with the traders caravan during the night, heading toward the oasis town of Palmyra, which Draven translated as *Heart of the Desert*. From there, Draven would catch a supply run back to War and plead his innocence to Ogden. Once he knew the status of the crown, he'd meet us at the Overlook Inn in the Court of Love at the next full moon, assuming the Inn hadn't been abandoned. Before then, Arin and I had several weeks to transform me into my brother, make the crossing to the Court of Pain, infiltrate the council, locate Pain's crown, and escape again with it in our possession.

Of course, the more Arin discussed his plan, the easier he made it sound. But he didn't know Pain like I did. What if Draven was right and Arin shouldn't go? There was no use in telling him so. He'd already dug his heels in. Besides, his enthusiasm was infectious.

After three days traipsing through the desert, we reached Palmyra. Giant flowering trees flanked the roadways, cascading waterfalls plunged into misty ravines, and humid junglelike pathways snaked between ramshackle bamboo houses. And all of it was nestled in a fold in the desert, obscured by heat haze, making it almost invisible on approach.

Arrival into the town was marked by a bridge spanning a waterfall, suspended close to the plummeting falls. Waters churned in the plunge pool below, and all around, a cool mist rained. Arin stood in the rolling mist like a wet vagrant. He raised his hands, collecting water, and laughed, then shook his wet hair, drawing some odd looks from the local folks.

Draven chuckled and patted him on the shoulder. "It's good to see you happy." He sauntered off, saying he'd secure us lodgings.

I joined Arin on the bridge and lifted my face to the mist. After the heat and grating desert sand, the soft, cool rain kissed my skin like a soothing balm.

Arin leaned against the bridge railing and admired the sprawl of jungle-clad houses and milling people. "It's spectacular. I like this place."

I'd learned to treat all beautiful things with caution. I should have heeded my own rule when I'd met him. "It's charming."

"'Charming'?" He snorted. "It's magical." He pushed from the rail, spread his arms, and spun in the wet mist. His clothes, like mine, were filthy with sand. Both of us needed a bath, a comb, and a razor, but as he spun, his hair loose and messy, his face smudged with red sand, his eyes burned with their first real brilliance since I'd found him again in War.

I wanted to dance in the rain with him, wanted to count the stars with him, to discover new horizons, dream new dreams, sing new songs—all with Arin. The need became so powerful, it stole my breath and my heart, rendering both silent. I loved him, my prince behind the door. I'd always known, but only now did I allow myself to experience how deep that love went.

He saw me watching and slowed, turning shy. Impossibly, I loved him more with every beat of my heart and every glance he gave.

"You just going to stare?" he asked, dripping wet.

I leaned an arm against the rail. "I'm waiting for an invite."

There were others using the bridge, but they found their way around us, clearly having seen a waterfall before.

Arin bowed at the waist and then, straightening, held out his hand. "Join me, Fool."

I crossed the few short strides, took his hand, and reeled his body in close. We fit together as though we were meant to be. We danced to a tune of our own making as the mists swirled. Water collected on his lashes, then fell to his cheeks and ran like tears toward the corners of his grin. This man had no idea how he ruined me in the most remarkable ways.

People flowed around us, the waterfall thundered, mist rained. I touched his wet face, skimmed my fingers along his bristling jaw, grown to a stubble in the desert.

"Careful." He smirked. "Or people will talk."

"Let them." If I kissed him now, I might not stop, and while Palmyra was not the Court of War, it likely held the same regard to men flaunting their mutual attraction in public. As guests, we didn't need to find ourselves on the wrong side of another wall.

I love you. An easy three words to speak. Much harder to admit, when I knew I wasn't worthy of such love in return.

I stepped way, let our hands part, and nodded toward the resplendent jungle town beyond the bridge. "Draven will be waiting."

CHAPTER 9

*A*rin

AFTER WE'D VENTURED into the heart of Palmyra, we drifted through a jungle wonderland, from markets to a performance alley, to eateries and bars, which would likely come alive once the sun set.

A trader threw Lark a bright yellow fruit, perhaps sensing he had the character to throw it back. Instead, Lark caught it, plucked two more from the market stall, juggled them, then tossed each back to the laughing trader. The man dipped his head, then tossed one of the fruits back again, as a gift.

Lark dipped his head in acknowledgement and bit into it. "Hm, s'good." He handed it over, and I sampled its juicy crunch. It really was good. When I tried to return it, he shook his head and told me to keep it.

We wandered some more, as though walking through a vivid dream. I hadn't known such splendid places existed outside of my own flower-filled court.

Draven eventually found us again and steered us toward a bamboo cabin not far from the town's bustling heart, with a view of the main square. The cabin was a basic two-room, two-floor affair, with gaps where some of the bamboo walls met, but it would suffice for a few days. I didn't ask how Draven had paid for it, but I did thank him, brightening his mood. He'd been dour since our argument at the traders' camp.

"Join me in the tavernas tonight, both of you," Draven suggested, making an effort to smooth the cracks in our relationship. "We deserve it."

Some respite sounded perfect. "Lark?"

He'd propped himself at the cabin's window with his back to us and watched the bustling street. "You go, I'm too weary from traveling."

Lark had been paler of late, despite the sun. Some rest would do him good, and it gave me a chance to talk our situation through with Draven.

I agreed to go with Draven and ventured up the cabin's stairs. I washed, shaved off the beard, and dressed in the same clothes, vowing to rectify our lack of clean clothes tomorrow. Lark had already retired to a bedroom when Draven and I stepped into the night.

Draven and I sampled a few tavernas, then found an open-air eatery with flickering lamps at each table.

"I wanted to speak with you," Draven began, as we sat. "About us."

"I had the same thought—"

"Please, let me speak."

I sealed my lips and nodded.

He struggled to find the right words, and sighed. "Shall we order food first?"

We ordered, and as the bright, jubilant atmosphere

soaked into my body, the tension from the last few weeks began to ease. With plentiful food and water, and the two most important people in my life close by, it seemed as though we might finally be finding our feet among the recent chaos.

"I know I'm not who you want," Draven said. "Despite what Lark believes, I'm not a dimwitted fool."

"He just says those things, he doesn't mean them—"

Draven held up a hand. "I have eyes. I see the two of you together and I know we're not like that. But I want you to know, it doesn't matter. I will always uphold our vows. I will protect you, Arin. You have my heart, always. I love you." He leaned back in the seat and sighed. "There, it's said."

He loved me. And I loved him too, but not as he wanted. "Draven, I'm sorry."

"I know. Lark is..." He looked over the heads of the other customers at the bustling street beyond the eatery. "He's Lark."

"Well, yes, but... I don't want to hold you back. You should find someone who makes you happy. Someone you can forge a happy life with."

"I truly believed I had."

Oh dear. We had worked well together, when it had been just Draven and I. But that was before I knew Lark's truth, and that truth had changed everything. I couldn't take that back. I couldn't unlove Lark. Draven was the better man. Better than me. He'd saved me, saved us. He always tried to do the right thing; honest and strong. It was a wonder he tolerated Lark and I, when we'd both tangled ourselves up in lies and scheming.

"I understand my place and I will make peace with it, but I don't want this to be our end. I'll be your friend and ally, Arin, if you'll have me."

"Of course."

He raised his cup. "To new beginnings."

"Yes." I clunked our cups together and attempted to smile. "New beginnings." The singer didn't sound so sweet now, and the wine had warmed, turning a little sour. Draven's smile didn't last, and mine had begun to crack. We'd eaten, we'd said all that needed to say. Draven and I, whatever we'd had—it was over. "Do you mind if I retire? I'm tired. It's been a long few weeks."

He nodded and cradled his wine in his fingers. "You know the way back?"

"Yes, I'll be fine."

"Good night, Arin."

"G'night, Draven." It hurt. Even if we weren't meant to be together, we were friends, and I hadn't meant to be cruel. His gaze tickled my back until I'd turned a street corner, and I strode back the way we'd wandered, through revelers, dancers, and the performers Lark would have delighted in seeing.

I passed a silk shop and made a note to revisit it to commission Lark's purple and black courtly attire, then entered our cabin. All the rooms were dark but one—the bathroom at the top of the stairs. "Lark?"

"Back so soon?"

I climbed the stairs and stopped outside the bathroom door. I should tell him about Draven and I, let him know it was over. "Are you decent?"

"Never."

I rolled my eyes and slumped a shoulder against the wall. "I spoke with Draven. I think he'll be... all right. Eventually."

He didn't reply, and I didn't hear any movement from inside. There wasn't any sound of running water either. "Lark?"

"I'm thinking."

Of course he was. But if the water wasn't running, what was he doing in there? "About what?"

"About whether to invite you in."

I chuckled. "Well, if you're hesitating, that suggests no."

"Enter, if you like. It's not locked."

I wasn't sure I dared to. Yet, as I questioned myself, I lowered the handle and gave the door a small shove, opening it by a few inches, then a few more, unable to resist. A hammered tin bath dominated the bathroom. Lark was draped inside it, arms relaxed along its rolled edges, head resting back. He arched an eyebrow, then reached up and ruffled his hacked-at wet hair.

He'd cut his glorious black locks, reducing them to a messy mop. "What do you think?"

I clicked the door closed behind me, sealing us both inside the steam-dampened room. "In truth, I'll miss its length."

"Less to clutch." He wet his hands and ran them back through his hair, slicking it back, and with its length gone, the angles of his face gained sharper edges, enhancing the dramatic angular features the Court of Pain brothers shared. With shorter hair, he resembled Razak more than I cared to dwell on.

"You hate it," he said, dropping his head back. "I knew you would. This is a terrible idea."

"No, I don't hate it. It's just different."

He eyed me, still standing in the spot by the door, and his smile slowly grew. "I recall another bath, larger than this one. We shared it, briefly." He shifted, sloshing water, folded his arm over the edge of the bathtub, and propped his chin onto it. Only his shoulders were exposed above the bath's edge, but I had no trouble remembering the rest of his body from our night in my bed. He had muscle enough to wrestle me beneath his blade in his bedchamber. The memory was a fond one, strangely.

Water dripped from his fingers, leaving damp splashes on the timber floor. His every slow blink, every lazy glance, tempted me closer, and he knew it. "That bath was the first time I wondered if there was more to you than a prince with a stick up his ass. You seemed more real then than at any other time since we'd met."

"Until the cove."

"Until the cove," he agreed. "The Prince of Many Faces."

"I couldn't maintain my act around you—didn't want to."

"I know that now. At the time, however, I'd assumed you'd come to see the damage your muscle-men had inflicted during your beating."

I looked away. By Dallin, I'd hated having to do that. "I'd been trying to make our rift believable."

He waved my words away. "I merely brought it up to make it clear the beating did little to temper my feelings for you. If anything, it strengthened them."

He'd *liked* the beating? Was that a good thing? He fluttered his lashes, so smug and innocent at the same time. "You have feelings for me?" I asked.

"No, you're a vicious liar, a terrible juggler, and awfully ugly." His smile twitched. "I suppose you think me a true fool, hm? But surprisingly, even villains have hearts, and mine is somewhat bruised and beaten. But it knows it's wants."

My own heart thumped a little too loudly. What was he saying? "You're not a villain, Lark."

"I will be, if we're to execute your plan."

And with his hair cut short, his face more angular for it, I was already beginning to see the change in him. It would only be for a few days, but he would have to play the part of Razak flawlessly, including all that entailed. There was no doubt he could do it. But he feared it too.

Was all of this worth it? What if we ran back to the Court of Love and made something of a life among the rubble? But neither of us would be able to rest, knowing all we did, knowing Razak unrestrained would see countless dead and we could have stopped him.

"Arin." His tone had darkened, turned harsh. I'd heard it this way before, when he'd held a knife to my throat and threatened to fuck me. It sent a fluttering trill down my back and sizzled lust through my veins. I liked it.

"Yes, Lark?"

"Come here." He still rested his chin on his arm, was still submerged. Nothing had changed, only his voice.

I swallowed, or tried to, and started forward.

"Stop."

I stopped. What game was this now?

"So obedient," he purred. "A natural submissive."

I'd heard the term. Although I hadn't been the most adventurous when it came to the pleasures of my court, I'd observed from afar. Submissive appeared to be the partner who bowed to their dominator. And he was wrong.

"Don't be offended," he said. "Being submissive does not translate to being weak." He leaned back in the tub, sloshing water over its sides while allowing me a tantalizing view of his pale chest. His tiny scars were barely visible in the orange-hued lamplight.

He stretched both arms along the back of the tub, his attitude very different to the previous time we'd shared a bath. Then, he'd been guarded and suspicious—mostly my doing, as he'd had no idea who I was. But now, we knew each other, knew who we really were. I'd wanted him then, but it had been a shallow, physical need. Here, now, everything I felt for him ran far deeper, ran into my veins, wove through my blood, and beat through my heart.

I approached the tub and pulled off my jacket, flinging it aside, then started at my shirt, only to pause as I realized the tub wasn't large enough for two.

Lark's smirk had grown, knowing I'd faltered. "Now what are you going to do?"

"You can't stay in there all night." I spied a chair by the window and, resuming unbuttoning my shirt, I sat and waited, letting the shirt hang open. For some reason, anger had joined the gamut of emotions spinning inside me. He did this to me, made me crazy. I didn't even know *why* I was angry. Perhaps because this was his game, and I didn't know the rules.

"You're right." He plunged his hands underwater, swept them back through his hair again, and stood.

Water cascaded down his smooth back and firm ass. There was no ignoring his jutting dick. He had no shame, no hesitancy. He knew he was beautiful. It was like watching a mythical nymph rise from the lagoon, a creature so beautiful, I'd surely suffer for desiring it.

"Well..." He stepped from the bath and now stood stark naked in the middle of the bathroom, erect and splendid. "What *are* we to do now?" He placed a hand on his hip. The tease.

My mouth had dried, and my heart may have stopped. Or perhaps it had moved to my cock, because the damned thing was trapped, hot and throbbing inside my trousers, demanding attention.

"You think I'm just going to fall over myself for you?" I asked. At least my voice hadn't betrayed the desperate lust burning through my body, and my balls.

He chuckled and turned away, scooping up a black robe—

I'd no idea where he'd gotten it—then shrugged it over his shoulders, curtaining off the majestic view of his back, ass, and lean dancer's thighs.

Wait, was he leaving?

He strode for the door.

If he left, we'd have no privacy when Draven returned. But if I called him back, I'd be admitting how much I wanted him. That was his game, then. To make me reveal my desire, a desire we both clearly had, but he had to hear it. He wanted me to submit. And maybe I wanted that too, because when he took that earlier tone, when he held a blade to my throat, when I had no choice but to obey, I fucking wanted it.

"Lark?"

He stopped at the door, reaching for its handle, and tilted his head, waiting.

I stood and sauntered forward. "Is there a lock?"

His hand dropped. The lock snicked.

I didn't slow, didn't stop, and crossed the floor in a few strides, then turned his face toward me, slid my hand into his wet hair, cupping his head, and pulled him into a near-kiss. Our lips almost met, our breaths mingled, and his eyes blew wide, drinking me in. His cock nudged my hip, prompting me to move in, grinding close, but we still didn't kiss, just breathed, his slick chest against mine, water droplets cooling between us.

"Do you have a knife?" I whispered.

He swallowed, and with his cock pressed close, I felt its twitch.

"I can lay my hands on a similar blade." He stepped away in a twirl of dark robe and snatched something off the nearby washbasin. Metal flashed, and a razor's cold kiss was at my neck, my back at the wall, and Lark's smile turned devilish. "How's this?"

An electric lick of fear joined the heady emotional concoction running through my veins. He wouldn't kill me, but the look in his eyes suggested he would hurt me and we'd both like it. The time I'd struck him in his room, he'd asked me to do it, said we'd both enjoy it. And we had.

I snatched his neck, jabbed my thumb under his chin, and tilted his head up. I didn't have a knife, or any weapon, but I could crush his throat, stop him breathing. His brilliant, sparkling glare demanded I do it. He gritted his teeth, and as I squeezed, his black lashes fluttered. I didn't want to hurt him, didn't want to do this—

I let go, he gasped, then slammed a brutal kiss over and into my mouth. Somewhere in all this chaotic madness, I remembered the razor, but it was gone from my neck.

Lark's right hand plunged into my hair, his tongue thrust against mine, and it was all I could do to ride the wave of his assault, afraid yet desperate for more.

We broke apart, gasping, scorched by violent, fierce desire.

He searched my face, as though needing something from me. Permission? Or something else? "I don't care what it is, if you need it, do it."

His lips ticked, hinting at a smile. "You don't know the power you're giving me."

"I trust you."

His smile crumbled, and his beautiful face fell.

"What?"

Was it wrong, to trust him? His reaction was... unexpected. It kicked my heart into a gallop. Had I somehow hurt him all over again? "I trust you?" I hadn't meant it to sound like a question.

"Why?" He pushed away, taking several steps back, creating a cold void between us.

I wished in that moment that I understood him more, that whatever doubt he had, he'd tell me so I could erase it. "I just do."

"No." He pointed the razor at me. "Tell me why, Arin. I need to hear it."

"I trust you..." So many reasons, all of them muddled and complicated. Because he'd tried to save War's people by almost killing himself, because inside all his neurosis there was a good, kind heart, because he'd survived terrible things, only half of which I knew, and he still somehow smiled and danced. Because he was one in a million, more than that, because he was Lark, my friend, my... lover, my love. "Because I'm not a good person, and you're not a bad one, and together? Together, we're better for each other. I don't know. I don't understand it, I wish I did. But I know I trust you."

The front door slammed below us, rattling the boards.

"Arin?" Draven's voice sailed up the stairs and through the locked door.

The man's timing had never been worse. I blinked up at the ceiling, wishing the warlord away. "Yes?"

"Is Lark with you?" he called.

Lark shook his head and pressed a finger to his now-smiling lips. The shimmer in his eyes suggested he was planning something mischievous and downright wicked.

"No," I lied.

Lark strode forward, but this time with the sultry sashay in his hips, and as he was still naked beneath the robe, his body made it clear he hadn't lost interest in what we'd begun and I'd almost ruined moments ago.

"Is everything all right?" Draven called, now from behind the bathroom door.

"Yes, fine."

Lark slipped the razor into my hand. Its weight was solid and real.

He leaned in, cheek to cheek, and whispered, "Turn around."

I'd face the wall, if I obeyed. I blinked at him, locked my gaze with his. His fingers tugged at my trousers, jerking my hips. He loosened them off, then slipped his warm hands around my waist and stroked down. Firm fingers dug into my ass cheeks, nails biting. "Turn around, Arin."

I knew what he wanted. I wanted it too. Flashes of our time in the library came back to me as short, sharp memories, his hand on my cock, the other on my mouth. But Draven was behind the door, and perhaps this was cruel. Lark's breath whispered at my ear; his cheek, then jaw skimmed mine. Every touch set me ablaze.

He jerked my trousers down. They pooled around my boots. He looked up, into my gaze. "Turn around, Prince of Hearts."

"Arin?"

"Draven, all is well," I growled.

Lark clutched my waist and turned me.

"Brace," he whispered. I raised an arm, leaning against the wall. Then he was gone. A glance back revealed him at the washbasin cabinet. I bowed my head and tried to slow my heart and my breaths. If Draven heard, he'd know... But he wouldn't hear.

Lark's gentle fingers plucked off my shirt, then those same fingers kneaded my ass, so exposed. By Dallin, how could I do this? Draven was so close, already hurting from being shunned, but Lark's fingers digging and massaging, separating and squeezing—it was too good to stop. His left hand came around, gently pressed over my mouth, while his right hand—now slick—dipped between my ass cheeks and his fingers stroked my hole. I jolted, the moan almost slipping free. He was going to fuck me, and fuck me hard. I had to be silent. Fear, anticipation, and excitement mingled like a drug, shifting all reason away and sense away.

Lark's right hand grasped my cock, fingers tightening. I shuddered and panted through my nose, the assault so sudden, there was no time to prepare. He pumped, ramping up delicious friction. His cock nestled between my ass cheeks, sliding up my crack, teasing its way deeper, separating my ass until his rocking motions stroked his hard dick over my hole, promising more with every stroke.

Crackles of heightened pleasure tingled my nerves. I might come too soon, already skimming the edges of ecstasy, but Lark knew, like he always did, and when he let go of my cock, he timed the thrust of his dick to push in at the exact right moment to muddle my mind and body. Pressure widened, tightened, Lark's breaths sawed at my ear, his hand trembled over my mouth and briefly, the tightness was too much, the invasion too exposing—then his cock skimmed some internal part of me, making my own dick jump, twitch, and pulse, unwinding my tension.

His hand tightened, trying to stifle my guttural groan. If Draven heard us, I'd gone beyond caring. Lark had me now, hand at my mouth, cock in my ass, and I'd never felt anything like it, as though my body was awash with waves of white fire. He eased in and out, stoking the fire. By the god Dallin, could I come like this, without my dick being touched?

I thought I might, then his right hand with its two fingers and thumb clasped me anew, and I fucked his grip while he fucked my ass. I was coming undone, mindless and free, burning up from the inside. I cried out behind his hand and spilled with no hope of stopping it. Juddering, rippling waves rode me higher. Cum wet his fingers. His breath scorched my ear.

"Bite me," he growled.

I'd do it, do anything. He tucked a finger against my lips. I opened my jaw and clamped down into pliable skin, and Lark's thrusting became frantic. There was no muffling the slap of his upper thighs on my ass.

"Harder," he ordered, his voice a vicious growl.

I dug my teeth in, bit as hard as I dared. Blood spilled over my tongue, alarmingly coppery, and I let go, afraid I'd hurt him too much.

Lark moaned in my ear, his thrusting stuttered, and there —the moment I'd wanted from him, his final release. His hips jerked, body shuddering. Gods, was there anything more rewarding, more satisfying, than having the man I knew I loved so thoroughly enraptured that he spilled his cum for me?

The bite, his blood. I tasted it still.

It was pain. He needed pain to climax.

My thoughts spun as he panted behind me.

The scars on his chest... were they from Razak, was every cut a memory of his brother bringing him to climax?

He lowered his hand, allowing me to breathe again, and placed his bleeding fingers on my hip. His dick was still seated inside, it's widening pressure curiously satisfying.

"A bath, my Prince of Flowers?" He nuzzled my neck, the both of us slick with sweat, oil, and fluids. A bath was definitely called for. And perhaps, by the time we were clean and dried, Draven would be asleep.

"Yes," I whispered.

Lark chuckled and eased himself free. Warm wetness trickled from my hole, down my balls. Perhaps I should have found it uncomfortable, but he'd finally been honest with me, holding nothing back.

Lark had been my first, and I was glad for it.

He sauntered to the tub, dipped his fingers in the water, then ran the hot faucet and perched on the tub's edge. His cock had lost some of its rigidity and lay against his thigh. I straightened from the wall, wincing a little around a small sizzle of heat in my rear, crossed the floor in two strides, and kissed him messily on the mouth. He laughed against my lips, kissing me back. He and I, it felt right, it felt as though we belonged, despite neither of us having a place to call home.

"I trust you," I whispered, "because I love you."

Lark's expression softened, saddened even, and when he looked down into the bath's steaming water his eyes glistened with unshed tears. Had he ever known love? The unconditional kind? He would now, with me. He didn't even have to love me back. That was his choice. But I would fight for him, protect him, and love him with all my heart. If anyone dared hurt him without his permission, they'd have my wrath come down upon them, because there was no greater force in the shatterlands than love.

CHAPTER 10

$\mathcal{L}$ark

Love.

Strange how, now I had it, I knew I'd never felt it before.

Arin loved me. He trusted me. I'd wanted that, but it was terrifying too. Love and trust meant pain, when it eventually came to an end. Which it would, because despite all the poems and songs, love always ended.

We bathed together, Arin's soft skin against mine, his mouth and hands exploring. I kissed his smile, and other parts, relishing in having him close as we sloshed too much water from the tub and dropped all pretense of not caring for each other, for Draven's benefit.

It was only when we stumbled from the bath, towel-dried and love-drunk, that Arin remembered Draven and his guilt soured the mood.

I tied off the robe left in the cabin for its guests and

ventured from the steamed-up bathroom in search of the warlord. He'd left, probably when he'd realized Arin had not been alone behind the bathroom door.

I returned to my prince in bed and found him gloriously naked and spread on the sheets like a feast I'd have no trouble devouring. "Draven's not here."

"Oh, well, that's good, I suppose." He saddened but brightened again as I shucked off my robe and joined him. I'd learned how he liked it when I nuzzled his neck and stroked his hip.

He writhed, ticklish and jubilant, and laughed, clutching my arm as though to lever me off. Our tussling turned heated, gaining an edge I'd gladly exploit to hear him moan and whimper. I'd never known a man to come so alive beneath my touch. Or perhaps I'd never cared to notice before. I cared now, cared so much it made my heart and thoughts race.

He'd told me he loved me, trusted me, and now I knew it, I had no idea what to do with that, so I did what I knew best. I worshipped his body with my mouth and tongue and cock, making him cry out and gasp, clutch the sheets in his fists, bite his lip, and spill his cum. I'd never get enough, and would have happily pleasured him all night, but the moment he spooned himself against my back, tucking close, and mumbled words of love so casually, I stroked his hair back from his face and watched his lashes flutter closed, listening to his breathing slow.

How could someone so perfect love me? He would realize his mistake, eventually. Until then, I'd take all the love he was willing to give and cherish it like the most precious gem in all the world, more precious than Razak's four crowns. I doubted my brother had ever known such love as this.

I fell asleep alongside Arin and woke to the calling from market stalls and clatter of carts outside the window.

Arin sat at a desk, scribbling a note. His shirt gaped, and he'd swept his hair back in a messy tail. Whatever he studied, it had him transfixed. I watched him, admiring the view while the sun poured through the window and made his golden hair shine.

"Ah, you're awake. Here, I've made a list." He picked up his paper and read aloud, "Clothes, for us, outfits for our performance. I spotted a tailor last night. They'll have silk. We must look like princes *before* we arrive in the Court of Pain. Then, a haircut. You need one. A professional one. Yours is—" His smile twitched. "—interesting. Does Razak have any distinguishing marks? Tattoos, scars?"

I flopped my head back, already overwhelmed. "Is breakfast on that list?"

Two raps sounded on the door moments before it creaked open and Draven filled its frame, answering my concern as to where he'd gotten to. His gaze absorbed me, clearly naked beneath the bedsheet, and Arin, haphazardly dressed at the desk. It didn't take much to piece our night together.

He didn't appear furious; his eyes were tired, and his lips tilted downward. Experience with cuckolded lovers had taught me the quiet ones were the ones to watch for a knife in the back.

"I'm taking the next supply train back to War," he said.

Arin shifted on the chair. "When does it leave?"

"Tonight."

"So soon?"

"There seems little point in delaying when there's nothing here for me."

Arin shrank some, his heart taking a beating. I flicked my hacked-at hair and flashed Draven a smile, drawing the warlord's ire away from Arin. Draven was bitter; he'd had his heart broken. I'd give him some time to hurt, but if he came at Arin with any more guilty blows, I'd put a stop to it. "Dinner then, the three of us," I offered, forcing some brightness into the room. "As a farewell."

Arin brightened, and Draven huffed a soft laugh and smiled. "Fine then, Lark. But you're paying."

I shrugged. I had no idea how I could pay, when I had no coin and nothing to call my own. Even my clothes were borrowed. But I'd figure it out.

"All right then," Draven drawled. "Dinner, before I leave." He closed the door again, and Arin and I listened to his clunking footsteps descend the stairs, then the front door creak and slam.

"Do you think he knows?" Arin asked.

Draven was sometimes slow to catch on, but not *that* slow. "Are you truly asking or jesting?"

He slumped in the chair. "I hadn't meant to be so cruel."

"Hm, but you're so good at it."

He flung me a droll look, then narrowed his eyes. "Stop."

"What?"

"With the look."

"I don't know what you mean." I blinked and fluttered innocent lashes.

"Get dressed. There's lots to be done."

"Well?"

"Well, what?"

"Is breakfast on your list?"

He sighed, then scribbled on the paper. *"Breakfast with Lark,"* he announced, then showed me, by which time I'd left the bed and padded bare-assed across the room. I perched on the edge of his desk, legs crossed at the knee. He made a valiant effort not to look at my crotch, but I'd left him little choice.

He dragged his gaze from my stiffening dick, up my chest, to my eyes. "What's for breakfast?"

I plucked his list from his fingers, tossed it aside, and leaned in. "I think you know."

LATER IN THE DAY, we visited the tailor's, had my measurements taken, and placed our order with promise of payment to come on delivery, then wandered the sweltering jungle-oasis town. The atmosphere was much like that of the trading caravan, the people open and friendly; even more so than in Arin's court—they'd all had barbed smiles. But the people here were honest with their expressions and their welcome.

With the town being tucked into a ravine, it remained sheltered from the sun's powerful rays, and it meant the evenings came early. We wandered into the performers' area as the day began to cool and the shadows drew long, and the bars, restaurants, and nightlife began to stir awake. Draven had brought Arin here the previous night. He'd thought then how I might enjoy it.

I did.

Players took to the streets and danced and sung; some juggled. One man swallowed fire on the end of a sword— something I might have to try; I was comfortable deep-throating most things. Arin left my side to go looking for Draven. I remained, tapping my foot to the jubilant music, eager to dance. It had been a while since I'd danced for my own pleasure and not because of someone's demands.

A great many things had ended with Arin's court's demise, not least my four years of freedom. His plan to infiltrate the

Court of Pain had merit, but it meant walking back into a prison, when I could walk away.

One of the street-players plucked an instrument much like a fiddle, but it was shorter than those I was familiar with. He used a small bow and glided it over the strings. He caught my eye as he played, smiled, and when his playing finished, he made his way through the crowd.

"You play?" he asked.

I searched for the ulterior motive in his gaze, some reason why he'd isolate me from the crowd, but found only kindness. "A similar instrument, yes. You're very skilled."

He offered me the fiddle. "Try?"

I'd been waiting for an excuse to get involved. I took the instrument and tested its weight, getting familiar with its feel. When he handed me the bow, he made no mention of my three fingers or how they might impede me. I plucked a few strings, then scattered a quick tune into the air, attuning myself to its flighty notes. Being lighter than the instruments I'd learned on, this little fiddle leant itself well to movement.

"It is, indeed, a beautiful thing."

I attempted to hand it back, but the kind stranger shook his head and smiled some more. "Play." He stepped back and bowed.

"If you're sure." He didn't have to ask twice. I hadn't played since Arin's court, and the moment I stroked the bow across the strings, my heart sang for the loss of my love of music. I coaxed a slow, sultry tune from the instrument. It drifted in waves and seduced its way into the hearts of those nearby. It seemed fitting in this hot, crowded, loud, and colorful place. And while I became aware of crowd's attention turning my way, I didn't play for them. I played for me, and the more I played, the more the music enveloped me, and the more my heart soared.

This might be my last chance to express the truth of me. And Arin was right. I'd never wanted to be the bad player in the game of courts. Neither had he.

I caught sight of the smiles, the glittering joy-filled eyes, and then the dancers, and soon I was among them, lost to the music, to its control and its freedom. Arin was there, his face in the crowd, blue eyes bright and grin brilliant. Draven was there too. The stoic warlord smiled a little. We had our differences, but he was a good man, a good friend in a world where friends were few, and good men rare.

Another face caught my eye—one not smiling—but as I spun, coming back around to find the hooded male, he'd vanished, swallowed by the dancing crowd.

The tune came to its natural end. I raised the fiddle and bow, breathless, quivering, but so alive, and the applause roared like a breaching wave. Handing the fiddle back to its owner, I thanked him.

He grasped my arm. "The passion lives within you. Never lose it... Makes you strong."

I thanked him again, and while trying to riddle out his prophetic words, I ambled back to Arin's side.

He threw an arm around my shoulders. "You are beautiful when you play."

"Am I not beautiful at all other times?"

He laughed and when the pair of us stumbled toward Draven, the warlord rolled his eyes, keeping his grin. "And on that note, it's time we eat."

Dinner, I'd forgotten. I had no coin. I'd only had a few moments to make my excuses, when Arin slipped clinking coins into my trouser pocket. Where he'd gotten it, I had no idea. It meant I wouldn't have to ruin our evening, and his glittering blue eyes told me he knew it.

We found a nearby outdoor eatery, where the music still

played and a crowd bustled at the bar area, bringing with it a celebratory atmosphere even our grumpy warlord could not resist. It was a fitting end to our interesting expedition across the desert.

We raised our glasses, toasting to new horizons and new beginnings, and with the moon high overhead, the moment of Draven's leaving arrived too soon. He lost his smile and cast his gaze toward the exit.

We'd had our differences, he and I, but we also couldn't have made it this far without him.

I stood, chinked my cup with his, and gripped his shoulder, peering into the man's warm, kohl-defined eyes. He was a handsome bastard, I'd give him that. "I wish you luck, my friend, and fewer sandworms on your return journey."

"And you. Don't let Pain take your spark, Lark."

I grinned. "We'll make a poet out of you one day, Warlord."

He gripped my arm, we said our silent goodbyes, and I left Arin and Draven to their farewells, giving them space to speak alone.

Draven had saved Arin; he'd been there for him when my actions had almost ruined all of us. He deserved a proper goodbye.

Mingling with the crowd at the bar, I sipped my cool wine and caught sight of the hooded man—the same unsmiling man who had been among the crowd when I'd played earlier. He seemed familiar. I studied his face in profile, assessing why he'd caught my eye a second time. He looked up, and his glare locked with mine a few beats too long to be casual.

He knew me.

Which meant he likely knew Arin.

Arin and Draven remained at the table, heads bowed close,

unaware we were being observed. I turned my attention back to the unsmiling man. He'd left the bar and was several strides away, heading toward the open street and its stream of people.

Hopefully, his presence meant nothing and I'd imagined his interest, in which case I'd apologize for what I was about to do. I downed my wine, pushed from the bar, and fell into step behind him.

Most folks ambled and dallied in the sultry night air, but my watcher strode with purpose. He had a destination in mind. Falling into a jog, I wove through the thickening crowd. The sooner I caught up with him, the sooner I'd return to Arin. The night was still young and full of possibilities, especially with Draven's departure.

Earlier in the day, I'd spotted an open-air bathing waterfall. A midnight dip with Arin would be the perfect way to spend a few hours.

The watcher had vanished. I stopped and scanned the faces of those in the crowd. None belonged to him. He must have taken the side-street with its row of bamboo-houses leaning on each other like drunken friends. The street abruptly ended in one half of a collapsed bridge that had once spanned the plunge pool of another waterfall. The falls still roared behind it.

I slowed at the street's entrance. All the houses were dark, and some near the waterfall sagged on their foundations, consumed by the mist. The watcher hadn't gone that way. His attire had been too heavy for a desert-dweller. He didn't live in these cabins.

I'd return to Arin, tell him of our stalker. We'd have to be more careful during our last few days in Palmyra.

A dry, calloused hand slammed over my mouth from behind, and something jagged and sharp dug into my waist.

"Easy now. Don't scream. Scream, and you'll bleed. You don't want this to get messy, Zayan."

I whimpered behind his hand and struggled enough to convince him I'd be an easy catch. But what he couldn't see, and what he'd never know, was how my smile grew.

CHAPTER 11

ark

"There, easy now, stay calm."

By the spread of the man's hand over my mouth and chin, he was large, muscular—likely the same man I'd followed. I panted hard and pretended to be the obedient victim.

"You're not going to fight, are you?"

I shook my head.

His grip eased from my mouth, and the blade poking at my side disappeared. It had to be now, while he assumed I was caught.

I slammed my head back, striking something hard but soft enough to buckle. He grunted, reeled, and I spun, caught the flash of his knife, grabbed his wrist, and snapped it back. He barked a cry, and the knife slipped from his fingers into mine.

With the main street and its mingling crowds a mere few strides away, this was not the place to cut a man. I skipped back, caught the watcher's eye, and pirouetted on my heel—and bolted for the misty falls. A well-timed trip gave my pursuer hope he might catch me, and a glance behind revealed he was chasing me. The fool. Whoever had sent him hadn't told him what I was capable of, or he wouldn't allow me to lure him into the dark.

I slowed near the broken bridge. Its one-sided span ended alongside the plunging falls, rotted and decayed, just like the houses. Any safety rail had long ago fallen into the pool below.

"Nowhere to go now, pretty." He stalked forward. His face was scarred, like my handler Danyal's had been. Each mark a murder, and the watcher had three. He came from the Court of Pain. But how had he found me?

I shivered, soaked through from the rolling mist, and made a show of chattering teeth and trembling.

"Give me the knife." The watcher reached out. "Come now."

I took another step back. The slick timbers creaked. "Who sent you?"

"There's only one who has that authority."

Razak.

Clearly, iron bars meant nothing to my brother. He'd proven that in War. If he had his claws in Justice's court, then he could hire bounty hunters, like this one.

"Your reward?" I asked.

"What else, but coin?" He sneered. It wasn't just about coin with this one. A cruel desire made his wrinkled eyes shine. "Coin enough to see me right. So come now, let's get you home, ready for the prince's return."

Then Razak wasn't yet back in Pain. Good. This was all good.

The watcher inched closer. The bridge shuddered. A crack sounded. "Come to me!"

Go to him. As though my fear of Razak was so great that I'd surrender myself here and now, to a killer's mercy. Sometimes I wondered if my brother knew me at all.

The knife felt solid in my hand, real, balanced, as though it had always belonged to me. I smiled, and the watcher's eyes narrowed. He sensed a change in our dynamic. He was the hunter, and I the prey? But my smile said otherwise.

"Come here you wretched fool!" He lurched.

I could have danced aside and shoved him off the edge of the broken bridge, but as my heart raced and hot blood burned through my veins, I needed this. Needed to make him hurt, and hurt Razak through him. I sidestepped and caught his shirt in my left hand, stopping his unbalanced fall.

I'd saved his life. His expression said as much, and he might have thanked me, had I not thrust the dagger into his neck—once, twice. Scarlet blood spurted, the man's mouth opened in a shocked *O*, and it was only now he truly saw me, truly *knew* me. Wasn't so easy a catch now, was I?

He groped at the air. Thin fingers skimmed my shoulder, desperate to cling to a life fast draining out of him. He grabbed my arm, tried to pull me into his dying moments. I slashed his forearms, forcing him back, separating us. He reeled again. His boots slipped on greasy boards and for a few breathless moments, he teetered on the edge of the broken bridge.

A man's life hung on the end of a thread, a thread I held. I could have pulled him back, although it was unlikely that gushing vein would heal.

"When Razak joins you in whatever damnation I'm about to send you to, please do give him my regards." I kicked his chest. He rocked, thrust out his bleeding arms, desperate for help, but as he danced, the boards underfoot snapped and the watcher vanished over the side.

The waterfall roared, swallowing any scream. The mist rolled, unperturbed. He was gone. The only evidence he'd ever existed was his bloody knife clenched in my hand.

I wiped wetness from my face. His blood or mist, it didn't matter.

It was time to find Arin.

CHAPTER 12

$\mathcal{A}$rin

DRAVEN and I embraced as friends. He wrapped me in his arms, and I pulled him close. It felt wholesome, as though our friendship might survive all this insanity. He smiled, let go, and gathered his single traveling bag from the ground. The supply caravan behind him was noisy, full of kareels and carts, wagons and traders. Draven cast his gaze over them and at what would be his new home for several days, until he reached Ogden's court and the true journey began.

"We'll meet again at the Overlook," he said, tossing the bag over his shoulder.

"We will."

"The next full moon. You had better be there, Arin," he teased, but there was enough weight behind the order to suggest he'd hunt the four corners of the courts if Lark and I weren't at the Inn.

I nodded, fearing my voice might break if I replied. I hadn't expected his leaving to hurt.

He grabbed the reins of a large, grumbling kareel, settled on its saddle, gave me a single nod, and then plodded into the moving caravan. A strange kind of panic gripped my heart as I watched him go. What if Ogden had him killed... because of me?

He looked back once, threw a wave, and smiled when I raised my hand. Then he was gone, lost in the disturbed sand, somewhere under the stars.

We would see him again, and by then, we'd have Pain's crown and Razak would be stopped, either in Justice's clutches or we'd find a way to finish him for good. It was good, positive progress. The kind of progress we sorely needed.

I returned to the bar where I'd last seen Lark, but he hadn't returned. He hadn't been at Draven's farewell either, I'd assumed to avoid an awkwardness between the three of us, but now I wasn't so sure. He'd been gone a long while. He'd likely returned to our cabin.

I hurried through the crowds, eager to get back to him. The fluttering sense of panic Draven's leaving had left me with hadn't subsided. If anything, it was growing worse. I flung open the cabin door, and of course, there he was, seated in a chair near the back of the main lounge with just one lamp for illumination. "There you are!" Relief stopped my heart's flutter. "Draven is on his way." I closed the door behind me, sealing the general nightly hubbub outside. "I'm sure Ogden will take him back in. The king liked him. It was me he despised."

Lark rose from the chair, not having said a word, and as the lamplight crawled over him, dark splatters marked his pale face. "You're hurt—" I swept to him, touched his cheek.

Blood, I was sure of it now. His lips did that typically Lark smile by ticking up at one corner.

"I'm not hurt," he said, his voice thick.

"You must be." Splatters dashed his neck and his shirt. So much of it. Then I saw his right hand, and the knife, both coated in what could only be blood. If he wasn't bleeding, and he wasn't hurt, then someone else was. "What happened?"

His gaze skipped over my face, my eyes, and his ticking smile died. He turned away and set the knife down on a sideboard, propped back against it, and folded his arms. "We have a problem. One less problem than we had earlier in the evening, but a problem, nonetheless."

So much blood. The more I looked, the more of it came to light. What had he done? "Lark, did you hurt someone?"

"He deserved it."

"But you're not hurt?"

"I'm fine."

His voice remained flat, cold, hard, devoid of all emotion. I approached him. In the single lamplight, his face remained hard too. He said he wasn't hurt, but someone had attacked him. "The man you hurt, can he identify you? Should we leave?"

"He won't be identifying much of anything." His smirk grew. Pride and satisfaction lifted his voice. He'd hurt his attacker, likely killed him, and he was pleased about it.

"Are you *surprised*?" he asked, seeing my expression and thoughts I'd been unable to hide.

"No, I..." The truth landed hard. He'd killed a man. The blood was still drying on his hands. But he behaved as though he'd experienced a mild inconvenience on his way home, something as frivolous as crossing the street. I knew him capable of murder. None of this should have been a surprise. But there was knowing, and then there was *seeing*.

He straightened and crossed the cabin, stopping almost close enough to touch. His energy had turned aggressive, confrontational. "Should I have brought him here, to talk over tea? Is that what you would have done, Prince of Flowers?"

"No." My heart thumped. "I mean, if you say he deserved it, then he did."

"I'd believe you, if you weren't looking at me as though you don't know me."

Blood. I could smell it on him, sharp and metallic. I stepped back. Not because I didn't trust him, I did. I just needed a moment to gather my thoughts.

"You seem to have mistaken me for an innocent man. Arin, the bounty hunter is not the first man I've killed."

"I know that," I snapped, stumbling away—not from him, never from him, but from *this*, from my own reaction.

"Do you? Because you seem to be having a difficult time with this. If you've painted a picture of me as an innocent man who needs a white knight to ride in and save him, then you'll be sorely disappointed."

His laugh was cruel, so like Razak's.

I hadn't meant to make the comparison, but perhaps I should have. I'd been quick to dismiss any comparison with Razak as wrong, but perhaps I'd also ignored some aspects of Lark's personality that made him who he was. I'd narrowed my view, not wanting to see the messy, morally challenging parts of us, and that was my fault, not his.

"Am I suddenly too much for you now you see the blood on my hands?" The cruel edge remained in his voice, but it wasn't there to hurt me. It was there because he was hurting, because he thought I was turning away from him. He believed I was too good for him, and he was *nothing*. Words others had told him. Words he took to heart.

Damn him, he wasn't going to succeed in pushing me away because of a little murder.

"I once burned a butterfly under a magnifying glass," I admitted, blurting the words.

"What?" *What*. One word, but my confession had shocked the cruelty from his voice.

"I don't know why, just that I could. I had the means and I wanted to see what happened." I turned. He'd returned to the sideboard, and the wicked smirk was gone.

He was my Lark again, his face stained with blood, but still my Lark. "Did you enjoy it?" he asked.

"I hated myself after. And there was a time I told a girl to meet me in the hedge maze. I wanted to see her naked, see what I was missing. When her breasts and other things did nothing for me, I claimed it was her fault. She cried, so I yelled at her and sent her away, then had her expelled from court."

Lark's dark chuckle lightened the mood. "Hm," he purred, "tell me all your filthy secrets, prince."

"We'll be here until dawn." I strode across the floor and stopped in front of him. I could still smell the blood, there was so much of it. Whatever he'd done, he'd made the man suffer. "My point is, I'm not a white knight. And when I saw the blood, my first instinct was fear *for you*, then you tell me you've killed a man. I needed a hot-moment to process that. If you want to get sassy about it, please do. Now my shock has passed, I'm rather enjoying your ire. And mine. Which is new."

His catlike black eyes slow blinked, studying me, assessing, reading between the lines, trying to unpick my thoughts when I'd just laid them out for him. He didn't trust me, not yet, not like I trusted him. "Razak is hunting us from inside Justice," he said, his voice precise.

"Well then, we'll have to be careful until we adopt our roles in a few days. And if anyone else gets too close, you'll dispatch them like you did the last one."

He swallowed and huffed a silent laugh. "I want to kiss you, but I'm bloody—"

I parted his knees, slotted myself between them, and smelled the blood on him again, saw its speckles on his face. Someone had dared attack him, meant to hurt him. "Was he going to kill you?"

"He'd killed before, but no, he wasn't going to kill me. He planned to take me back to Pain, to await Razak."

Which would have been a spiritual death sentence, if not a physical one. "Fuck him then."

Lark's grin bloomed. He touched my chin and in a soft voice, he whispered, "I'd prefer to fuck you."

"As we have a few days until the tailor finishes our princely disguises—" I leaned in and nudged his mouth with mine, teasing the kiss to come. "—and we can't go outside—" His bloody hands clutched my hips. "—it seems we have some time to kill."

His lips brushed mine, so soft, but they could be sharp too. I knew what he was, who he was, and while I couldn't pretend not to be shocked, it all made up Lark: the man I loved, the good and the bad and all the messy, complicated parts in between.

"I feel I must warn you," he whispered. "I've been thinking of little else but getting my hands on you since dispatching the bounty hunter."

Pain, violence, it aroused him, and in any court outside of his, he'd have been considered wrong for those feelings. He wasn't wrong; he was brilliant and perfect, dark and delicious. He was beautiful and deadly, my beautiful lie. But the lie was the one he told himself. He wasn't nothing. He was everything.

"Hungry, are you?" I asked.

He roamed his hands up my back, fingers feeling their way, while leaning in, as though to seal our kiss and begin what we both knew was coming. "So hungry it hurts."

I ground my hips, rubbing against his rigid erection. Like this, Lark was a drug; he did things to me I had no control over, made me want things I hadn't known could elicit pleasure. I really had been lost behind a door, until he'd opened it.

His stained fingers skimmed my face, and I didn't care how the murdered man's bloody scent clung to him. Perhaps even liked it, if I were honest. But overthinking now would get in the way of feeling, and nobody made me feel to the depths of my soul like he did. As though we were the whole world, and nothing existed outside of his touch, his mouth— now on my neck while his hands fought to get inside my clothes. He tugged and pulled, stripping off my layers, and then his hot mouth was on my chest, tongue swirling, his hands expertly bringing me to hardness.

"How do you not find me repulsive?" he whispered, dropping to his knees.

Did he believe he was? Not Lark, the man everyone at the Court of Love had admired. Lark, who commanded every gaze the moment he walked into a room. I looked down; he looked up from my navel, where he'd been fluttering kisses, and his expression was so raw it hurt my heart. I grabbed his mop of hacked-at hair and hauled him into a furious kiss. I'd make him forget all thoughts like that one so he never had them again. I shoved, slamming him against the sideboard. He hissed. His knees spread, bracketing me close, and he met my kiss with his own ferocity. Something toppled off the sideboard, perhaps the knife. I tore at his bloody shirt, needing to taste him, to swallow him, to have him inside me, all of him at once. But before that, I had a question to answer, and it was damned important.

I clutched his face in my hands, leaving him no choice but to see me and see how much I meant this. "You want to know why?"

He seemed pained again, as though he might dread what came next. After everything, all my mistakes, my messes, my failures, he believed he was the one who didn't deserve me? "Because I love you." I'd said it before, but it hadn't seemed enough.

His blunt teeth dipped into his bottom lip and his eyes widened. "You truly love me?" he whispered.

Gods, I'd expected him to be happy, not look as though I'd torn his heart from his chest. "I suppose that secret of mine is yours now too." I chuckled, trying to make light of my confession in the hope it stopped him hurting.

He lunged and kissed my mouth slowly, sliding his tongue in, seeking acceptance, confirmation, and the truth. Did he think I was lying? I clutched the back of his head and deepened the kiss, needing him to know I didn't confess such things lightly. I *did* love him and if he didn't believe my words, then I'd make him feel it, because while our words sometimes deceived, our bodies did not.

I tugged his clothes apart, freeing them of buttons and laces, and then reached his warm, flushed chest with my hands and mouth. He tasted sweet under my tongue and quivered beneath my lips. I didn't know what I was doing, just that I needed to feel him in every possible way. He braced his hands to either side of him on the sideboard, bending backward, giving me all of him to tease and sample. His shirt was gone, his trousers hung open and clung to his hips, and in a moment of indecision, I stepped back, admiring how he sprawled there, panting, hard and desperate. He was beautiful before, but now, stained by blood, his beauty gained a razor's edge.

"Like what you see?" he asked, eyebrow arching.

I flew back in, clutched his hair in one hand, and wrapped my fingers around his neck, making him gasp and freezing him rigid. "You make me wild, make me insane—" I pushed the words against his panting mouth. He liked it when we fought, when it hurt. And perhaps I did too. I freed his neck and dropped my hand to his hard, weeping cock. I still had him by the hair, and his wide eyes drank me down while I gathered the smooth wetness from his tip and slid my hand down his length. It wasn't enough. Closer, I needed to be closer.

I dropped to my knees and took him deep, hearing him spit a curse. His hands plunged into my hair and twisted, sparking pain as he tugged, driving his cock deeper between my lips, over my tongue, down my throat. I gagged, choked, and even that didn't matter. Lark lifted my head, checking my face, my smile, then plunged back in. I spluttered around his width, unable to take his full length. But it wasn't all about swallowing him deep. I wrapped my hand around his base and pumped, then worked my tongue, muscling around his tip, combining sucking and stroking until his moans deepened to guttural panting. Gods, yes, I wanted him to come, to lose himself in me, but he needed more, he needed that sharp edge, that painful bite, to tip him over the edge.

The knife lay on the floor beside us. Bloody, forgotten. All I had to do was pick it up and cut him. Like Razak had, time and time again. He'd had my Lark under him, kept him prisoner, bound and chained him. He'd fucked him, hurt him, made him bleed. And I... couldn't do that.

Lark cupped my face, pulled me off his cock, and drew me to my feet. "What's wrong?"

"Nothing. It's nothing—" I lunged and kissed him as though my kiss could burn away the horrible things he'd endured.

Dropping my hand, I encircled his slick and straining dick, sliding down its length. He arched under me, driving his hips forward, and his dick into my fist. I had him now, pinned to the sideboard, attacking his mouth and his cock at once. I pumped hard, fast, desperately needing to feel him come undone. I thrust my tongue against his, taking everything he gave in return. "Come for me."

Dark eyes sparkled. His bruised, plump lips parted.

He was close, but he needed more. His breath stuttered, his body twitched and bucked, and his cock—so hot and hard, desperate for release—leaked pre-cum. His gaze begged when his words could not. This moment was its own kind of torture; he rode the very edge of orgasm, and I could keep him there, keep him from falling... Was that what Razak had done?

I snarled the Prince of Pain from my head, nuzzled Lark's neck, sucked his skin between my teeth, and bit deeply. Lark cried out, clutched my head, my ass, and warm, smooth cum hit my wrist. We swayed, rocking as one, riding his climax together, and gods, I was so primed, it would only take a touch for me to spill. And as though Lark knew, he grasped me through my trousers, gave several rough, messy pumps, and I came within moments, spilling in my undergarments against the heat of Lark's hand.

We clung to each other, breathless, sweat-soaked, and wet with cum and blood.

Lark's soft fingers skimmed my jaw, then tilted my chin up. "I am far from done with you."

CHAPTER 13

ark

THREE DAYS and nights we lay together, eating when we fancied, indulging in physical pleasure, dozing side by side, but as with all good things, it came to an end too soon.

On the third day, a note from the tailor arrived at the house, confirming our outfits were complete. I left Arin sleeping, visited the barber to style my hair exactly as Razak wore his, then collected the clothes for which Arin had already paid—he'd pawned his ceremonial joining dagger for a small fortune, a fact I was rather glad Draven didn't know.

While he continued to sleep, face down on the bed, arms and legs akimbo, I stripped, showered, and applied the new clothes, complete with a long black tailcoat, embossed with silver and purple. The quality matched that of Razak's own tailors, and once dressed, I stood in front of the full-length mirror, staring at my brother looking back.

It was real—suddenly and violently real.

I swayed and reached for the nearby dresser top. My brother followed. Gods. I turned my face away from the mirror. My gut flipped, churning. Nausea rolled up my throat, hot and acidic. *He wasn't here, I wasn't him.* I lunged into the bathroom, dropped to my knees, and dry heaved nothing into the toilet bowl, thankful I hadn't eaten.

I had to do this. I had to pretend to be him, to laugh like him, sneer like him, smile like him. I had to *be* Razak. I clutched the bowl and tried to swallow my heart back down where it belonged.

Being Razak was like any other act, any performance. He wasn't me, and I wasn't him. Just an act, another lie, a performance that would eventually end. They always did.

"Lark?"

"I'm fine," I croaked.

Arin crouched beside me, messy and perfect, with a sheet wrapped around his waist. He offered a cup of water. The sheet slipped. He clung awkwardly to it with one hand, while the other held out the water. "We don't have to do this."

He was wrong. This had to be done.

My dreams were worsening—dreams of storms, and laughter, of falling into oblivion, where I'd be shattered into countless pieces. The nightmares meant something; they told me Razak was winning.

"We could go back to my court, see if there's anything left to salvage, just you and I."

I took the cup and sat on the bathroom floor, cradling the cup in my lap. "He'll find us." The bounty hunter was just the beginning. "He'll never stop. We'll forever be looking over our shoulders, forever running." I sipped the water, finding it clean, cool, and fresh, and shook my head. "I don't want that life, do you?" He didn't reply, didn't need to. "We must do this."

Arin nodded. "I'll be with you."

Taking him into Pain... My honey and sunshine, my Prince of Flowers. I feared what it might do to him, what *I* might do to him. "Perhaps Draven was right, and you shouldn't go."

His smile froze on his lips. "It's not up for debate. I come, or we don't do it. I'm not leaving you alone in this."

"Very well, Your Highness." Arguing with Arin was pointless; he knew how I liked it. In fact, Arin might have been the only person in the four courts to truly know me. It was strangely freeing, having him see me, the *real* me. Not having to hide my ugliness, my wrongness.

He stood, reached down, and helped pull me to my feet. I swayed a little. His firm hand clutched my shoulder, steadying me. I did need him with me, because if I went back to the Court of Pain alone, I'd shatter. He was right; I couldn't do this alone.

"It'll just be for a few days." His voice was soft, but the ferocity in his eyes made it clear there would be no negotiation. Had I been of a stronger mind, I might have shoved him against the wall and reminded him which one of us controlled the other, and he'd let me.

"What?" he asked, the warmth in his cheeks ruining his mean glare.

"Your tone when you're mad is exceedingly arousing."

He chuckled and led me out of the bathroom. "You find *everything* arousing."

"Only when it comes to you."

He pretended to frown. "Remind me, how many people in my court did you seduce?"

"Most of them, and those I did not fuck, I fucked over." I flopped onto the bed, forgetting that I wore my new clothes and resembled my brother. I'd have to practice his mannerisms during the next few days.

Arin would need to purchase us passage to Pain's borders, and from there, we'd walk into Pain's central city as though I owned it, and Arin would be my prisoner, slave, pet? Certainly not the prince peering down at me now.

"Did you truly?" he asked.

Ah, this man, he'd work all my secrets from me and then I'd lose all my mystery and magic. "No, I did not engage in carnal desires with half the people I was accused of dallying with. Some rumors may have been embellished."

"By you?" He snorted.

"As if I'd do such a thing!"

Arin sprawled on the bed beside me, and we both lay back, staring at the cracks in the bamboo ceiling. The general clatter and hubbub from the street sailed in through the ill-fitting window, chatter and laughter. I'd become accustomed to the sound. Soon, there would be only the sound of rain on windowpanes.

He sighed. "We should leave in a few days, or we'll miss meeting with Draven at the Overlook Inn."

"I know."

His fingers twined with mine. "I wish I could slow time. I want nothing to happen, so that everything slows, but at the same time, I want to share the world with you."

His words formed a lump in my throat. Nobody had ever spoken to me in this way. All the showered praises had been fake, and when applause had rained, it had always been shallow, almost meaningless, compared to the fireworks Arin sparked alive within me now.

"Afterward, we'll have all the time in the world," I said, sounding like him. If we succeeded in stopping Razak, we'd be free to do as we pleased, go where we liked—to run in his meadows, dance in the rain, make love under the moon on his secret beach. Hope. What a wonderful thing it was to have it.

"Yes." He smiled, squeezing my hand. "We will."

If we survived.

THE LAST OF Arin's coin paid for passage on a huge metal mechanized wagon-train to Pain's borders. We left the next day, boarding our own private booth inside a large, cylindrical carriage made of what appeared to be hammered steel. A metal beast of an engine spewed hissing steam. It pulled the snake of carriages and thundered along metal tracks. At the front, at its nose, a huge triangular shovel swept waves of sand away. Sand washed by our carriage window, as though we tunneled beneath red water. I'd never moved so fast or inside such a machine. It took a little while to acclimatize to the rocking and rattling.

Arin clung to the opposite bench seat. Our knees touched.

He'd purchased a suit of white with gold-threaded embellishments for himself. Not as grand as his princely attire, but still a sight to see, and a reminder of his lineage. In comparison, in purple and black, I was the thunder to his sunshine.

There were a hundred things I wanted to say to him, a hundred more I wanted to do with him, but the clock was ticking again, my time running out with every desert mile the metal beast consumed. In the end, I said none of it, fearing it may sound like goodbye.

This wouldn't be goodbye. Nothing would change between us. Just a few days home, in Pain. A few days playing Razak.

But... it would change. Because Arin didn't know my life, he didn't know the Court of Pain. I couldn't shake the feeling we were about to make a terrible mistake.

"Arin."

He stared at the window, his jaw grinding.

"Arin?"

"Sorry. Yes? I..." His smile collapsed. He smoothed his trousers instead, or dried the sweat from his palms. "I'm a little anxious, is all. And this machine on tracks isn't helping."

"There will be things that I say and do when we're in the Court of Pain. Promise me you won't believe them."

"I know you'll have to lie. It's fine." He scooted onto the bench next to me, tucking himself close. The booth was only large enough for four people, seated two by two. "I've weathered your lies before. For many years, in fact. It's just a few days."

But this would be different. I'd be different, and not just because of who I had to pretend to be, but because of how much Pain changed me. He knew me as Lark, his courtly jester, and even though he believed he'd seen me as Zayan, that act had also been a lie.

He hadn't seen me as Razak's pet, paraded on the end of a leash, or left cuffed to a bed. I'd return as Razak, but I'd have to pretend Arin was my prisoner, my pet. He would take my place at the end of *my* leash.

We'd prepared, he knew, but... gods, this felt wrong. "I'll try and protect you from the worst of it."

"Lark, I can withstand a great deal. Don't assume I'm weak, like everyone else does. You know me better than that."

"I do. But there's believing you know what you're about to walk in to and then there's experiencing it. Nothing prepares you for Pain."

"I can take whatever you give as Razak." He twisted on the seat, pressing his knee to mine, and scooped up my mutilated right hand, cradling it carefully in his gasp. "You've endured a lifetime of torture. If I can't survive a few days, then I'm surely not worthy of you." He tried to smile again, and this time it stayed, softening his eyes.

"Worthy?" I laughed, dismissing his silly notions about my worthiness being anything special, and took my hand back. "I am the least worthy person of your affection, trust me." I turned my gaze toward the window of swirling red sand so I didn't have to see his disappointment. One day he'd realize what he felt for me could be explained away as infatuation, obsession, desire, but not love. His heart was meant for a better man than I. He'd learn that soon, once he saw my home, saw the real me.

"Have you had any thoughts about where Pain's crown is?"

"It's in the city vault," I said. We'd passed through the worst of the desert dunes and as the sand settled, the view to the horizon cleared, revealing heavy, black clouds choking the sky. Silent lightning cracked the clouds. That was my home. "The royal vault houses the court's riches. The crown will be inside it. Few can enter. Just selected council members, and Razak."

"Have you ever been inside?"

I coughed a short, cruel laugh. "Fuckboys are not permitted near the court riches."

"Don't do that."

I faced him, drawn by his icy tone. His gaze had cooled, and his smile was long gone. I'd thought him distant before, when he'd looked at me this way, but in truth, he was guarding against revealing too much in his expression. "You put yourself down," he said. "You believe you're worthless. You're so much more worthy than me, Lark, and I know I can't make you see it, but one day you will, you'll see yourself as I see you."

"The ugly behind the beautiful?"

"Stop." He lunged, capturing my face in a firm hand and pinning me to the back of the seat. "I will kill him for how he's treated you." He threw a leg over my lap and straddled my thighs, and suddenly my whole world became Arin. He was in my lap, holding my face, peering into my eyes, pinning me and smothering me at once. So fierce, so strong, so full of righteous fire.

"You want to kill the man I look like?" I smirked.

"Do not jest. I hate how I hear him when you put yourself down. It's wrong. He's wrong."

I grasped his hips, marveling at their perfect fit in my grip, and lifting my chin, I peered into his eyes. "Careful, or you'll stain all that princely white."

His snarling lips softened and twitched into a smile. He shifted, relaxing into my hold, and trapped my legs under his ass. The fine fabric clutched at his crotch and thighs, tightening in all the right ways.

"Promise me—" His mouth teased my lips. "—that whatever happens, you will not blame yourself."

He rocked forward, brushing against my growing erection, also pinned and about to become exceedingly painful. "That's a big ask."

"Promise me." He rocked again, crushing my cock in the most delectable way. The pain of pressure throbbed.

"I promise," I hissed between my teeth.

He looped his arms around my shoulders and tilted his hips, grinding higher.

"Are you getting off on me, Prince?" I asked.

"Do you think we can indulge?" He glanced at our booth's closed door. People sometimes walked in the narrow walkway outside. I hadn't seen anyone in a while, but the odds were that if he had his trousers around his ankles and my cock up his ass, we'd surely be interrupted. As much as I wanted to feel him under me, over me, anyway he liked, I also didn't want to be thrown into the desert for a second time.

"Regrettably, I think we're almost at our destination."

He slammed a kiss on me instead, thrusting his tongue in, assaulting me in a full-body wave of lust that left us both breathless as soon as he staggered back to his feet. His dick bulged in his loosened trousers. "The white fabric is appropriately flattering."

He followed my gaze. "Gods. Look what you do to me." He gestured at his trapped cock, as though anyone needed directions to see it when it really couldn't be missed. "I didn't think to order undergarments too."

A laugh burst out of me, made worse when he shot me a look of pure annoyance, reminding me of the frustrated prince who had failed at juggling.

"The more you sit there and laugh—"

I stood, grabbed one of the swinging handles above our heads with my left hand, and peered into his eyes. "There's an easy way to deal with this. Hold on."

"What?"

I dropped my right hand and made quick work of his trousers' golden fastenings, then before he could protest or argue, I went to my knees, pried his dick free, and had it deep in my mouth, my tongue cupping its warm length.

Arin's growling groan was all the permission I needed. I took him deep, sliding him down my throat, then partially withdrew, using my two fingers and thumb to pump as I sucked and lashed with my mouth and tongue. It had to be fast; we ran the risk of a passerby seeing us. I had him teetering almost immediately. He pushed back, trying to drive himself deeper and deeper, chasing the high. His free hand screwed into my short hair, twisting, igniting darts of pain and lust through me. I moaned around his dick, pulled my lips free, and jerked him off, his cock flushed, its tip leaking. He moaned and trembled, clinging to that handle and my hair. I pumped harder, my grip slick around his veined length. Arin threw his head back. "Going to..."

I sucked him back into my mouth, sealed my lips around him, and pumped. His breaths sawed, his body strummed like the strings of a violin, he shuddered, his grip switched to the back of my head, and Prince Arin spilled salty cum over my tongue while bucking, trying to drive himself deeper. I gagged around his dick, swallowed, and took more, his cock pulsing between my lips.

While he trembled, I sucked him clean, swallowed every drop, and straightened to look him in the eyes. The glare he returned was one of pure masculine satisfaction.

I wiped my thumb across my lips and flopped back in the seat, leaving Arin standing there a few moments, dick hanging out of his fine clothing, spent and ruined.

"Best put that away lest you give some passing lady a fright."

He fumbled himself back into his trousers. When he settled back on the opposite bench, he no longer gripped the seat as though his life depended on it, appearing thoroughly sated and relaxed.

"How was it?" I asked, and as his grin broke out, I added, "Fucking Razak's mouth?"

His face fell. "That wasn't— I wasn't thinking that."

"No?" He must have, for a moment. Razak on his knees, his cock down his throat? Had he liked it?

"Lark—" he began, desperate to explain.

I leaned forward. "You had better start thinking it, because your life depends on believing I'm my brother."

Arin stilled, ground his jaw, making his cheek twitch, and cast his gaze out of the filthy carriage window. "I know."

Did he? He had better remember this moment, and how he'd just fucked Razak's mouth, because he'd need it, where we were going. Pain could make the strongest man as weak as a kitten. It wasn't about muscle, or reputation, or righteousness. Pain was fought inside the head.

He'd need to cling to the memory of taking Razak on his knees, cling to the power it gave him over my brother. And I'd cling to my Prince of Honey and Sunshine, and hope the storms didn't devour him.

CHAPTER 14

*A*rin

RAIN WASHED sand from the carriage windows. The sky had turned black and War's sand dunes had given way to rows of brick buildings. Houses for the city workers, I presumed. Each one was sparse and basic, no color, no personalization, just brick after brick, each built on top of the next.

The darker the skies fell, the quieter Lark became. He stared out of the window too, and the darkness paled his face. He was coming home, but this was no jubilant return. I could only imagine what thoughts went through his head.

This would test us, but I had faith. He steadied me, and I anchored him.

The carriages clattered, shunted, and rattled to a screeching halt, and a shrill whistle rang out.

We'd arrived.

I slipped the pair of cuffs from my pocket—purchased

from a Palmyra trader—and handed them out to Lark. He ratcheted them around my wrists, then took a pair of fine purple silk gloves from his pocket and slipped them on. Two stiffened additions hid his missing digits.

Now, I was his, and he was Razak.

This was it. The beginning of the lie. Perhaps the greatest lie we'd ever have to tell. Our last lie.

Lark opened our carriage door and stepped down onto the station platform. I wiped clammy hands on my jacket and followed. A few passengers glanced our way. We'd drawn attention when we'd departed, due to our strange clothing, but it was different here. Here, our clothes marked us as nobles. But my white and gold marked me as the prince of a fallen court, and I stood among them, like day is to night.

"I'll see if we can hail a carriage outside the station before we draw too much attention," Lark said, striding forward into the main thoroughfare where hundreds of people gathered.

I nodded, following along, thoughts reeling at the strange world around me. Everyone wore black. The walls were grey, the floor too. There wasn't a flash of color anywhere. Lark pulled on my bound wrists, hastening me through the people as they went about their day, their faces blank and their eyes cold.

More and more people observed our passing. Any moment, someone would call out, they'd stop us, and know we were imposters.

We hurried out of the station, onto a sidewalk. Carriages lined up, waiting for their fares. Black horses stomped heavy hooves on wet cobbles. Rain lashed both beast and man, but nobody appeared concerned. They all marched on, weaving around each other, as quietly and orderly as ants, with no minds of their own.

"You!" Lark declared, striding toward the largest of the coaches led by four horses. "To the towers, and hurry!"

"Sir?" Rain poured over the driver and ran in streams from his wide-brimmed hat.

"Don't you know your prince when you see him?" Lark snapped. "Hurry now, I'm without my own transport and have matters to attend." He grabbed me, hauled me against his side, then shoved me toward the carriage. "Climb in."

I stumbled, missing the driver's response behind the noise of water hammering on the carriage roof, but he must have been convinced. No shout came when I climbed in through the door. Lark closed the door behind us, the crack of a whip sounded through the noise, and the carriage jolted on.

"Do you think he believes us?"

"I think he knows it's not worth losing a finger over if he's wrong."

Rain glistened in Lark's short hair. A few drops shone on his stark face. He'd only said a few words as Razak, but they'd been enough to witness the layers of his lies at work. His voice had been different, and now, he sat differently. Tight, upright. His face seemed different too, leaner somehow, although perhaps that was my imagination. His eyes had lost their mischievous gleam and turned viciously cold. He was a master magician, his performance stunning. If I didn't know he was my Lark, I'd have been fooled.

"I wish we did not have to do this," he said, his soft briefly softening, shattering the lie.

"A few days. Find the crown, and then we leave. Nobody is going to challenge us in a few days."

It would take at least that for word to reach Justice of Razak's apparent return. Nobody was going to challenge Lark as Razak. They wouldn't dare.

"With luck, I'll keep you in his room," he said. "You'll be safe there."

He hadn't looked at me, perhaps afraid to. "You don't need to keep me safe," I reminded him.

His eyes flashed a warning, sharp with Razak's cruelty, then softened. "Please, don't fight me on this."

I reached out with my cuffed hands to grip his knee, the only part of him I could reach without shifting seats. I'd do what he asked. He knew this world, better than I ever could. But I'd also protect him, and if the lie became too much, damn the crown; we'd walk away, and keep on walking, to the ends of all four courts if we had to.

The clop of horses' hooves slowed and the carriage drew to a halt.

Lark eyed the closed carriage door. The carriage rocked as the driver climbed down.

Lark didn't move.

"If the driver opens the door, we're safe. If a guard opens it, then we're about to be arrested."

I took my hand back and stared at the door. We were safe. Zayan did not exist here. Only Razak and his prisoner, the Prince—*King*—of Love.

We would succeed. We had to, and that was all there was to it.

The door jerked open, and the driver bowed low. "The tower, my prince."

Lark hesitated a beat, blinked, and stepped down. A nearby aide handed him an umbrella.

"Come along, *Arin*." He snarled my name and didn't deign to look behind him as I stumbled out.

An enormous fan of black steps rose up to huge glass doors, opening into a building that was so high, it seemed to bend above us and then vanish in the clouds.

I'd never seen monuments built into the sky. Light blazed from its countless windows. However was it constructed? To its right and left, there were more of the same design, although not as tall. Rain patted against my face as I tipped back to admire them.

The blow to my face whipped my head around. Fire flushed across my cheek and tears sprang to my eyes. I staggered, almost fell. Hands clamped around my arms like more shackles and rattled me on the spot. Lark's sneer filled my vision. "Did I not give you an order, prince?!"

My mouth fell open, words all gone.

"Move!"

He threw me at the steps. I sprawled against the jagged stone risers. Then his grip was on my arm again, dragging me upright, alongside him. His fingers dug in, and my side burned, my face throbbed. The assault had come too fast, too hard. I hadn't been prepared.

The doorman stared, his face impassive.

"Open the door," Lark growled.

The man lurched from his spot and grabbed the door. "My apologies, my prince. We were not expecting your return and I—"

"Where are my advisors?"

The man gaped. "I don't... I—"

"I'm surrounded by fools." He hauled me through the doorway into a huge double-height foyer. A sparkling chandelier hung high above us. Encrusted with amethysts, it fractured its own light and cast purple shards about the cavernous space. "Inform the court of my return," his voice boomed, filling the foyer and the ears of everyone who turned to watch.

We climbed a staircase sweeping to a second-floor galleried landing. I'd managed to find my balance and was led along like a dog on a leash. People stopped and stared. This was clearly unusual, even for Razak. Were they fooled? Did they see their prince and his prisoner? Was it enough?

Some of the glances narrowed, less than impressed. We were on display. What happened now would set the tone for the rest of our visit. We had to make it believable. *I* had to make it believable. I was a king, albeit of a fallen court, but still a king.

We arrived on the wide landing atop the stairs, the perfect stage for my performance. I yanked my cuffed hands free of Lark's grip. "I'm the King of Love, not your plaything."

Lark whirled. "You're whatever I make of you and certainly no king."

Yes, this was good. A quick glance to the entrance foyer revealed an entranced audience. The Prince of Love, a prince from another land, was in their city, their foyer, brought here by their ruler. A rare sight, indeed.

"Get on your knees." Lark sneered.

I laughed. "I'm not kneeling to you."

He swooped in; his fingers locked around my neck, trapping all the air in my lungs. I reached for his grip with my cuffed hands.

"Then I'll make you." I'd seen cruelty on his face, I'd seen lust, but I'd never seen this before. Madness.

Tears swam in my vision. My chest burned, as if my lungs were filled with broken glass. I struggled, tried to fight him off, but already, a darkness throbbed in my peripheral vision.

There was nothing left of my precious Lark in his eyes. Razak, the Prince of Pain, had me in his grip, and he wouldn't hesitate to kill me. He'd killed before. I was nothing to him. I couldn't fight, I had nothing left to fight with. I tried to yell, to roar at him, but no sound made it past his chokehold.

My knees struck the floor, and Razak still choked me. Was any of it real? Had Lark always been Razak?

No... but he'd always been capable.

He let go. I collapsed, gasping, drifting somewhere far away, but not far enough that I didn't hear Lark's laugh. So like Razak's, there was nothing to tell them apart.

CHAPTER 15

ark

I DID NOT WANT to be here, seated at the head of the council table while Razak's closest advisors peered at me, through me, demanding attention I had no wish to give them. Arin was, presumably, in Razak's room—where I'd told the aides to take him in his semi-conscious state. I wanted to be there with him, not here, with these people, wishing they'd all die a slow, painful death. Perhaps I could hang all four from the hanging tree before Razak returned and kicked me off his throne? But hanging them as Razak was pointless. Nobody would bat an eye. To hang them as Zayan though... To see them kick and writhe at the end of the rope, as my mother had, as Justice Ines had. These people, who'd watched me leave bloody footprints as I'd danced, watched me hang on the end of Razak's leash.

"Razak?"

I met Malvina's steel-grey eyes. She'd been Umair's advisor, but since the king had vanished years ago, she'd stepped into the role as Razak's advisor. Wily, brutal, if she had a heart it was made of stone. She had despised me from the moment we'd met. Had it not been for Razak's protection, I'd have hung at her order long ago.

She wasn't sneering now. She didn't see Zayan when she met my careless gaze.

"You seem out of sorts this evening," she said. Her grey hair had been twisted and pinned up high, as though she had styled herself a crown of silver.

The crown... I was here for Pain's crown. I needed to focus and not lose myself in the lie.

I couldn't ruin it now, when Arin and I had just begun— and after Arin's foolish spectacle in the foyer. I'd almost... I stared at my gloved hands and curled my fingers. I'd almost choked Arin unconscious. My heart thumped. I could have killed him, in that moment. The lust had been real. I'd worn the clothes, called myself Razak, and as soon as I'd stepped from the carriage, I'd become my brother.

"Razak?"

"*What?!*"

"Your success in War?" She slow-blinked, carefully masking her fear.

"My success at what?"

"Did you secure the crown?"

They knew then, they knew about Razak's plans to secure the crowns. They'd talked about it, all of them, while I'd been on my knees beside Razak, in this very chamber. So I'd suspected they'd known something of his mission, but hadn't known how much.

"Of course." I shooed her apparent concern away. All four council members looked at me with varying degrees of concern and suspicion. I'd been summoned here, to explain how I'd captured Prince Arin. But the longer I stayed under their scrutiny, the more my mind frayed at the edges. I'd have been fine if Arin hadn't baited me. I'd had everything under control until I'd had my hands around his neck and *liked* it.

"You know, I do believe I'm feeling out of sorts. Perhaps I am ill, caught something during my stay in War's godsforsaken heat."

"And Justice? They didn't hold you for long?" Malvina asked, the voice for them all.

"Clearly." The reply came from Bendrik, the youngest on the council. His father had been a trusted advisor to Umair. Bendrik always wore a flat cap, and even now, it sat on his head, its peak shadowing his narrowed eyes. When his father's heart had given up, Bendrik had adopted his father's seat and his station and apparently proven his worth. I knew him as the man who leered at Razak and rubbed his own cock beneath the table when he thought nobody was watching.

Razak had told me once, during one of his more talkative nights, how he'd had Bendrik whipped, and Bendrik had *liked* it. I wasn't entirely sure if Razak and Bendrik had some kind of relationship outside of the council, and hadn't cared, until now. Hopefully, I wouldn't need to know the answer.

These people knew a whole lot more than me. They likely knew *why* Razak was securing the crowns, but I couldn't ask them without giving my ruse away. I had to tread carefully in my questioning.

Getting one of these council members alone to wring some answers out of them could be an option—Bendrik perhaps, he seemed the most obvious target—but Pain's crown had to remain my focus, and keeping Arin safe.

I had to get back to him.

"I'm tired from traveling. Tomorrow, I'll be more like my usual self, I'm sure." I pushed from the chair and strode for the door, done with these fools. Tomorrow, I'd visit the vault, collect the crown, and be gone. Nobody called out, nobody stopped me. I'd done enough to convince them I was Razak, but it wouldn't last. Malvina would be the one to uproot my lies.

Just a few days.

I hurried into the stairwell, climbed to Razak's floor, and swept along the corridor. The door was unlocked. I dove in, eager to see Arin, to know he was all right.

He wasn't on the large purple-and-black draped bed, not in the bathroom either, after I checked. One door remained. The door that was always locked, the door with the key on the outside. A key that sat in the lock now, waiting for Razak to turn it.

I knew its sound so well—*clunk, click*—knew it meant pain was coming for me.

I flicked the lock, hearing it a thousand times in my memory, but this time, I had the key in my hand, and inside the room, Arin lay out cold on the bed, chest rising and falling. His princely clothes hung askew, scuffed, and his golden hair had tangled about him, but otherwise he appeared fine. In a strange, dreamlike flash, I saw myself in his place, bound at the wrist, stripped naked, sprawled and waiting. Sometimes Razak came straight for me, sometimes he went to the window, sometimes he smoked his pipe, and sometimes nothing happened. He just stood, and stared, the anticipation more agonizing than the deed itself.

But I wasn't on that bed, and Razak wasn't here.

I huffed out a shuddering sigh.

They'd cuffed Arin to the bed post, as was expected. I hated that cuff, hated that he was here, that he saw all this: the real Zayan behind all my acts.

I grabbed a chair from the nearby desk, placed it at the

142

foot of the bed, and sat, watching him sleep. After a while, I dozed, and between one blink and the next, Arin sat up, eyeing me sharply.

I dipped my chin and stared back.

He blinked. "Lark?"

"No."

"What?"

"Razak. Not Lark. We don't mention that name, we can't."

"Are you all right?"

My laugh fell silently from my lips. "No, not in the least."

He tried to shift, but the cuff snapped at him. He tugged at it. "Is this necessary?

"If we're disturbed, you cannot be found wandering about as a free man."

Slumping, he huffed and winced, then fingered his cheek with his free hand. I'd struck him *hard*. Harder than I'd meant to. He noticed me watching and held my gaze. "It's just a bruise. Don't blame yourself."

"What were you thinking?"

"In the foyer? It wasn't working. We needed to do more, to make them see us, see Razak and Arin. *Nice* wasn't cutting it."

"Nice? I threw you to the ground outside." I'd grabbed him, handled him roughly, thrown him around as though he were nothing, as though he were... Zayan. By the gods. I slumped over and pressed my hands to my face while my stomach knotted.

"You know I'm right," he said. "It needed more. We had to convince them."

He stroked his neck and winced. I'd choked him with my own bare hands. And what he didn't understand was how I'd *liked* it.

I shot from the chair and strode to the window. I couldn't

143

stand this. Old bruises given to me long ago flared up, brought to life by my own memories, even after so long. Arin was in my bed, wearing my cuff, rubbing his throat. I was looking in a mirror, only seeing an innocent man there instead of the nothing boy who deserved it.

"I can't do this," I whispered.

"We're doing it."

"You're going to get hurt." The power I had, wearing Razak's clothes, standing in my brother's shoes, choking out the Prince of Love for all to see— The rush had almost seen me finish Arin.

I couldn't be around him, not like this. Everything was muddled in my head. I'd hurt him.

"Lark."

"It's fucking Razak!" I rubbed my head, trying to force the thoughts and feelings away.

"Lark, damn you, look at me!"

So fierce, my Prince of Flowers, cuffed to my bed and kneeling there as though he wasn't a rabbit trapped in a snare with the wolves circling.

"We're doing this, it's happening," he said. "We only need to make it out the other side."

Was that how I'd looked, tied to the bed, baring my teeth like angry prey? No wonder Razak fucked me. The same need roared so hard and fast through me now, it rocked me back against the barred window. I'd bend Arin under me, wrap his golden hair in my fist and fuck him from behind, then cut him, and gods, I'd come so hard, deep inside him, making him mine.

Was that my desire or Razak's?

I braced a hand against the window frame and bowed my head, keeping my back to Arin, and tried to will my body under control. Was I losing my damn mind?

What if I took the crown tomorrow, wore it, and told the world who I was? Zayan, Umair's bastard son, come to claim Pain as my own. I'd hurt them all, everyone who had hurt me...

I rocked, head down, cock so damned hard it would only take a few strokes and some well-timed spike of pain for me to come. I didn't want to be like this. I wanted to be back in the Court of Love, pulling cards from sleeves and picking pockets, dancing through the night, weaving fantasies for bored lords and ladies.

"If I wasn't damn well cuffed here, I'd come to you."

"Trust me, you do not want to be around me right now."

"Don't I? What makes you think I don't know what you're going through? This is getting inside your head. I can see it. I want to help. Tell me what you need."

"Nothing from you."

"Lark, what do you need?"

"What do I need?" I tipped my head back and blinked at the ceiling. "I need to fuck you so hard, it'll hurt the both of us." I needed to hurt him, and myself, punish him for making me do this, punish me for liking it. Everything was a blur, a mess I couldn't escape. I didn't want to be Razak, but also, I did. I wanted to be Lark, but didn't. And in the middle of all that was Zayan, the boy who played the fiddle and sang for coins in his cap.

"Do it," Arin said.

"No." My pulse thumped in my throat. "I'm not an animal."

"Do it," he said again, louder.

He didn't know what he was saying. This place, it was eating at my mind, and it would eat at his too. I couldn't hurt him, not like I wanted to. It would break us, ruin us, tarnish his shine.

Rustling fabric drew my eye toward the bed, to him, where he untied his trousers and grasped his cock in his free hand.

He was hard?

He glared, holding my stare while he held his cock.

I shoved from the window, bit my gloves free and tossed them. When I got to the bed, I made quick work of my trousers, shucking them loose. Arin turned, poised on his knees, his right arm held taut by the cuff, his left hand stroking his dick.

I opened the drawer in the bedside cabinet, removed the oil, and climbed onto the bed. The smell of that oil summoned with it a thousand different memories. I snarled them away, jerked Arin's trousers down his thighs, and exposed his round, firm ass.

There was no time to think; if I paused and let the thoughts inside, the floodgates would open.

Grasping my cock, I oiled it, spread Arin's ass, and pressed my dick against his hole. He gasped, clenched, and I stretched him open.

Arin swore. The hand that had been on his cock shot to my thigh, trying to lever me back. It was too late for that; I was in him now. His tightness burned us both—good. I withdrew, heard his exhale, and thrust again, hearing him gulp.

He tried to rock forward, to escape. I clutched his hips, withdrew, and slammed in once more, balls deep, riding a burst of pleasure and pain. He let out a gasping, choking moan. It was too much, too deep. I knew it was. It hurt him. I thrust again, needing to move, to have his hole choke my dick, to have him writhe and pant.

"Wait..." he breathed. "Lark, wait—"

I slumped over his back, grasped his lagging dick, and pumped hard and fast. His hole clenched, throttling my cock.

He shuddered, muttered to the gods. "Lark, yes..."

Faster, I pumped my hand and rocked my hips, fucking him from behind while he fucked my fist. When he spilled, I let go, clutched his hips, and fucked him like I hated him, like I was Razak and he was Zayan, cuffed to the bed, taking it, because he had no choice. Balls and thighs slapping, I grunted like a damned animal, and pounded like one too, faster, harder. I needed to come, to spill deep inside and make him mine. Fuck pleasure, this wasn't that. It was revenge.

I let go of his hip and bit into my own thumb's soft flesh. A ripple of ecstasy ran through me and turned to delicious sparks, spilling down my back. I cried out around my teeth, buried in my hand, and slammed deep into Arin, my dick pulsing its seed.

Deeper—I needed to be deeper, needed to touch his soul. I jerked his ass desperately close with each releasing wave.

A surge of self-loathing rolled over the numbing come-down. What was I doing? I wasn't Razak. But I'd hurt Arin, I knew I had. I pulled free. Creamy cum dribbled from his raw hole. I'd gone too far. Had he asked me to stop? I couldn't remember. I'd hurt him, like Razak hurt me. Quickly tucking my cock away, I stumbled for the door.

"Lark, wait, don't go—"

I fled through the room, flicked the lock behind me and took the key, then left Razak's bed chamber, left the corridor, and the floor, taking the stairs down to the ground, and ran outside, down the steps. Rain-soaked streets welcomed me. I disappeared among rivers of people, anonymous but for the royal clothing, but few even cared to peek from under their umbrellas. Rain slicked my hair to my face, glued my clothes to my clammy skin, and chilled me to the bone. I walked and walked, taking streets I hadn't visited in years.

And then, when I came to the corner where a boy had

once played a fiddle and sung for coin, I stopped, as though searching for him.

Little had changed. Trash cans and soaked newspapers banked high in the nearby alley. I should have brought a fiddle, then I could have played, and begged for coin, and killed the next man who tried to lure me away.

I looked at my hands, looked for my two missing fingers, my gloves—I'd forgotten them. People stared now. Did they know? Could they see the truth of me? I slunk back into the shadows and leaned against a wall, using it to hold me up.

Why was I here, why had I walked all this way? Who was I really searching for? I wasn't damn well going to find the answers on the corner of a nameless street.

And I'd left Arin.

Would he hate me?

It didn't matter. I had to get back before anyone noticed I was missing.

I emerged from the alley and stepped back into the flow of people. I had to hold it together until tomorrow, until I got the crown, then we could leave, and all of this would be another nightmare to add to my collection of broken dreams.

A hand shot out from a figure I'd passed and grabbed my wrist. I looked up, into old, familiar eyes.

"Now what would you be doing here, young prince?" Danyal smirked.

He'd gained another scar on his cheek, another murder since we'd last met, under the Court of Love's oak tree at Arin's mother's funeral pyre. The sudden appearance of my handler sent my thoughts reeling. A knot of panic almost choked off my voice. I swallowed it down and yanked my hand back, or tried too, but his grip hardened, crushing my wrist. "Unhand me, Danyal, or suffer my wrath, and we both know you won't enjoy the punishment *I* inflict." I put every-

148

thing into the act, all I was capable of, and glared back at the man who had known me as Lark *and* Zayan. If anyone was going to see the truth, it would be him.

His eyes narrowed. Razak did not march off for walks in the rain. Did Danyal know the significance of the corner I'd just left? Had he followed me here? There had always been a ruthlessness to my handler, a sharp-eyed keenness, as though he'd seen or done things that would turn Razak's blood cold. I'd rarely lied to him, not needing to, and only when Arin and I had become closer. But even then, I suspected he'd known the truth—somehow.

He searched my eyes for too long. He wasn't afraid, because he knew. He sniffed and straightened, then freed my arm. "Let's get you back to the tower, where you belong."

"I'm fine walking."

"It is the least I can do, *Prince*." He bowed, and the crowd swept away at the word: *Prince*, creating a void nobody wanted to touch.

If he knew, and if he planned to tell the council, then I had a single carriage ride to kill him. If I didn't, he'd expose Arin and I. Arin's life depended on Danyal's death.

A carriage pulled up. Danyal nodded to the driver, then opened the door. "Razak?"

I didn't have a weapon, only my hands. Danyal was a proven killer. He'd be armed. But I had the advantage. He wouldn't kill me, not even if he knew the truth. Zayan belonged to Razak.

The ride back wouldn't take long, but it also didn't take long to choke a man.

We climbed into the carriage. Danyal closed the door and settled opposite me.

He stared, unblinking. He didn't need to say the words; his appraising gaze did it for him. He stripped my lies bare.

Few men or women had such power. I'd likely never know how he'd been able to read me so easily.

He slow-blinked and leaned forward. "What are you doing, Zayan?"

"You are mistaken—"

He grabbed my hand and spread my finger stumps, as though I needed reminding. "Your lies cannot hide what's been done to you, boy."

I snatched my hand back, lunged, and smacked his head against the carriage bulkhead, rattling his consciousness. But it didn't last. He swung, landing a punch in my side, then twisted, hauling me down to the floor, under him. I kicked out, caught his leg, dropped him to a knee, and brought *my* knee up, impacting his middle. As he grunted, slumping over, I cracked a fist into his nose. Blood spurted. He reeled, clutching his face. I grabbed him by the shoulders and flipped him under me and pinned him to the carriage floor, reversing our positions. He became wedged in the narrow space between the seats, and while he struggled, my hands slotted neatly around his neck.

Blood from his mashed nose ran down his face, under my fingers. He whipped his head to one side, dislodging my grip, and he landed another punch in my bruised side. Pain snapped. I gasped, and I clung to the carriage seat, then bared my teeth. "You willing to die for this?"

He struggled back to his knees, coughing and wheezing.

The old bastard had a whole lot of fight in him, I'd give him that.

He raised a hand, panting. "Don't want to hurt you," he mumbled.

The carriage had stopped. Were we already back at the tower? Any moment the driver or an aide would open the door. They couldn't see Razak brawling with a commoner.

I sat up, straightened my clothes and hair, winced around the crackling heat in my side, and flashed him a long, withering look. If he talked, it would not end well for him.

The carriage door jerked open.

"My Prince, we have arrived." Danyal gestured toward the door, then used the same hand to wipe blood from his nose. He hadn't used my name, hadn't yelled for guards, and the aide wasn't at all interested in Danyal, just me.

I dropped down and hurried up the stairs, reapplying my act with every step.

All I had to do was get through the night, steal Pain's crown, and leave with Arin.

And if anyone else got in my way, I'd remind them exactly how Prince Razak ruled the Court of Pain by swinging their wretched bodies from a tree.

CHAPTER 16

*A*rin

EVEN IF I could escape the cuff, there was no escape from
the room. Lark had locked the door. I yanked on the damn
thing anyway, pulled and tugged until my thumb had rubbed
raw, but it was no use. He'd left me here.

I slumped on the bed, defeated.

This room was his. I'd seen it on his face as soon as I'd
woken to find him sitting at the end of the bed.

The bed itself was plain, the walls grey, and there were
bars on the window. A prison, not a room. I'd spent a few
hours here and already despised it. He'd spent years, with a
single door between him and Razak. How had he not lost his
mind?

Lark needed me. He didn't know it, he thought locking
me away would keep me safe, keep me away from his court
and his life. But he couldn't do this alone. It was too much,
even for him. He was coming apart. He'd become his enemy,

his tormentor, his nightmare, and he was so afraid of it and what it did to him. I saw it all, because I knew him, loved him, but I couldn't damn well help him if he ran.

If he'd just have stayed after he'd brutally fucked me, I'd have told him how I'd liked it, needed it even. Yes, it had hurt —still damn well hurt—but I could take whatever he gave, if it meant he'd realize I was here for him. I'd always be here for him.

A key clattered in the lock. I twisted on the sheets, angled toward the door, wearing nothing but my wrinkled shirt and fine silk jacket. At least it appeared as though I'd been thrown here and discarded, which was the point. If whoever was about to come through that door was anyone but Lark, I'd fight them with all I had. Kill them if I had to.

The door swung open and Lark strode in. He glanced at me, then away.

"Thank Dallin," I sighed.

Without meeting my gaze, he lay down on the bed beside me, rested his head on the pillow, and took a drag on a slim black pipe. His clothes were ruffled and dark in places, wet. His hair was wet too, and disheveled. And when he'd climbed onto the bed, he'd favored his side, as though he'd been hurt. Something was wrong—more wrong than everything else around us.

He handed me the pipe. "Forgive me?"

"Don't apologize for something I asked you to do." I took the pipe, sealed my lips on its slim end, and breathed in. Sweet smoke laced the back of my throat, numbing the aches he'd left me with. Pennywort. I recognized its odor from the times it would waft under my father's chamber door. "Also, no apology is necessary when it felt so good."

At his sideways glance, the tension between us dissipated.

"We don't have time to do this," he said, softly. "We need to leave. Now."

"What happened?"

"The man who collected your courtly secrets, Danyal—we met on the street. He followed me, or it was just by happenstance. Whatever his reason, he did not believe I'm Razak." He raised his right hand and waggled his two remaining fingers. "We fought. He's tougher than he looks."

I took another, deeper drag on the pipe, slumped against the headboard, letting the lightness carry me away, then handed back the pipe. "Did you kill him?"

"I ran out of time."

The both of us getting high didn't solve anything, but damn, it felt good to drift a while. Things seemed clearer, simpler. "We can't leave."

"Arin—"

"We've come this far. We need the crown."

"Danyal *knows*." He twisted at the waist, hissed at his pain, then finally looked me in the eyes.

"You're hurt?"

"It's nothing compared to what will happen if we're discovered."

He could never be Razak, I realized. Not to me. Razak's eyes were cold, flat, and that chilling emptiness went all the way down inside the Prince of Pain's soul. Lark's cool harshness was genuine. He played his brother well. But I knew him too well, I knew his heart. His heart was always true. It was in his music, in his smiles, and in his eyes, when he wasn't guarding all of those things—like now.

"He'll tell the council. We have hours, at most."

I shrugged. Had I not been high, I might have cared more. As I was detached from most feelings, the solution didn't seem difficult. "Then get the crown now."

"I can't. It's in the vault," he said, then winced again and lifted his shirt, revealing a red, growing bruise spreading down his side. "Damn that old bastard." He gave the bruise a soft poke and hissed. "It'll be fine. I've had worse." He drew on the pipe and flopped his head back, blowing smoke out. "Pennywort has its uses."

I wanted to kiss his chest, kiss the bruise, make it go away, and lay my hands on him, but that was the pennywort too. I *always* wanted to kiss him, but not when all the four kingdoms were at stake, and our lives. "You're a prince, start thinking like one," I told him instead.

"Meaning?"

I held out my hand, and he handed the pipe back. "Nobody is going to stop Razak from visiting the vault whenever he pleases," I said. "You just fucked me over, now fuck them like you know Razak can. There isn't a single person in this building who is strong enough to stop him."

He looked at the window, its bars, out into the endless rain.

"Except Zayan," I added, then smiled, feeling tipsy. "And Zayan's not here, remember?"

"Do you truly believe Zayan is strong enough to stop Razak?"

The softness and insecurity within which he asked almost broke my heart. "I *know* he is."

I'd told him before with words, under my touch, every time we'd kissed. But this time was different. Perhaps because of this room? This time, he heard my words, and he believed them.

"If I go now, they won't know I've taken the crown until the morning."

He lunged, caught my face in cool hands, and kissed me on the mouth. Pennywort sweetened his lips. I opened up, wanting more. His tongue roamed, teasing, and the throbbing ache he'd left me with pulsed anew. He smelled of rain and wet stone, and when I wrapped my free arm around him, he leaned back, offering his neck. Unable to resist, I mouthed a kiss under his jaw, my lips warm against his cool, wet skin. He shivered, soaked through, or perhaps it was my touch that sent tremors through him.

He moaned and pulled back enough to peer into my eyes. "I should drug you more often."

"Hm, or just fuck me so hard we both think clearer."

His smile bloomed, shattering the lie that he was anything but my Lark, my fool, the man I loved with all my heart. "You are too good for me."

"Me, good?" I snorted. "Never."

He laughed, shuffled off the bed, scooped the gloves he'd discarded from off the floor, and tugged them on as he strode for the door, reapplying the disguise one more time.

"Oh, Razak?" I called. He turned, hip cocked and shoulder lifted, his expression so sly I almost laughed aloud. "Won't you bring me your crown?"

He swept low in a dramatic bow. "I'll bring you whatever your heart desires." He left, the lock clicked, and I flopped back on the bed, chuckling, warm and relaxed. The pennywort had me, but that was all right. I'd needed it. We both had. Lark always knew what I needed. I'd been afraid I'd lose him, then he'd walked back in and flipped the world upside down, just like he always did. *He* was a wonder, my Prince of Storms.

We were going to be all right. I knew it. He'd get the crown, we'd sneak out, and with some luck, we'd be gone by dawn.

I pulled on the pipe, letting the drug ease the remaining

nerves and dampen the pain, then set the pipe aside. Its affects would clear by the time he returned. I'd be ready.

Yes, we were in our enemy's court, but we were in control. I slumped back, closed my eyes, and drifted. Gods, I loved him so much it hurt. Once this was over, we'd go home, to my court, and it didn't matter what was left, we'd make something of it. I'd ask him to join me, officially, in the proper way, make him a real prince, and surely it was the pennywort going to my head, but I wanted happiness for him, whatever that meant. We'd dance in the meadows, and we'd dream of freedom.

The door rattled.

I opened my eyes and peered at it through a haze of pennywort. "Back so soon?"

It rattled again.

"Lose your key?"

He didn't reply.

My heart thumped, trying to clear the pennywort's weight slowing my instincts. This felt wrong. "La—Razak?"

Someone or something slammed into the door, nearly shaking it off its hinges. I twisted and tried to get to my feet, but the cuff yanked me back. When a second blow struck the door, it flung open.

Three men poured in.

None of them were Lark.

CHAPTER 17

ark

ARIN ALWAYS HAD THE ANSWER. I shouldn't have fled the room, should have stayed with him, should have known he'd know what to do and say. *I* was the problem, not him. But I'd work on that, once this was done. And we were so very close to being done...

Get the crown, return to the tower, collect Arin, and leave before dawn. Any delay would see Danyal reveal my lies, and if that happened, any chance at freedom would slip through my fingers, as would Arin's life.

He'd been right, though. I couldn't have done this without him.

Razak's royal carriage clattered along at speed. With the aid of the carriage's grand exterior, whoever greeted me at the vaults would have no reason to doubt my identity. Once inside, all I had to do was locate the crown.

A glance out of the veiled window showed the rain had

eased, and the clouds had parted. The moon hung suspended over towering buildings, and an occasional star fought through the midnight gloom to shine against the odds. That star was my hope, my Arin. I'd have given anything to be strolling through his flower meadows at midnight as I'd used to, my only concern whose secret I'd pluck next. Those days and dreams had been so much easier. But Arin's court was long gone, like the other courts would be gone if I failed now.

The driver slowed the horses and the carriage, jarring my dreams, and came to a halt outside a building I'd heard of, but never seen. I peered through the window. I'd assumed the vault would be the grandest of all buildings, a public display of wealth and knowledge. But its single-story façade was the smallest of all its towering neighbors. A large iron portcullis barred a huge timber door.

Two guards flanked the portcullis. Two guards between me and the crown.

All I had to do was play the part of Razak, and they'd let me through. As Arin had said, nobody would dare stand in Razak's way.

Two gas lamps lit the vault's steps, and with just the moon above, plenty of shadows would help conceal any roughness I hadn't had time to fix from Danyal's assault.

Remembering Arin's words—*begin acting like a prince*—I waited for the driver to open the door.

If Arin were here, he'd smile and tell me we would succeed. And like a fool, I'd believe him.

The door clunked open.

"The vaults, Your Highness."

Razak wouldn't hesitate. So I didn't either. I climbed down from the carriage and up the steps, toward the portcullis, anticipating their opening, *believing* my lie. I was Razak and nothing stood in my way, not even these iron bars.

I'd almost reached the top of the steps when I caught the guards' sideways glances.

Believe the lie.

I am Razak. Prince of Pain.

The guards averted their gazes.

Chains clattered out of sight and the portcullis began to lift. I levelled my breathing, but my thudding heart grew louder. The timber door groaned open. My heart thumped a beat in my throat: *Im-pos-ter*, it drummed. The truth had no place here—only lies. I was Razak, and Razak did not stop or slow for anyone.

I passed through the entrance into a sumptuous foyer of purple and black silks, ornate chairs, and a vast dark mahogany desk, carved like a wave.

"Ah, sire!" A man scuttled out from behind the desk. His full-length purple gown flowed around his legs, round glasses rested on his long nose, and he'd tucked his shaggy brown hair behind both ears. In the soft lamplight, I'd thought him in his middle years, but as he dipped his head in a small bow and looked up, his face bore no more age lines than mine. Perhaps he was a low-level administrator, or a trainee custodian of the vaults.

His hand vanished into the fold of his gown. Did he mean to draw a blade?

I faltered, having no blade of my own. My frantic heart skipped and old instincts urged me to run. He produced a ring of keys and swooped ahead, toward another impressive door. "Valdan is away this evening. We weren't expecting a visit so soon after your last," he said.

I arched an eyebrow. Valdan was likely his senior. This was good. An apprentice wouldn't notice any discrepancies in my behavior. "Then you shall assist me."

"Yes, yes of course." He dipped his head again, submissive,

and hurried to open the door into a long corridor. Multiple steel doors led off at intervals, each one sporting its own heavy lock. Those were private vaults, belonging to nobles. The royal vault would not be as accessible.

We walked on—the apprentice ahead—toward another door at the far end of the corridor.

I was almost there. Once inside, the crown shouldn't be too hard to find. They'd probably have it on display, awaiting the King of Pain's return. Razak was not yet king, not without our father's blessing, or confirmation of his death. And as Razak and the council had no confirmation of either scenario, he had no right to claim the crown. It *would* be here. There was nowhere else in the court it could be.

The apprentice rattled his keys in the next door's lock and swung the door open. Another corridor stretched deeper into the vaults, leading to yet another door at its end. It was the largest door of them all—this one carved with a simple design of four interlocking circles. The apprentice stopped, folded his hands in front of his gown, bowed his head, and waited.

Clearly, I was supposed to do something. Were there words, a phrase, some kind of ceremony?

I glanced over, and the apprentice gestured at the door. "Your key, Your Highness?"

"My key—yes! My key." I patted my outfit in theatrical fashion. "I seem to have mislaid it."

He blinked. "Oh."

"You possess a spare." I made it a statement, not a query.

"I, well, this is unusual." He patted his gown as I'd earlier patted my empty pockets.

"Are you mocking me?"

His face flushed, then proceeded to drain of all color. "You?! No, my sire, prince, lord. Goodness! Not at all."

Now, if I were me, I'd have half a dozen ways of seducing

him to get my desired outcome—getting through the door. But Razak was not me. He didn't seduce, and he didn't threaten. He cut off fingers, without warning.

I killed the thin smile on my lips. "I do not have time for this. Open this door immediately or there will be consequences."

"Well, I just…" He glanced back the way we'd come, searching for assistance.

I arched my eyebrow in a Razak-like way. "Who are you looking for? Because unless it's the king, *my father,* then I do not see who would be foolish enough to refuse me access to my own vault, except you. Please enlighten me, if I am wrong." I knew all too well how politeness from Razak was a prelude to agony. I assumed others among the court and the staff knew the same. It was always better to agree with Razak.

"No. Of course. One moment." He fumbled his keys, searching for the correct one.

Finding the key, he slammed it home in the lock. This could have ended very differently for him, and he seemed like a nice fellow. Thankfully, neither of us had to experience whether I'd have gone so far as to take a finger.

Multiple locks clunked and the door swung inwards, revealing a decorative iron spiral staircase. I stepped onto a metal tread and began the tight, corkscrewing descent until reaching the ground floor, swallowed in blackness, with no edges or light source. The darkness pushed in, so large and so heavy I almost tasted it. It was the weight of countless riches, of a million secrets—the Court of Pain's infamous vaults.

This had to be it, all its riches were about to be revealed.

"O-one moment," the apprentice stuttered, reaching for a heavy lever protruding from the wall. He clanged the lever down, and one after another, great panels, hung high above us, tilted forward, directing ambient moonlight from vaulted skylights down onto a cathedral of wooden crates.

Row upon row of shelves stacked with paper folders, each one marked with a letter and number. So many, they stretched far into the distance. The apprentice pushed on, and I trailed behind, trying not to react to stacks upon stacks of files. There was gold too, I noticed. In crates, stored three high, each single crate the size of a man. There was enough coin here to finance the penniless Court of Love for years, or buy an army, or do whatever Razak wished.

"I'll take you to the letters," the apprentice said. The stacked shelves muffled his voice, made the space intimate, despite its size.

"Letters?"

"No?" he asked, glancing back and slowing. "Oh, it's just... You always begin there. Should we not—"

Any further mistakes, and he'd suspect something was wrong. "The letters, yes. Lead on."

He walked a brisk pace, gown swishing about his purple-slippered feet. A name for him would have been useful, but how to ask when I was supposed to already know the man? *The apprentice* would have to do.

We passed shelf after shelf of bulging folders. I glimpsed names, dates, numbers. Birth records or *all* records? So many secrets, so much knowledge, so much wealth. The sight, the smell, the sound, it sent a thrill through me. I'd never see its like again. A vault of knowledge. All the answers at my finger-tips, if I'd known where to look. But I couldn't lose sight of why I was here: the crown.

"Here," the apprentice announced.

He reached a wall of small, locked drawers, took a key from his loop, and opened one drawer, then pulled out the long, metal container from inside and set it down with care on a nearby table.

"I'll give you your privacy. Please call out, if you require assistance." He bowed and hurried away.

Privacy, for letters? I dipped my chin, opting to remain silent lest I give my general awe away, and once he was out of sight, I turned to study the lockbox.

Why would Razak visit the vault to read letters, and visit regularly enough for it to be expected by the staff? I flipped the lid and scanned the contents. A lock of black hair, a faded blue flower, likely too fragile to manhandle. And a neat stack of letters, tucked into the far corner. Each was addressed to Razak with an intricate *R*.

If Razak thought them precious, then they would be. Curiosity almost had me stuffing them down my shirt. But letters, as intriguing as they might be, were not why I was here. Still, a quick look wouldn't hurt, to keep from alerting the apprentice to any unusual behavior.

The first letter, the one on top of the stack? No. Too obvious. Razak would hide the most important to him at the bottom. I eased the last latter out from beneath its stack. Purple wax stained the paper's aged ochre hue—the royal seal, long-since disintegrated. These letters were years old.

I carefully unfolded the fragile paper. The signature, with its elaborate swirls, drew my eye first.

Umair.

The King of Pain.

Razak's father. And mine.

This letter was the closest I'd been to my own father since he'd laid a hand on my shoulder and watched my mother swing from the hanging tree.

I skimmed the swirling penmanship, picking out vital words: *Justice, key, balance, regret,* and *power.* Umair had written to Razak multiple times. I searched for a date, but the edges were so worn and creased, if there had been a date mark, it had long since faded away. These letters might contain secrets we needed. They could prove invaluable. I grabbed a few at random, shoved them into my pocket, then froze.

At the bottom of the box, hidden beneath the letters, lay a sketch of a woman. She sat, straight-backed in a chair too grand to be common, but too plain for a throne. Sweeping eyes seemed kind, and her dark as night hair was styled high. The sketch was drawn with confident strokes. But it was her smile that arrested.

I touched the paper, as though to touch her, then flipped it over.

My beloved Umair had written, the calligraphy the same as the king's letters. *May we meet in the meadows.*

"Sire, forgive me—"

I slammed the box closed and slipped the sketch into my pocket, out of sight from the keen-eyed apprentice.

"Your coachman has requested you er—" He swallowed. "—you return to the coach."

"And why would I entertain obeying such an order from my coachman?" I laughed, hoping it didn't sound as weak to him as it did in my head.

"It seems the council—"

"Remind him," I snapped, "he's here on my orders." My time was fast running out. Mention of the council likely meant Danyal had informed them of my ruse. "And remind me, where is the crown?" It didn't sound as casual as I'd have liked, but the tone suited Razak's general impatience. There was no time to dally. I needed to make progress.

"The crown?" he asked, eyebrows pinching together in a frown.

"Yes, the crown."

"Is this a trick?"

I tilted my head, acutely aware that my heart had stopped and tripped my thoughts with it. "A trick?"

"I..." He swallowed again. "It's just... Well—"

"It's a simple question. So answer it."

He appeared to consider his next move carefully. Perhaps he suspected something in my mannerisms, and this was a ploy to get me to out myself, but if that were the case, he wouldn't be as nervous as his trembling hands suggested. Or was there some other reason for him to hesitate. Did he not know where the crown was?

"Follow me," he said, before pirouetting and diving deeper into the vault. I strode behind, glancing over racks of items and documents. Everything gleamed, dust-free. Surely, one apprentice didn't keep all this clean and tidy?

We passed by a rack labeled *Court of War Benefits*. Benefits? Benefits to whom? I slowed. The apprentice marched on. There wouldn't be another opportunity like this. I'd never see the inside of this vault again. Just a quick look?

I flicked open a folder, spotted names listed in order, A through E, and numbers— *Wait*. My gaze hooked onto one name. *Draven*. Why would Draven's name be on a list, in a folder, in the Court of Pain's vaults?

The next column highlighted gender, and then age: 6.

A different Draven then, there would, of course, be more than one person with such a name.

I stole a few sheets, tucked them against the small of my back, and strode on, without missing a stride. I'd pocket a few gold coins before I left too. Arin and I would need them once we escaped Pain.

The apprentice approached a large, glass display cabinet.

He stopped and stared.

I stopped too. Everything stopped—my heart, my thoughts.

The glass box contained a plump purple cushion, a cushion with a circular indentation. But no crown. I kept my face blank, even as my heart plummeted and all my plans fluttered away like scared birds.

The crown wasn't here.

The apprentice didn't appear surprised by the crown's absence, so I assumed Razak wouldn't be either. But I was. If the crown wasn't here, then all of this—our lies, our disguises, returning to Pain with Arin—was for nothing.

It *had* to be here. Where else would Razak keep it?

No, it had to be in this vault. Was this a damned test? Was the apprentice fucking with me? "Assume I don't know where it is," I said, keeping the quiver from my voice. "Tell me what you know."

The man blinked behind his glasses. "I don't understand."

I backhanded him, sending his glasses skipping across the floor and knocking him against the display case. "You're not supposed to understand! Just answer." Nausea slithered, wetting my tongue and making my ears throb.

He cupped his flushed face. "I don't know!"

Clearly, a lie. He knew a great deal. His whole world was knowledge. He pottered around this vault with all these files and documents, coins and secrets at his fingertips. "Tell me and I'll reconsider your punishment."

"I— The letters!" he blubbered. "It was just the once. You left them out— I saw, I didn't mean to look."

Letters? What did they have to do with the crown? "Are you suggesting it's my fault you snooped through my personal items?"

"No, no! I was tidying them away, it's what I do. I tidy, and I saw... I saw the words."

"What words?" I clamped my hand around his neck. *Choke him,* a voice said, a voice so like Razak's that he could be behind me, leaning over my shoulder. *Choke him, he'll like it. They always do.* My fingers crushed tighter, as though through a force of their own.

"The crown," he wheezed.

"The crown what?"

"Umair..."

This was getting tiresome. "Umair what? Explain!" *Choke him harder.*

"He took it!" He clawed at my grip, face flushed, eyes weeping. "The king took it! In the letters... says he took it with him."

Umair had been absent for years, almost a decade. He had vanished not long after he'd forced me to watch him murder my mother. If he'd taken the crown with him, it could be anywhere.

But Razak knew where it was.

He wouldn't be doing all this now if he didn't know exactly where Pain's crown was and how to get his hands on it.

One thing was clear, the crown was not in the vault.

Panic made the nausea swirl, but I still gripped the apprentice's neck, still crushed him in my fingers, his life mine.

"Took it with him *where?*" I snarled.

"To Justice, to find the key! It says—in the letters— The letters were open, and I *didn'tmeantoreadthem!*"

Justice? The threads always returned to Justice.

Razak had said Justice knew about the crowns, the key, and they'd kept the knowledge a secret. And now Umair had taken Pain's crown there ten years ago.

The King of Pain hadn't been seen since.

Was Umair dead or imprisoned?

The apprentice thumped at my arm, then gripped it and clung on, like a drowning man. I didn't want him dead, I didn't want to hurt him, yet that voice in my head—*choke him, make him see death, make him beg for it.*

I tore my grip free and backed away.

No, this wasn't me, I didn't want this. *Razak, it was Razak. In my head, my life.*

I was him, but not. And I was losing my fucking mind! I laughed. It didn't matter. The crown wasn't here. Our father had taken it. Perhaps Razak had a personal reason to kill Justice Ines? Did Justice have the Court of Pain's crown? Was that their secret?

I whirled back on the wheezing apprentice. "Why Justice?" I asked. "Why did Umair take the crown there?"

He flinched and clung to the glass case, afraid of *me*. "He believed Justice guards a power."

"A god's power, Dallin's power?"

He nodded and rubbed his neck. "But... forgive me, you know all this."

I did? *I did.* Razak knew. "Of course." I straightened my clothes and hair, realigning my lies.

The Crown of Justice wasn't the only crown in their court. I hadn't failed, not yet. There was still a chance, but not here... Not in the Court of Pain.

The apprentice dropped to one knee and bowed his head. "Forgive me. I accept whatever punishment you deem appropriate. Hurt me, it's all I deserve."

"Hurt you?" I didn't have time for this. The crown wasn't here. We had to abort the plan and flee Pain before its bars closed around us. I turned on my heel. "Ten lashes of the whip should suffice."

"Sire?" he called.

"Do it yourself. You may find you enjoy it. And don't read my letters again!"

The crown wasn't here. It hadn't been in Pain for years, which was why Razak always wore the prince's crown, not the king's. I should have known! If he'd had access to a king's crown, he'd have worn it at every opportunity.

I grabbed a handful of gold coins from the crates and hurried up the spiral stairs.

I had to get to Arin. I didn't have the crown, but I had information which could prove almost as valuable. Arin would know what to do next. We'd return to the Overlook Inn, meet with Draven, discover the whereabouts of War's crown, and then we'd decide whether we could still stop Razak from getting his hands on all four crowns. Although, the fact Pain's crown was in Justice's Court did not bode well. My brother was there, *exactly where he needed to be*, as he'd delighted in telling me.

Damn him.

"To the tower," I called to the coachman and jogged down the portico's steps.

He tipped his cap and held out a sealed letter, damp from rain. "A runner brought this, Sire."

I snatched it from his fingers, climbed into the carriage, and tore open the letter as the carriage got underway. *Prince Razak, Attend the council chamber as a matter of urgency.* The council was the last place I needed to be, especially as they likely knew I'd lied.

I scrunched the letter and tossed it from the window.

If they knew I was Zayan, they'd kill Arin.

Panic prickled my veins. Once back at the tower, I'd order the coachman to wait outside, collect Arin, and we'd ride out of this grim city, leaving its endless rain and Razak's influence behind for good.

The nightmare was almost over.

Coins clinked in my pocket. I plucked one free and rippled it across the backs of my left hand's fingers. Gold shimmered. I had enough gold in my pocket to keep Arin and I clothed and fed for weeks. We could walk away tomorrow, and perhaps we should. With no court and no army, just Arin's optimism, my charm, and Draven's blades—assuming Ogden hadn't tossed him back out into the sands—what could do we do to stop Razak anyway?

Luck would only get us so far. And eventually, that luck would run out. I tossed the coin, watched it spin in the air, and snatched it into a fist.

The sands... Wait. The documents, the names.

War threw their unwanted things into the sands.

Draven's name in Pain's documents, War's less-than-perfect children were tossed away, and Draven refused to speak of it...

A son. Draven. Age 6?

There was more here, threads of truth weaving together, crafting a picture I did not like.

But Draven didn't lie, he wasn't cunning or sly. Yet when I'd been drugged and dying on War's temple floor, Draven had chased Razak and the crown. He'd reappeared later, without either.

Had he been working against us this whole time?

No, that wasn't Draven's way. He couldn't fool me. But that name on the documents, the child's age, and Draven's dead son. What if the son wasn't dead, what if Razak had him, using the boy as leverage over Draven?

Age 6.

War tossed their broken things away.

People went to extremes for love.

I loved Arin, and I'd do anything for him; I'd lie, cheat,

kill. Was it such a stretch that a warrior of War would do the same for his child?

It was all theories, no proof. But what if I'd missed it, because Draven was... Draven. Handsome to look at but not complicated. And Arin had missed it, because Arin had married the man, a man he did not love. His own guilt would blind him to Draven's misdirection.

But *Draven*, a traitor?

I had to tell Arin my suspicions, show him the documents. We'd discuss it on the journey back to Love.

Regardless of Draven's possible betrayal, Arin would want to go to Justice with all we knew. He'd argue they'd listen. But all the courts were corrupt, suggesting Justice would be too. We had to leave Pain, meet with Draven, confront him, if necessary, and we'd regroup from there.

In the meantime, only one thing mattered: Arin. And getting him to safety.

The carriage rocked to a halt. Without waiting for the aide, I climbed down and caught the driver's eye. Rain pummeled his leather cloak and wide-brimmed hat. "Wait here. We have one more journey to make tonight."

"Aye, Your Highness."

I swept into the tower. It was still late, or early, and while a few people loitered in the foyer, the building was quiet. I climbed the stairs, two risers at a time, up and up, to Razak's floor. The doors groaned open. I slipped between them, breaking into a run, breathless and dizzy. "Arin? We—"

At a touch, the door swung open—unlocked. No. Broken.

I stumbled, slowing. The door to my room hung open too. That one I *had* locked. "Arin?"

I flew in, still hoping Arin would be on the bed, sleepy-eyed from pennywort, but the bed was empty, its sheets askew. The cuff's chain had been cut, not unlocked. They'd come prepared.

Arin was gone.

They knew—*they knew!*

They'd taken him. They'd taken Arin, my sunshine and honey, my Prince of Flowers.

Pain had him, the council had him, someone had him!

I thrust my hands into my hair and reeled, falling against the dresser. My dresser. My room. My prison. My bed. My chain, my life.

Arin wasn't here.

My insides coiled. Pain stole the air from my lungs, as vivid and sharp as the lash of a whip.

I clung to the dresser, rocking it.

In the mirror, Razak sneered. *It's all you deserve.* He'd done this. Somehow, even from a whole other court, he'd reached out and crushed the one good thing in my life.

I grabbed the mirror and threw it. Glass rained in jagged shards across the floor. It wasn't enough. I tore the drawers from the dresser and flung those too, the sheets from the bed, everything, and screamed. Arin's soft floral scent slapped the madness aside.

I was losing my mind...

No, not yet... Not yet.

I was a prince. I was Razak.

Arin had been taken, but I'd find him.

He couldn't have been gone for long.

They'd taken him, not killed him, or I'd have returned to a bloody body.

They needed Arin.

To get to me.

I flew toward the door. Arin would tell me to stop, to think, to plan. But I had a role to play. It wasn't over. If I blustered in as Zayan, they'd hang us both. And that wasn't ever going to happen.

I straightened myself, my clothes, and breathed.

I could do this.

They had Arin. They had suspicions but no proof. I'd go to the council, I'd be Razak, and if they'd hurt so much as a single hair on his head, I'd fucking butcher them all.

CHAPTER 18

*A*rin

PURPLE SILK DRAPED from the ceiling in wide strips, like curtains. An image of four interlocking circles adorned the chairs and curtains. I'd seen the same design elsewhere in the court, subtle, yet obvious. Pain's courtly insignia. I'd imagined Pain would have chosen a scythe or a lightning bolt to represent it, something more pain-like than circles.

I'd been told to dress, then rough-handled here and shoved into a chair in front of a long table, as though I were to be judged, but this was not the Court of Justice.

Although I'd never seen Razak's council, the people staring from behind that table were surely them. All but one appeared much older. They'd probably served as advisors for Razak's father, King Umair. If they were anything like Ogden or even my own father, then I was already the foolish Prince of Love who'd led to my court's downfall. Were they complicit in its downfall? Did they know Razak's plans?

"How did Razak come to capture you, Arin?"

"*Prince* Arin," I corrected the older woman.

A sharp smile flashed across her lips, there and gone again in a blink. She studied me, and with each passing moment, her glare pushed me deeper into the chair. "I'd assumed, as Albus's son, you'd be intelligent enough to recognize when you're not in a position to make demands."

"And I'd have thought you'd be intelligent enough to realize capturing and holding me in such a fashion will incite Ogden's wrath. I am of War's court. Kidnapping me warrants retaliation." My words barely ruffled her curled white hair, bunched atop her head and pinned there in strict fashion.

"Ah yes, the joining." She said it as though she'd tasted something foul. "So like a child of Love, to assume the shatterlands revolves around you."

This woman wouldn't know love if it smacked her between the eyes.

"Ogden will not come for you, Arin," she added matter-of-factly. "You are a prince without a court, and frankly, it is only your warlord husband keeping you from being tossed into the sands and left there to desiccate, like the rest of War's rejects."

I'd known I was little more than a name, but it still stung to be so easily dismissed.

Her gaze skipped over my shoulder, fixing on someone lurking behind me. I twisted, to get a look, when a fist slammed into my jaw. Fire flash-burned up my face, knocking me sideways and almost off the chair. Blood pooled under my tongue.

They hadn't needed to strike me. I wasn't resisting.

They'd torn me from a bed, flung me into mismatched clothes, and brought me here, already their prisoner. *None* of this was necessary. Unless it wasn't about me.

I licked blood from the inside of my cheek and spat.

"It is not Ogden we're interested in, or you," the cruel woman explained, then leaned forward over the table, trying to force me deeper into the chair under her icy glare. "How did Razak capture you? I'm intrigued to know the logistics."

This was about Lark. Did they not believe his act, was that why I was here? "Ask him."

The woman's hollow eyes sucked what little warmth there was from the room. "He'll be along in a moment," she said. "We'd like to hear your account first."

Then Lark was coming here, and whatever I said, they'd ask him the same, searching for inconsistencies in our replies. They clearly suspected not all was well with our performance. Yet, if they knew Lark was pretending to be Razak, he and I would already be dead.

Wherever Lark was, he had better have the crown and a plan for how to get us both away from Razak's council.

All I could do was delay them.

"I don't know what you expect me to say. The last few hours in War were chaotic. Razak poisoned the wine. He was discovered, arrested—"

"Where's Zayan?" she snapped, not interested in my play-by-play account of events.

I dabbed at my sore cheek. "Who?"

The second blow was no less painful for being expected. Blood swelled, and this time I spat it onto their polished black marble floors instead of swallowing out of politeness. I eyed the bastard with the fists, but he was careful not to meet my gaze. He had orders to look away, like everyone else in Pain.

"Your fool," the woman explained. "Or have you forgotten the spy who assisted in the destruction of your court? Razak's brother. He attended your joining alongside our prince."

179

"That fraud," I snarled. "What of him?"

"Where is he?" she asked again.

"I've no idea. I'd prefer never to see that traitor again."

The third blow tipped me out of the chair and onto my knees. Blood dribbled from my lip and nose. Numb inside, I watched it drip and pool on the floor and tried to ride out the pain. Each drop of blood was another moment passing, another heartbeat in time. Each passing moment was a win.

"I see you've stolen my pet." Razak's bitterly cold, clipped voice filled the council chamber. I looked up, choking on fear —Razak was here! He'd returned from Justice?!—then saw the purple gloves. Relief chased the heady fearful rush away. I blinked, clearing my vision, and wiped blood from my chin. Razak's smile said it all: He was in control.

He strode on by, stopping at the end of the long council table. "I'll forget for a moment how you dared summon me here like a dog on a leash, and ask instead, why has Love's prince been taken from my room without my permission?"

Slumping against the chair, I kept my eyes downcast, careful to school all emotion from my face. Lark was a marvel, his performance so perfect the council had no choice but to believe him. I couldn't ruin this as well as everything else.

I'd feared they may have caught him too. But no, he was here, and his lies would wrap around them all as they had done in my court.

Did he have the crown? He must have. We just needed to keep up the act, as we had in the foyer. Make them *believe* we were enemies. "I'm not your pet."

"I did not give you permission to speak," he snapped back.

I chuckled for them all to hear. "Do you hold the reins to this court, or does she?"

Lark came at me like a hawk with its talons out. His hand arched over his shoulder and came down in a vicious slap, leaving me breathless and reeling, my vision spinning.

And now we were even, I supposed, after I'd made a show of assaulting him in his chambers so many moons ago it seemed like another lifetime.

I peered through swimming tears and caught his furious glare, almost believing it. He marched back to the table.

His lies were formidable. But I'd learned to seek the softness in his eyes, and it had been there, buried so deep no other could see it.

"Your return, Razak," the woman began, "does not match witness accounts."

"What does it matter, Malvina? I'm here, and I brought you the Prince of Love." Lark flicked his fingers toward me. "The *how* is a mere distraction. Results speak for themselves."

There appeared to be a power play at work here. Malvina was respected; the others had been silent this entire time. She and Razak had likely clashed many times before. "The how is important, as we must now consider how to maneuver you into Justice," she said, keeping her voice level. "Where you claimed you'd find the keys. Not here, dallying with the boy. Prince Arin is the distraction. Get rid of him and focus on breaking Justice. This power game of yours is becoming decidedly tiresome."

Lark braced both hands on the table and peered down its length at them all. "It is no game. Order me again and Justice Ines's corpse won't be the only one hanging from a tree."

Finally, Malvina balked. She stiffened, lifted her chin, and leaned back, switching from aggression to submissive in moments. "That will not be necessary, my prince. I merely have your own well-being at heart."

My chuckle slipped free, and I dabbed again at my split

lip and cheek. My face burned, but I'd live. We both would. Lark had these people dancing to his tune. He was damned good at what he did, even as it galled me to admit I'd been his victim too.

"Are we done?" he asked. When nobody replied, he strode to me, hooked me off the floor, and dragged me toward the door. "After this unnecessary interruption, I'm not to be disturbed for the day."

"Razak, there is one more request," Malvina called. "Won't you remove the gloves?"

Lark half turned his head.

Her tone had changed again. The fear we'd all heard moments ago had shifted into curiosity, and something more.

She knew.

Lark's glance caught mine. His eyes narrowed, and in that brilliant head of his, he juggled our options. Draven had said Lark would always be the last man standing, and he was right. This was his world. He knew how to play them, how to twist them. He knew their secrets, their lies—he had to. He always knew which card to play, and if they didn't have the right cards, he'd have one tucked down his boot. Magic. He'd know what to do.

He flung open the door and shoved me through. "Run."

Run? That wasn't a plan. I bolted, with Lark a step behind.

"Stop them!" Malvina shrieked.

We spilled down a stairwell, spiraling down and down so fast the torches flickered, and the only sound was that of our hammering feet and hearts. A door slammed above. Thundering feet joined the sound of our own.

"Run?" I panted. "Really?! That's all you've got?"

"They know," he growled, chasing down each step after me. "Danyal told them. Damn him!"

"The crown?"

His sneer thinned even more. "Not there."

I stopped on a half-landing. "What? But you said—"

Lark grabbed my arm and shoved me into motion again. "I was wrong. But I did discover information we'll need." He slowed. "There were letters—"

"Get them!" someone several flights above yelled.

"We have to get out of here first." He pulled me down the steps after him. "When we reach the foyer, run outside. Don't stop. There's a carriage waiting at the steps. It will take us to your court, your home. Do you understand?"

So he *did* have a plan. "Yes."

We reached a door, and he spun me into his arms, chest to chest. His gloved fingers skimmed my face. "I hurt you?"

"It's nothing." I smiled, letting him know we were fine. "All part of the act."

The marching of boots drew ever closer, but Lark hadn't opened the door. He studied my face, while his own shifted from desperation to determination. He wiped blood from my chin, turned, and flung open the door. "Go."

We had an audience of administration workers, but none tried to stop us. News of the truth hadn't reached this far. Beaten and disheveled, I was the perfect distraction alongside Lark's portrayal of his brother. He caught my arm again and pulled me through the gawking crowd. "Come along, Arin." Nobody seemed alarmed, and the guards had yet to reach the ground floor.

We hurried outside and down the steps. A glossy black coach waited. Lark opened the door, glancing behind us. "Get in, hurry."

I grabbed the handles and climbed in. My jacket snagged on something. I twisted, caught sight of Lark's hand in my pocket, and frowned up at his face.

He smiled. "For your new life."

"What?" I shoved my hand into my pocket and grasped a handful of gold coins. What was this? My heart hiccupped.

Lark slammed the carriage door closed between us.

"Lark?" I tried the handle. It didn't budge. My heart lurched again, tripping inside my chest, sensing the wrongness unfolding in front of me. "Wait, the door's stuck—" I pulled and shoved. It creaked but didn't give.

"To the border. Don't stop for anything," Lark barked at the driver.

What? No. Not without him. "Lark!"

He backed away from the carriage.

"Wait!" The window. I grasped the metal latch and heaved the window down, but it wedged halfway. "Lark, wait. The door's stuck. Tell the driver to wait." I knew, of course I did. My heart knew, but my head refused to believe it. He was leaving me.

His gloved fingers slipped the carriage key into his pocket.

He'd locked the door.

I couldn't open it *because he'd locked it.*

A whip cracked the air and the horses lurched the carriage forward. Why was he doing this?

Lark stepped back again and bowed his head. Resignation softened his eyes. But satisfaction hardened them too.

"You bastard! Open this fucking door!"

His eyes widened, some kind of panicked thought occurring to him. "Don't trust Draven."

"What?" I yanked on the door. "Lark, what!?" I thumped the top of the carriage. "Driver, stop!"

The carriage hastened. *Don't stop for anyone or anything.*

"No!" I couldn't see him outside the window. We'd moved too far already. I grabbed the half-open pane and leaned through the slim gap, trapped to my chest. "Lark?" It was too late. The carriage was taking me away and I couldn't stop it. "Why?" I called back. Lark didn't move. He stared back, and by Dallin, I hoped this hurt him, because he was tearing out my heart.

The horses' steel shoes clattered on wet cobbles and the carriage clanged, rattling around me. Lark stood watching, hands clasped in front of him, waiting.

"Damn you!" Damn him for taking my choice! I'd have stayed with him, faced the council with him, stood beside him. And he'd known it.

Guards poured from the tower's front door and raced down the steps.

"They're coming! Run!"

He didn't run, didn't try and fight them. He raised his hands at his sides, his stare still on me, and the guards rushed him.

"No!" I kicked the door, but like before, it didn't give. And when I looked again, they had Lark pinned to the ground.

Lark had just saved my life, and all it had cost him was his.

CHAPTER 19

ark

It had been the right thing to do.

As the guards manhandled me back up the steps and into the main foyer, my heart was at peace. Arin was safe. And in the grand scheme of things, he was the only thing in this wretched life I cared for.

If I'd have left with him, they'd have chased us down. But I'd realized it too late to properly say goodbye, to warn him, and to tell him I loved him.

"Hold him!" Malvina barked from the galleried landing above the foyer.

The guards jolted me to a halt beneath the sparkling diamond and amethyst chandelier. Pain's administrators gathered around. We had an audience. They probably saw the council arresting Razak. He'd be furious if he knew the charade I'd put on. I smiled... Good.

"Remove his gloves," Malvina said.

I rolled my eyes. The theatrics were unnecessary. We all knew who I was. The guards tugged my gloves off anyway.

"His right hand. Hold it up."

The guard on my right raised my hand for all to see.

"Oh, how terrible," I drawled and waggled my remaining fingers. "It seems you have an imposter in your midst."

"Zayan," Malvina growled. "It *is* you."

"I prefer the name Lark, these days."

The smug smile on her lips was a horrible thing to witness, as though a slug had crawled there and died. "Credit where it's due, you had us fooled," she said.

"You never would have known, if not for Danyal."

"Danyal? No. Not him." She leaned against the rail and took all the time in the world to study me, captured and at her mercy.

Danyal hadn't betrayed me. Interesting. Although, regardless, I was caught.

Bendrik carved his way through the gawking crowd, slithering like the snake he was. He eyed me with equal measures of intrigue and lurid satisfaction. "You really are a remarkable creature," he said, making the compliment sound sordid. "He shouldn't be wearing those royal clothes," Bendrik said. "Strip him of his lies."

Rough hands tore at my coat, jerking me about. They tore the garment away. The expensive clothes had been a delight to wear, but in the end, I was only a prince of a gutter, not a court. Fine silks did not belong on me. The shirt went next, torn free, popping buttons. Someone thought to force me to my knees, and so, there I was, arms spread, naked to the waist, almost all of me on display. There was no denying it now. My body told the truth of me. It always had. Missing fingers, scarred chest. I was Zayan, Razak's dog on a leash.

Bendrik studied my torso, running his gaze over the many

light scars, then came forward. His appraising gaze had an unwelcome hunger, the same kind of hunger I'd seen in the eyes of the men who had bought me on the street. He caught himself at the last moment, stopping short of touching me, and looked up at Malvina. "I'll watch him, while you get word to Razak."

He'd do more than watch. "I demand Justice," I said, raising my voice so it filled the foyer.

Malvina laughed. "Demand all you want, Zayan. Your voice is worthless here."

"I'm no longer invisible. I have a name. I'm Umair's son, as much as its inconvenient for you. There are witnesses." Several of which surrounded us now. "You can't silence them all. Zayan exists, Razak acknowledged me as a half prince. Charge me, cuff me, but balance is all. Justice will be heard."

Everything pointed toward Justice. Umair's letters, Razak's plan, the crown. I had to go there next, and I'd take a leaf out of Razak's book and make Justice work for me. If I made enough fuss, Justice would come, my voice would be heard—balance was all—and they'd take me back to their court for judgement. Exactly where I needed to be.

And Arin would be far away from it all.

They could hurt me all they wanted, but they wouldn't kill me. Whip me, cut me, fuck me. None of it could touch my heart, not when Arin carried it with him. With him safe, I was immune to pain.

"Very well," Malvina agreed. "Take Zayan away until we hear from Razak. And Bendrik, make sure to lock him up tight. That one has a knack for escaping."

I smirked up at Malvina. "I promise to behave."

CHAPTER 20

ark

IN THE PAST, Bendrik had circled Razak like an annoying fly. Always a yes-man, eager to please the prince. Razak had once told me, while high on pennywort and feeling conversational, how Bendrik had believed they were friends.

Razak didn't have friends, only tools and enemies.

As I'd been given over to Bendrik's "care," I'd need to get the measure of the man, and fast. He'd have a weakness. Everyone did.

His thoughts on me, as Zayan, ran along the same lines as everyone else's. I was the inconvenient secret, now not-so-secret. I belonged to Razak, but that didn't mean I was untouchable. As I was probably about to discover.

Considering Bendrik was a council member, his chambers —curiously on a sub-ground floor—were dressed like a king's, overflowing with silks and velvets. A wood-burner throbbed waves of heat, making the large space stifling. Perhaps

Bendrik had some War blood in him, hence the heat. Although it seemed unlikely, when the courts had always been divided.

"There's no point in trying to escape," Bendrik said, leading me and my guards through his chambers. "The world knows who you are now."

"And who am I?" I asked, struggling with that question myself.

"You're a criminal. Through here," Bendrik told the guards, opening a second door into another vast space dominated by a huge half-sunken pool. The square pool had marble steps leading up to its edges. Lavender scented water steamed inside. The reason for Bendrick's cleanliness fetish became clear as soon as I took in the rest of the antechamber. Chains hung from the far wall. A rack of weapons and tools gleamed. And on a mahogany table, an array of implements was displayed.

Ah, Bendrik was *that* member of the council. The one who did their dirty work.

He nodded toward the far wall. The guards wordlessly escorted me to the chains, and holding my arms out, they clamped the shackles around my wrists.

"That will be all." He gave each of the guards a gold coin, probably for their discretion. They left, and the door closed, sealing us in absolute silence. No windows, not here. Screams wouldn't penetrate these walls.

I glimpsed the drain in the floor. People had died here, in this room. They'd bled and screamed and pleaded. If Bendrik sought the same from me, he was about to be disappointed.

Bendrik dipped his fingers into the bath, then shook excess water from his hand. "Would it surprise you to know you've featured in many a dream?"

"*You'd* be surprised by how little surprises me."

He looked over from the bath's steps and huffed a soft laugh. "After all these years as his, I can hardly believe you're here."

I let my gaze linger on the table and its shining metal tools. Clearly, Bendrik liked his games. But his words unsettled me more than the sight of his tools. There was a fine line between obsession and madness—I walked it daily. Obsession, infatuation, I could handle, but madness was slippery and difficult to manipulate. As Arin had once said, madness could not be reasoned with. But it could be molded.

He approached and again admired my chest, with its speckled scars. I breathed slowly, despite my hammering heart.

Bendrik would have to enact his fantasies fast, before Razak learned he'd adopted me. My brother's wrath when it came to his own personal toys was legendary. Razak did not share.

Bendrik reached out. His warm fingers skimmed my chest, scattering gooseflesh in their wake. This man and I were roughly the same age, but he'd been raised in Pain's court, had his every whim met, been told he was above all those beneath him who worked to keep the court and its hungry cities thriving.

"Prince Razak told me, Zayan, how he'd lay you on your back and cut you." His fingers skimmed some more, sweeping down to my hip. "He said you'd only come with a knife and his cock inside you."

I gritted my teeth and fluttered any feelings away. What was one man's lust, when I'd toyed with so many?

"Each of these scars is a testament to your ecstasy," he went on, skimming his fingers up, over where my ribs jutted from having my arms pulled back. "Each one a mark of pleasure and pain. The truth of it is quite beautiful." He peered into my eyes. "As are you."

Razak had told Bendrik all this about me to torture him, knowing Bendrik would *never* get his hands on me.

Yet, here I was, caught and exposed. Razak wasn't here to save me from Bendrik's desires. Chained, with little hope of escape, I *did* need my brother. And that was a more disturbing thought than having this man drool all over me and potentially stick his cock into whatever hole and crevice he pleased.

My top lip curled of its own accord. "Fuck me, and he'll take a finger for each time your cock violates his property."

Bendrik stole his hand back, curling his precious fingers into his palm. "Oh, I know." He leaned close and whispered, "You might just be worth it."

He sashayed backward, his hungry gaze admiring me with every step. "I have some matters to attend. I'll return soon. Rest now, save your strength. And do not worry, this will not be a task. You're going to enjoy our time together."

I rather enjoyed my freedom too, but he wasn't about to give me that.

He left the room; only the sound of my own heart disturbed the quiet. I gave the cuffs an experimental tug. Even if I could slip my right hand free, as I had to escape Razak's cuff in the past, the left wouldn't give as easily.

The table of nasty-looking tools was several strides away and far beyond my reach.

I wasn't escaping the chains without Bendrik's help. He'd have his fun with me, and eventually, he'd want more. Men always did. That would require he uncuff me...

His pleasure was his weakness, and my strength.

All I had to do was endure and wait for an opportunity.

The exact same as I'd been doing my whole life.

CHAPTER 21

*A*rin

I FUMED IN THE CARRIAGE, at Lark, at myself, at the whole world.

The sun rose, dragging blue skies over a distant, hilly horizon. We passed through villages, over bridges, down roads, on and on, farther and farther from Lark. I'd tried to sleep during the night, but every time I'd closed my eyes, I'd seen Lark on those wretched steps, waiting to be captured. He could have run. Why hadn't he?

He'd *allowed* them to capture him.

The more I fumed, the more I hated—and *loved*—him.

For a new life, he'd said. He'd saved me. But I didn't need saving, I needed Lark.

He'd sent me off with coin in my pocket and didn't expect to see me again. He didn't know me at all, if he thought I'd walk away. He *should* know me. I thought we'd gotten past all the lies and misdirection. He should have told me his plan, should have *asked* me. We could have talked it through. Although, he hadn't known the council had seen through his act, so he hadn't planned to shove me on the carriage without him. That realization must have come to him in the tower stairwell. But still...

And his parting words: *Don't trust Draven.* What was I supposed to make of that? Draven was all I had left who I *could* trust.

The galloping horses slowed and the carriage drew to a halt. Through the window, fields and forests covered rolling hills. I hated that too, because it meant I was so far away from Pain that the rain and storms couldn't reach me here. Lark couldn't reach me.

The coach rocked, the driver jumped down, and slotted his key into the lock.

I kicked the door open, lunged at the reeling driver, grabbed him, and flung him against the side of the carriage. "Take me back!"

"Can't do that," the man grumbled. His hat had knocked askew, half covering his face.

I grabbed his neck and squeezed, then felt the press of something hard and cold in my side. Some kind of weapon. Driving a royal coach like this, he'd of course be armed. The driver nodded, advising I let go.

With a snarl, I freed him and stepped back. He aimed the tip of his short sword at my chest.

I raised my hands, backing up further. "You have to take me back."

"My orders were clear. You get off here."

"I have gold." I sunk my hand into my pocket and pulled out a fistful of gold coins. "Take it. And take me back." He glowered. I flung the coins at his chest, and the stubborn bastard still glowered. "You don't understand, I have to go back."

He lowered the sword and righted his hat. "Ain't worth my life to go against the prince's orders."

He turned his back and swung himself onto the driver's seat.

He was leaving? There was nothing here, no houses, no people. Just a few grazing animals and a whole lot of trees. "Wait... The man who gave you those orders? He wasn't even Razak! He's not your prince, so your orders mean nothing. I know it sounds insane—it *was* insane. But it's true. So take me back and I'll prove it."

He gathered the reins.

"Stop! What am I supposed to do?"

"Ain't my problem." He clicked his tongue, geeing the horses on.

"You can't leave me in the middle of nowhere!"

"Yargh!" He snapped the reins and lurched the coach forward.

"Hey!"

Clouds of dust churned in the carriage's wake. I attempted to jog after it, but gave up when my heart and head throbbed as one.

The dust settled, the coach was long gone, and I stood alone on the road with no idea where I was. Assuming this was the border between Love and Pain, then I had one choice. Walk back into Pain or return to Love.

I turned on the spot. Behind me, the sky was dark, heavy, laden with storms. Ahead, white clouds drifted. Ahead was my home, whatever that meant now.

My heart demanded I walk back into Pain, but my head... My head knew I couldn't do that. I had no power there. I'd been Pain's victim since Razak had destroyed my court, and that hadn't changed. If I went back while Lark was in chains, they'd capture me, and his sacrifice would be for nothing. As much as I hated what he'd done, and how he'd gone about it, he may have been right.

Ahead, my home waited. Ruined, desolate, but mine, nonetheless. I'd meet with Draven at the Overlook, as we'd planned. But I didn't have Pain's crown. I didn't have anything to show for our efforts in the Court of Pain. Just a pocket full of gold and a hole in my heart.

I couldn't help Lark from inside Pain. But perhaps, if there was anything left of Love, I could use it to save him. At least I'd have Draven.

"Damn you, Lark!"

The grazing animals startled and ran into the woods.

It hurt, all of it. Being here without him, when he should have been at my side. Knowing he'd pushed me away to save me. And knowing, wherever he was, he'd be hurting too.

Tears blurred my vision, put there by rage. I snarled them away, picked up the coins I'd thrown at the driver, and stomped toward Love's blue skies. Fine then. He'd left me no choice. The shatterlands and their courts be damned. I'd always save Lark before I saved the world, because this world wasn't worth saving without him in it.

I WALKED until stumbling into a nameless little town. Its market and farming people were so far removed from my court they didn't recognize me, or the white and gold jacket. Nobody asked why I happened to be dressed half like a noble and half like a vagrant in trousers that didn't quite fit, probably assuming I was a lord who'd been robbed on the road. I looked like one, with my bruised, unshaven face. After renting a room at the inn, I visited a small clothing store, one of several little stores along the narrow, winding main street.

The owner helped pick out clothes more suitable for traveling and less likely to mark me as being wealthy enough to rob.

I'd expected to feel some regret as I handed over the princely coat as partial payment, but I mostly felt relief.

"Er, sir? There's some letters, 'ere." The store owner handed them back. "Looks important. Don't want to forget 'em."

"Thank you." I left the store and glanced at the documents as I stepped into the street.

The topmost letter bore the words *Dear Razak* in swirling penmanship.

Ice water spilled down my spine, as though the rotten prince was here, watching. I glanced about, checking nobody had seen, and tucked the papers into my new coat. Lark had said something about documents, but I hadn't thought to check all my coat's pockets—just the one I'd caught him with his hand in.

After returning to the inn, I ordered soup, bread, and mead at the bar and tucked myself into a corner to read the papers.

There were three letters, all to Razak from his father. The other documents appeared to be lists of names. The first page had gotten wet while I'd been on the road, blurring the bottom half's contents, making it illegible. I'd study it later. For now, the letters demanded my eye.

With my belly full, the fire blazing, and the inn's bar filling with background chatter, I began to read.

Umair spoke of a search for power, and reading between the lines, he'd travelled to a crypt, buried in ice. He mentioned a font or well several times, claiming it would

make things right, and *return the world to how it should be*. In one
letter, the king was scathing—ranting at Razak. Blaming him
for the ruin of Umair's heart. Umair was careful with his
words, probably in case the letters were read by anyone but
Razak. The more I read, the more it became clear the King
of Pain had been writing to Razak from a faraway land, a
land of ice, where he'd been searching for something he
called the font. He believed it could put right an event Razak
and he both shared, an event he blamed his son for. He
called Razak wretched, a mistake, said he was spoiled like
rotten fruit.

My own father had many, many problems, but he'd never
cursed me in such a manner. I'd always been loved. There was
no love in these letters. If anything, the King of Pain spoke of
this font as though he coveted that more than the love of his
own son.

In the final letter, Umair wrote:

*Keep Zayan close. You both will be all that is left of me, if I do not
unite the keys soon...*

He'd made no mention of keys in the previous letters and
hadn't mentioned Zayan either. His tone had changed. This
letter almost sounded like a goodbye. For all Umair's scornful
belittling, these letters were likely the last words of Razak's
father. A father whom nobody had seen in many years. Whatever Umair's mission, it appeared as though he'd failed and
probably perished in his quest for the font.

Perhaps Razak was following in his father's footsteps,
trying to find him and this *font*? Umair hadn't mentioned
godlike ambitions, such as those of his son. His motivations
had been to set right events of his past, not to hoard power,
or covet godliness.

I reread the letters again and again, searching for anything
I'd missed among Umair's words, until the oil lamps had

burned through most of their fuel and all but a handful of patrons had left the inn.

The barman rang the bell for last orders. I tucked the letters away and set my sights on the documents titled *Court of War Benefits*, complete with a long list of numbers, names, genders, and ages. Most of the entries appeared to refer to young children. I scanned the legible sections. Lark must have stolen the documents for a reason, but I failed to see it. When I reached the Overlook Inn, I'd show Draven. He'd know.

Between my ex-husband and I was a whole lot of road and several days to cover it before the next full moon.

I finished my mead and retired to my room. Tomorrow, I'd purchase a horse. And then onward, to whatever remained of the Court of Love.

It took four days and nights of riding before I passed through villages I'd been paraded along as a child. Then, streamers had flown from cottage windows, petals had been thrown over us, and the entire village had turned out to greet us. Most of the cottages appeared empty now. A few stray dogs rifled through discarded bags. Cottage doors hung open, banging in the breeze, and all the flowers had wilted in their gardens.

I'd passed several travelers on the road. One had told me to turn around, claiming there was nothing worth visiting on the road ahead. Those people had carried their belongings in small carts. If they were heading for War or Pain, then they'd have a harsh welcome. A farmer carting dead animals had spoken of how he couldn't afford to keep his farm, now the markets had closed.

None of the people knew me as their prince. If they had, they likely wouldn't have greeted me so kindly.

The deeper into Love I rode, the more desolate the land became.

Draven had carted me out of these lands, bleeding and unconscious. I hadn't witnessed Love's fall, until now.

Razak had done this. He'd dismantled my home and my reign, secret by secret, lie by lie. These people weren't bad. They hadn't deserved his wrath. Was it just about the crowns or had something more personal driven Razak to burn my court?

Whatever his motive, a jail cell in Justice was too good for that monster.

Anger boiled in my veins, growing hotter with every abandoned cottage I passed.

"Yargh!" I galloped my horse through another empty village, around fallen branches and abandoned belongings, until we raced through the town that hugged the palace gardens, and there, high up on the natural bluff, the palace towers jutted.

I pulled the horse to a sudden halt, making the animal screech and dance.

A shell of the palace remained, but it was blackened and hollow. Multicolored flags no longer fluttered from crumbling spires. My once magnificent white and gold world was now nothing but a rotting carcass, picked clean by Razak. The Court of Love had been flawed and shallow and on its knees, but I could have saved it.

Should have saved it.

I dismounted, tied the horse to a fence post, and walked into the meadows. The flower heads all hung low. Their stems turned to dust in my hands. One lone butterfly danced in the air, seeking a bloom yet to die—a hopeful creature.

"What have I done?"

If I'd been a hero, I'd have killed Lark the first day we'd met, as boys, instead of trying to outsmart him and his brother.

But I couldn't kill a man, and certainly couldn't kill Lark, not even as strangers. Why kill a wounded creature if it could be saved?

I'd been naive and foolish, and later, I'd been selfish. My people had paid the price.

This was about more than my love for Lark. I had to stop Razak from ruining lives. He could not be permitted to steal the crowns. My love for Lark, brilliant as it was, and my need to save him, would have to wait.

As dusk swept in off the ocean, I collected my horse and walked it back toward the town. A single swinging lamp illuminated the Overlook Inn's door, like a beacon in the night.

If Draven wasn't already inside, he'd be along soon.

Hopefully, he carried with him better news than I. We needed it.

CHAPTER 22

ark

TWO DAYS I'd hung there, like meat.

Bendrik had decided to savor the time we had together. Or he hadn't yet decided how best to fuck me. Either way, I'd begun to wish he'd get it over with before boredom did me in. Fuck me, cut me, do something. But he'd mostly stared, then stroked his metal tools, and sometimes his cock through his trousers, as though ashamed I might see how all of this aroused him.

I was allowed out of the cuffs two times a day, to clean up and relieve myself, but each time, he'd watched, like an overzealous nurse.

Today, the third day, Bendrik's return stirred me from a half-sleep, suspended by aching wrists and tingling fingers.

He smirked and made his way over, so pleased with his toy.

He tugged off his coat and rolled up his sleeves, as was a

habit with him, then tossed his flat cap onto the table of tools and ruffled his hair. He returned in good spirits, but his mood would quieten. Then he'd dally over his instruments, gaze at me, get hard, and leave.

The pool steamed behind him, making the air thick with humidity.

"Water?" I croaked.

"Ah, yes. Of course. We can't have you dehydrated."

He kept the dungeon stifling. I sweated out any hydration within hours. I wasn't sure if it was part of his game. Perhaps his blood ran cold. Gods, when would this end?

"You know, I thought you'd be more interested." He lifted the glass of water to my lips. I guzzled all of it, without stopping to breathe. He might disappear all day again, leaving me gasping like yesterday.

"Interested how?" I asked, after he took the empty glass away.

He set the glass down, then turned and skipped his gaze up my bare chest. The desire in his eyes betrayed all the ways he wanted to indulge, but some kind of barrier was stopping him. It wasn't fear. He'd tortured people before, of that there was no doubt.

"Oh, you mean my cock?" I smiled. "Perhaps you haven't provided ample stimulation?"

He smiled back, but there was intrigue in his gaze too. "Razak said you usually respond favorably, eventually."

Eventually. After he'd had his hand on my cock long enough for me to imagine I was somewhere else, with someone—anyone—else. I responded to Razak because if I didn't, he wouldn't stop. Besides, this situation was very different. Bendrik wasn't Razak. He thought he was, pretended he was, probably got himself off to the thought of fucking my brother, but Razak would never stoop so low as to have this one pleasure him. I knew my brother. He had standards. Bendrik was too desperate, too needy, too far below Razak, intellectually, to be of any interest to him. But he'd have told Bendrik stories of all the ways he'd fucked me, because he'd have known how Bendrik desired me.

Hm, there was an idea.

"Don't you think these cuffs are unnecessary?" I asked, giving them a rattle.

"I like them." He studied his table of weapons, deciding which one would cut me the best, only to later change his mind.

"The small one, the paring knife," I suggested. "Start with that one."

Startled at my suggestion, he glanced over.

"Easier to wield for delicate work."

The man was so hard in his pants that a patch of darker black gave away his cock's need. He picked up the smallest knife and again looked at me. Was he waiting for permission? If delayed gratification was something Bendrik struggled with, I could help him with that, if he let me go.

"Wouldn't you like me more if I danced for you?"

His eyebrows lifted. "Dance?"

"I'm bored." I shrugged, rattling my chains. "If you want me hard, then let me off the leash and let's play."

His smile grew, but he returned to admiring his knives. He'd seen me attack Razak before. He knew I was fast. But he also really wanted my cock stiff for him. It's not much fun when your partner yawns during foreplay.

Did he think we might form a bond? Captor and captive, perhaps?

"Come now." I tilted my head and raised my coyness level. "I have many skills, as I'm sure you've heard. Cuffing me is a waste of both our time, when we could be having a lot more fun fucking each other. How do you like it? You seem the careful type, methodical. You enjoy control. Uncuff me, and I'll get on my knees and beg you for cock."

"You'll say anything for a chance to escape."

I frowned, playing at being hurt. "And I thought we were friends, Benny."

He huffed a laugh and still didn't look up.

Playing coy wasn't getting me anywhere. I'd yet to figure out what Bendrik wanted from me. It was time to change tack. I wiped the smile off my face and poured a little ice into my veins instead, summoning the act that had gotten me this far, for better or worse. "Look at me," I snapped.

He straightened and whipped his head around.

Oh, I had him now.

He didn't want me, that's why he'd been delaying. He wanted Razak. I should have seen it sooner. I hadn't, because he didn't know. This was new to him. Well then, now I knew how to have him work for me. "You want me hard? Then stop procrastinating and get over here. Make it happen."

"Don't do that."

"Do what?"

"Be him."

"What? You don't like it? I think you do, and that's why you're over there, behind that table. Are you hard, Bendrik? Can you feel your cock pulsing? You want to hurt Razak, you want to fuck him until he chokes. I know what that feels like. I can make it happen for you. I look like him—"

"It's not like that." But he'd fallen quiet; of course it was *like that*. A chance to fuck Razak? By Dallin, even Malvina would salivate at the idea.

"What did he do to you?" I asked. "Did you try and seduce him and he laughed you off? No? Worse? He humili-ated you."

Bendrik winced.

I laughed, using Razak's awful, dark, slippery laugh. Whatever this was doing for him, it had *my* blood flowing south. I shifted my hips, drawing his eye to how my trousers failed to hide a growing need of my own. *Look over, look at the man you hate and want to fuck, chained to your dungeon wall.*

"What did he do?" It had to be something typically Razak. But Bendrik had all his fingers, so not that. Something a young and up-and-coming member of Pain's court would despise.

Bendrik lifted his gaze, and all the soft uselessness drained out of him, leaving the raw man inside. He had some flare, some fight in him, and it showed in his new snarl. Possessed by a sudden urgency, he unbuttoned his shirt, then whipped it off and sauntered over. Sharp brown eyes searched mine. His cheek twitched. "He had me whipped." His voice grated. "In the tower foyer."

But that wasn't all of it. There was more. Public punishment was just another day in this court. No, something else had happened, something to make Bendrik despise Razak, but want to be seen by him too, admired, even loved by him.

"What did he do?" I whispered, leaning forward, and then, knowing Bendrik's mind was back in that moment, I whispered again, "What did *I* do to you, Bendrik?"

His gaze turned glassy, his head now full of memories. And by Dallin, the man's cock jutted like a flagpole, without him so much as touching himself.

He pushed in, plastering his body against mine, hatred and cocks trapped between us. "You laughed... when I... when they saw, when everyone saw..."

"What did they see?"

He rubbed against my hip, dry-humping me through his clothes. "How I came for you, right there. You laughed—"

His hand clamped around my neck. *"You laughed and walked away.* I came, right there. In front of everyone!"

"You want to fuck me, Bendrik? Then uncuff me." I wheezed. "Do what you've done in your dreams a thousand times."

He reached up. One cuff clicked. My arm dropped. He reached up again and the second cuff sprung open. Suddenly free, I clasped his face in both hands, ignoring their tingling, and slammed a kiss full of vicious bites and furious desperation on his mouth. He knocked me against the wall. His teeth pinched my lip, sparking pain.

I had him distracted, almost wild with lust.

What I needed now was a weapon. His table with its display of knives and implements was several strides away. Too far to reach without suspicion.

His hands dropped, grasping my dick. "You're hard," he mumbled around my tongue.

I was hard because I knew how this ended.

I grasped his chin, jerked his head back, and marched him backwards toward the pool. "What do you want to do with me? Fuck my mouth, my ass, come all over me? The possibilities are endless. Hurt me, cut me—"

His eyes lit up. As I'd suspected, he'd carve up Razak, taking his time, and it didn't matter that the fantasy wouldn't be real. He'd gone beyond thinking, or fearing the true Razak's wrath. Bendrik had dreamed of this for a long time. Nothing would stop him living this fantasy. His desire for Razak was his weakness, and it would get him killed.

I turned away, grabbed a whip from the table's selection with my right hand, and slipped a knife down the front of my trousers with my left. I'd have to be careful. The blade was unsheathed, and the knife was snug against all my best parts. But it wouldn't have to remain there for long.

Facing Bendrik, stroking the whip, I nodded at the pool behind him. "We'll get to this. But first, get in."

He glanced behind him, uncertain. If he began to think, then he'd doubt everything that was happening, and I'd lose my control. Bendrik thinking was not part of the plan. He had to remain distracted. I shoved him in the chest, toppling him backwards, over the edge of the pool and into the water. He emerged moments later, spluttering, shock all over his face.

I waded in, moving fast, moving as though he were my prisoner and I the prince.

"Wait—" He raised a hand, thinking to hold me, believing he could stop me—stop Razak.

He'd already lost.

I took his hand, put it on my cock, and looped the whip around the back of his neck, jerking him up close. "You wanted me aroused. Now I'm fucking aroused. What are you going to do with me, Benny?"

His gaze jumped about my face. His body screamed for sex—his pupils were blown, his face flushed, his breaths racing. He wanted to fuck and hurt Razak, to lick and bite and taste him, to land his whip as revenge for Razak humiliating him. He wanted to make me cry out, make me bleed. So many marvelous things, but men like him thought with their dicks, and I had his in my skilled left hand.

I stroked, making him groan and mumble. His blush spread down his neck, beneath his clothes. He'd forgotten I'd pushed him in, forgotten I was Zayan and what that meant. I was all his dreams about to come true.

He backed through the waist-high water, letting me steer him by the dick, and bumped the back edge of the pool.

I lunged for a kiss, pumping him hard. The whip didn't matter now. I dropped it and sunk my right hand into my trousers, careful to keep my fingers from the nasty little blade's edge. Pleasure sizzled through my veins, as well as lust, desire, and need, and somewhere inside all of the madness a voice screamed at me to stop—the voice of reason, of morals —but it was too late.

Bendrik panted around my assaulting kiss. His hips bucked, driving his dick into my fist.

I'd heard it said once, that killing a man was one of the most difficult things to do.

I'd never found it that challenging.

I sliced the small knife up his left forearm, unzipping the flesh from wrist to elbow.

He grunted, but I had him under me, his body shuddering from ecstasy, heady desire, and the siren song of lust. He didn't notice the new, fiery burn in his arm. Pleasure blurred the edges of pain, made everything seem lesser. The burn he'd felt in his arm might even heighten his desire. His dick, trapped in my grip, approved.

I reached behind him, dropped his dick, switched the knife to my left hand, and grasped his dick again with my right, all under the guise of an embrace. We kissed like lost lovers, as though we'd been starved of each other.

He didn't know he was dying.

With the little knife now in my left hand, I dropped it below the water's surface, snatched his hand from off my back, and while we were still engaged in the deadly kiss, I glanced down, saw my target, and carved the blade up his arm.

Steam from the bath carried with it a warm coppery smell.

"Yes, Bendrik," I crooned in Razak's lethal voice, the one that forewarned of terrible things. "Come for me, fuck my hand now and cut me later, make me scream and writhe." I touched the man's paling face, holding his gaze under mine. He saw Razak, and this was everything he'd ever wanted.

He moaned, bucked, and shuddered. Cum warmed the water around my hand.

There were worse ways to die than at the height of pleasure.

Bendrik shuddered and gasped, slumping into my arms. Then he must have seen the water, and how it had turned scarlet. He froze.

I shuddered my own relieved sigh and whispered, "With every beat of your heart, you die a little more."

He shoved against my chest. I lurched back and smiled at my handiwork. Bloodred water swirled. His forearms were painted in red. Disbelieving his own eyes, he raised his arms from the water. Blood streamed back into the pool.

"What have you done?"

I backed toward the pool's steps, and chuckled. "Everyone makes the same mistake."

"You... You... Help!" he cried. "Someone, help me!"

He swept forward, washing a wave ahead of him, but lost his footing and slipped under the surface. The red water sloshed.

Nobody would hear him. That was the purpose of this room. People died here. I'd have died here. But not anymore. Benny would be the last.

He thrashed back to the surface, locked in panic's clutches, got his feet under him, and sprang backward, away from me, and clung to the pool's edge, fixing me in his terrified sights.

I backed up the steps—never taking my eyes off him—and sat on the last step. "Everyone assumes my brother is the worst of us." I poked the knife against my finger, then pointed its tip at him. His skin had turned blue, and he shivered, despite the heat. It wouldn't be long now. "Razak kept me leashed for a reason. What he fears, so should you."

His mouth opened and closed, but no words came.

The pool had turned a deep red, the air rich with the smell of blood, like spilled wet coins in the rain. *Wet coins on a street corner, a fiddle tossed aside, a stranger's hands burning up my skin.*

Benny tried to fight, but all remnants of life snuffed out of his eyes, and his grip slipped. He bobbed into the water, floating face up, eyes open, both forearms gaping.

The chamber was silent once more.

I left the pool and grabbed a towel from a nearby rack, then Bendrik's shirt from over a chair. I threw it on and buttoned it up as I left the dungeon for his bedchamber. There, I found boots, fresh trousers, and a handsome brown jacket that suited me just fine. I searched his dresser drawers, discovered some tape, and fixed the stolen knife to the small of my back.

His flat cap lay on the bed, tossed there prior to visiting me.

The reflection in the mirror didn't know who I was as I passed by. Not Razak, not Zayan, not Lark. I ruffled my hair, donned the flat cap, and buttoned up the jacket. With my hands in the pockets, my head down, cap hiding my face, I'd pass for Bendrik at a glance.

Another lie, another disguise. It didn't matter. I was nobody.

In stories, kings and queens lost their heads.

All I had to do was cut the head off this beast to bring it down.

And the next head in the Court of Pain belonged to Malvina.

CHAPTER 23

rin

As a child, I'd been too young to explore my local town without an escort, and after Lark's arrival, I'd locked myself away. But I was here now, albeit far too late.

At least not all life had vanished. Some cottage windows were lit from within, including the Overlook's. I pushed through its heavy door into a warm, welcoming bar area. Two other customers hunched at tables. A huge fireplace crackled and spat, and the innkeeper with a ragged head of salt and pepper hair matching his beard flitted behind the main bar. I paid for several nights' stay, a bath, and food, tipping the man generously with Lark's gold coins. These people needed the coin more than I.

After a bath, shave, and food in my belly, I settled at the bar, feeling more like myself than I had in weeks, and waited for Draven.

"Where you from?" the innkeeper asked, rubbing a cloth around a tankard to dry it.

"Oh, here. I lived here. Before..."

"Before," he grunted, no need to elaborate. "Well, I appreciate the custom. Don't know how much longer we can carry on. As you can see, there ain't much custom left. Supplies don't arrive. Folks assume we've already closed."

I tried to smile, but smiles didn't come easy anymore. Not with guilt weighing on my back. "It will get better."

"We can hope."

"Yes, we can." I sipped my mead and slunk lower on the stool. If only I could do more, but where to start? Father had had his advisors. I hadn't been crowned king. I didn't know the processes, the people. Four years behind a door had crippled any chance of building trust with the courtly advisors, and even if they'd survived the fire, how could I find them? And what could I do that would amount to more than a drop in the ocean?

"Arin?"

I lifted my gaze to the barmaid with plaited brown hair and bright, intelligent eyes. I knew her, but with everything that had happened, I struggled to place where from.

"Ellyn..." she said. "I was er... I was a kitchen maid. In the palace."

"Ellyn, yes!" We'd talked a great deal, sometimes at length —about Lark. I'd admitted to her how he was a beautiful lie, beginning our spiral into madness. "Of course! Goodness, how are you?"

"I'm er..." She balanced empty bowls on her arm and poked self-consciously at her messy hair. "Well, you know. I'm alive. So there's that." The bowls almost slipped from her arms. I lurched to grab them, and we fussed, securing the stack on the bar. "May I... hug you?

Would it be inappropriate? I'm sorry, I just— You're here!"

"Uhm, I suppose, but please keep your voice down—"

She threw her arms around me, rocking me back a step, and squeezed as though we were lifelong friends. Her hair smelled of wood ash from the fireplaces she'd been stoking and baked bread from the kitchens.

"I'm so sorry," she whispered, prying herself away. Tears gleamed in her eyes.

"Whatever for?"

A shy laugh fell from her, or perhaps a sob she tried to hide. "Lark, I... I didn't know who he was. You have to believe me. I had no idea. I trusted that rat." Her sadness waned, and the tears dried without having fallen. "He lied to me, to everyone. I thought... I thought we were friends. And all that time, he was *that horrible prince's brother*."

Her bright eyes turned fierce with rage. They'd been close. But not close enough she knew the real truth beneath Lark's lies. "It's all right. He fooled us all." I'd known Lark was lying, even when she clearly had not. I'd kept the information from her, so in part, I was as guilty as Lark.

"He ruined everything." She swept at her apron.

"Well, Razak was mostly behind—"

"He always had something about him, you know." She looked up again, and her mouth twisted, then pinched. "That sly little smile of his, like he knew things we didn't, as though he knew all our secrets. The bastard."

"Well, he did."

"Yes, but... Argh!" She grabbed her bowls and puffed her hair from her face. "I have to get back to work, but later, would it be improper if I sat with you a while?"

"I'd be delighted for the company. I'm waiting for a friend who may not arrive tonight."

She curtsied—thankfully nobody noticed—and hurried off, returning a little while later after I'd moved to the lounge area at the back of the main bar. Here, the seats were comfortable and the fireplace ablaze.

"Jay has let me off early, assuming we don't suddenly get a rush of customers." She flopped into the chair opposite mine. "It's so good to see someone from... before. Most everyone has left."

"Let me buy you a drink?"

"Oh, no, I—" She spotted the coins. "All right then."

I handed her a coin and she returned from the bar moments later with two tankards of mead. "I got the good stuff Jay keeps for his best customers, and himself."

We settled in and chatted like normal people. It was good, although my guilt was never far away. She'd lost someone she'd cared for in the palace fire. Her eyes had shimmered with unshed tears again when she spoke of her. Then she raged about Lark, blaming him. I tried to interject with Lark's reasoning, but she was spirited in her character assassination and had no room for excuses. She clearly needed to voice her rage. Her ire was appropriate, considering how close she'd believed she'd been to Lark.

Lark had used her like he had everyone else in my court, but there may have been more of a genuine connection there.

"So, you're back," she said. "I assume you're going to rebuild the court?"

We'd grown comfortable in our chairs. The fire burned low, and we were on our third tankard of mead. Ellyn had a friendly manner that made her easy to speak with. She also didn't hold back on voicing her thoughts. And right now, her glare demanded I pick up my fallen name, don my crown, and ride off to battle with the Court of Pain. If only it were that simple. My name was all I had left. I couldn't fight a war with that alone.

"I do not know how, in truth."

She fluttered a hand, dismissing my concerns. "Just your being here will bring hope back to our hearts."

Would it? Why would anyone look at me and think me capable of saving them? "I suppose, but I... I can't stay. Razak's plot didn't begin and end with destroying my court. He's seeking some far larger power, and he has to be stopped."

I told her everything. We talked into the morning hours; we talked about Lark's true purpose, about suspecting his lies, about falling for him, and I told her how I'd somehow come to care for the deceiver in my court, despite knowing he was my enemy. I told her about Draven, the Court of War, the fact I was technically married, and I told her how we'd tried to locate Pain's crown, to stop Razak in his tracks. And how we'd failed. It flew out of me, and when I was done, my voice was hoarse. Throat sore and heart aching, I sat back and blinked dry eyes at the rising sun through the inn's dusty windows. So much had happened in just a few short months. My whole world had turned upside down. And I had nothing to show for it. Not even Lark.

Ellyn looked as exhausted as I felt. I waited her assessment. She'd blame me for all of it; I certainly did.

"Lark's such a fool," she sighed.

"Well yes, but so am I."

"The difference is, you tried to do the right thing. He just —" She waved her hand. "—looked out for himself."

No, this had never been about Lark. He didn't know how to look out for himself, believing he wasn't worth the effort. "He did what he could. He's not free, like we are. He never has been. Not even when he'd danced and played in my court.

Having seen just a small piece of his world, it's very different to what we're used to."

"Maybe," she conceded. "So what are you going to do about it?"

"Until Razak is stopped, there's no use in rebuilding my court. He'll burn it all down again. His mission to make himself a god must be stopped. Everything else will come after."

"Everything else like... saving Lark?"

I sighed and dropped my head back. We'd talked all night, and my heart was raw and exposed. I wasn't speaking as the Prince of Love, but as just me, a man somehow swept up in all of this. A man who had made mistakes. "I know what I should do, but what I *want* to do is hire the next passing coach to go back to him, no matter the cost, or the hopelessness. It would likely be suicide. But I think of him alone and I..." The weight of feeling pushed down had my voice creaking. It hurt, knowing he was hurting too, so far away.

"That's because you're a good man, Arin." She reached across our table and took my hand.

"So is he, beneath all the—"

"Pantomime? Drama? Theatrics?"

"He's actually very sweet, when you get to know the real him."

Her right eyebrow arched. "When he's not lying and manipulating us?" She chuckled. "I remember when I told him what you'd said, about him being a beautiful lie. He was told he was loved by a hundred different people every night. But he never believed it. When I said those words you'd spoken, I saw his eyes light up. It was as though I'd given him a gift, like he'd never been given a gift before. I didn't understand it then, but I do now."

Beneath all Lark's layers, he had a strong but vulnerable,

fierce but damaged heart. That heart deserved to be loved. And now, with Lark alone in the Court of Pain, I feared he might unravel further, and I wasn't there to stop him, to tell him he was loved, to show him there was hope, even when all around, the storm clouds drew in. "I need to get back to him."

Ellyn squeezed my hand again and let go. "You have it bad."

"Am I so obvious?"

"Definitely." She raised her almost empty tankard, prompting me to lift mine. "To love. The best we can do is hope to survive it."

"To love." We clunked the tankards together. "And surviving."

CHAPTER 24

*A*rin

ELLYN and I grew familiar during the next few days. Her company was a delight and took my mind off impending commitments I had no control over.

On the third night, as I helped Ellyn clear tables at the inn, a familiar voice grumbled from the front of the bar area. Its deep monotone lured me from the back, into the lounge.

Draven stood at the bar, wearing a black shirt over rusty red trousers and black boots. The sheathed daggers at his hips marked him as a warrior. There was no chance he'd have been robbed on the road. For the dirt and dust in the creases of his clothes and on his face, he'd been on the road a while.

"Draven!"

He jerked his head up. "Arin, you're here. And... tending tables?"

"I'm helping out." I set my armful of cups down and started toward the warlord. His smile grew, lighting up his

223

darkly lined eyes. He pushed from the bar and wrapped me in his broad, unyielding arms. I hugged him close.

"It's good to see you." His voice rumbled, and its familiar resonance did more to soothe my thoughts than any mead.

I breathed him in, reminded of hot, sultry nights I'd spent in his court, among his people. "You too." It meant a lot, knowing I wasn't alone. I'd spent too long alone in the past.

We separated and Draven slapped a hand on my back, his warmth as comforting as an open fire. "I've missed you," he admitted.

"And I you," I said, finding it to be more true than I'd expected. Ellyn caught my eye, loitering nearby, pretending not to be watching. "Ah, Draven, please meet my friend Ellyn."

Draven smiled and offered his hand. Ellyn swooped in, took his hand, then curtsied.

"Uh, miss, you don't need to bow." He chuckled, lifting her to her feet. "I'm just a lord."

"Forgive me, I know who you are. We haven't met but I saw you at Love's ball," she gushed. "I mean, we all *saw* you. It wasn't just me. Looking, I mean." She pulled her hand back. "It's a pleasure to finally meet you. Lark said some things, but half the time I didn't know what was true with him, so I'd much prefer to meet you for myself."

Was she blushing? Just what had Lark told her? Something scandalous, apparently.

Draven's smile turned comical. "What did Lark say about me?"

She blurted a laugh. "It's best you don't know."

"Ellyn is—was—a friend of Lark's. We've become reacquainted while I awaited your arrival."

"Where *is* Lark?" Draven asked.

"He didn't make it out of Pain."

Draven paled. "He's dead?!"

"No! Gods, no. I should have worded that differently. Nothing like that. Get settled in a room, refresh from traveling, and meet me for dinner? We have much to discuss."

Draven nodded, then thwacked me on the arm, hard enough to bruise. "I'm glad you made it here, Arin. Whatever has happened with Lark, we'll right it."

My voice lodged in my throat. I nodded and watched as the innkeeper Jay—who had been half-listening nearby— offered to escort Draven to a room. They left through the back stairs moments later, leaving Ellyn and I alone at the bar.

She side-eyed me. "He's very handsome."

"He is."

"And you're married?"

"Politically," I corrected. That was a very important distinction.

"But you love Lark?"

I winced. "It's complicated."

"Not really." She shrugged. "Get a bigger bed."

I laughed and tried to will the growing heat from my face. "You mean keep both?"

"Why not? Lark likes Draven. They've already, you know." She made a grasping motion with her hands.

By Dallin, I could see why she and Lark got along so well. "Molded clay?"

She laughed and whacked me on the arm in the same spot Draven had assaulted moments ago. "You know what I mean!"

"I'm afraid I do." While we waited for Draven to return, I ordered drinks at the bar and considered how to explain how Draven and Lark fit in my life. "It's not so simple," I explained. "I like Draven—love him even—as a friend. What I feel for Lark is very different."

"Oh well, that's a shame. I mean, I'm not really into men, but you know, those two together?" She fanned her face. "You wouldn't walk straight for a week."

I spluttered a sudden laugh, spilling the drink I'd just picked up. Ellyn swooped in with a cloth and laughed along. She and Lark must have been very close for him to tell her about Draven.

"Did you and Lark ever...?"

"Oh no, we didn't." She pulled a face. "We weren't *like that*."

"Never?"

She settled back down on the stool and turned serious. "He didn't whore himself out as much as he made everyone believe. Those rumors suited him, gave him power."

"Yes, I suppose they did." I knew fragments of his past, knew some of what he'd done to survive.

We fell silent for a while, both of us thinking of Lark. She'd be thinking of the past too.

At least Razak wasn't in the Court of Pain. Razak was the only one who had true power over Lark. They'd punish him, though, and he'd already been hurt so much.

"You miss him, don't you?" Ellyn said. "More than you missed Draven."

I swallowed, careful to keep the creak from reappearing in my voice. "You have no idea."

"Yeah, I think I do."

We fell quiet again, the mood turning melancholy. She'd lost her love in the palace fire. I almost wished I could go back and do things differently. Although, I still wouldn't have killed Lark. So perhaps we'd always been destined for this path.

"Why so sad?" Draven boomed behind us. He smelled of soap and fresh clothes. His wet hair had been smoothed back, accentuating his dark, desert features. "We're here, aren't we? Let's make the most of that while we can. Dallin knows we need it." He ordered more drinks, and with his great booming voice and broad grins, the somber atmosphere lifted. "Lark is alive. That's good," he said. "Tell me."

"Yes, I mean— He's definitely alive." I refused to think anything else.

"He's Lark." Draven shrugged. "I've told you before—"

"He'll always be the last man standing." Although, the cost of that survival might be too great.

"See, you do listen."

I mustered a real smile this time. "Sometimes."

He thrust a drink into my hand. "Get that in you. I have good tidings to report. Then tell me your adventures in Pain, which I'm sure we'll need more mead for, or wine, even. Wine would be better."

"We have wine. I'll get it," Ellyn offered, rising from the barstool. "I'll leave you two to catch up."

She left to fetch Draven his wine, and I turned my attention back to the warlord, taking a swig of mead. "Please tell me there's good news regarding War's crown?"

"There is." He grinned. "I know where it is."

"Is it safe?"

He nodded. "After Razak tried to steal it, Ogden locked it away. Razak didn't get it. It's safe, Arin. Razak won't get his hands on it anytime soon."

The relief was so visceral it made my head spin. I chuckled and enjoyed my mead with fervor, finally feeling good. If War's crown was safe, then perhaps all was not lost.

Ellyn returned with several bottles of wine and left to

tend tables. Draven downed his mead in one go and refilled his tankard with generous glugs of wine.

"Ogden didn't throw you in a cell?" I asked.

"No. On one condition." He drew in a deep breath. "I've rejected our joining as a sham."

"Oh." My smile fell. "I mean, I suppose that was to be expected."

"You sound disappointed."

"No, I... Not disappointed exactly, more regretful." I touched his thigh, startled some at its firm warmth. "I did not set out to hurt you. I'm sincerely sorry."

"If Lark hadn't returned at our joining, we might have had our moment, but he was always in your heart."

Hearing him speak of the things I'd struggled with was a relief too. He understood, of course he did. He was a good man. A good friend. Better than me.

He placed his hand on mine and squeezed. "What happened in Pain? Did you get the crown?"

"No. It's not there. Lark did discover some letters. I've read them, have them with me in fact. You're welcome to take a look. Umair was searching for a font of power too, like Razak. He went to Justice to find it, taking Pain's crown with him. As far as anyone knows, he's not been seen since."

"Then you think Umair is in Justice?"

"I don't know." It seemed a stretch. Justice had always been the pillar upon which the courts leaned. If it was found to be corrupt, then all laws would collapse. "I don't understand why they'd keep him there and not tell anyone."

"Unless he's dead?" Draven suggested, coming to the same conclusion as the rest of us.

"If he's dead, and they know, Razak has good reason to go after them," Draven said, thinking aloud. "If Razak has evidence Justice were engaged in foul play, then he has leverage against Justice's court."

"Which gives him power there, like he had in War." And my court. Secrets were Razak's main weapons, and our undoing.

Draven nodded. "It seems likely he'll get his hands on Justice's crown." Draven peered into his wine. "Well, fuck. That's a whole lot of bad right there."

"At least he doesn't have War's crown." Thank Dallin War's crown was safe. And now Ogden was aware of the threat Razak posed, the Prince of Pain wouldn't get near it. Not even with his spies in every court. War's crown was safe, for now.

"Right." Draven gulped his wine and winced. "What happened to Lark?" he asked, glancing over. "You seem pissed. What did he do?"

"What makes you think he *did* something?"

He snorted. "Trouble runs through his veins. And he wouldn't know a good thing if it hit him in the face."

"We were discovered, we fled. He locked me in a carriage and sent me here. I couldn't stop him. He stayed behind, knowing they'd capture him and wouldn't waste time coming after me." Was I pissed? Yes. Saying it aloud again brought it all back. His locking me in the carriage, his face as he'd watched me leave, as I'd hurled hurtful words at him.

Draven twisted on the stool and frowned. "Lark sacrificed his freedom for yours?"

"Yes, that's exactly it. The prick."

Draven blinked, huffed an impressed laugh, and scooped up his drink. "I didn't think him capable of caring for anyone but himself."

"You've never forgiven him for the fall of my court, have you?"

229

"Your heart is kinder than mine, Arin. It's why—" He cleared his throat. "It's why I care for you like I do. You're willing to forgive terrible things."

I'd forgiven Lark because I knew the events that brought down my court weren't of his design. "I don't forgive without reason. Lark is as much a victim as I am. Perhaps more so."

Draven smiled, but his smiles were always warm and this one wasn't. "I wish you'd find someone more worthy of your heart than Lark."

Lark was more than worthy, but Draven didn't see it. Few people did. Lark didn't show his true self to anyone, so how could anyone truly know him?

"I love him," I said. It really was that simple.

Draven winced. "Does he know?

"I told him."

"Did he tell you he loved you in return?"

"No, but... It's not about that. It doesn't matter if he..." I rubbed my face. The wine was going to my head, loosening my tongue, blurring my thoughts. "It doesn't matter. I love him. He knows it. And that's all. I don't expect you to understand."

"Why?" He stilled. "Do you think I haven't loved?"

"No, I mean..." His frown turned into a glower. "I'm sorry, of course you have." He'd had a child. A son. And while I did not know much about having children, love was surely a part of raising them.

"I've known love." He turned away and sent his gaze out of the window, to somewhere far away. "Lost it too."

Of course he'd loved. For a Prince of Love, I didn't know much about it. "You never talk about them."

"What is there to say? It just prolongs the hurt. I'd hoped, you and I... I'd foolishly thought I might find love again with you."

"Draven—"

He waved my words away and drank his wine. "It's fine, really. And I understand, when you say you love him, I understand that, Arin. Don't assume I don't because I don't show it."

"You're right. I'm sorry. What happened to them?"

"We were joined young and the boy came along soon after. He was..." His voice quivered. "It's over now."

I shuffled a little closer and laid a hand on his arm. "If I could give you that love again, I would."

He raised soft eyes. "Renouncing our joining didn't dull my feelings. I'd have you as my husband again in heartbeat."

I didn't want to hurt him, but at the same time, I didn't want him thinking there was anything between us beyond friendship. "You're a good friend, Draven."

"A friend, yeah." He chuckled darkly. "Who you'll fuck when Lark isn't around."

That wasn't fair, but I let it slide. He was hurting, probably from mention of his son. We drank in silence, and if I didn't change the subject soon, I'd ruin both our evenings. This was supposed to be a positive meeting, a chance to put our heads together and decide how to move forward.

"You said there were letters?" he asked.

"Oh, yes, and these." I pulled the documents from my pocket, unfolded them, and slid them across the table. "Lark found these documents in Pain's vaults. It appears to be a list of names, numbers, and ages. Most are young, under thirteen. Do you have any idea what it pertains to?"

Draven angled the papers toward him and scanned the information. "Court of War Benefits? These are people."

"Yes." I leaned closer, bumping his shoulder. "Mostly children."

"What happened to this section?" he asked, referring to the water-damaged top sheet.

"Ah, Lark didn't tell me he'd stashed them in my pocket when he shoved me in the carriage. When it rained while I was on the road, they got soaked."

"Had you read it before it was damaged?" Draven shuffled the papers, scanning them again. They didn't seem to mean any more to him than they did me.

"No, as I said, I didn't know I had them. He gave me coin too, told me to have a new life. Can you believe him?" I clipped my tone, refusing to go over the same emotional ground about Lark until I saw him again. I'd rage at him then. "He said something strange about you though. I'm not sure it makes any sense."

"What was it?"

"He told me not to trust you."

Draven's eyes widened. "Not to trust *me*?" He laughed. "That's rich, coming from him."

"I thought it strange as well."

"It's not *that* strange." He folded the papers and slid them back across the bar. "He knew you were meeting with me. He also knows we are—*were*—intimate. In all likelihood, he was jealous, perhaps afraid we'd rekindle our connection."

It was possible. Lark had never believed he was good enough for me. He probably saw Draven as a good match, thinking himself unworthy, no matter how many times I told him how I was the unworthy one.

Draven turned his head and his gaze dropped to my mouth. We sat close, too close, our shoulders touching. I'd moved forward to examine the papers and hadn't thought anything of it.

I cleared my throat, grabbed the papers, and shifted back.

"I don't know what that list means," he said, looking away

again. "Benefits implies Pain uses those people for something. But as to what, it doesn't say. Lark told you nothing else?"

"There wasn't time." We were missing something, something obvious. "It's strange how he went to the trouble of handing them over. The letters have importance, so these documents must mean something too, I just don't know what. Perhaps their meaning was in the ruined section?"

"It will come to you," Draven reassured. He raised the wine bottle. "In the meantime, more wine?"

I offered my empty cup and Draven refilled it. "It's almost like before, but without the heat, and sand in every crack."

"*Every* crack?"

Our laughter washed away the earlier tension. "Our issues aside, I'm glad you're here, Draven. Truly. I spent a long time alone, and it turned me into someone I have no wish to be. I know we've had our trials, but I'd like to remain friends, if you'll have me." Goodness, if my loose tongue were any indication, I must have mixed too much wine and mead.

"I'm glad to hear it." He chinked his cup with mine. "And that's worth celebrating." Waving Ellyn over, he asked for a third bottle. "Won't you drink with us, Ellyn?"

Ellyn glanced back at Jay, he gave permission with a nod, and soon all three of us were fast consuming Jay's supply of fine wine in front of the fire, with Draven telling raucous tales of how he and his friends—in his rowdy pre-mature years—had been trapped outside War's huge gate and had to climb back in, risking their reputations and their necks.

We laughed and jested, drank more wine than was right, and Ellyn told of the time Lark had allegedly tupped a well-known lord's son, leaving him quite enamored and declaring his love for the Court of Love's fool. In response, Lark had partnered the lord's son with a stable hand, and the two had been joined a year later. Rather than laugh at Lark's matchmaking, my heart's ache grew, seeking its other half. My love for him was a potent thing. We hardly knew each other, except from all his notes and silly tales he'd posted beneath my door, and how I'd heard his soul in his music, seen him vulnerable while asleep on the pillow beside mine. The simple parts of Lark were where his truth shone. I missed that about him, and I missed him.

"Arin, are you all right?" Draven asked, interrupting my thoughts.

I turned my attention from the window and back at the pair. "My apologies, I... I think I'll retire. I fear I've had too much wine. It's making me melancholy."

"I'll come with you."

Draven began to stand, but I waved him down. "Not necessary. I'm not so intoxicated I can't make the stairs."

He raised the wine bottle and waggled its remaining contents. "Or you could stay and finish this with us?"

Ellyn yawned into her hand. "I really must get to bed too. Two late nights are more than enough."

"I refuse to let this go to waste." Draven upended the bottle into his cup. "G'night, the both of you."

"Will *you* be all right getting to bed?" I asked him.

He laughed, as though I were mad to suggest he couldn't handle his drink. "Don't you worry, I'll be the first down for breakfast."

Ellyn walked with me up the stairs and along the landing. "My room's just a little ways down here," she said, then tripped on her own feet. We fell together against the wall, tangled up in limbs and laughing. She stilled, looking me in the eyes. "You have kind silvery eyes, Arin. I see why he likes you."

"I don't know what he sees in me, truthfully. If he sees anything at all."

She snorted a chuckle and extricated herself from my hold. "He won't tell you he loves you. He can't."

"He can't love me?" I asked, ignoring my heart's lurch.

"No, silly. Telling anyone he loves means telling the truth, and the truth frightens him. He almost lost his mind once after that beating you gave him. He lives in fantasy, it's his life. Truth shatters his illusions and reminds him who he is, where he comes from. He never shows his pain..." She trailed off, as though saddened by her own words. "Gosh, so much of him makes sense now I know who he is."

"You're very profound when drunk."

Her snort ruined the affect, somewhat. "When you spend hours peeling potatoes, you have time to think."

We laughed and swayed our way back toward our rooms but stopped at the sight of two men and a woman gathered at the end of the corridor. Other guests, I supposed. Perhaps business was picking up. Strange, how they all wore identical riding cloaks. Strange too, their deep shade of blue.

"Can we help you, sir?" one of the men said.

I straightened. "You're in front of my door, there. That's my room." I reached out. I could probably open it and slip by him; he'd left enough room.

"Goodnight, Arin," Ellyn called.

"G'night—"

One of the strangers grabbed my wrist. "Arin, Court of Love's prince, you are hereby detained—"

This was ridiculous. I yanked, but his grip held. "Sir, let go of my arm—" The other two lurched in, grabbed my shoulder, and spun me around. "What is this? You can't do this. Are you charging me with a crime?" The blue cloaks, the color of Justice. Of course! I was too intoxicated for this.

"You're detained under charges of conspiring with Razak

235

to raze the Court of Love, to infiltrate the Court of War, the attempted poisoning—"

"What?!" I dug my heels into the floorboards, but two of the three had locked my arms under theirs, and they far outmuscled me. "Stop! Wait!" They marched me down the corridor. "At least let me collect my belongings?" I didn't have any, but I needed time to think, to stop my head from spinning and to think of a way out of this, even if it included climbing from a damned window to escape them. This was insanity. I hadn't done any of those things against my own court or War's. I'd tried to *stop* Razak.

"Hey!" Ellyn cried behind us. "Stop there, you can't take him. Arin!"

Draven would stop them. We'd get to the foot of the stairs, he'd see, and he'd wield his daggers, stopping them in their tracks. They'd reconsider my arrest then.

We stumbled to the bottom of the stairs.

Draven stood at the bar, already close, still finishing his wine.

"Draven!" I called, struggling anew in the men's grip. "Help me."

He didn't move.

"Draven?"

He stared into his tankard. Couldn't he hear me?

"Draven, they're arresting me. Tell them it's wrong, tell them—" I bucked and writhed. "Let go, let me go!"

He lifted his eyes and stared with no surprise, no anger, barely alarmed, as though he'd been waiting for this. As though he'd... known.

I twisted and tried to fix him in my sights, but Justice's enforcers shoved me through the inn door and outside into cold night air, where a prison wagon waited, its horses chomping at their bits. No, they couldn't put me behind bars.

Alone. Trapping me behind another locked door. Not again. I'd spent years behind a door, locked away. I couldn't do that again.

"Draven!"

I couldn't go in there, in that wagon with bars on the window. Locked away again. "No, stop! Don't. This isn't right. Draven!" Why wasn't Draven doing anything, why wasn't he stopping them?

An enforcer flung open the wagon's rear door, and the pair threw me inside. I sprawled onto my hands and knees, turned, and sprang at the door.

It slammed closed, plunging me into near darkness. I fell against it, then hammered a fist against the scored wood. The only light came through the narrow window. This wasn't real, it couldn't be happening. It was a dream, a nightmare.

Arrested as a conspirator against my own court, against the Court of War? How?

I peered through the window. "You're making a mistake."

The inn door opened. "Draven, tell them!" Yes, he'd tell them now, and they'd unlock this door.

Draven said something to one of the enforcers. They nodded. Yes, yes, this was it, they'd let me go. Draven strode toward the wagon. The light from the inn's windows washed over his grim face.

"Draven... stop them."

"I'm sorry, Arin."

Sorry? Sorry for what? Whatever this was, he didn't want it to happen, but he'd known it was coming. None of this was a surprise. He wasn't fighting, raging, demanding my freedom.

Because *he'd known.*

Our meeting at the Overlook Inn had been arranged weeks ago. Only three of us knew. Me, Lark, and Draven.

Draven had told Justice I'd be here. Draven had brought them here, *for me.*

"You did this?" I hissed.

He'd *betrayed* me. They'd take me to Justice; they'd put me on trial as a traitor to the Court of War and my own court. They believed I conspired *with* Razak! And Draven had aided them? I didn't want to believe it, not Draven, but his face and its guilt showed the truth.

His cheek twitched. "There was no choice. I don't expect you to understand, but I am sorry."

I recoiled from the window. I didn't know who he was.

This man I'd trusted, who I'd loved as a friend, had turned me over to my enemies. The betrayal burned so deep it turned ugly and vicious. I spat, but when the spittle dashed his cheek, it wasn't enough. "You're no friend!"

He wiped his face and held my gaze. He didn't explain, just stared, his gaze flat. Did he not care? I was looking at a stranger.

"How could you?!"

The wagon jolted, throwing me against the window's bars. "Draven, why?" The wagon rocked and jolted. I clung to the bars, needing to know what had possessed him. I'd done nothing to him, nothing except... almost kill him, and join with him then cast him aside. And break his heart?

He hung his head. "Take Arin away."

Don't trust Draven. Lark had known, somehow. He'd known.

But it was too late. I had trusted Draven, and he'd burned my trust to ash. "Damn you to the bottom of Dallin's great ocean."

The wagon carted me off. Draven and the Overlook shrank in the distance, until they were blurs through the filter of my tears. I bowed my forehead against the cold bars. I was going to Justice, and there, I'd be tried for treachery against my people.

I should have been relieved; Justice was balance, and balance was all. I knew I was innocent.

But I also knew the courts were corrupt. And in all likelihood, Justice would be too.

I'd be tried as a traitor, and my only defense was truth.

In a court of lies, the truth was worthless.

CHAPTER 25

ark

NOBODY NOTICED me stride by them in the tower's narrow corridors. I was Bendrik, why would they question me? I had the swagger, the confidence, the clothes, and the flat cap to top off my flawless act.

The majority of the council—except Bendrik and his pleasure pool—lived in the main tower. Malvina's chambers would be among theirs, and as she'd been on the council since Umair's reign, she'd have one of the larger, luxurious accommodations.

I knew the floor, knew the rooms on the corner of the building were the largest.

While chained to Bendrik's wall, I'd lost track of time. I couldn't be sure what hour of the day or night I'd be greeting her—and was beyond caring. I had Bendrik's blood on my hands and a desperate need to destroy all those who had watched me dance until I'd fallen to my knees, bleeding and raw both inside and out.

They all deserved to die.

This whole fucking court should burn, like Razak had burned Arin's.

If Arin were here, he'd tell me to stop, tell me this crusade wasn't worth the risk of getting caught. I knew it, laughed at it, didn't care. My one regret was that Razak wasn't here so I couldn't choke him with my leash in his sleep. It would happen, one day, eventually. I'd see him swinging from that hanging tree.

But I was getting ahead of myself.

I tried the first luxurious room, found it unlocked, and ventured inside, but whoever it belonged to didn't have Malvina's ambience, or her perfume, with its lemony notes. The memories tumbled... Her cloying perfume, her acrid laugh. The idea of vengeance tasted sweet. She'd be behind the next locked door, I was sure of it. If I'd had a hairpin. I could have crafted a pick, but as there was no time to hunt for one, I tried what would have been Draven's method and slammed my shoulder into the door, rattling it on its hinges. Once, twice, pain flared, and on the third try, it sprang open, spilling me inside. The lemony spice hit me, rolled over me, trawling memories up from the depths I'd buried them in.

"You!"

She stood in a gown by her bed, her hair a grey mass about her pale face. She brandished a letter opener, or a stiletto dagger.

"Oh, I'm so terribly sorry, did I interrupt your beauty sleep, Malvina?" I veered right, around the end of her bed.

"You will be sorry, Zayan. I knew we should have killed you."

"Hm, no, you wouldn't have. We both know why."

Razak was here with us, even now. Nobody could kill me, only him. Everyone knew it. I belonged to the prince. He'd made me untouchable, fuckin' immortal. I lunged from the end of the bed. Malvina swung the blade down, and I skipped right, then grabbed her thin neck.

The punch was unexpected—deep into my right side. The hatred running like hot fire through my veins stuttered, and a horrible knowing filtered through the rage.

A black, slim handled dagger protruded from my side. Strange, I didn't feel it.

I shoved Malvina away and grabbed the dagger's handle.

"Help! Help me!" Malvina bolted.

I grabbed for her but brilliant fire blazed up my side, turning my scream into a silent gasp and dropping me to my knee. This was the part where Arin would have told me he was right, and I should have listened. I laughed as I yanked the cold blade from my insides. A horrible knowing sent shivers down the back of my neck. A flash of scarlet painted the dagger's blade with a bright warning.

This wouldn't kill me, would it?

Blood spread, soaking into my stolen shirt. I clamped my left hand over the wound, trying to stem the flow, to stop the blood from draining out of me. Strange, how not so long ago I'd wanted to see my blood flow, to see it spill from my veins to spite Razak.

"Put the dagger down," a man said, a voice I knew. Danyal approached with Malvina hanging back, by the door. "You goin' to kill me with that needle, boy?" Rain sparkled in his grey hair.

I knew this was bad. I should have fled after killing Bendrik, but my freedom hadn't seemed as important as hurting everything Razak believed in, everything he appeared to care for. I could have done it; I could have destroyed the council.

Danyal was closer now, just a few strides away. He held out his hand. "Give me the dagger."

If I gave him the dagger, it would be over.

Blood leaked between my fingers, clutched to my side.

"If I die," I rasped, "he'll punish all of you."

"But you'll still be dead," Danyal said. "Revenge is worthless if you're not alive to savor it."

I slumped to both knees but held the blade aloft. My arm sagged, my aim wavering. A heated *thud-thud* radiated from my side, trying to beat me down.

Danyal crouched. His pockmarked face and cold grey eyes told of a hard life. The scars in his cheek marked him as a murderer. He could lunge, grab the blade, and cut my throat. I wasn't even sure if Razak's threat was enough to stop a man like him. A man who had the look of someone with nothing left to lose.

"Zayan?"

Surrendering the dagger meant surrendering my life.

I couldn't. Not again. I couldn't go back to being chained to Razak's bed, to being used by the Court of Pain.

I flipped the dagger, turned it on myself, and pressed its edge to my throat. And here we were again, death and I, old dancing partners. I didn't want this, not anymore, but I had no choice.

Danyal's glare soured. "Easy..." He spread his hand, palm out.

"Just let him do it!" Malvina growled like a rabid dog. "The court will finally be free of his threat. Razak will return and thank us for it. Trust me. Do it, Zayan. Slit your throat. Join your wretched mother in oblivion."

My lashes fluttered. The blade's cool edge clung to my skin.

"The traitor's son," Malvina said to me. "You should have hung alongside that bitch."

Danyal's cheek twitched. He half turned his head, almost as though he might reply, but then his gaze came back to me. "I knew your mother," Danyal said. He lowered his hand and rested his arm on his knee. "You're much like her."

My lip quivered, ignoring my attempts to contain the rising swell of choking emotion.

"She wouldn't want this for you."

Tears blurred my vision.

She'd died because she'd tried to save me, she'd died *because* of me.

Danyal held out his hand. "This is not where it ends. She did not give up her life so you could end yours here. Give me the knife, Zayan."

I barely knew this man, and what I did know of him came from our brief monthly meetings outside the Court of Love, in which I'd spill my secrets for him to carry back to Razak. That was the extent of us, yet... there was more warmth in his eyes now than I'd gotten from anyone in this court. And with blood leaking from my side, the thudding in my head, and all the world telling me it was better off without me in it, Danyal's kindness was a beacon I needed.

"I won't hurt you." He reached out. "I give you my word. I'll never hurt you." Rough fingers encircled mine, then pried the dagger from my loosening grip.

With it gone, my strength left too. I gasped and slumped onto my hand. What would happen now? Another bed, another chain, await the return of my brother and his punishment, lose another finger, a hand this time? Dallin, I couldn't survive it again. I'd tasted freedom, and that made my prison a thousand times worse.

"What will you do with him now?" Danyal asked Malvina.

I struggled to lift my head, to see what fate Malvina had for me. She gathered her gown tight to her legs and peered down her nose at Danyal. "That's not of your concern." She sniffed. "Remove him. He's bleeding all over my rug."

Such a nice rug too. Laughter bubbled inside, then from my lips. What a shame, she'd have to throw out the rug.

"He's quite mad," Malvina chimed.

"But what choice did you give him?"

The strange softness in Danyal's voice drew my splintering thoughts back to him. Malvina didn't see how he tightened his grip on the dagger. She was too busy scowling while I ruined her rug.

Danyal stepped back and in one precise slice, slashed the blade across her throat. Blood gushed. Malvina choked, staggered, grabbed her neck, and reached out with her other hand for someone to help her.

She made it three steps, collapsed, and lay shuddering, trying to breathe while drowning in blood. Like with Bendrik, with the bounty hunter, and so many before them, I watched her die and didn't feel a thing. Except perhaps anger that she hadn't suffered for long.

Danyal scooped me up and tucked me against his side. "It's all right, Zayan. I'm taking you away."

A thumping began in my head and poured down my neck, making everything hurt. "Where?"

"Somewhere safe."

Safe. There was nowhere safe in the Court of Pain. Not for me.

We made it outside, into the corridor. I slumped, shivering and heavy. "I can't—"

"Yes, you can, Zayan. The wound is deep, but I know where there's help. Stay with me and I'll keep you safe. I promise you that much."

Stay with him. I didn't know who he was or why he was doing this, but it didn't matter, because I was falling and not hitting the ground, dreaming while awake. If I closed my eyes the nightmares would come.

Then the darkness washed in, wave after wave, pushing me down and down and down. Whoever Danyal was, my fate was in his hands.

CHAPTER 26

ark

A GENTLE ROCKING stirred me from broken dreams. Horses' hooves clopped nearby and the clattering of wheels on a road surface suggested I lay in a wagon. Sunlight pricked through gaps in the canvas slung overhead. Dust motes swirled. It was peaceful, warm. Unlike the dreams I'd left. I breathed and blinked and didn't want to move—moving meant facing everything from before.

I wedged my elbow under me, but when I tried to sit up, heat throbbed through my chest. Gasping, I flopped back down and plucked the blanket from over me. A thick, blood-stained bandage had been bound around my middle. Nausea spun my thoughts and flooded my mouth with saliva. I dropped my head back and blinked again at the canopy. Where was I? Who was driving the cart?

Sunlight meant we weren't in the Court of Pain. Or if we

were, then it was a long way from the city. How long had I been out?

My head and body throbbed, aching and sore. The rocking motion lulled me somewhere between sleep and wakefulness.

Someone had patched me up and had carried me out of the city. I was safe, they'd said.

Safe.

Danyal, my handler.

He'd killed Malvina. Danyal, who knew my mother and said he didn't want to hurt me. We'd fought when he'd found me in the city, so what had changed?

Had I been wrong about him this whole time? It seemed unlikely. I was rarely wrong.

Yet Danyal's recent behavior did not fit with that of Razak's cruel handler.

The wagon trundled on. Swathes of bare forest swept by the back of the cart, and when the sun dropped, a bone-deep chill set in. I pulled the blanket tighter and drifted, dreaming of pools of blood and the horror on Arin's face when the black carriage had taken him away. He'd despise me for forcing him to leave and that was probably for the best. Even if I missed his brilliant grin and the way laughter sparkled in his eyes like sunlight on Dallin's ocean.

Those few days we'd had in Palmyra had been the best days of my life. I clung to their memory and kept them with me as night set in, and so did the dreams.

THE DAYS that followed were a stream of nightmares and memories merged together; the past was the present, where I stood on a street corner singing for coin, playing my fiddle to fill my belly. Then Razak's touch branded my chest, and my soul. I woke wrecked and shivering, with my own screams echoing in my head.

A fever, someone said. *Malnourished, weak.* Then the voice I knew to be Danyal's would tell them they were wrong, and that I was stronger than they realized.

I didn't feel strong.

When I woke again, a campfire licked at the dark, and through the flames I saw Danyal. He sat opposite the campfire, stirring a steaming pot. The wagon was parked up behind him, and to my right, a lone horse chomped on a shrub at the forest's edge.

The fire roared, but my back was exposed to the forest, and an icy cold. I shifted, trying to tuck the blanket tighter.

"Are you back with me?" Danyal grumbled, in the same monotone drawl he'd used to ask me what secrets I had that month for Razak.

This was very real then. I hadn't been sure, until he'd spoken.

"Water?" I rasped, my tongue thick.

He poured some water from a leather pouch into a wooden cup and handed it over.

After struggling to prop myself up on a trembling arm, I took the cup and sipped.

"You'll be all right," he muttered, to me or himself.

Why was he being *nice?* "What do you want?" He must want something for saving me. We weren't friends, and he wasn't a good man. The marks on his face made that clear. Was this about Razak's bounty? Danyal seemed the sort to sell anyone for coin, and I assumed Razak had offered a great deal of it.

He returned to his upturned log, sat, and smiled into his pot of simmering broth. "I don't blame you for being suspicious. You don't know me, but I know you, Zayan. I *knew* you. What they did to you, to you both..." He shook his head and clamped his mouth shut.

I hunched over, pulled the blanket over my shoulders, and huddled closer to the fire. "You knew my mother?" He'd said as much, I remembered that.

"I did. I helped her escape the court when you were just a babe."

The memories of my mother were few and far between. I recalled her voice, telling me I was her lark, and the tune she'd hum with me tucked in bed. I'd been too young to understand the world then. And it was only when I was older, when Umair had sent people to find us, that I'd witnessed my world crumble. My good memories were buried beneath all the bad. "Tell me of her."

"She loved you. You were her whole world. She'd have pulled the moon from the sky and given it to you, if she could."

"Until I killed her."

"Is that what you think?" His gnarled face screwed up even more. He glared as though hating me, but I was beginning to suspect that was how he looked at the best of times.

"If it wasn't for me, she'd have survived."

"No, boy. Is that Razak talking? Did he tell you that?"

"I don't recall." But it was likely. Much of what I knew of my past came from my brother. He'd shaped the truth, twisted it, turned it into the stories he wanted to tell. Perhaps when it came to telling tales, we weren't so different.

"She worked in the court as an administrator, close to Umair. And when the king's wife perished, your mother, with her kind heart, tried to ease Umair's burden. I warned her. Kindness does not belong in the Court of Pain. But she disagreed. She was adamant the king had goodness in him.

Then she vanished and returned some months later with a babe—you. She did not speak of Umair after that. A light had died inside her. She lived at court for a time but confessed to me how Umair had taken an interest in you, his son. So, we plotted her escape."

I recalled none of this, nobody had said a damn word about my beginnings. I'd always been the traitor's son and nothing more. I listened now, absorbing each piece to build my own picture of the past.

Danyal had fallen silent, and although he appeared as gruff and distant as I'd always assumed him to be, his hesitation spoke of deep emotion. "How do you know this?"

"I worked alongside her."

That seemed... unlikely.

He huffed a short, sharp laugh. "I know, this is not the face of an administrator. But I was, in my youth. She escaped and I made sure you and her were hidden, but as you know, the court is loyal to the crown, and Umair eventually discovered my deception. I warned your mother and fled, both of us going our separate ways. I lost contact with her and lost myself for a while. Turned to... darker things, to get by."

Darker things to get by. I knew that road and where it led.

"I later learned she'd been found and captured, with you. And I tried..." He stirred his broth, then tapped the stick on the side of the pan. "I tried to get back in, but I was different by then, a changed man, with scars to prove it, and the courtly doors were closed to the likes of killers. By the time I eventually did find a way in, I was too late, and she hung as a traitor." He fell silent, but that silence was loud with feeling. "You vanished not long after. You'd escaped, and that was a good thing. I thought that would be the end of it."

"But it did not last."

"No. Razak found you, sealed you away, where I couldn't

253

get to you. If I asked after you, suspicion turned my way, so I stayed, I listened, I watched... and when you were sent to the Court of Love, I volunteered to carry messages back and forth. Razak didn't know our connection. He didn't know I was close with your mother, or how I'd worked as an administrator for Umair, alongside her. Nobody did. The young, brilliant man I'd been had died with her. I became what you see now, but I watched you."

"You could have told me."

"We'd both changed so much. You were nineteen years, devious, sly, too clever for your own good, and you had the Court of Love dancing to your tune. Razak had molded you into a stranger, into his spy. If I told you what I knew, spoke of your mother, the traitor—from seeing what you were capable of, you'd have handed me over to Razak. The risk was too great. So I vowed to watch for you from afar, for your mother."

He'd known all this and said nothing. All the times we'd met, and I'd thought him Razak's man. I'd looked into his eyes and seen a killer there. "You're a damned good liar, Danyal."

"So are you. I believed Razak had turned you. I heard someone fitting Bendrik's description had been seen near the council chambers *after* his body had been discovered. If it was you, I had to know. I had a suspicion I knew where you'd go next. That's when I heard Malvina's cry for help."

If Danyal hadn't arrived when he did, Malvina would have fled, and I'd have bled out on her precious rug.

He'd killed her though, for me.

"Thank you." Such small words didn't feel like enough. *Thank you for bringing my mother back to life, if only for a few moments, and thank you for saving me.* "Thank you," I said again, croaking it.

"It wasn't enough. Soup?"

He talked, while I sipped soup from a bowl and listened to tales of how my mother had known there was a wrongness at the center of the Court of Pain. She'd seen how the court exploited its people, taking their lives, their wealth, and hoarding it—bleeding its own citizens dry.

The last she'd seen of me was that night on the hill, with Umair at my side, his hand on my shoulder. She must have been desperate in those final moments, but I remembered her being fierce.

I was glad Umair was dead, lost somewhere in Justice's sordid past. My only regret was that I hadn't been the one to kill him.

"You must never take your own life, Zayan. Not when you mother fought so hard for you to have one."

Taking my own life wasn't a decision I'd come to flippantly. Backed into a corner, holding a blade to my neck had had been all the control I'd had left. "You sound like a friend of mine. He would not be please with any of this."

"Ah, Love's prince." Danyal's smile suggested he approved. "You did well to get Arin out. The Court of Pain is no place for a man like him."

"He'd disagree with you. And believe me, he's not the fragile prince most everyone believes him to be. He's no meek-minded emotional fool."

"Then it appears he's a good match."

"*Was* a good match." I'd sent him away and made sure it had ended, for his own good. By now, he'd have long discovered the documents and realized Draven's duplicity. Arin had a sharp mind and a keen sense of survival. He'd survive.

Danyal talked some more, but the cold drew in and when he stoked the fire, I laid alongside it, closed my eyes, pulled the blanket closer, and sketched a picture of my mother in my mind. To know she'd been kind, loyal, and fierce... She'd been good, in a world that treated goodness like a disease. I'd known in my heart, but I'd been left with only bad memories. Danyal had given me some good ones.

If there were good people in the world, people willing to fight for what was right, like Danyal, like Arin, then not all was lost.

CHAPTER 27

ark

MY STRENGTH RETURNED over the coming days, thanks in part to Danyal's catching and cooking wild critters and broth. He'd set up camp in the wilderness, far outside the cities and close to Justice's borders, which accounted for the dramatic swathes of trees, steep inclines, and frosty nights. Danyal chastised me for my thin appetite, and as there were no hungry children here willing to steal my food like there had been in the desert camps, I was forced to eat like I hadn't in years. He seemed to imply I might suffer from self-loathing, to which I replied I loved myself more than most. He had a gruff laugh and a kind personality, hidden beneath all the grizzled, snarling exterior.

But as the days cycled on, and the wound in my side healed, I grew impatient.

Neither of us could return to Pain. I'd likely be hung, drawn, and quartered in War, and I couldn't go to Arin. The meeting at the Overlook Inn had long since passed. By now, he'd be putting his coin to good use and crafting himself a new life. At the very least, he was safer than when he'd been with me.

There was only one way forward, one fate I couldn't walk away from. We'd been tangled together since my mother's death and it would always be like that, until I stopped him.

Razak.

If I could cross into Justice's lands, there was a chance I could learn of my brother's fate, and perhaps stop whatever he had planned. The letters had indicated Umair and Pain's crown was somewhere in Justice, and Razak had allowed himself to be caught and transported there. Weeks had passed since then. He might already have the crown and be free, but either way, I had to know.

"Can you get me into Justice?" I asked Danyal.

He skinned a critter he'd trapped in the brush and was skewering it to roast above the fire. I'd learned he was a man of few words, unless I asked about my mother. He'd talk for hours about her. I owed him a great deal, not least my thanks. But I couldn't remain here, hiding out in the woods forever.

"Why?"

"Razak has a plan and I fear its only winner will be him, while the rest of the shatterlands suffers. He must be stopped."

"And it has to be you who stops him?"

I stared at the fire and recalled how my mother had tried to do good, tried to make Umair see the wrongs. She may have failed, but I was still alive, and as Danyal had taken great pains to tell me, she lived in me. I owed it to her to make right the wrongs. Nobody else was going to. "I know my brother. I can get close to him. I may be the only one who can."

"Or, you could leave well alone and live your life a free man?"

"He has bounty hunters looking for me. There is no freedom while he's alive."

"Ah, then it's revenge you seek."

I couldn't deny it. I wanted to wrap what was left of my fingers around Razak's neck and watch the light fade from his eyes.

"You don't need to say it, I see it in your eyes. You want to tear him apart, and I don't blame you. But I will caution you. That desire for revenge almost got you killed. If you walk back into that world, I may not be there to save you again."

"I cannot hide in the woods and eat whatever that poor creature is for the rest of my days." I laughed, and he seemed affronted. Had he planned for me to stay here, with him? "Did you think I would?"

His grizzled face fell. "I want to see you safe, Zayan."

"From all you've told me of my mother, she'd want me to stop Razak. Tell me I'm wrong, and I'll stay."

He cursed under his breath.

"I thought so. So can you get me into Justice?"

"Since Razak outed you as his brother, you've become notorious."

"Then I'll disguise myself. Can you get a blue gown?"

He rolled his eyes. "They're Justice, not the Court of Love. They are not so easily fooled by a pretty face and flattery."

"Have you visited there?"

"Visited? Not of my own free will."

Well, now I was intrigued. "You were arrested?"

"I was detained, served time in their jails."

"Then you *can* get me inside."

He grumbled his frustration. "I've just pulled you from

certain death, what makes you think I'll throw you back among the wolves?"

I smiled. "Because you know I'm right, and besides, we belong with the wolves."

"Zayan, you belong somewhere far away from all this, where you can be yourself for you, and nobody else."

"Perhaps, one day, when I'm free of Razak. But not while he's drawing breath and his heart still beats."

"Can you imagine a life like that, with your Prince of Love? Do you want a good life?"

"Maybe, if I deserve it. And if he'll have me." Did I dream of better things? Not before meeting Arin. I hadn't known anything outside the Court of Pain. I hadn't even seen a meadow to know such a thing existed. His world, his court *had* been a dream.

Danyal sighed and scrubbed his hands down his face. "She'd hate this. She'd want you safe. And that's what I vowed to do."

"But she'd know I'm right."

He lifted his head, and from the resignation on his face, I knew I'd won. "I'll get you into Justice."

THE COURT of Love had never believed in borders. They'd allowed all to come and go freely. War had its infamous walls around its court, and few wanted to enter Pain. But Justice was altogether different. Mountainous peaks jutted from vicious crevasses and savage gorges. It was said that Dallin had grown so furious with the shatterlands, he'd struck it from above, and Justice's land had taken the brunt of his wrath, shattering into jagged fragments. Thus, the shatterlands were made, and the court of Justice built upon its wound, as though to fix it.

Dallin had always been a story, but when Danyal left me with the wagon in the tree line and crossed the enormous swinging bridge from one side of a cliff to the other, with nothing but a bottomless drop into thick mists below, I wondered if I'd been too quick to dismiss Dallin as a myth. An atmosphere of foreboding hung over the chasm, as though a great beast waited below, in the mists, eager to devour anyone unworthy, who dared cross into Justice.

I wrapped a thick coat around me, and hidden among the trees, I waited for Danyal's return. A campfire was forbidden, lest the scouts see the smoke and investigate, so I was left to shiver alone.

Of course, my thoughts wandered to Arin. And so came the guilt for sending him away. He'd be all right. He was the most capable man I knew. Nothing fazed him, not even me. And I'd tried. He'd fought Razak, faced a sandworm, defied his father, and briefly commanded War's warriors. He'd find a way to move forward, he always did.

But I wanted him by my side. He'd lean into me, tell me he burned the wings off butterflies, and I'd wonder if he was jesting or truthful. He always had me on the backfoot, was forever a surprise. He was my magic in a world sorely lacking wonderment, and I was his beautiful lie.

Perhaps he'd confronted Draven, made the warlord spill his secrets, and they'd fucked with all the hate and spite I knew him capable of harboring. But no, Arin wouldn't. He was careful with his heart. A heart I'd likely crushed.

Danyal clomped across the bridge, making it swing. I watched from the tree line, until he'd left the bridge and veered off the road.

"They'll let you in," he mumbled behind his thick scarf.

"As Zayan?"

"Yes, as Zayan, or Lark. Whatever name you choose." He climbed into the driver's seat and gathered up the ice-encrusted reins. The horse snorted clouds from its nostrils and trotted on.

That Justice should just *let me in* seemed unlikely. After everything I'd done? "Are you sure?"

He glared from the corner of his eye. "If I were unsure, we'd be riding in the opposite direction."

I pulled my collar up and hunkered down into my coat's thick folds. "It's just... as you said, I have something of a reputation. It seems suspiciously fortuitous that they'd let me in uncuffed and free as a bird."

He chuckled. "Would you prefer they arrest you?"

"No, of course not."

"Then don't question it. Be grateful. Going in as yourself gives you leverage the rest of us common folks don't have."

"How so?"

"You're Prince Zayan. Don't forget that."

"Half a prince, when it suits everyone else."

"Half is enough in the shatterlands."

The horse shied at the bridge, and I didn't blame it. Mist swirled far below the timber slats.

"Gee-up." Danyal clicked the roof of his mouth, urging the animal on. It chewed on its bit and threw its head but walked on. If it bolted, it would take us down into the mist with it. I peered over the edge and fancied I saw reaching hands swirling in those clouds, like the souls of the dead clamoring for life.

We crossed without incident and passed beneath a watch-tower, its glass turret fogged from the inside. I couldn't see the guards, but the weight of their gazes crawled over us. Noemi had come from Justice, and she'd been good. Hopefully, there were more like her inside this frigid realm.

Snowflakes dallied in the air and danced around us. Soft, at first, puffed by the breeze. But soon the wind picked up and the snow began to push us forward. I believed in magic I could see and touch, not in the supernatural. Yet when I glanced behind, driving snow had blurred the road and the tower, as though both had never existed.

We'd entered into Justice, and there was no going back.

ark

JUSTICE'S CASTLE had been constructed long ago of blue-tinted granite blocks, high atop a jagged peak. Its battlements jutted into snow-laden clouds, like the sharp fronds of a crown. A winding track led us around snow-dusted boulders and by the time we'd reached the portcullis, our horse puffed and wheezed.

Aides bundled us into a large, vaulted ceilinged entrance hall that stretched deep into the mountain. Great arches acted as doorways leading into further rooms. I glimpsed a library, a lounge, a dining hall. But in the center, a fanned staircase swept up to a split landing, serving the castle's two main wings. Impressive was too small a word. War's temple had been impressive. The size and grandeur of this space was extraordinary.

A woman in a blue cloak and hood glided out from one of those side arches and studied me from head to toe, and while she maintained a smile, it was a struggle. "Prince Zayan, you must be tired from your journey."

I glanced down at myself and then at Danyal. We'd spent the last few weeks living in the woods. Slushy snow and grit caked our boots. Our clothes were unkempt, we both smelled like horse, and we looked as though we'd escaped one of Justice's jails and should probably return there.

"Please excuse our attire," I said, slipping into a more regal tone of voice, to match my title. "We had some misfortune on the road. Bandits stole everything. Terrible, truly. Even the clothes off our backs. We had to get by through the kindness of strangers, hence our borrowed attire."

"I see." Whether she bought the lie or not, it didn't matter. We were their guests and so far, it appeared we'd be treated as such. "Well, let's get you refreshed. My name is Justice Sonya." She dipped her head.

"I know who you are. We met briefly at War. You refused to delay my brother's incarceration."

Her head twitched, just a little, and her smile tightened like the knot in a noose. "That's right. Forgive me, you were dressed very differently then too."

I swept a hand toward Danyal. "May I introduce my advisor, Danyal. He'll be staying with me."

Danyal grunted, then remembered some of his old administrator's manners and dipped his chin. "Pleasure."

"Of course, we're pleased to host you both. Right this way."

Pleased, indeed. How strange that I should be welcomed while I assumed Razak was behind bars somewhere inside this castle. I'd ask after my brother later, but for now, I needed to orientate myself so I'd be ready for when our hosts inevitably turned on us.

Danyal and I were given connecting rooms, so vast and

luxurious they could have been for the highest of royals, with sumptuous furniture and ridiculously large beds. It had to be a trick. Seduce us with luxury, then rip it away later? Razak often played such games. Still, I'd enjoy the vast bed and private bathing rooms while I could.

My room came with a young man of early twenties with fluffy red hair that fell in curls against his cheeks. He stoked the fires, and later, when I returned from bathing, he presented an armful of fresh clothes, then poured tea from a silver teapot. I eyed him in the mirror, curious. Buttoned up in blue and grey, he spoke only when spoken to. What had he been told about me? What could he tell me about his home and its people?

Shirtless in front of the mirror, I raised my arm and examined the tender but healing knife wound in my side. Two weeks in the wilderness and Danyal's fattening me up had healed it well.

"You can ask," I told the aide, catching his reflection eyeing my back.

He straightened and made his way over with a tiny cup and saucer. "Tea?"

"You are the first to ever serve me tea." I took the cup. "Thank you." The drink was sweet and hot, with a lemony bite.

"What happened?" he asked, while trying not to gaze at my chest.

"I fell," I said. "Onto a dagger. Terribly careless."

"You fell onto a dagger?"

Leaving the mirror, and him, I examined the clothes he'd laid out on the bed. Purple and black, of course. I was here as Zayan, so I should look the part of Pain's half prince.

"Did you really fall on a dagger?"

Bless this innocent man. He'd likely grown from a boy,

closeted in this castle, stifled by Justice's many rules. "What do you think?" I teased.

He considered my question, then lifted his head. "You know, we don't tell lies in Justice."

That was good to know. Honesty was a rare commodity elsewhere. I shrugged the purple shirt on and buttoned the pearls into their hooks. "Noted. Did Justice Sonya tell you not to talk to me?"

"No." He averted his gaze again.

"But she told you something?"

"Yes."

"And what was that?"

"Not to trust you. That you'd lie."

I laughed and scooped up the fine, heavy jacket, embroidered in purple silk, clearly made for a prince. Strange, how they'd had the clothes tailored and waiting for me. They couldn't have known I'd be coming, yet they seemed well-prepared for my arrival. "She's right. I'm untrustworthy, and I have been known to lie on occasion." I could have a lot of fun with this one.

I finished dressing as the aide looked on while trying *not* to look and returned to the mirror. Zayan. *Prince* Zayan. Danyal thought the name gave me power, but I wasn't so convinced. A name did not make a prince.

"Lying's not always so bad," I said.

"Yes, it is."

He was adorable. "What's your name?"

"Theo."

"All right, Theo. What if I told you your eyes are too close together, your hair is an uninteresting ruffled mess, and we'd better hope there's a growth spurt still to come as you don't have much else going for you." He gaped, and heat flushed his face. "Or—" I turned to face him and propped my ass against the dresser. "—your eyes are enchanting, your hair is quite the statement and I daresay your best feature, and if you don't dance with that body like yours, it's quite the crime."

Now he glowered and folded his arms, halfway between furious and intrigued. "I don't understand. Which is it?"

"Both."

"It cannot be both. One is true."

"One man's lie is another's truth."

"That doesn't make sense."

"Maybe not here, within these walls, but outside of them, you'd see." This one would be a joy to teach the worldly ways of courts outside of his own, where truth didn't always have to ruin magic, and lies could be spun for good. "My point is, there are other ways besides those of Justice. Keep an open mind, and you'll see them, Theo."

I left him staring after me and knocked on the connecting door to Danyal's room. "Oh, and if you like, I can teach you to dance. That part was true."

The door opened and Danyal's imposter stood before me. Almost like Danyal, but buttoned up in a slick red and black suit. His hair had been smoothed back, making his grey eyes startlingly penetrating. "By Dallin." I laughed, and his grizzled face scrunched into a frown. "Forgive me, it's a surprised laugh, not a mocking one."

"Last time I wore anything like this I worked in the court. I hope you appreciate how uncomfortable I am," he grumbled.

"Appreciate it? Frankly, it was worth it just to see you dressed like a lord." I offered him the crook of my arm. "Dinner awaits."

DINNER in the Court of Justice was not like the sparkling, fancy affair of those in Love's court, nor the raucous chaos of War. Pain didn't host banquets, reserving gatherings for public punishment. Justice's dinner had us all seated around a circular table. The only status symbol was a throne encrusted with sapphires, not much larger than the other chairs around the table. Queen Soleil's, no doubt.

I settled in my assigned place with Danyal beside me, and as our wine glasses were filled by silent aides, we awaited the arrival of the remaining guests. All of them were strangers, and all were dressed in blue. Likely Justice's equivalent of lords and ladies from nearby fiefdoms.

Justice Sonya took her seat and sent her fake smile sailing my way. I was beginning to think she didn't like me. In fact, most everyone here avoided meeting my gaze, having heard of my reputation. Would they gossip later? Perhaps Theo could be persuaded to tell me what rumors swirled regarding my brother and me.

The door swept open as it had a dozen times, but this time I knew the man who strode in. Black pants, red sash, hair bundled back but with a few deliberate plaits swinging free.

Our gazes met. Draven's stride faltered. His kohl-lined eyes blew wide, his mouth opened, but then one of the most beautiful women I'd ever laid eyes on swept through the door behind him, demanding every gaze in the room. Everyone stood, including me. She wore a gown of pale blue, with a sheer veil ghosting her face and a sweeping cloak of water-like silk edges in white, as though shrouded in frost. Justice's sparkling crown gleamed and sparkled atop her head of golden hair, right there in plain sight, for all to see.

Queen Soleil's beauty was well-known outside her court, but I hadn't expected the tales to fall short. Her arrival tripped my already spiraling thoughts, leaving me scrambling to catch up, by which time Draven had taken a seat far across the round table and was making a concerted effort to ignore my efforts to catch his eye.

If he was here, where was Arin?

There were no more spaces at the table. If Arin were visiting Justice, he'd be among the nobles at this table. Had Draven met with Arin at the Overlook and something transpired between them, accounting for Arin's absence? Was it because of the documents I'd found featuring his name? I had to speak with him.

Soleil took her place at her modest throne, and in a soft, musical voice she said, "Balance is all." And with that, we sat.

Soleil announced me as a Prince of Pain. All gazes obligatorily turned to me—all but Draven's. Why was he avoiding me? I narrowed my eyes at the warlord. What was he hiding? I thanked the queen, my fellow guests, and we began to dine.

"Danyal, after dinner, I need you to track that warlord down," I muttered so only Danyal heard. "I must speak with him urgently."

"The one in red and black?"

"His name is Draven and since arriving, he's been desperate to leave. I need to know why he's here, and why he's avoiding me." If he'd done something to Arin, I'd slit his throat, and unlike Arin, I wouldn't miss.

"How much *persuasion* is permitted?"

Soleil glanced my way. The Queen of Justice—the woman whom every single person in the shatterlands answered to. Commit any wrongdoing and be discovered and Justice would come for you. I covered my mouth, faked a cough, and spluttered, *"Don't kill him."*

"Understood."

Draven's anxious fidgeting suggested he wouldn't come

willingly, but while Draven was a formidable muscular force, Danyal was clever and vicious. He'd be able to handle the warlord.

"Would you like to visit your brother?" Soleil asked, appearing at my side.

I jolted, caught scheming. It was a good thing she couldn't read minds. I saw a shadow of a smile through her veil. Blue eyes skewered me to my chair. Did she mean see Razak now? Surely not. "I will need to see him, yes, thank you."

"Tomorrow." She turned to leave.

"May I ask, is my brother in custody?"

"Yes. Prince Razak is far too dangerous to be allowed to roam free while awaiting trial."

That was a relief, at least. There was only so much power he had behind bars. But it still begged the question why they'd allowed *me* to walk among them, eat at their table, dine with them as a guest. This didn't seem the place to ask, and I didn't want to trigger any kind of protocol that might see me thrown into a cell alongside my brother. Better to keep quiet and let my curiosity go unanswered for now.

"If that is all—"

"Warlord Draven is here," I blurted, stopping her from moving to the next guests.

She glanced across the table. "Do you know him?"

"You could say as much." I'd had his cock in my mouth and loved his husband. I'd thought I'd known him, but recent discoveries suggested otherwise.

"Zayan, this is not the place for Pain's scheming," she said, quite clearly, despite the veil. "I hope you understand that while here, inside these illustrious halls, you will behave in such a manner as is expected by Justice."

Those were a lot of words for mind-your-own-fucking-business. I bowed my head. "Of course."

"Your brother will await your arrival in the morning."

She glided to the next guests, leaving me to turn my gaze back toward Draven. He'd finished three glasses of wine and poured himself another now. I stared, willing him to see me. What if Arin had demanded answers, and he'd hurt him to keep whatever secrets those documents held from being exposed? He was capable. If Draven was beholden to the Court of Pain, would he sacrifice Arin to protect himself? Damn it, if only there had been more time to explain my concerns to Arin. I'd thought the papers made it obvious something wasn't right with Draven, but Arin's absence now rattled my nerves.

"Danyal, when you were an administrator, did you come across the word *benefits* in relation to children, and what it meant?" I asked.

"For children, no. But benefits means leverage. A benefit is something or someone that can be used for the Court of Pain's gain."

I'd thought so. "And if I were to discover some documents pertaining to Court of War benefits, and a list of names, what would that mean?"

"A list like that would mean those people, or others connected to them, are controlled by the Court of Pain."

That had been my suspicion. But how deep did the control go? I didn't want to believe Draven had aided my brother in the Court of War, but if he had, then everything we'd told him, every moment we'd spent with him, every plan, every confession—Razak likely knew it all. We'd told Draven *everything*, even my plan to infiltrate my brother's court.

He finally looked up. I stared through him. The table and its guests faded away, and he squirmed like a worm on a hook, then downed another glass of wine.

Oh, he knew.

He stood, bumped the table, and almost toppled his wine. "Excuse me."

Damn it, he was leaving. I couldn't escape the dinner without drawing attention. "Follow him," I told Danyal. "Find out what room he's staying in. Don't let him see you. Report back to me later."

Danyal nodded and slipped away, unnoticed.

I'd pay Draven a visit when I wasn't being watched, and he was going to tell me everything, including Arin's whereabouts, and if he lied, then our friendship was about to get very personal.

ark

Danyal did not return all night. When Theo arrived in the morning to stoke the fires, I asked him to find the whereabouts of my advisor. I then returned to the main hall to await Justice Sonya, who would be my guide into Justice's dungeons.

"Good morning, Prince Zayan." She bowed her head and offered her polite smile.

"Where's my advisor?"

"I'm sorry, I don't—"

"Danyal, he joined me for dinner last night and did not return to his room."

"Oh." She seemed surprised. "Perhaps he lost his way?"

I returned her thin smile with a frosty one of my own. "*Perhaps* you might send someone to look for him?"

With a flutter of hand gestures, she sent her own aide

away to discover why Danyal hadn't returned and promised to keep me informed. "These corridors and winding staircases really are difficult to navigate," she said, escorting me down a stairwell into the castle's bowels, deeper into the heart of the mountain. "This castle is so old it's said Dallin himself lived here." Her tittering laugh fluttered down a long, grim corridor lined by oil lamps tucked into sconces, desperately trying to fend off the dark. She might believe all of this was amusing, but I'd lost my sense of humor around the time Draven had arrived at dinner, acting as though we were strangers.

Metal doors clanged. We passed locked door after locked door, each with just a small slit to peer inside. Some prisoners moaned for help, others glared through their slit in silence, some begged and pleaded their innocence.

I kept my eyes forward, grateful I hadn't yet found my way to such a punishment. It was one thing to be chained to a bed, quite another to be locked in permanent darkness.

Sonya led me to the end of a block, slipped a key in a door lock, and swung the iron door open. The rectangle of light highlighted my brother, who sat against the far wall of a narrow space, arms draped over his drawn-up knees, head back, eyes closed. The air smelled acrid, damp, and despite all he'd done, a pang of pity had me feeling sorry for him in this dire place.

My life would have been easier if I didn't have a heart to care.

"Thank you," I said, dismissing Sonya.

She bowed her head and returned the way we'd arrived, then waited at the end of the hall, presumably to make sure I didn't do anything untoward to her prisoner.

"Hello, brother." The cruel familiarity of his voice

vanquished the flutter of pity. His eyes remained closed, but the corner of his lips ticked into a half-smile, like a fishhook. "It took you long enough."

I stepped inside, and his eyes opened. Dark pupils swelled, fixing on me. He cocked his head, gaze roaming, assessing, scrutinizing beneath my skin. "They dressed you like a prince, how wonderful."

I knew his games. He'd slither his way into my mind if I let him. "I know about the crowns."

His smile died and he slow-blinked, as though uncaring.

"And I know Umair blamed you for the death of his wife, your mother."

Razak's lip curled. He brought his knees closer to his chest and turned his face away.

Yes, that one had hurt him. "I know you're following our father, trying to finish what he began."

"You know nothing," he snarled.

"You will fail."

A sharp laugh fell from his lips. "Found your confidence, Zayan? Do you think those fine clothes make you my equal? You are nothing, just my shadow. Shadows die when the lights fade."

"Which one of us is behind bars? Which of us is caught?" I crouched and met his glare at the same level. We were brothers, it was true, and outwardly it seemed as though our roles had been reversed. I was the free prince, and he the pauper in chains. He'd never looked so unassuming, so pathetic as he did in filthy prisoner clothes. But he was right; despite appearances, nothing had changed between us.

His smile grew again. "Indeed, which one of us *is* caught?"

I nodded toward his wrist and turned mine upward. "No chains."

"I don't need steel to chain you, brother. I'm in your head, in your blood, in your body. You're mine in every way. I click my fingers and you dance." He snapped his fingers, and like a fool, I flinched. He was right. I was chained in my mind, but I'd be free of him soon.

"Are you so deluded to think me still owned?" I asked.

"I'm right."

"I'm never dancing for you again."

From inside this cell, he couldn't do anything except bark and snarl. He'd been here weeks, languishing in the dark. For all his bluster and scheming, Queen Soleil would punish him. Justice's esteemed members of the jury would find him guilty. He'd hang.

I straightened, done with him, and turned to leave. "I'm going to watch you swing on the end of a noose—"

"Why do you think Soleil allows you to walk freely in her court?"

In a few more steps, he'd be out of my life forever. I just had to walk from the cell. But why had Justice allowed me inside, as a Prince of Pain, knowing I'd brought down Arin's court and accompanied my brother to bring down the Court of War? The question had unsettled me since we'd passed over Justice's long, unnerving bridge. Surely Razak couldn't be behind the queen's leniency. His reach couldn't extend beyond these bars to the queen.

"Our mutual friend saw to it," he added, so damn pleased with himself.

We didn't share any friends. He couldn't have orchestrated my freedom here, it wasn't possible. He was lying.

"Turn around." His chains rattled and clanged, and when I turned my head, he'd risen to his feet. The ragged clothes hung off him; he'd rarely looked so pathetic, but his presence still spiked my heart with fear. "You believe you're free? You'll never be free. After what I'm about to reveal, you'll get on your knees and beg to suck me off—"

I lunged and when I squeezed his throat, he choked under my grip, and climactic pleasure rippled through me. The rage came so fast, burning so brightly, I had no control over it. I *needed* him to hurt. Gods yes, to kill him, now that would be true freedom.

He clawed at my grip, mouth gaping, and wheezed, *"Arin."*

Arin's name on his lips jolted through me like a static shock. I let go and stumbled away. "What of Arin?"

He coughed and hacked, braced against the wall, and it was all I could do not to dive back in and slam his head against the bricks, end him right there. But he'd said Arin's name, he knew something. "What have you done? Where's Arin?" I knew, didn't I, somewhere inside. I'd known all along. Razak had cards left to play, and Arin was my obvious weakness.

He grinned, enjoying his moment, his win. "He's here."

Not possible. "He's not—"

Razak slumped against the wall; his smile turned into a dark chuckle. "He was arrested for treason against his court and attempted treason against the Court of War."

No, I'd sent Arin away, to keep him safe. Nobody knew where he was. "You're lying."

"Oh no, brother, this is all real. Our mutual friend saw to it, and he saw that all charges against *you* were dropped. You're my victim, a pawn, used and discarded. Poor Zayan, so weak, he danced for me because I fucked him over and over again, like the willing little victim you are."

No. The room spun, my thoughts untethered. I grabbed the doorframe to keep my legs from buckling. Arin had been arrested? Arin was here? "No, you're lying! I sent him away, I saw to it. You couldn't have gotten to him—"

"He's here," Razak snapped. "And unless you find me Pain's crown, I'll see to it he dies, found guilty of his many crimes. Those are your choices. So fuckin' dance for me. I own you. You will obey, you will kneel, and you will do everything I say to save your precious Prince of Love!"

I fled the cell, running blind as my brother's laugh chased me down.

"You'll be back!" he yelled. "You always come back!"

Sonya saw my approach. "Zayan? Are you all right—"

"Arin." I grabbed her shoulders and dug my fingers in, reeling inside, so damn afraid for Arin. "Is it true? Arin's here?"

She writhed. "You're hurting me."

I let go and staggered, unbalanced and adrift. "Arin? Please, tell me." Acrid panic burned my throat. "Tell me. Is he here, in one of these cells?" These horrible, dark holes with bars. No, he couldn't be here, not my honey and sunshine prince. Alone, in the darkness. Lost. *Please let it be a lie, please let Razak be wrong.*

Her lips clamped closed.

She nodded.

"No, no, no, no." I reeled, falling but standing still. Arin was here. Arin had been arrested, made out to be a traitor. Alone, captured, lost in the cold. How long?

I'd sent him away, I'd abandoned him. I shouldn't have. I should have stayed with him. I paced while my whole world fell apart around me. If Arin was here, then everything had changed. Razak had won.

We could have run together. But I'd pushed him away, sent him to the Overlook Inn alone... straight into Draven's arms.

Draven. Whose name had been on the documents. Draven, who had been at our sides this whole time. Draven, a benefit to the Court of Pain, *to my brother.*

Draven... our *mutual friend?* No, it wasn't possible. It couldn't be. But I'd sent Arin to him, and Arin was now here...

Draven was Razak's man. Draven had betrayed us, betrayed Arin.

This was Draven's doing. He'd played us this whole time. He'd always been Razak's man, from the very beginning. The memories tumbled, one after another, unraveling truths I'd been so sure of. Draven's smirk at Love's ball, his singling me out, the letter he'd supposedly received alerting him to my identity. *You're him, the traitor's son.* He'd known exactly who I was when he'd had his cock down my throat. Razak had told him everything he'd needed to know, including how to catch my eye. He'd been at our sides this whole time—*he'd married Arin.*

"That cocksucking bastard!"

He'd fucked my throat knowing Razak had sent him. I scrunched my hands into fists. There *had* been a third man in Arin's court, another imposter, and I hadn't seen it. Bumbling, heroic, passionate Warlord Draven.

I coughed a bitter, crazed laugh. The son of a sandworm had played me.

When I got my hands on him, I'd make him pay, make him wish for death. But before that, I had to see Arin, to know he was all right.

Sonya had watched me pace and rant, warily backing away, but as my gaze fixed on her, she froze with her back pressed against the wall.

"Arin's not here," she blurted. "He's in the eastern wing. Please, Zayan, please don't hurt me."

"Hurt you?" I snarled, and slammed a hand against the wall beside her head. "Take me."

"I'm not supposed to reveal—"

"Do not test me, Sonya. You will not like the result. *Take me to Arin.*"

CHAPTER 30

rin

I MEASURED time by the deliveries of slop in the bowl they slid through a locked flap in the door and when they came to take the bucket I used to relieve myself in. It had been long enough that the single chain and cuff had rubbed my wrist raw, and my eyes had become so accustomed to the gloom that every time the door opened, light flooded in and my tears squeezed free.

I had hoped for a chance to voice my defense, at least make a plea of innocence, but after the wagon had arrived in Justice's icy castle and I'd been unceremoniously marched down to the cells, nobody had come.

Behind a door again. Alone again. Pacing back and forth, eating their slop, pissing in a bucket, pacing back and forth... My feet were raw too. They'd taken my boots. So silly a thing. Why take my boots?

I'd stopped jumping at every door slam, every yell or howl

from those in the neighboring cells. It wasn't days. I was certain of that much. It had to be weeks. I paced and ate and relived myself, and paced and ate and sometimes half slept, when the cold floor didn't gnaw on my bones. Over and over, day and night and day.

Alone.

Again.

Alone with the guilt of my mother's suicide, my father's murder, the blaze that had destroyed my court. Alone with the knowledge I should have done more, been better, stopped Razak. Alone with broken dreams of Lark on a clifftop, playing until his music died, and so did he.

A man could lose his mind in the dark. Alone. Locked behind a door.

Again. Pacing. Again.

"Arin?" Dark-lashed, elegant eyes gazed through the open slot in the door.

It couldn't be? Had I dreamed him. "Lark?"

He vanished.

"Lark, wait?" I unfolded my legs, stretched creaking muscles, and climbed to my bare feet. Was he truly here?

"Open the door," Lark ordered, in a voice full of thin, barely contained rage.

"I can't do that," came a woman's reply.

"You did it for Razak and he's a lunatic. Open the door, Sonya."

"Prince Zayan, I have explicit instructions not to allow you inside Arin's cell—"

"Lark!" I surged forward. My chain snapped tight, dancing pain up my arm. I reached the narrow window. "Don't fight them." If he pushed them, they'd throw him in chains, and I needed him free. One of us had to be. Silence fell outside the door. *Don't do anything rash, don't provoke them.* "Lark?"

His beautiful eyes appeared at the window again, wide and full. Then they narrowed. "I'm getting you out. I'll talk to Soleil."

"Lark." I didn't know what to say. I'd missed him, missed him so much it hurt even more now he was here and I couldn't touch him. Then I remembered the last time I'd seen him, standing on the Court of Pain's steps, watching his coach take me away. The rage flared like a monster, consuming my fear in its flames. "You asshole! You put me on that carriage!"

"I'm sorry."

"You prick."

"I was wrong."

"You broke my heart." A sob choked off the words and then a horrible, heavy silence fell between us. His lashes fluttered down. I hadn't meant to hurt him, but he'd hurt me. It didn't matter. None of that mattered. "I'm so happy you're here."

He looked up, and the fierceness in his glare burned anew. "I'm getting you out."

"Don't do anything foolish. Please? I cannot bear it if they arrest you too."

"Which one of us is the fool?" His smile lifted his voice.

He'd do whatever he wanted, whatever he thought was right, and nobody could stop him. Not even me. I loved that about him, despite how it infuriated me. "Lark?"

"I'm here."

Now wasn't the right time, but I had to say it. He had to know—he had to *believe* it. "I love you. And it's fine, if you... if it's different for you. I just want you to know, I love you. I've always loved you. You drive me crazy because I love you."

He reached through the tiny window, fingers spread. I stretched as far across the cell as the chain allowed and pushed my arm out, but our fingers didn't meet. I tried to reach him, I really did. The chain held me back.

He withdrew his hand and peered through the narrow window again. "Arin?"

"Yes?" Would he tell me he loved me now? It didn't matter if he didn't, but if he did... it would give me hope I could cling to in the dark. I needed to hear it, selfish as that was. I loved him, there was so escaping it, no denying it, even if it did hurt. But if he loved me back, that meant everything.

"Did Draven do this?" he asked, and my heart thumped a little quieter. Of course he wouldn't tell me he loved me; Ellyn had said he couldn't. It didn't matter. He was here.

"Draven?" I asked, hating the name.

"Yes. Did he do this?" His voice held a thread of menace. He already knew the answer.

"It was in those documents, wasn't it?" I asked. "On the first page? They were ruined after you shoved them in my pocket, and I didn't make the connection. Something on that first page told you not to trust him. I didn't know. I didn't see it..."

"I'm going to kill him."

"Ahem," the woman outside with Lark said, apparently listening to our every word. "Please do not discuss potential crimes in my presence."

Lark turned his head. "Are you going to arrest me?"

"We do not arrest for crimes yet committed. But you had better hope Warlord Draven does not die anytime soon, as you've just indicated your desire to kill him, with witnesses."

"Lark," I said, snapping his gaze back to me. "Do not give them fuel with which to burn you with."

His gaze skipped downward. "Yet they make it so easy," he teased.

Gods, if—when—I got out of these chains, I was going to kiss him so hard it would leave him dizzy. "You know that time you said you didn't need a white knight to save you?"

"I recall."

"I could really do with one now. Do you know any?"

"I know a fool?"

"I'll take a fool over a knight."

"Well then, Prince of Flowers, we have a deal." His eyes softened, turning sad. "I have to go. I will free you. Whatever it takes."

"Lark, just— Please, stay safe?"

"Always." He left, and my heart tripped. I didn't want him to go, didn't want to sit in the dark, alone. The walls shrank around me. But Lark was here, and that was everything. He was brilliant and bright and clever—so clever. He'd fix this, somehow.

"Arin?" He'd returned to the window.

"Yes?" Hope lifted some of the dread off my back.

"You do know you have my heart?"

Was he saying he loved me?

"You've always had it," he said. "From the moment we met."

My throat was too raw to speak, so I nodded instead and hoped he knew how much it meant—how much *he* meant—to me. If Lark was mine, then there was nothing in this world we couldn't fight together.

He vanished again, then a door slammed somewhere far off, but it didn't seem as dark as before now I had Lark's love to light the way.

CHAPTER 31

$\mathcal{L}$ark

"TAKE ME TO QUEEN SOLEIL." Sonya seemed a reasonable woman, all things considered. But as we climbed the endless stairs leading from Justice's prison cells, I couldn't decide if her obstinance was deliberate or if she genuinely couldn't help.

"You'll need to complete a request to have a meeting with the queen, expressing your reasons for such a meeting. You cannot simply meet with our queen."

"And how long will my request take to be processed?"

"Between five and seven days."

Soleil was the only one who had the authority to free Arin, but if Justice wouldn't grant me an audience with her, then I'd have to manufacture one.

Or return to Razak… But if I returned to him now, he'd win. He was in control, despite being locked behind bars. That had to change if I had any hope of beating him.

I couldn't fight Razak alone. I needed Arin beside me, but to free him, I had to play Razak's game and find Pain's crown.

This was a mess, all of it. Draven, Justice, Arin.

I should have known my brother had accounted for everything, even my apparent freedom to find him Pain's crown.

Sonya and I emerged from the cells and found Danyal waiting in the main entrance hall, joined by two guards. He wasn't restrained, but his glare suggested he'd had a rough night.

"What is this?" I strode over with Sonya in tow.

"This man claims to be your advisor," the guard on the left said.

I frowned. Danyal clearly wore the colors of Pain. "Why has he been detained?"

"He was caught lurking in the private residences."

"I wasn't lurking," Danyal groused. "I was walking. Last I checked, walking wasn't a crime."

Walking, indeed, was not a crime. "Is he under arrest?"

"No, he was kept overnight for observation."

"'Observation'?" I arched an eyebrow at Sonya, but her stoic expression made it clear everything about Danyal's detainment was apparently normal. He'd been kept overnight for *walking*. It was more likely they suspected us of scheming or wrongdoing and had kept him to hamper such efforts. If they didn't want us here, why invite us in?

"I apologize for my advisor's gross misconduct in walking the wrong way. I'm sure he'll refrain from doing so again, won't you, Danyal?"

"Surely."

"Good. Now that's settled, we'll be in our chambers." I nodded for Danyal to follow and marched from the hall. "Did you find Draven's room?" I asked under my breath.

"Yes."

"We'll make it appear as though we're behaving, and then I want you to take me. Once there, stand watch at the door, and do not enter, regardless of what you hear. Are you comfortable with this?"

Danyal glanced side-on. "What did he do to you?"

"Betrayed Arin and I in the worst way."

He nodded. "Then I'm comfortable with whatever you decide to do."

I'd already asked much of him. He didn't want to be here, but he'd come all the same. Such loyalty was rare, and I'd never expected to experience it for myself. "Thank you, Danyal. For everything."

"Are we likely to leave Justice as free men?" he asked.

I thought of Arin in one cell and Razak in another, and somewhere, Pain's crown waited for one of us to find it. Arin would be free, I'd make sure of it. But as for the rest of us? I didn't have an answer. "Are any of Pain's people free?"

"No, but you could change that."

"Me?" I laughed. "I look like a prince but don't mistake me for one. Nobody follows a gutter whore." He gave that gnarled, snarly expression which meant he was about to argue or impart some grim wisdom. "All right, here we are," I said brightly, for the benefit of anyone who may have followed us. We entered my room, closed the door, and waited several beats. Boots thumped outside, then faded away.

I nodded once at Danyal. "Take me to Draven's room."

"Are you sure about this?" Danyal whispered. "The warlord ain't small."

"Size isn't everything, Danyal. A man like you should know that." I grinned and knocked on Draven's door.

"Who's there?" came Draven's deep grumble.

"*Aides, sire, come to freshen your room*," I crooned in a soft, accented voice.

"Come."

I opened Draven's door. He looked up from the chair by the fireside, saw me, and lurched toward the fireside set. I scooped a vase off a nearby sideboard and flung it with well-practiced accuracy. It smashed over his head, raining water and flowers over his shoulders. He grunted, staggered, almost fell into the roaring fire, and reached for the poker.

"Let's dance, then, *traitor*."

I snatched the poker away from his fingers and spun, cracking it against the backs of his knees. He barked a cry and dropped. I straddled his legs from behind him, clutched the poker in both hands, pulled it down over his head, and yanked it up, under his chin, against his throat, jerking his head back against my chest.

I had him.

His hands flailed, trying to grab behind him.

He choked and snarled, growling like an animal. I yanked tighter and pressed my cheek to his. "You think you know me, Draven? Do you believe Razak told you everything, or just what he wanted you to hear? You have no idea who I am or what I'm capable of. But you are about to find out. I'm going to hurt you in ways you can't imagine. My only regret is Arin isn't here to witness your death."

He roared, reached back, caught my arm, and bent double, throwing me forward over his head. I hit the floor, flat on my back, blinking up at Draven's rage-twisted face. Damn his strength. I smacked the poker across his jaw, and as he reeled, I flipped onto my front.

Draven bolted for the bedside cabinet—probably going for a weapon. I had to stop him now.

I ran after him, swung the poker like a bat, and cracked it across the side of his head.

He tripped, spilling onto the bed. I snatched a fistful of shirt, pulled him around, and jammed the poker's tip under his chin, clamping his jaw shut.

"Stay down," I panted.

He glared but didn't struggle. He could have reached out and gripped my neck; we were close enough, and his arms were free at his sides. But he didn't move, didn't try and push me off, just panted and glared, surrendering under me.

"Do it," he snarled through gritted teeth.

Blood dribbled down the side of his face.

"Kill me," he added, in case I'd missed the point.

I wanted to. A step back, a final swing, and I'd shatter his skull. But why had he stopped fighting? He could kick me off, wrestle me for the poker. We stared at each other, breathing hard, each waiting for the other to make the next move.

"Under the bed," he said, dropping his chin as much as the poker allowed.

"What?"

"Check under the bed."

What trick was this?

"You're going to want to see," he said.

I huffed. "I've knelt in front of you once before, Warlord. I'm not doing it again."

"I won't hurt you, Lark."

What was this? He seemed sincere, but he'd always been sincere. "Oh fine." I shoved off him, putting space between us, and kept the poker pointed at him. "If this is a trick, I will rip your balls off and roast them on that fire."

He gave an exasperated growl, dropped to his knees, hauled a traveling case from under the bed, and shoved it across the floor, toward me.

I stopped its slide under my boot. It didn't look important. Just a deep-sided tan leather case.

"Open it." He slumped back against the bed and dabbed at his bloody head. "Do it, Lark. And then kill me. It's all I deserve."

"If it's full of scorpions, so help me Draven—" I kicked open the lid.

The Court of War's black and red crown hadn't lost any of its vicious aesthetic for being dumped into a simple traveling case. Was this a fever dream, because Draven could not have one of the four courtly crowns hidden under his bed. Not even Draven was that foolish.

"Say something," he demanded.

"I'm speechless, and believe me, Draven, rendering *me* silent is quite the accomplishment."

He snorted. "Yet there it is."

He'd had the Court of War's crown all this time? "You bastard."

"I know." He dabbed at his head and winced when his hand came away glistening with blood. "So kill me. Do it now. I won't fight. Just tell Arin I'm sorry?"

I lowered the poker to my side. Why had he done this, why was the crown here, why had he betrayed Arin and I? Even now, with the evidence in front of my eyes, I still didn't believe it. I knew people, I used people, and to do that, I understood them. I *knew* Draven. He wasn't a liar. Something had made him one. "Why?"

"My son."

The name on the document, a Court of Pain Benefit. Draven and his son. My heart swooped. Of course, it had to be for love. No other force could be so destructive. "He's alive?"

Draven nodded, then flinched. He flicked his dark eyes up

but couldn't hold my stare. "He shouldn't be. He was born with a... His foot is mangled— It doesn't matter. It never mattered to us. We tried to hide him, but Ogden gave them both, my wife and my son, to the sands. She died from exhaustion after getting our boy to a place she believed was safe. But the Court of Pain has been harvesting our castaways. They took him, put him in an orphanage. That's where he is now."

"Six years old." I remembered the document, and the child's age. Old enough to already be in the workhouses, day and night, working to fill Pain's vault with gold.

Draven looked up. "You saw Arin's documents."

"Just the name. I didn't know for sure what it meant."

"Razak told me my boy was alive, and if I wanted him to stay alive, then I had to go to the Court of Love. I was to report back on you, the courtly fool, but then he asked for more and more, and eventually, he had me report on... Arin."

"Did he order you to wed Arin?"

"No, not that! I swear it." Horror paled Draven's face. His lips quivered. "I meant our vows, the joining was real, at least to me. I wanted it to be real, even as every day I lied to Arin."

"All this time, Draven... We searched for that crown, you told us Ogden had it safely stored away, when you clearly took it!"

He hunched forward and his big shoulders shrank around him. "I chased Razak from the temple, and I meant to stop him, I really did, but he said he'd kill my boy. He handed me the crown, told me to ship it to Justice, to my own name, and we would er... We agreed to meet here."

While I'd lain dying, poisoned, and Arin fought to find the antidote, Draven had been conspiring with Razak. "You *shipped* the crown to Justice?" It was so absurd, I had to ask again.

He nodded.

I backed away from the man who had looked me in the eyes and told me a hundred lies. Arin and I had planned to steal Pain's crown, and he'd been right there, listening to our every word. We might as well have had Razak alongside us.

Draven could have stopped us, could have told us he already had a crown. If he'd handed War's crown over, we'd have tossed it into the ocean, and none of this would have happened. Arin wouldn't be imprisoned and I wouldn't have had to suffer Bendrik's twisted affections. Although, Bendrik's death had been a high point of the last few weeks.

"This is a relief, honesty. Telling you all this." He clutched his chest. "It's been eating me up inside."

"A relief? Oh, how fucking nice for you." I dropped into the chair beside the fireplace and set the poker down. "Fuck, Draven."

"I know, I know... My son was just a babe when Pain took him," he croaked. "I thought him dead. Razak gave me hope again. He told me I'd see him. You've no idea to fear someone dead, and then have them returned. It's like, it's like a dream made real."

All the rage drained out of me, leaving me numb. "Razak does not deal in hope, Draven. You'll never see your son again. He'll never give him back."

He squeezed his eyes closed, and his tears fell. Good. But my glee from seeing him hurting didn't last. The whole damn thing was tragic, and I didn't even have it in me to rage at him.

"He was born different," Draven said. "They blamed Cherise, my wife, and... I couldn't do anything. Ogden saw to it they were thrown away." Draven spluttered a sob, then choked the rest back. "It's always been our way. The sand takes them, and nobody talks of it. It's as though they're erased from our memories, but not mine. I've never forgotten my little boy."

My gaze dropped to the jagged fronds of War's crown, sticking up from the traveling case.

"I had no choice. I had to obey Razak."

"I know what it feels like to be under my brother's thumb. But you could have said something, you could have told us. We'd have helped you."

"No, if Razak learned of my betrayal, he'd kill him. He doesn't care at all, he'll cut his fingers off, send them to me, and then his head. By Dallin—" Draven sobbed again and buried his face in his hands. "I didn't want to hurt Arin. Or you. I thought you were like the rest of them in Pain. Then I learned of your missing fingers and I... I knew Razak was capable of carrying out his threats. It seemed better if we all just did what he wanted."

"Better? So much better to have Arin arrested. I assume that's what you chose to do?"

"Razak wanted you, Lark, not Arin. But you didn't come to the Overlook. And so, Arin was the next best thing." Draven wiped angrily at his face. "It's terrible, what I did. I know that. But I had to try. I'll always try. My boy has nobody..."

I'd had nobody once. I knew what that felt like too, to be alone in a world so large it threatened to swallow me every time I dared look up. I couldn't stay angry at Draven, not for loving his child. I knew that love. Had the situation been reversed and Arin had been the one in danger, I'd have done anything to save him. Still would. "I nearly killed you. Still might."

Draven nodded, accepting his fate. "If I die, Razak will leave my boy alone."

"Unlikely, now he's in my brother's sights. Our only solution is the same as it's always been. Kill Razak."

"I'm sorry, Lark, for all of it. So sorry..."

"Arin is the one you should be apologizing to."

But at least now I knew the truth. And we had War's crown. That had to be worth something. And Razak didn't know I had it in my possession. The crown gleamed in its case. I leaned forward, staring into its barbed design.

"What can I do? How do I make this right?" Draven asked, red-eyed, bleeding, and slumped on the bed.

"Razak is more dangerous now than he's ever been. He's orchestrated all of this. Three crowns are close, and we're still trying to fathom his plans."

"Then you're not going to kill me?"

"I *need* you, Draven. I can't stop Razak alone, and you have as much reason to want him dead as Arin and I. No, I'm not going to kill you. Razak clearly wants all of us here. He's using Arin as leverage against me, and your son as leverage against you. He's behind bars, but we're still his tools." We could use that, turn it on him. I just needed to figure out how.

Draven nodded, trying to get on board. He'd shaken off his tears. "What does he want?"

"Pain's crown."

"It's here?

"Umair brought it to Justice while searching for a power and that's the last anyone heard from the king. I need to get Arin out of that cell, but Soleil isn't likely to let him go. Razak has something on Justice, leverage he's using against them too."

"This court is different. It *feels* different. As though we're always being watched. Like there's something in the walls... It feels wrong."

I'd felt it too; it felt like secrets. Something was very wrong with Justice's court. "Justice is hiding something. Razak knows what. He knows enough that they want him locked up but can't kill him, lest he spills all his secrets on the gallows. I have to go back to him. If I can find Pain's crown, it'll give *me* leverage over Razak. He needs it. With it, I'll demand Arin's freedom."

"So where is it?"

"He's going to tell me."

I stood and kicked the lid closed over War's crown, sealing it away once more. "Justice is looking for any excuse to put us all behind bars. Hide that somewhere more appropriate than under your bed." I opened the door and nodded for Danyal to enter. "Danyal, this is Draven. Draven, please meet Danyal." They glowered at each other like a pair of angry bears. "I'm sure you'll get along fabulously."

"And we're not killing the warlord now?" Danyal asked.

"No. It's complicated, but he's on our side. Mostly."

Draven arched an eyebrow at Danyal. "How much does this man know?"

"Enough. He killed for me. You can trust him. I want you both to find Noemi. She may help us, if she's free to. And she's the only one who's gotten close enough to Razak to stab him."

This was good, this was progress. We had War's crown, but Razak clearly had his own plans in motion. Plans we needed to disrupt.

"Lark?"

I looked back at Draven, seeing a man beaten down by his own actions. I understood now, why he hadn't run from the sandworm. Understood him a great deal more. Razak had made him a victim, like he had all of us.

"Free Arin," he said.

"You know I will."

He knew love, and he knew what it meant to do anything to protect it. I'd stop Razak, but not to free the people of Pain or for the prosperity of the shatterlands. I wasn't a hero. I'd stop Razak because he'd hurt Arin and would hurt him again. And for that alone, Razak deserved to die.

CHAPTER 32

ark

"BACK SO SOON, brother? It was inevitable. You've always needed me." Like before, Razak sat at the back of the cell, arms propped on his drawn-up knees, and peered at me, content and at ease with his surroundings. He appeared comfortable. Of course he did. He believed he pulled all our strings.

I could do this. I could talk with Razak without letting him inside my head. The only control he had was that which I gave him.

It sounded good, in theory, but when I stood inside his cell, and its gloom threatened to drag me inside with him, all my carefully woven notions of indifference and control unraveled. He only had to look at me for my body to recoil yet desire his approval, his acceptance. His touch.

I glanced behind me, back into the small doorway lit by

flickering oil lamps. Sonya had left, moving far enough away that she wouldn't hear our conversation. We were alone.

"All right." I stepped inside his cell. "I'll do what you want if you have Arin released."

"First, tell me, did you kill Draven for his treachery?"

How far did his reach extend? Would he know a lie? Not before this meeting ended. "He's no longer a concern."

Razak chuckled. "Shame, he was one of my favorite toys. So easily manipulated. Find the right screws and—" He motioned using his thumb to drive a screw into the dirt. "—they so easily give. He spilled all the secrets about you—so desperate was he to keep his son alive. He sent letters from Palmyra. The poor man seemed rather emotional over Arin choosing you, and then, of course, he revealed all the details of how you plotted to steal my crown from my court. How did that go for you?"

I hated him, hated every word that fell from his lips. "Bendrik is dead. I slit his wrists while he came in my hands. Malvina is gone too."

His smile vanished. "You killed Malvina?"

"Cut her throat."

He sent his gaze far away and flexed both hands into fists. "The council will be in turmoil. Oh well. They've served their purpose." His small laugh spoke of his uncaring heart. "How did it feel, brother, drawing the blade across her throat?"

He didn't need to know how Danyal had been the one to kill Malvina. Danyal was the wild card I had up my sleeve. "Meaningless. But Bendrik's death was positively climactic. Were you aware he had an unhealthy obsession for you?"

Something dark and hungry flashed in Razak's eyes. "You pretended to be me."

"I infiltrated your court, played at being you. I wore your

clothes, sat in your chair at the council table." I knelt in front of him. "And honestly, brother, I liked it."

"Did Bendrik fuck you?"

"He never made it that far."

"Good. Tell me how he died. Tell me everything."

I told him all of it, from the moment Bendrik trapped me in his dungeon to how the pool turned red with blood. By the time I was done, Razak had dropped his head back against the wall and closed his eyes. I knew that smirk. My tale excited him; the bulge in his trousers was evidence of that.

"I regret I wasn't there to relish in his demise as you clearly did. But reuniting the crowns is far more important."

I propped myself against the wall beside him, almost touching, shoulder to shoulder, and ignored all the instincts screaming to run. If he relaxed, he'd be more inclined to tell me things he perhaps shouldn't. Things like *reuniting* the crowns, suggesting they'd been together before, and that having them together was important again.

My tale still echoed in the dank air and now we were close, an electric tension sizzled between us. He turned his head. "You've come a long way from the soft little traitor's son you were when I first adopted you."

It almost sounded like pride, but it could equally be resentment, or disgust. He might loop the chain holding him to the wall around my neck at any moment, or he might praise me, tell me how good I'd been. I rarely saw the blow coming, whatever form it took. His smile was as difficult to read now as always.

I should have brought a blade, could have cut this throat...

"You love me."

It wasn't a question.

"Of course."

"Then say it."

"I love you."

He laughed. "No, do better."

I swallowed the inexplicable cloying lump in my throat. "I love you." They were just words, just three little words. Arin had my heart, and that was the truth. Razak had nothing.

He grasped my chin and held me an inch from his face. "Again."

Saliva pooled around my tongue. *I love you. I've always loved you.* I pushed passion behind it, made it sound real, but that passion was fueled by hate, not love. They weren't so different. *You saved me from the gallows. I owe you everything. I love you, brother.*

Was it enough? My heart hammered, pounding in my chest and my ears. He slammed a kiss on my lips, thrust his tongue in, and I could do nothing to stop him. So I kissed him back, forcing some meaning into it. I swept my tongue in with his and kissed him as though he were the sweetest thing I'd ever tasted, even if his kiss did burn like poison. I'd done worse than this. And for all its passion, it didn't touch my heart. The kiss ended naturally, and he pulled away, clutching my face in both hands.

He might break my neck, might tell me he loved me. I never knew how this ended.

"Get me the crown, and I'll let you have your prince, but we both know you will always be mine."

"Always," I whispered.

His soft, liquid chuckle coiled around me, trying to slither inside. He pressed his forehead to mine. "The crown is here, with my father," he whispered. "Locked in some deep, forgotten part of this wretched place. Find Umair, and you'll find the crown."

Umair was here?

"Is he alive?"

"No." He withdrew and rested against the wall again, his passion snuffed out. "He discovered their secret and they locked him away for it. They won't do the same to me. You're going to ensure it."

"What *secret*?" I dared ask.

"The key to everything." He smirked. "Hurry along, brother. I'm growing tired of this cell. It's time I wore my crown."

CHAPTER 33

rin

THE DOOR CLANGED, rousing me from an exhausted slumber. I rubbed at my crusted eyes and saw Lark in the doorway's brilliant glare.

In my sleep-addled mind, he glowed, like a mythical creature come to save me, but then, of course, reality washed back in. My body ached, my stomach clenched, and I remembered this was no dream. But Lark was here.

He stepped inside my cell, and sores be damned, I shot to my feet, lunged, and flung my arms around him. My chain clattered, trying to pull me down. Lark rocked, and his arms swept around me. He smelled of amber and jasmine, of flowers, of home. His warmth soaked through my ragged clothes. He felt real and he was here, and by Dallin, I couldn't stand to be alone another moment more.

Tears fell and I didn't care. I sobbed and didn't care about that either.

"It's all right. You're not alone." He stroked my hair and hummed a soft little tune. "I'm sorry, I haven't come to free you, not yet." His lips brushed my cheek as he spoke. "But I am working on it, I promise."

"It's all right, it's fine..." It wasn't, but none of that mattered, because he was here and in my arms and that was everything. "Please." I sobbed and laughed and brushed the wetness from my face as we parted. "Some good news? You must have some?"

He turned his head and nodded at the guard, dismissing him. He left the door open and probably wouldn't go far.

Lark swooped in a second time, wrapped me in a hug, and nuzzled my neck. "Missed you," he mumbled.

"Gods, you feel so good." It had felt like weeks since I'd had any kind of company. Longer, since we'd separated in the Court of Pain.

"Forgive me?"

"No, and yes." I blinked fast, clearing the blur in my vision, and clung to his arms.

He leaned back and his little, fragile smile broke my heart wide open. I'd always forgive him. The sharp edges of his brother's disguise remained, but his hair had gown some, turning ruffled and loose. His clothes were fine, now that I could see them in the light. Purple woven through black, and he wore the jacket loose, as though he didn't care for it. "You look good."

"Hm, Danyal had me eating forest critter for weeks, and it's surprisingly fattening."

I laughed and bumped my head against his. I yearned to have him alone again, in my arms, in a bed, the two of us without a care.

The room tilted; the floor tipped. I clung to Lark, heard him ask if I was all right. "Dizzy, that's all." He sat me down and scooted up next to me, so warm, I couldn't stop from leaning against him.

"You must eat, Arin."

"Don't care for it."

"I know where Pain's crown is. I'm going to get it and get you out. A day, maybe two."

I rested my head on his shoulder and closed my eyes. It was good he had a plan to get the crown, but right now, I just needed him here, with me.

"My prince of honey and sunshine was not made to be kept in darkness." His fingers teased through my hair, and it felt right, having him here.

I mumbled a sound of agreement and shuffled closer. If I closed my eyes and ignored the *plink-plink* of dripping water, I could almost imagine we were in my meadows. The sound of the ocean was a distant memory, but I hadn't forgotten all of it. If I dreamed hard enough, I'd hear it again, and taste salt on my lips.

A melody drifted on that sea breeze, a sweet little humming sound. I sighed and listened to Lark's spellbinding tune. Then, like the brightest of lights in the darkest of places, he began to sing. The tune was soft and delicate, like butterfly wings on that sea breeze. I'd never heard him sing, not like this. He'd recited poems and limericks, made fun of the rhythm, but this was something else. *"I remember the times we had together, the laughter and the joy we shared, but now the memories are all I have left, and it's more than I can bear,"* he sang, his voice hauntingly beautiful. *"The fire has gone out, the night is cold, and my heart is heavy with sorrow, but I know that someday we'll be together, and I'll wait for that tomorrow."*

He hummed the tune as a chorus, then began again. His voice chased away the dread and the cold and the despair. It likely sailed outside my cell too and echoed down the prison corridors. He'd told me magic was in the wonder, in the not knowing. *The world is dark enough, it needs a little magic to light the way.* Lark was my magic.

I'd ask him about the words, and the melody. But for now, all I wanted was for the tune to carry me far away from this nightmare and make me dream of the days we'd walked in the meadows together, and nothing and nobody could take that away.

CHAPTER 34

ark

I SANG my mother's lullaby over and over, falling into its waking dream. I sang until my voice grew hoarse, because not singing meant letting the silence in. I'd never feared the quiet before. It had always been a part of my life. But with Arin dozing against my shoulder, his world reduced to four walls and bars over a narrow window, the quiet threatened to swallow him. His mind wouldn't last much longer. He was not meant for places such as these.

But I was.

I stopped singing, and the hungry silence rushed in.

It was time.

After easing from Arin's side, I gently laid him down, climbed to my feet and left his cell without looking back. If I'd looked back, I'd have stayed. It pained me to leave him, but this had to be done. I hurried down the outer corridor, each step silent, and snuck by the guard, unseen.

Ahead, the stairwell led down as well as up toward the castle halls. I took the steps down, descending into darkness. Razak had said Umair was far below, as deep as the foundations, deeper perhaps. Find the king, find the crown. Once I had the crown, I had a degree of control over Razak.

As the gloom pushed in, I stole an oil lamp from its sconce and hurried on. Down and down, around and around. The stone risers blurred, my breath misted, and a chill tightened my skin. There were no oil lamps here. The darkness became so thick that should my oil lamp snuff out, I'd be blind. But that wasn't going to happen. I wouldn't be down here long.

The staircase corkscrewed deeper into the mountain. I didn't slow, didn't stop. If I were to be discovered, it would be over. Everything—Arin's freedom, the crowns, defeating Razak—hinged on finding Umair, and with him, Pain's crown.

I hit the bottom step and stumbled into darkness. My breath misted in the cold. I raised the lamp, fought off dizziness, and studied the thick gloom. My lamp's efforts illuminated a stone pathway, and after a few steps, a rock wall emerged, turning me right. Those walls had been left chiseled rough. This was nothing like the polished blue-silk-wrapped rooms in the castle high above me.

This was where Justice kept its secrets, deep inside the mountain where nobody would find them.

Pushing my light against the cloying dark, I walked on.

There was no sound, save that of my own racing heart and the lamp's spluttering.

No doors either. Just a tunnel toward darkness. But all tunnels led somewhere.

This had to be it, didn't it?

Ice dusted my clothes and nipped my fingers. I tucked my left hand inside my jacket, keeping it warm. The shivers trembled my hand holding the lamp, making the oil in its reservoir slosh and the flame splutter. If the lamp extinguished now, I'd struggle to find the path back.

I wasn't thinking about that, only moving forward.

Shivers turned to convulsions. It was too damn cold.

I hummed the lullaby. It was all I had—that and the lamp —to keep the darkness at bay. I sang it like my mother had sung it for me, and the darkness gobbled up my voice. The dark was so large, so thick, it seemed to be a living thing, watching me pass through, singing, with my single tiny flame. *"The fire has gone out, the night is cold, and my heart is heavy with sorrow, but I know that someday we'll be together, and I'll wait for that tomorrow."*

If I'd had my violin, I'd have played it and chased the dark away. But I only had my voice, and so I sang and shivered and walked, moving further and further from Arin, from Justice, from the shatterlands, from reality. Shadows moved in the darkness, swirls of dark on dark. My voice quivered. I stopped, listened.

It was nothing—just my mind playing tricks.

My halo of light washed over a vast wall barring the way. The wall was so large I couldn't find its edges. Markings gleamed on its surface. I raised the lamp, illuminating a dull, painted scene. A puff set the dust free, and color exploded. The art spoke of battles and bloodshed. I raised the lamp, moving it along the scene. Four crowns came into sight, placed in a square. Whoever had made these markings had crafted similar art in War's great pyramid temple. Here, like there, people knelt beneath the crowns, as though in worship.

No, not in worship. Their eyes— They'd been hollowed out, chipped from stone and left that way, without detail. These people weren't worshiping the crowns, they were their slaves. The crowns themselves seemed peculiar. They almost appeared broken, or that could have been cracks in the ancient art; my flame was too poor to see in any great detail.

Perhaps the scenes in War's pyramid had not been about just War's crown. Perhaps they'd been echoes of a past, and a warning for whoever ventured down here. But why hide such a thing so far beneath Justice's castle? Was this the great secret Razak had spoken of? It didn't seem too great a thing. Certainly not enough to warrant hiding it.

"My heart is heavy with sorrow, but I know that someday we'll be together, and I'll wait for that tomorrow," I sang softly.

My light slid across the art and pooled into a gap where the stone had crumbled away, exposing a hole. I crouched and angled the lamp inside. A breeze sucked at the flame, almost spluttering it out. A sense of space loomed beyond. There was a room on the other side of the wall.

Perhaps the wall was a door, and with my small light, I couldn't see its edges.

I'd come this far. I couldn't turn back without Pain's crown. If Umair had found this, he'd have made his way through, seeking the font on the other side.

On my hands and knees, I shuffled through the cramped, jagged hole and clambered out the other side into silence. A teasing wind encircled me, but the darkness didn't wane. If anything, it was heavier here, and beat against me in silent waves.

There had to be lamps or torches... something to light the way.

I stepped forward, once more using my tiny light to push the dark back. My toe struck rock—a channel of some kind. I followed it, then found a candelabra topped with half burned candles. I uncapped my lamp and lit the wicks, casting a larger glow, encompassing another collection of candles. I moved down the line, lighting each one, until I'd made a path of light to a column and the beginning of enormous stone blocks, stacked like giant steps.

This place had the feel of giants, like War's great walls and its enormous gate. I'd felt so small.

A sack of rags had been dumped on the second step. I raised my lamp, drew closer, and as the light highlighted the mound, familiar features took shape. Boots clad a pair of legs. A long coat draped from narrow shoulders. He'd had a face, but it was gone now, ravaged by time and obscured by dust. And on his lap sat a silver crown, studded with purple amethysts.

"Hello, Father."

My voice echoed in waves, coming back around, and then faded.

I climbed the first giant step and raised my lamp again. Light licked over amethyst gems and tarnished silver points. I'd thought War's crown was brutal, but Pain's was the most elaborate of all—and the sharpest. Thorns jutted from its sides, each one hungry for blood.

It gleamed, untouched by dust or dirt, as though it had been crafted just yesterday. Whereas time had devoured the body of the man who held it.

I climbed the next step and knelt beside him. He and I wore almost the exact same clothes, but his coat was long and woven with intricate purple roses. A coat fit for a king.

In the shifting shadows, I could almost see the ghost of his face. My memory filled in what decay had taken.

Umair.

"I wish I could say it's a pleasure to see you again, but time has not been kind."

I remembered the weight of his hand on my shoulder, steering me toward the hanging tree where my mother waited. Hands that were now bracketed against the crown. No, not bracketed—fixed in place by those vicious thorns.

But he wasn't chained here. It was as though he'd stopped to rest on the steps and never moved again. There were no signs of a struggle, no weapons on him, or nearby. I looked back at the enormous wall, now lit by the candelabra.

He'd come here, to this strange place, seeking a power, but he'd died here, with the crown on his knees. Why?

A small corner of paper poked from his coat pocket. I reached in and plucked it free. "You won't be needing this." The paper dusted my fingers, disintegrating under my touch. I set the lamp down and eased the paper's folded edges open.

My dear Umair, if there were one thing I'd wish, it would be for more time, but I see now we do not control our fates, and mine has come for me.

You must not blame our dear boy. He is but a babe, an innocent. I know this will be difficult. I know you will hurt, but I must walk again in the meadows. I wish you could have seen them. Perhaps one day, we will walk together again. Your beloved wife, Jocelyn.

It was strange, to read such softness directed toward a man I'd only ever known as cruel. Jocelyn had clearly loved him, and Razak.

He'd died brokenhearted, and alone, on a fool's errand for a power that probably didn't exist. He'd abandoned his son, blamed him for his wife's death, and left Razak behind, passing his hatred and spite on to him. All because of love.

I gently refolded the letter and tucked it back out of sight.

The crown drew my gaze.

Its barbs gleamed. I touched a fingertip to a spike's thin edge and felt its bite. The part of the crown designed to hug the head bristled with vicious points. However it was held or worn, it would cut its host.

I eyed Umair's coat. "Apologies, but that is a very fine coat and frankly, I deserve it more than you." I tugged and pulled it from his desiccated limbs. His body slumped to one side, and something brittle clattered down the steps, echoing all around like a ringing bell. I raised the coat in candlelight, lamented its beauty, and tossed it over the crown. "At least you gave me one good thing, Father." After bundling the coat and crown under my left arm, I picked up the lamp.

Whatever this place was, whatever truth Justice had hidden here, it had cost Umair everything, and Razak was on his way to joining our father on what was very likely a pointless quest.

My lamp shone over giant steps leading higher, into more darkness above. If I climbed them, what awaited at the top? Another painted wall or the real reason Umair had come all this way only to die on these steps?

My lamp's reservoir was half full. I had enough oil to last the return journey.

There were secrets here. Secrets Justice didn't want told. If I could discover them, I'd have the same power as Razak, perhaps more.

Razak knew why Umair had died on these steps, he knew why our father had forsaken everything for a power he'd tried to find. If I was going to stop Razak, I had to know what he knew.

I began to climb.

With the crown and lamp to maneuver, I struggled after making it up five of the gigantic risers. On the sixth, the lamplight washed over the base of a huge pillar—one of many holding up a vast portico decorated with molded flowers. War's stone, and now flowers? Was it a coincidence these courtly elements decorated a hidden temple beneath Justice, or deliberate? It was said, long ago, Dallin brought the courts together to give them their crowns, and harmony reigned. I'd never believed it. How could Pain and Love find harmony? How could War and Justice set aside their differences? Yet, this strange place had echoes of such a balance.

Balance is all.

I ventured beneath the arch, using the lamp's halo of light to guide me, and entered a huge, arena-like space, so large the lamp's light didn't touch any sides. I'd walked onto a stage. The deeper I ventured, the more peculiar this place became. Was it enough just to know it was here? Would Justice free Arin if I revealed I'd been here?

Only if I knew what it all meant, and I didn't. Not yet.

Grit scuffed under my boot. I glanced down and kicked more sand aside, revealing swirling patterns beneath. Kneeling, I swept more away, chasing the swirls in a far larger design, until coming to a point at the circle's center and the words: *Balance is all.*

The crowns, balance, the shatterlands' people on their knees... The pieces were all here, but why?

I stood and eyed my boot prints in the dust. Razak knew, like Umair had known. I had the crown. It would have to be enough.

"You'll have to keep your secrets," I told the quiet.

A blast of wind surged. Sand whipped around me, blasting my boot prints away. My lamp spluttered, the flame clung on. "Wait!" The flame died, plunging me into darkness. The other candles must have snuffed out too. The wind vanished as suddenly as it had arrived, leaving me alone, panting in the silent dark.

I'd have to find my way back in the dark?

No, no... perhaps some of the candles below, near where I'd crawled in, still flickered.

Something skittered to my right, pebbles falling...

If I just walked ahead, I'd come to an edge, eventually. I had to.

This was... fine. Get to the top of the giant steps, and there would probably be light below.

More pebbles trickled, this time from my left. Something was out there, moving around me.

"The fire has gone out," I sang softly, wincing at the prophetic words. *"The night is cold, and my heart is heavy with sorrow, but I know that someday we'll be together, and I'll wait for that"*—the ground jolted—*"tomorrow."*

A thunderous rumble trembled below. A roar grew louder, like the roar of the waves near Arin's secret beach. But there was no beach here, and no waves to roar. The ground gave a sudden jerk, almost spilling me to my knees. I swayed, clinging to the crown and unlit lamp. Stone grated on stone, tilting, slanting. I staggered, stumbled.

"The night is cold."

An almighty crack sounded behind me.

"And my heart is heavy with sorrow."

Sand hissed, like a thousand snakes. The floor shifted, tipped, and vanished from under me. My insides swooped upward, then my feet struck the ground, slamming me to the ground. The crumbling, cracking, and hissing grew, encroaching all around. The dark amplified all sound. Icy dust touched my lips and burned my eyes. Grit burned under my hands. Too much, it was all too much. If the walls crumbled in, I'd be crushed here. Nobody would come, Arin was caught, Draven had his son, I had nothing—

Lightning bolted from the dark. It pierced my chest and plunged into my heart like a needle through lace. Dark turned to blinding light. I gasped, arched backward, and reached out for help, with nowhere to go and nothing to see.

I was ablaze but so cold, alight but unharmed.

This was it.

This was the font that had driven Umair to die down here and pushed his son toward madness. This was the thing they all sought, the secret hidden beneath Justice. And now it was *in me.* My breath froze in my lungs, my heart turned to stone in my chest—still there, but heavy. And the power held me in its embrace, so blinding, as though I held a star in my hands.

It wasn't bad, or good, but it was powerful. And it wanted *me.* It desired and burned and roared for more. Lust and obsession, gluttony and greed. It surged through my veins, promising freedom, and all it wanted was love and life and passion.

I buckled under it and wrapped my arms around me. If I let it in, nobody would stand in my way, no law could stop me, no bars would hold me. I'd never be chained again. And I wanted that. To be free, to be strong, to make others pay for the agony I'd endured. To take vengeance on the world that had taken my mother, taken my life and beat me down to dust. I wanted them all to hurt, to pay—

But it would be wrong. This strange power, although starved, was a beautiful thing. By Dallin, I wasn't strong enough to hold it, control it. It would burn me up. I wanted it, desired it, craved it even, but my heart wouldn't survive. *I* wouldn't survive.

I tried to push it out, to fight the onslaught, but the more I fought, the more it churned. It would be easier to let it win, to take it and make it mine, to twist it, to climb a throne and make the world kneel at my feet. Easier to embrace it as mine.

"Zayan!" Razak's cry pierced the maelstrom. "Take my hand!"

I lifted my head and looked through the lashing tendrils of light. He reached down, hand extended, his face full of fear

—for me. How was he here? Why wasn't he in his prison cell? It didn't matter, he'd come to save me.

If I didn't take his hand, I'd lose to the light. And this couldn't be my end.

"Brother!" His eyes burned. "It's killing you! Take my hand!"

Was he really here? Or was this some fantasy I'd summoned to save my sanity? I lived in fantasy. Made each one mine. But I couldn't live here. Power like this was not meant for gutter whores like me. I loosened the crushing hold I'd locked around myself and reached out.

"Yes, take my hand!" Razak stretched closer, fingers splayed.

Razak was my only way out.

"Take it, brother."

He lunged, grasped my hand, and the moment my mangled hand met his, the onslaught of light and hunger and lust pushed from me *into* him. He lurched backward, struck by its blow, and dragged me with him. We tangled together on the floor, discarded there in a sudden, gasping quiet.

A woman stood over us with a flickering lamp. I blinked at her veiled face. "Soleil?"

"The seal is broken," she said. "The crowns are too close. We must return and send the crowns far—"

Razak's laugh cut her off. His laughter rolled with a thick, ironic knowing.

I crawled off him and stumbled to my feet, needing to move, to breathe and feel my heart beat in my chest. "The light?" I spun. "Where is it?" We were still in the clutches of the dark arena but with Soleil's light illuminating a gaping hole in the floor. Guilt pushed down while shock left me reeling. Had I done this? Had I... broken the seal?

"Thank you, Zayan." Razak remained on his back on the

floor. He lifted his hand, and turned it over, admiring it. "This gift is quite remarkable."

Gift?

"What have you done?" Soleil said *to me*.

"I..." What *had* I done? I'd been lost, drowning. I'd reached for Razak...

"Yes, yes, this is what perfection feels like." Razak thrust out a hand and a whip of savage cold slammed down my spine. I dropped, gasping, and felt my brother's touch plunge deep inside, violating the most vulnerable parts of me. My love, my heart, my soul.

Our touch—I hadn't stopped the light, I'd passed it to him. I'd *wanted* him to have it, because I couldn't bear its weight.

"Oh yes." He smirked and rolled onto his side, propping himself on his elbow with his left hand still extended, fingers clawed, as though he gripped my soul. "Thank you, dearest brother. You've just made me a god."

He crushed his hand into a fist, and I screamed.

CHAPTER 35

rin

THE CELL FLOOR SHUDDERED, stirring me from a restless sleep. The Court of War had quakes in the earth, from sand-worms tunneling around their foundations. But this was Justice. There were no giant worms here. Were there? I dozed again, drifting, dreaming, until the screech of the cell door yanked me back to wakefulness and a guard stomped in.

He knelt, slipped a key in my shackles, and the cuff clattered loose. I looked at it, there on the floor, then at the guard. Was I dreaming again? I'd dreamed Lark had come and sung a lullaby. Or had that been real?

"You're free to go." He grabbed my arm and hauled me to my feet.

"What?" This didn't make any sense. I brushed grit from my sore wrist, finding it light without the chain holding me down. "Why?"

"I always find it best not to ask them's in power," he

grouched. "Come along. I've been tasked with getting you cleaned up. Let's get to it. We've got some work to do."

While I wasn't going to argue, the ease with which I'd been freed didn't seem real either. Was this another part of another dream? Gods, why couldn't I think clearly?

What could make Justice turn around and free me without a trial? Only Soleil had such power. Had the queen realized my innocence?

The guard guided me through the cell door, and I blinked into sharp light.

"You there." Draven marched up the corridor with a second, older man following behind. "Let him go."

I hadn't seen Draven since the prison wagon had carted me away from my home.

The guard said something along the lines of he'd already freed me, but all I could see and hear was Draven. His stoic expression gave little away, and his clothes marked him as a lord of War. Had he come to gloat? He stopped, focused on the guard, demanding to know where I was being taken.

I didn't think, just swung my fist, connecting it triumphantly with his jaw. He barely rocked, but the blow did whip his head to the side. And it felt good, even as pain shot down the back of my hand. Satisfying. "Betrayer." I spat at his boots.

He flinched. "I deserved that."

"I see why Lark likes you," the aging, grey-haired man said.

I'd seen his weathered face before somewhere but couldn't place where. None of this made any sense. "What is happening?"

"My name is Danyal," he said, dipping his chin. "I'm Lark's *advisor*."

Lark had an advisor? What kind of advisor?

Everything moved too fast. I was out of the cell, apparently free, and now Draven was here. And this stranger. I couldn't trust either of them, not without Lark's word. "Where *is* Lark?"

"I came to ask you," Draven said. "He went to Razak, to find the er..." He glanced at the guard. "The *item* Razak has been searching for. That was yesterday."

He'd gone to Razak and hadn't been seen since? Oh no. For all Lark's wonderful bravado and his promises to free me, Razak was his one fear, and his weakness. I was free, which meant Lark had done *something*. "I have to speak with Lark."

I'd started forward when the guard caught my arm. "You can't go anywhere until you're checked over by a healer and cleaned up."

"You said I was free." I pulled my arm from his grip.

"My orders were to free you and take you to your room. That's what I'm going to do."

"I'll take him," Draven said, reaching out.

I whirled on him, the anger bright and sharp. "If you so much as touch me I will fight you, and I will not stop until one of us is no longer moving. Do you hear me, Draven?"

I stepped forward, intending to go find Razak's cell myself and demand where Lark was, but the floor and walls tilted and my head spun. Draven lunged, trying to scoop me out of my fall. I shoved him away and glared, then staggered back and fell against the wall. The dizziness would clear soon. "I need a moment."

The guard, Draven, and Danyal stared.

"You need decent food, clean water, and rest," Draven said, then shrank away when I leveled my stare on him. This was *his* fault. He'd done this to me.

"I'm sorry," he muttered. "I explained to Lark... The things I did, I never meant to hurt you."

"You explained to Lark, and I'm... what? Supposed to forgive you now, because he did?"

"He didn't forgive me, actually. He said it was you I needed to apologize to, so here I am."

It wasn't enough. He'd put me here, in chains. It would never be enough. Gods, why was it so hot in here and when would the shivering stop?

The guard muscled in and caught my arm again. "Continue whatever reunion this is in your own time. I've got a job to do. Talk and walk, if you prefer, but I'm getting this man to his room."

The walk gave me time to go over all I knew, which wasn't much. Lark had come to me, he'd sung a haunting song, or had I dreamed his visit? Everything had fragmented in my head, memories and dreams mingling. But I was free, that much was true. Lark must have freed me. Did that mean he'd found the crown and given it to Razak? All the questions chased themselves around my head. The guard left me in a warm, comfortable room, with a roaring fire and fine clothes folded on the bed. He said a healer would be along and left.

I blinked at my bright, clean, blue and white alien surroundings, then down at my filthy hands and clothes. I didn't want to be here, didn't want any of this. It all felt wrong, as though I was a stranger inside my own skin.

A knock came at the door. "Arin, it's me."

Draven.

I dropped onto the edge of the bed and buried my face in my hands. If my head would just stop spinning, I could think. Lark... Where was Lark?

"You shouldn't be alone," Draven said, still shut out.

"I'd rather be alone than with you."

"I'm sorry."

"You had me arrested."

"Allow me to explain?"

"Go away." I needed Lark. Only Lark. I needed his hand in mine and his soft voice in my ear. This place, with its creeping walls and clanging doors, Draven and his lies, Razak pulling all our strings—it was too much. The smell of wet rot wafted from my clothes and my whole body trembled. I chuckled into my hands. I was losing my damn mind and I really was alone.

Breathe.

I had to breathe, to slow everything down.

Lark had found the crown. He'd given it to Razak. Razak had pulled whatever strings he held in the court of Justice and had me released, just as Lark had said he would. That must have happened, for me to be sitting on the bed.

"Damn it, Arin. If you don't answer me, I'll kick this door in. Hit me again. I don't care. You need help." Draven thumped on the door. "Arin? You shouldn't be alone."

"Open the damn door, if you must!"

He pushed in, then stopped halfway to the bed, pinned under my glare. Danyal, the stranger, was no longer with him.

"I don't trust you," I said. "I don't know who you are. Why did you do this to me? To us?!"

"Razak has my son."

His son? "I don't..."

Oh, the names on the documents. His son's name had been among those listed? "Tell me everything."

He talked and talked, About the letter from Razak outing Lark as my court's fool; the demands from Razak to do more, discover more, lie more; and finally, to accuse me of treason against War and ultimately to bring me to Justice as leverage against Lark. Draven had done it all to protect his son. As he talked, he heated water over the fire and readied the wash-basin, and all I could do was watch and listen and try to forgive him, but it was too raw, too much. A good man would forgive him.

"I needed you to know. It was wrong," he said, when he was done. "I regret every lie, every hurt I've put you through. I'm sorry, Arin, truly."

"Was our joining a lie?"

"I almost wish it had been."

So did I. I nodded and had no idea what to say. I'd trusted him, and he'd been lying to us from the beginning. I couldn't forgive him. Might *never* forgive him.

"I'll go. When this is over, and you're safe with Lark. You'll never have to see me again."

"Don't wait. Leave now."

Gulping, he turned away and left the room. When the door swung shut behind him, I covered my face and sobbed, furious, hurt, lost, and so damn tired. I'd be all right, I just needed to wash the filth off and find the pieces of myself so I could put them back together.

With the tears drying, I washed the prison dankness off, shaved my face clean, and dressed in the fine clothes. A pale, blue-eyed, golden-haired prince stared back at me from the mirror, but he was hollow. I tried to remember how to be the Prince of Love again, but I didn't feel the same as before. Some part of me had been torn out and tossed aside. It wasn't all Draven—it was *everything*.

I needed Razak out of my life, out of all our lives.

A knock sounded on the door. "Draven, so help me, if you do not give me time to think I will swing at you." I yanked the door open—and found a young red-haired woman staring back. "Noemi?"

Her blue eyes shone, brittle with fear, but her voice, when she spoke, was as solid as ice. "You must gather your belongings and leave. Immediately."

"What's going on? Are you all right? You were arrested in War. I wasn't sure I'd ever see you again."

"Prince Arin, there's no time." She glanced behind her and wet her lips. "You must leave. Take your troupe with you."

"My troupe?"

"Warlord Draven, Lark? They didn't travel with you?"

"Yes, but no. I mean, I was arrested. I've only just been released."

Her mouth fell open. "I... I'm sorry, I did not know. They didn't say. Of course they didn't... Regardless—" She smoothed her blue cloak down, sweeping away the kinks. "—there's no time for this, you must go—"

"Noemi, do you know why I was freed?"

"No, Arin. I'm sorry. I don't know anything. Just that, please—you must go. Take the west bridge. And hurry. The bridges will soon be cut." She took a step back into the corridor and glanced over her shoulder a second time, clearly concerned she'd be seen. She wasn't supposed to be here.

"What's happening?"

"I fear something terrible."

Others spilled from their rooms into the corridors, coats on and cases under their arms.

Draven emerged from the room next to mine. "Noemi... What's happening? Have you seen Lark?"

"No, you're the only ones I've seen. I came to you, only to you. And you must go. I'm sorry. I can't say any more. Leave, and everything will be all right." She backed away again, desperate to leave.

"Lark is missing," I said, hoping to keep her here. She knew more but was afraid.

"I don't..." She blinked.

"We can't leave without him," Danyal said, emerging from Draven's room. A piece of the past flashed into my mind—a man standing beside Lark, beneath the old oak tree outside my palace. He was the man Lark had told my court's secrets too. He worked for the Court of Pain.

Draven had told me War's crown was here. Pain's crown was here too, assuming Lark had found it. Justice's crown was, of course, nearby. And my father's crown of Love? What if that was also close? Razak had taken it long ago... But it seemed as though all the pieces had begun to fall into place. Draven's story told of how he'd sent himself War's crown, sent it here. What if Razak had done the same? "Noemi, tell me. Was there a package sent here, several months ago now? Sent for Razak's attention?"

"I'm sorry, I don't know about any packages. I have to go—"

"Wait." I stepped into her path. "Is this because of the crowns?"

She stiffened, fighting her fear back. "Please, you must go."

"The crowns are here, aren't they? Razak brought them together." Yes, that was why we were all here. Razak had maneuvered Draven, me, and Lark. He'd planned everything down to the finest detail. Then, with my freedom and Lark's absence, one thing seemed obvious. My heart sank. "Is Razak free?"

She didn't need to answer; the truth was clear in her fearful eyes.

Justice had set Razak free.

WE STARED at the empty cell that had, until a few hours ago, held Razak.

"There's no fucking justice here," Draven growled.

An open cuff lay on the floor. None of the guards had seen him—we'd asked—and none appeared to know who had released him. It seemed as though the Prince of Pain had evaporated from behind his bars like mist. And nobody cared either. The guards all bustled about, distracted by calls for aid and a commotion elsewhere in the castle.

"How does someone as conspicuous as Razak disappear?" I whispered.

"They have help," Danyal said.

Then Justice was as corrupt as all the other courts, it had to be.

I turned my gaze to Noemi, still with us but conspicuously quiet at the back of our group. The crowns were likely here, and Razak was free and able to do as he pleased. Everything he'd wanted, had planned, had come to pass.

Had we already lost?

Several more guards ran by the end of the corridor. Did nobody care their prisoner was missing? Someone had to be in control of this circus, someone must have been able to stop Razak. The only person with enough power in Justice was the queen herself. "Queen Soleil must be informed of Razak's escape."

"Arin, please." Noemi wrung her hands and averted her gaze. "You must leave."

She bit her lip and shook her head. Danyal and Draven saw it now too. She knew more. "You helped us before, Noemi. Your own people arrested you for it. Something is very wrong in Justice, and you know it." I gently touched her arm, prompting her to look up. "I'm asking for help. I'm asking for you to do the right thing—"

"This is the right thing, to save your life. He said you must go!"

"*He...* What do you know? Is it about Lark? Do you know

331

where he is?" My grip on her arm tightened, and she stepped back, pulling free. If she knew the truth behind what was happening here, then she perhaps knew where Lark was.

"Arin?" Draven said from behind me. "She doesn't know anything."

I ignored him. Noemi bumped against the wall, and I stepped closer. "I will find Lark, whatever it takes. If you know where he is, tell me."

"Love is the most powerful of the courts," she whispered. "The most balanced."

I braced an arm against the wall, fencing her in. "Yet my court was the first to fall."

She blinked bright blue eyes. "It's why Razak undermined yours first. He knew, without Love underpinning the shatterlands, the others would soon fall. It has always been known by Justice. Much is known within these walls. Balance is... all."

I leaned close, so close she had nowhere to go, no escape. Noemi had helped Lark in the past. She'd helped me to realize the truth of Lark. And she knew the truth of what was happening now. *"Tell me everything."*

"Arin, let her go," Draven warned, but he didn't get to level righteousness on me after all the wrong he'd done.

"Dallin forged the crowns and created four courts," she said. "But it wasn't for harmony as the tales suggest. He didn't want peace. The courts were made to be at odds, forever in conflict, circling each other in a terrible, bloody dance. War, Justice, Pain, Love, they can never be balanced. Dallin did all this to guarantee the crowns would forever be kept apart."

"What happens when the crowns are brought together, Noemi?"

"I do not know, for certain. There is nothing in the libraries. I looked for weeks once I was freed after serving my punishment. But there is not just nothing. There is an absence of information. The truth has been erased from Justice."

"But you have an idea?"

She nodded, glancing over my shoulder at the two men and then back into my eyes. "I think... the crowns are a key to something hidden deep in the past. Something so terrible it's been erased so none would seek it."

"But Razak *is* seeking it."

"His father did too. I'm certain Umair was shut away and forgotten because of it."

The letters. Razak knew his father had been killed by Justice, and he knew what his father sought. Now he had the crowns close by, the key within his grasp. But a key to what? Razak had said he wanted to be a god. What secret could be so powerful? "And why must we leave now?"

"The tremors? You've felt them? I think... I think whatever secret the crowns unlock has been opened."

"Then..." I eased back, giving her room to breathe now she was finally spilling her court's secrets. "The font has been found?"

She nodded. "Cracks have appeared in the castle walls. Everyone is being told to leave, not just guests. I fear Justice is falling too."

I was right, Razak was winning. Even now, as we raced to catch up, he was out there somewhere, laughing at everyone. "You said *he*. Who told you to come and find us? Who told you to make sure we leave?"

Her eyes fluttered closed, and she whispered, "Razak."

Damn her. We'd wasted so much time already. "Where is he?"

"Arin." Tears glistened in her eyes. "It's too late. Please, just go..."

"It's never too late to do the right thing." I started back down the corridor. There had to be a way to find him. Where would he go? The crowns. He needed those wretched crowns. "Draven, you said you have War's crown?"

The warlord hurried into pace alongside me with Danyal behind us. "Yes, in my chambers."

"Good. Then whatever has been set into motion, he can't yet have full control? Noemi?" She followed too, keeping pace as we raced from Razak's cell. "Tell me where Razak is. Where did you see him?"

"An aide summoned me to the library. He waited there, and said you'd only listen to me, and that I was to see to it you left or he'd kill you."

"He keeps trying. I'm not so easily pushed aside."

"I think... I *know* where he's going." She raced ahead, blue gown rippling. The castle gave a trembling shudder underfoot. "Follow me, quickly. I fear we don't have much time."

We ran through Justice's huge, vaulted corridors, moving against a stream of people fleeing toward the main hall. Tremors continued, rattling grit and dust from the castle's vaulted ceilings. Whatever the reason, Justice really did appear to be coming undone.

Noemi stopped outside a door inlaid with countless tiny sapphires, like a scattering of stardust. An uncomfortable low-level resonating hum sounded from inside.

"Is this the queen's chamber?"

Noemi hesitated with her back to me and pressed a hand to the door. She whispered something like a prayer. "This court is the most sacred of places. In here, all our fates are decided."

"What's the noise?"

"You hear it too? I don't know."

"We should better prepare—" Draven said, attempting to stall.

Muffled voices came from beyond the door. I moved closer, hearing a voice I'd come to despise. Razak was inside. "Does he have Lark?" I asked, dreading the answer.

She nodded, and renewed rage set my heart ablaze.

Nothing and nobody was stopping me from saving Lark.

CHAPTER 36

rin

THE ROOM NOEMI had claimed was the source of all our fates resembled a theatre, with stepped benches around a central staging area. A lone podium stood in the middle of the floor, from which accused prisoners would stand, desperate to plead their innocence.

The most guilty of them all stood there now.

"Razak."

His clothes hung off him, so much so that I almost didn't recognize the prince beneath the filth. But there was no mistaking the crown atop his head, purple and black and bristled with jagged edges. Pain's crown.

"Are you a king now?" I asked coolly, while my thoughts raced to absorb the scene we'd walked into.

Blood streaked his pale face. But I didn't care about him, or Queen Soleil, on her hands and knees, as though bowing to

Razak. I cared only for Lark, standing behind his brother's right shoulder, like his shadow.

Lark didn't move, didn't look up, didn't acknowledge anyone. He stared at a point far away.

"Ah, of course they do not listen," Razak tutted and gestured at the inconvenience of having us interrupt him. "I said they wouldn't, brother." He spared Lark a glance before his gaze snapped back to me.

I kept moving, kept reading everything we'd interrupted. A veil obscured the kneeling queen's face, hiding her expression, but her shoulders heaved from sobbing. And the strange, bone-tremblingly deep hum grew louder now.

Razak pointed a finger at me. "You should not be here, Love's prince." He smirked, clearly delighted I was. "Let it be known, I did try and send you away, to save you. But now you've come, you may witness my rising."

As I gave him a wide berth, the bench behind him slowly came into sight. On it, laid out in a neat row, sat the three remaining crowns, including War's. Had Draven handed it over, after claiming he'd had it? I threw a glare back at the warlord, but he was too consumed with marching toward Razak.

"How?" Draven snarled. His face fell, and Razak's grin grew.

"You're entirely too predictable, Draven," Razak said. "Keeping War's crown under your bed? Really?"

Draven growled and lurched. I lunged and blocked him, holding him back, then shook my head. Something was very wrong here—more than the obvious—something I couldn't explain. A bone-chilling cold misted our breath and the chill of it tightened my skin. And the noise, it went on, with no beat, no pause, just an endless drone.

The walls gave a shudder, and with it, Razak's smile grew.

"Yes." Pain's prince laughed. "Oh yes! I'm going to bring it all down."

Lark remained unmoving, lifeless and empty, with his head bowed and his dark hair curtaining his eyes. He usually lit up every room he walked into. But his stillness didn't seem real, as though my eyes lied, and he wasn't here at all.

"Lark?" I asked.

He didn't respond. "Lark?" Again, this time without hiding my fearful quiver.

Razak pretended to finally notice his brother and barked a startling laugh. "It seems *Lark* is no longer with us."

Vicious hate and fear muddied my mind, trying to unbalance me all over again. But I couldn't lose here, not to Razak. "What have you done to him?"

"Saved him." Razak rolled his hand. "He was lost in the dark. Dear Soleil and I found him, and with him, the seal he'd broken and the power my father sought. The font of all desire."

Were we too late, after everything we'd been through? Was Razak about to become a god?

"You're just a man in a crown, Razak."

He laughed. "My father wished to bring my mother back from the dead. She hailed from your court, the wretched Court of Love." Razak hiccupped a laugh. "Did you know?"

"What?" His mother wasn't from Pain?

"You knew, you read the letters. He blamed *me* for her death. *Love*," he scoffed. "So tragically pathetic."

But I hadn't read all the letters, just the few Lark had grabbed. "I don't understand."

He snorted. "Of course you don't. Nobody *understands*. Everyone has it wrong. Except me. The dead are dead, as Zayan discovered when he plucked my crown from our father's desiccated corpse." Razak dipped his chin and pointed at the crown fixed on his head. "My mother's sickness meant she was far beyond saving, but Father would not accept it. He believed he could bring her back using the secret Justice kept from us all. He found it, you see, knowledge of their secret, deep in our vault. The evidence is all around for those who know to look, despite Justice's efforts to erase it."

"Razak, stop this—"

"Had they not hidden this vital piece of history, he'd have known you can't bring the living back from the clutches of death. Desire is not the same as resurrection." He grinned. "But I know its truth... He left me with scraps of information, pieces of a puzzle it took years to solve."

Razak stepped from the podium, enjoying his performance. Lark remained standing, unresponsive. I could feel his absence, even as I looked right at him. The man there was as empty as a reflection.

"Our souls, the parts of us that make us feel," Razak continued, clutching his hand to his heart as though he had one. "The essence of desire, of hate, of all the things that make us living creatures—*that* force is eternal, and that is the power and the truth Justice tried to hide. Isn't that right, Soleil?" Razak snatched a fistful of the kneeling queen's hair and yanked her head up.

He tore the veil away and tossed it into the air, where it fluttered back down to the floor beside the pair. With the veil gone, he'd taken her mystique too, turning her from a faceless judge into a mere woman, on her knees and beaten.

"You'll never control it," the queen snarled, clutching at his arm, trying to pry him off. "I should not have helped you. You're no god."

He threw her to the floor and marched back to Lark,

where he grabbed him by the neck and drove him to his knees.

My heart lurched. I started forward; Draven moved too. "Razak, Dallin help me, if you hurt him I will finish what we began in my court."

Razak snorted. "The court I burned as you lay bleeding? Oh, do stop pretending you and your dimwitted warlord are anything to me but a nuisance. I'm embarrassed for you. Truly." He stroked a finger down Lark's cheek, slid it under his chin, then clamped his neck, squeezing hard. "Another step, *Arin*, and I'll break Zayan's pretty neck."

I jolted to a stop, stopping Draven too. "You won't. You love him."

Razak's grin turned vicious. "As an only child, you would think that." He bent forward to study Lark's blank face, then lifted his glare through dark lashes.

Murder gleamed in Razak's eyes. I hung back.

Razak jerked his chin. "It has taken years to get to this moment, so *you will fucking listen,* Arin."

I clamped my jaw shut and glared.

"Dallin, the self-proclaimed god of this world before it became the shatterlands, sealed the font of all the combined essences, claiming it was too dangerous a power to be toyed with. But in truth, he kept it for himself."

Razak was surely mad. None of this made any sense. Yet, Lark had not moved or called out or so much as looked my way. He knelt, statue-still. Real, but not. Where was his smirk, his swagger, his fire? Where was my Lark?

"You needn't worry. Zayan is fine." Razak laughed, stepping behind Lark. He stroked Lark's neck, fingers dancing, and I knew he'd had him on his knees like this before, forcing Lark to do all the things Razak's horrible mind could conjure. "Perhaps even improved. He's far more *obedient* like this."

"Lark, please answer me." I needed something, anything, a sign he was all right.

"He's gone," Soleil rasped. "The scales of balance have tipped too far. This is the beginning."

Gone. Gone where? What did that even mean?

Razak tutted at the queen. "A demonstration, I think. I've been waiting a very long time for this. Watch, Love's prince, Warlord Draven, the administrator—yes, I know who you are, Danyal—and whatever that woman's name is, you at the back there."

"Noemi. I stabbed you in War, remember?"

He narrowed his eyes. "Oh yes. Thank you for that, Noemi. Your attack improved the believability of my incarceration. Now watch as a new god rises."

He thrust into the air behind Soleil and snapped his fingers together. Soleil threw her head back, let out a shrill scream, and her body arched. Razak hadn't touched her, but her wail spoke of a visceral agony. The scream came from inside of her and rose in an ear-splitting shriek.

Razak snatched his hand back, Soleil jerked, the cry cut off, and the Queen of Justice dropped like a sack of rice.

"Soleil?" I ran to her side and touched her shoulder. She breathed; her eyes were open, but dull and unseeing. She didn't respond at all, just stared somewhere far away. Exactly like Lark. "What have you done?"

Razak's thick laughter swirled around us all. "Oh, nothing really, just removed her passion. Without a will to live, you are nothing. And trust me, Arin, this is all the bitch deserves. The Queen of Justice saw to it my father rotted beneath her feet. I have long awaited the moment when her callous actions would be the catalyst for my glorious ascension."

"Enough!" I snapped, and shot to my feet. "You're not a god, Razak. You're a sad, broken boy of a man, lashing out because his father abandoned him. Stop it, Razak. Go back to Pain, sit on your throne, and make your council dance for you, if they'll have you. Your insanity ends here."

Razak blinked, then spat an unimpressed laugh. "Dance, you say? What a grand idea. Zayan?" He clicked his fingers. "My beloved brother. Won't you dance for your precious Prince of Love? And make it good. It'll be the last performance of yours he'll ever see."

Lark climbed to his feet, but his movements were jagged and wooden. He began to dance to silent music; he spun and dipped and swayed, pirouetting around us, and every glimpse of his face showed a flat, empty mask. But his eyes, those were the worst of it. His eyes were empty, soulless pits of darkness. His passion, his delight, and his love for dance, for music, for life... It was all gone. *Taken.*

It was worse than had he been killed.

"No, stop... Razak, stop!" I turned on the spot, tracking Lark's every step. This was wrong. This wasn't Lark. He wouldn't want this. Razak controlled him. It felt like the worst betrayal of all, like a violation of Lark's most precious self—as though Razak had stolen his soul.

Razak laughed and Lark spun, pirouetted, stepped, and swayed—a puppet dancing on the end of Razak's strings.

"You're a dead man, Razak," Draven threatened. "Lark, stop!"

Lark dipped in front of me, almost close enough to reach out and grab. And then—by some miracle—as he rose, mischief sparkled in his beautiful eyes.

I choked on a sob of relief that sounded like grief. The mischief was there and gone again, like a star streaking across the night sky, then he danced on, much to Razak's laughing delight.

Lark was still in there. More than that, Lark's dance was a lie. All of this was a lie.

"My beautiful lie," I whispered.

"He does not deserve this!" Danyal surged off his back foot. "You have no right, you pathetic excuse for a prince."

Razak's glee vanished, severed at the source. He eyed Danyal anew, and Lark danced—away from his brother, toward the display of crowns.

"Back for revenge, Danyal?" Razak asked.

Danyal strode on, moving past me, approaching Razak. "I helped Zayan's mother escape Umair's clutches. I've been watching over Zayan since the day he was born. He's more of a prince than you'll ever be, you rat bastard. You've tortured him enough." Danyal sneered, now only a few strides from Razak.

Lark stepped and spun, heading for the crowns behind Razak...

Noemi saw it too. With Razak's attention on Danyal, Razak missed how Lark's dance abruptly ended. He dashed toward the crowns.

Razak threw his arms up and laughed. "Torture? Now there's an idea! I am the Prince—excuse me—*King* of Pain. Oh brother?" Razak snapped his fingers. "Come, kneel and lick my hand for all to see." Razak whipped is head around as Lark snatched Love's gold and pearl crown from off the bench. Lark spun and tossed the crown into the air, toward me.

Razak let out a roar.

Time slowed. The crown spun overhead. I reached but caught sight of Razak in the corner of my vision. He reached out too, but not to stop the crown. He reached with his fingers splayed, toward me, like he had Soleil, and his twisted expression was all the warning I had.

Ice slammed into my chest and burrowed down my throat. I gasped, choked, stumbled—my body locked, and my every thought screeched to a halt. The crown crashed to the floor. I dropped, gasping. As quickly as the assault had begun, it vanished.

I looked up.

Lark's advisor, Danyal, stood between Razak and I, absorbing Razak's attack. Danyal's back arched, his body buckled, and a wail of agony left his lips.

Lark swooped in, grabbed me and then the fallen crown, and we bolted toward Draven and Noemi, toward the door. Ice still crackled in my chest, making each breath pull glass from my lungs, but I was alive and moving.

Danyal's screams went on, joined by Razak's furious roar.

We bolted from the room and raced down a corridor, out into the main lobby with its huge vaulted ceilings and dramatic sweeping staircase. Noemi sprinted ahead. "Hurry!" she called. "If we make it over the bridge, we can cut it behind us, trapping him here."

Jagged cracks split the corridor walls. Bricks plummeted from above. Dust blurred the path ahead, like smoke. Whatever power Razak had unleashed, it had unsettled the foundations the castle had been built upon. It was all coming down.

"I've got you," Lark said, hauling me along. His voice was steady, his eyes clear. Beautiful eyes, full of passion, fear, and hate. Everything that made him Lark. I'd been so afraid Razak had stolen his heart. "Arin, hold on."

I could, for him. Even as the ice spread through my chest and filled my limbs, turning them hard and cold. We ran, and walls crumbled around us. Stone slammed from above. *Run, just run.* I had Lark, and that was all I cared for. Let the world crumble, just so long as I had him in my arms.

We sprinted through the castle gate and outside, into

knee-high snow. The cold bore down, sapping the remaining warmth from my bones.

I fell to my knees, shivering. "What d-did he do to m-me?"

Lark gripped my shoulders. "Razak is coming. You feel him now, don't you? Inside? You feel his touch."

I felt the tightening mixed with welling panic. I nodded.

"If he gets you, he'll rip your passion from you—all your love, your wonder, he'll try and take it. I won't let him. He'll damn well take me before he has you. But you have to run."

"I know... I just...Everything's s-so c-cold."

Draven loomed. Snow flurries spiraled around him, dusting his dark black hair. Without a word, he scooped up my right arm, while Lark had my left, and together we all staggered on, following Noemi's flash of blue in the swirling snow. The sense of panic grew, turning brittle and sharp. I knew what it was now. Razak had touched some inner part of me. And it was his oily touch I could feel encasing my heart.

I glanced behind us. Snow was fast filling our tracks, but not fast enough. He was out there, coming for us.

If he caught us, he'd kill me and ruin Lark, make him dance forever.

We stumbled on, fighting the wind, the snow, and consciousness. The cold dragged me down, sapping my strength. It was all right though, because Lark was with me. And Draven—with Love's crown firmly in his grip.

When we came to the bridge, its swinging length stretched across the chasm, to I assumed a secure landing on the other side. Snow and mist swirled, obscuring the other side. We stepped onto groaning timbers and creaking ropes.

"Hurry!" Noemi called, her blue cloak the only beacon as she raced across the bridge and disappeared into the mist.

"You have Arin?" Draven asked. "I can help her cut the ropes."

"Go," Lark said.

Draven left me to slump against Lark, and the warlord paced ahead, soon disappearing in the whiteout too.

Lark panted in my ear. We hobbled on, surrounded by snow and the hollow howl of the bitter wind.

Razak's laughter sailed on that wind.

"Cut the ropes!" Lark yelled.

The mist parted, and I saw Draven and Noemi kneeling at the bridge's suspension ropes, sawing at the taut ropes.

Lark and I were almost there. Just a few more steps.

Lark let out a cry and dropped, taking me down with him. No, no... We were too close to fall now. I got my hands under me and glanced back.

Razak marched onto the bridge, his hand out, curled into talon-like fingers. Blood ran anew down his pale face. He brought his fingers in and beside me, Lark threw his head back, his mouth open in a silent scream.

"No!" I grabbed Lark's arm and hauled him along behind me, scrabbling off the bridge. "You can't have him!"

The invisible whip of Razak's stolen power looped around my waist and squeezed. I struggled, caught, almost frozen rigid, and once more felt the strange sensation of some vital part of me being hooked out of my chest, taking my will, my passion, and my heart. It burned in a way no physical wound could.

"Lark, catch!" Draven yelled.

I was frozen, unable to move, trapped in hollowing agony, but I could *see*. Lark snatched Draven's flying dagger out of the air, spun, and launched it across the bridge. It slammed into Razak's chest with a heavy, terminating thump.

Razak jerked, took a step back, and his devastating hold on me collapsed.

I dropped, but Draven had me in his arms in the next moment. His deep voice rumbled something about me being too cold, but he seemed so far away. And I wasn't really cold anymore...

"Cut it," Lark yelled. "Cut it now!"

"You're mine!" Razak bellowed. "I will come for you! I will take Arin's precious heart and crush it in my hands. You hear me, Zayan!? I'M COMING FOR YOU!"

The ropes twanged, unraveled, then snapped, and the bridge swooped away, vanishing into the mist, taking Razak's shocked, blood-streaked face with it.

I panted, propped up on an arm, and stared into the wall of white, expecting to see Razak loom out of it at any moment. But the world was quiet, except for my desperate heart trying to warm my veins. Snowflakes landed on my lashes.

"Is Razak dead?" Noemi asked.

She tried to wrap her cloak around me, but I shook my head. In Razak's absence, the strangling ice had waned.

"We're not that lucky," Draven replied. "We have to find shelter, get warm."

Lark flung his arms around me and hauled me into a hug. He trembled, like I did, and then his mouth was at my ear. "I thought I'd lost you, thought he'd taken you. I have you, Arin, I have you," he said again and again, over and over, not just for me, but for himself too. I hadn't felt fear inside the castle, not even when Razak had first attacked, or when he'd taken Danyal instead of me, but I felt it all now. Razak had almost torn us apart.

I hugged him as tight as my frozen muscles allowed. "I'm all right."

He desperately stroked snow from my face. "Are you? Are you sure?"

"Yes. I think so. I will be." But was he? His lashes were damp with melted snow or tears. He mustered a smile, but he was hurting.

"I'm all right too," he said.

"Promise?"

Draven stomped from the snow. "Come, before we freeze."

We stumbled to our feet in deep snow. "Well?" I asked Lark again. He smiled, but like before, it lacked warmth. "Promise." He turned to Draven. "Can you keep hold of Love's crown? You appear to have a habit of losing them."

"I've got it," Draven grumbled, wading ahead.

We plodded through the snow, following Draven's wide tracks. We shivered, wet and bruised. But we were alive.

Razak was, in all likelihood, alive too. I still felt some cold, barbed part of him inside me.

This was far from over.

$\mathcal{L}$ark

"It's over," I said.

We couldn't stop Razak. We'd tried and failed. In the past few weeks, Arin had been beaten by Pain's council, accused of treason, thrown into a prison cell, and almost had everything that made him brilliant ripped from his body. It *was* over.

The only thing we could do now was run.

"It's *not* over," Arin denied, speaking to our group as a whole. We sat huddled around a campfire, in the ruin of someone's home. Its roof had long ago fallen in. Draven paced behind Noemi, who stared at the fire as though she could will the answers from its flames. "Razak caught us off guard, my head wasn't clear, Lark was missing, and Draven, well... Draven had his own problems," Arin went on. "We have failed, and people died, that is true, and I'm sorry for that." He paused a moment, probably thinking of his court, his family, while I thought of how Danyal had thrown himself at Razak's mercy to save Arin. "But we just need to regroup, to heal, and to understand the power Razak has so we know how to beat it, and him."

Understand it? We couldn't understand it.

I'd seen it... Beneath Justice, I'd seen how it was too large a thing to be contained. The unleashed thing was desire with no boundaries, no limits. Razak had mastered it because, like it, he was a creature of endless wants. It was almost as though it had been waiting for *him*, its maestro.

And I'd given it to him.

"It doesn't kill them, not directly," I said, thinking of Soleil and Danyal. "It's worse than that."

All eyes turned to me. Draven even stopped pacing.

Arin rested a hand on my knee. It burned there, like a brand. Guilt, hatred, frustration, self-loathing—all the things Danyal had suspected of me—swirled around my head. Danyal was gone now too, gone like my mother. Sacrificed for me, the same as she had been. All the good people died.

Yet, I went on living. The most unworthy of us all.

I brushed Arin's hand off and stood.

They'd soon ask what had happened; they'd ask how Razak had come to be in possession of the crowns, the key to control the font. It was me. Like the fool I was, I'd handed him everything.

Arin wanted to ask; I saw it in his eyes.

"He takes his victim's desires," I explained. "Their will to live. He takes everything that animates us, makes us love and laugh, makes us different from beasts. And he tears it out. But they're not dead." I paced and stared at the ground, not at their faces, especially Arin's. I couldn't meet his gaze knowing I'd been the one to give Razak control.

"Lark... what happened?" Arin asked, like I'd known he would.

I shook my head. I couldn't tell him what I'd seen, how the seal had opened beneath my feet and swallowed me. I'd been lost there, in the dark, surrounded by nightmares. And then Razak had come, Soleil too, but it was Razak who had called out to me in the dark. And in the madness, I'd thought he'd meant to save me. I'd reached for him. He *had* saved me, like he'd said. And I didn't know what to do with that. With any of it.

I hadn't known the seal would open; I hadn't even known I'd stumbled upon such a thing.

And now he had control of it—some of it. We had Love's crown, and separating the crowns should weaken him.

We had to get the crown as far away as possible. Take it to the edges of the shatterlands and throw it into Dallin's Ocean. But that wouldn't stop him. I felt his stain on the part of me I'd never let anyone touch, except perhaps Arin. It made my skin crawl and my guts heave to think on it.

"Lark?"

I looked up. They each stared. "Yes?"

"I asked what happened."

Concern pinched Arin's eyebrows, and perhaps some anger too. At least he could feel anger. Had Razak's grip held, he'd be lifeless—worse than dead.

I waved his query away. "Nothing. He tried to hurt me. You saw how I pretended I was his so I might get a crown away from him. We have to take it far away. The farther the crowns are from each other, the weaker his power becomes. That was why the shatterlands were always destined to war and rage and oppose each other. The crowns control it, so the crowns must never come together." The wall art below Justice, with its four crowns and their soulless slaves, had made our potential fates very clear. "Dallin saw to it, until Razak learned of the truth."

And now Justice had fallen.

I couldn't stand to see the grief in Noemi's eyes. If she didn't yet blame me, she soon would. Razak couldn't have done *any* of this without me. I was the eye of his storm.

Umair should have hung *me* from the tree that day.

"I don't understand how he got to Soleil," Noemi said softly.

I knew. Soleil had feared the seal had been broken, not by Razak, as she'd assumed would happen, but by me. She'd freed him in exchange for his help in stopping *me*. Razak had likely been very persuasive. *He'd keep her secret,* he'd have said. Nobody needed to know about the power I'd discovered. They'd both stop me. They were the only ones who could. And they'd come, to do exactly that.

Until I'd given Razak everything he'd ever wanted.

"Do you know, Lark?" Draven asked. He'd been quiet since helping to build the fire. And he'd been watching me. Like Arin had. They all watched.

"It doesn't matter. It's done."

"She did not deserve that."

She'd killed Umair by locking him away. She'd kept an untapped source of chaotic power a secret beneath Justice's foundations. Soleil and her predecessors had erased almost all mention of it from the shatterlands, leaving only War's art and that tomb or temple buried beneath Justice's ice. And she'd broken her own vows of Justice by releasing Razak. She was not without blame. But no, she hadn't deserved to have her will torn from her. Nobody did. Except, perhaps, Razak himself.

"Let's rest," Arin suggested. "It's late, and we're cold. Tomorrow, things will be better." I snorted, and Arin shot me a devastating glare. "You have something to add?"

I turned my face away. "Tomorrow will not be better.

Razak cannot be stopped. Anyone who tries will be torn apart. He will come, and he will rule through fear. This has just begun. He'll go back to Pain, he'll take up Umair's throne, and he will make sure every living soul in the shatterlands kneels to him. You saw what Pain was like. Now imagine that across War, across Love and what remains of Justice. By the next full moon, all of Pain will be his. A month later, he'll claim Love and Justice. War will make a stand, but they will fall."

"He's just one man," Draven said.

I scoffed. "To underestimate Razak is to lose."

"Lark, we'll discuss this in the morning," Arin said, trying to placate me. But nothing was going to change, and the sooner they saw that, the sooner they could each go and try to find some peace somewhere far away where Razak might not find them.

"He's not a man," I said. "Not anymore. You know it, all of you know it. He's a god. Exactly as he planned. Hope cannot save us; love cannot save us. It's over."

Arin shook his head. "I refuse to believe that."

"Of course you do," I snapped, and hated myself for it as soon as Arin's glare failed to hide his hurt. I turned my back, found a shadowy corner in the old house, and tucked myself into it.

Snowfall dusted in through the broken roof while the campfire crackled and spat. We were alive; if we faced Razak again, we wouldn't be.

It was over.

WE MOVED on during the warmer daylight hours, but the damp and the cold were never far away and the forest I'd travelled through with Danyal by cart was harder going on foot. Draven and Noemi struck up some conversation, but Arin remained quiet, and I trailed behind, blowing into my cold hands while checking nothing tracked us in the snow.

After we came upon an abandoned longhouse, Draven managed to spark a fire in the old fireplace grate, and while he and Noemi discussed War's ability to attack the Court of Pain, Arin and I stewed in silence. He sometimes looked over, but every glance grew colder.

"I know what you're doing," he said. Noemi and Draven were deep in conversation by the fireside. I'd hung back by an ivy-strewn, filthy window, watching outside for any sign of movement. The snow had stopped falling and a serene monochrome stillness bathed the overgrown gardens.

"What is that?" I asked.

"Deliberately shutting me out."

Was I? Perhaps I was. But it was for his own good. Since my ruse in the Court of Love had been revealed, his entire life had been thrown into turmoil. I was his toxic trait.

"You forget, I see you," Arin went on. He leaned against the wall, making sure I had to see him. "I know exactly what this is."

"If you know me so well, then tell me what I'm doing."

He offered me a palmful of berries. Draven had caught and skinned some critters too, but Justice's lands were bitter and harsh. We'd need to find a proper town soon, fill our bellies, get fresh clothes. Although, I feared I might never shake Justice's chill. I shook my head, and he popped a few berries into his mouth.

"In that handsome head of yours, you're blaming yourself for everything," he said, after eating.

"It's not blame when it's fact."

He huffed a silent laugh, but there was no humor in it. "I

can't keep doing this with you, Lark. I tell you you're not to blame, but you don't believe it."

"Because you're wrong." It was out as a reflex, before I had a chance to think. Arin's soft smile faded away beneath his hurt.

"I wish you'd talk to me."

"We're talking."

"No, not like this. You know what this is?" He leaned closer. "This is us *before*. This is me, as the prince behind the door, and you, out there, doing your utmost to pretend everything is a fantasy. You're being shallow and hurtful because you're afraid. If there was a horse and carriage here, you'd shove me on it and lock the door."

He was right. I pulled a face but didn't deny anything.

"You see!" He flung a berry at my chest. It bounced off and hit the floor. "Do you not see how wrong that is?"

"Why is wanting to save you so wrong?"

He laughed again. "I can't do this with you over and over, Lark. You know my feelings, you know I'll do anything for you, but when you push me away every time something goes wrong, it's exhausting."

Noemi and Draven had fallen silent, probably because we'd grown loud. We were all tired, hungry, and cold, but this was something more. His weariness went soul-deep—weariness for me.

"Then don't." Once more, the words were out, like the lash of a whip I couldn't take back. It felt good, knowing they hurt him, seeing him wince, pushing him away. It felt good because I *was* saving him. If the stubborn fool would just let me save him. But that wasn't Arin. He'd argue, he'd fight, and he'd come right back around again... Although, from the saddened look on his face, perhaps this time he wouldn't come back.

He slumped against the wall. "I want to love you, I do love you, but you have to let me in, Lark. I can't love you alone."

Two sides of the same coin. Pain and love. "Let you in? What do you think is inside me that's so worth seeing? The man his brother fucked for much of his adult life? The man who brought down the Court of Love? Who could have saved your mother and didn't because he was far too occupied with a future betrayal? A man who at every key point in Razak's grandiose plan has been absolutely pivotal to his success?" Noemi and Draven both stared now. Good. Let them hear this too. "Draven had a son to protect. He was driven to help Razak because he had no choice. I had a choice, and I broke that seal beneath Justice. I did that." Arin's eyes widened. I couldn't stop now; he had to know everything. "I was there, Arin. I took Pain's crown right to it, and with the other crowns so close, it was enough. My brother came for me, and I let him. When he placed Umair's crown on his head and lashed out like a whip, it was me he attacked first. I nearly lost myself to him. How do you think I was so able to mimic being empty? I let him in, and the worst of it is, I'll always let him in. He knows it. He'll hurt me, and I'll beg for more. I'm your weakness. And he is mine. I do not deserve your friendship, or your love. I'm nothing, yet people keep dying for me. I won't let that happen to you. So no, Arin, let's *not* do this, whatever it is. Because we all know how this story ends, and the villain does not win the hero's heart."

Arin frowned. "I will not fight for us alone."

Good.

"Then don't fight for us at all."

He was meant for so much more, like a prophesized knight from a sweeping tale of love conquering all. But he couldn't be that person with me dragging him down. This was clearly the only sensible way to proceed—taking his love out of it. And mine.

I bowed my head and caught Draven's disapproving glare in the corner of my eye. He could glare all he liked. I was doing this for all of them. Better for me to be alone than have Razak rip out their souls.

CHAPTER 38

rin

I DREAMED of Lark playing his fiddle on the clifftop again, but this time when I called his name, he stopped playing, turned his head, and tipped over the edge of the cliff to spite me. I woke spluttering in the dark and listened to the unfamiliar sounds of people clattering and talking a floor below. We'd found an inn, and Noemi had used her position as a member of Justice's Court to secure lodgings.

Damn Lark.

I'd meant what I'd told him. I wasn't fighting for us alone. If he wanted to walk away, so be it. I wasn't going to stop him, not anymore. I loved him. We both knew it. But he either didn't believe me or didn't believe he deserved to be loved. I couldn't watch him tear himself apart and had no idea how to help him when he pushed me away.

It had been several days since we'd fled Justice's court.

Noemi and Draven had been gathering information, while I'd been growing more and more restless. We could do more to stop Razak, and we had to do it fast, but how?

I ventured from my room late in the morning, and of course, found a small commotion surrounding Lark in the main bar. He was flipping coins, delighting his small crowd with his effortless magic tricks and sleight of hand. I propped myself against the bar, just out of sight behind him, and watched him dazzle his ensnared audience. I also saw him pocket a few coins.

As his show wound down, I stepped up to the bar beside him, took the stolen coins from his pocket, and handed them back. "Never trust a magician."

"They wouldn't have missed them," Lark said, mischief making his smile dance.

"Regardless, the coins aren't yours."

"Shall I sing for coins instead? Would that better suit your morals, Prince of Hearts? If we don't find some coin soon, I'll be doing more than singing. Unless you'd like to volunteer? Some would pay good money to sample those peachy lips of yours."

This was how it was going to be now. Right back where we'd begun. "Don't do this."

"Do what?" He gave a cutting grin, goading me.

"Never mind. Where's Draven?"

Lark tossed a coin onto the bar—a coin I hadn't seen him pilfer away, but clearly he'd hidden it somewhere else on his person—and ordered a drink. He asked if I wanted to partake and rolled his eyes at my head shake. "I'm waiting for our illustrious warlord, actually. He claims to have news."

"So you stole their coins to squander it on beer?"

He pursed his lips, waited for the barkeep to leave his

drink, then took a sip with a smirk. "So judgmental. Is Justice rubbing off on you?"

"You're a scoundrel when you're like this."

"I'm *always* like this."

He was punishing me, and it hurt, but I wasn't going to show him how much. "Listen, I've been thinking these last few days. We should all go back to Love. It's not all lost. We at least have a foothold there, and perhaps we can make enquires as to my father's advisors—if there's anyone left."

"Yes, fabulous." His smile flashed. "You do that."

The inn door rattled and Draven stomped in, kicking snow from his boots and shaking off a new blue cloak. I wasn't sure what to make of it, but as he made his way over, he spread his arms, clearly pleased with the garment. "What do you think?"

"It's very..." I began, then stalled.

"Blue?" Lark offered.

"Well, they don't make red ones here, obviously."

"Did Noemi buy it for you?" Lark asked, drinking from his tankard and leaning back against the bar.

"She did. She's very kind."

Lark threw me a mocking glare. "Strange, don't you think, how she hasn't bought us new cloaks?"

I saw where Lark was going with this. "Perhaps she will?"

"Hm, yes, I'm sure."

"What?" Draven groused, sensing we were conspiring against him. "Do you want cloaks? I can ask."

"You have news?"

"Yeah, but first, are there more of those?" He nodded at Lark's drink. "You're going to need it."

Lark found another stolen coin he'd squirrelled away and ordered Draven a drink.

"Noemi has the news actually, but she's busy with the townsfolk." Draven accepted his drink and planted himself at the bar beside Lark. "Razak is alive. He entered a household not far from our route, killed the lady of the house, tortured the husband, and robbed them of coin and their horses."

Lark peered into his drink, all his humor and jest having evaporated.

"There's more," Draven grumbled. "He has an aide with him. Someone from Justice."

"Who?" I asked, dreading the answer.

"A young man; just a servant, as far as Noemi's been told."

"Is it Theo?" Lark asked, his voice strangely tight.

"Yes, I think." Draven arched an eyebrow. "How did you know?"

"Lucky guess," Lark growled.

Lark knew who Theo was and was in no mood to tell us.

"What's his next move?" I asked.

"He took the road to—"

"Pain," Lark said. "His seat of power. Once there, he'll burrow in like War's sandworms. He'll be impossible to get to. We had our chance."

"No, actually." Draven sighed and looked to me. "He's headed to Love."

"What?" I asked. There was nothing there for him.

Lark clattered his tankard down. "That doesn't make any sense. Why?"

"We have my crown," I added. I checked on it every day, not trusting Draven. His boy was still in Pain's clutches and Razak knew Draven was alive. Razak would use Draven again, but this time Draven would tell us.

"Is there anything there he'll use as leverage against you, Arin?" Lark asked.

"No, there's nothing left. He made sure of that."

"Well, he must think there is, else he wouldn't be going. For him to wield the font to its full potential, he needs Love's crown. He has no option but to lure us out of hiding. Are you sure there's nothing left you care about there?"

"Nothing. The palace is gone. I didn't know most of the court enough to care, there's only..."

Oh no. I closed my eyes, cutting off Lark's penetrating glare.

"Only?" he prompted.

"I'm sorry, Lark. It's not me he's luring." I opened my eyes. "Ellyn's there."

Lark's eyes widened. "Ellyn? I thought..." His voice stuttered. "I thought her dead." He hunched over his drink, gripping it tight, then with a roar, threw it at the back of the bar and flung himself from the stool. He flew out of the door, slamming it behind him, leaving just a few dallying snowflakes spiraling in the air and the inn's other patrons staring after him.

Draven leaned over the bar. "Innkeeper, my apologies, let me help clear that—"

"Let me." I stepped in. "Draven, go after him. Make sure he's doesn't... hurt himself."

"Me? Shouldn't you go?"

"As things stand between us, I'd make things worse."

Draven grumbled something along the lines of not wanting his throat cut and swept after Lark.

I helped the barkeep clear up the spilled drink, but even as I focused on that menial task, Razak's icy touch skimmed the back of my neck. He knew exactly how to get to Lark, and how to get to *me* through him.

The shatterlands were not prepared for Razak. He'd already reduced two courts to rubble. War was next. We could—should—go there, explain everything, demand Ogden rally his armies, and march on Pain. It was the only way to stop Razak. Ogden was our last chance and Razak's final barrier to break. We had Draven, Noemi, me, and Lark. Four representatives of four courts. We could do this, if we worked together. But right now, Lark and I were drifting apart.

CHAPTER 39

ark

BRILLIANT SUNSHINE MADE the quaint Justice townhouses sparkle. I stood by the town well, shivering to the bone, and peered far down into the well's bottom. The water hadn't frozen down there, but it would be bitterly cold.

Ellyn was one of the most capable people I knew. She'd see Razak coming. If he thought her an easy target, he'd be in for a shock. That's if he was truly going to Love, or just throwing us off his trail.

"Don't do it," Draven called, gingerly navigating across the icy street.

"Don't do what?"

He lurched, slipped on some ice, caught himself, and stumbled all the way to the well, then clung to its wall and peered down into its gloom.

"Do you think I mean to jump?" I asked.

"Do you?" He caught my frown and fumbled. "Arin feared you might..."

I laughed. "Then he does care? Be at ease, warlord, I'm not going to fling myself down a well. Besides, that would be a ridiculous way to die."

"I don't know what to think with you," he grumbled.

"I just needed a little air. Sometimes it feels as though Razak's hands are still around my throat."

"I dare not imagine."

Arin had sent him out in some foolish attempt to placate me, no doubt. "You can go back," I said. "You've done your part."

"Lark, if you keep pushing Arin away, one of these days, he'll believe it."

"I think that ship has sailed. I cannot be what he wants me to be. I won't put him in further danger. And don't you prefer it this way? You can have him back, or have your fickle affections moved to Noemi?"

The warlord glowered. "You're a real bitch sometimes."

"Here's a thought. Maybe you should shove me down the well and tell Arin I jumped? Kill two birds with one stone? Arin will grieve in your arms, and I'm out of your lives for good—"

The backhanded slap came out of nowhere, not least because I hadn't been looking for it. Fire raced up my face. I gasped, more stunned than hurt. "By Dallin, you tease."

He shook out his hand. "Are you done with this childish kareelshit? You need to go back in there and apologize to Arin for being a dick so we can all get on with the business of stopping Razak."

"I'm fairly certain he did not instruct you to hit me. Although, he does have form—"

"He should have. Because it's the only fucking language

you know. So fucking listen, Lark. Arin loves you, and if you fuck that up like you seem desperate to, you will break his heart and yours. If it takes a slap for these words to find a way inside that complicated head of yours, so be it. You're hurting and afraid; we all are. Do you know how to get through that? With friends, Lark. With Arin."

I blinked at the warlord. I'd underestimated him, on occasion. Like now. He appeared to be here, fighting for Arin and I, when his easiest option was to let us fall apart.

"At least you have someone," he snapped, hammering his point home. "My son is alone in some awful Pain workhouse. He probably doesn't even know I exist. But I'd do anything for him. *Anything*. I miss him with my every breath. I wouldn't wish that on anyone, and if you let Arin go now, you'll regret it for the rest of your days."

"That's the problem, isn't it? How many days do I have left with Razak determined to come for me? If he catches Arin, he will rip his passion out, his fire, his *heart*, and I can't —I will not—see that happen. Not even for love."

"Then live those days, Lark. If you let him steal your heart now, he's already won. And I know you don't want him winning anything."

I pressed my cold hand to my burning face. "I forget sometimes, how you're not as dim as you pretend to be."

He laughed, showed me his middle finger, and stomped back across the street.

"Blue looks terrible on you!" I called.

He disappeared inside the inn, leaving me alone with thoughts that swayed from Arin to Razak to Ellyn.

I couldn't save Ellyn; I could only hope she was wily enough to see him for the fiend he was and escape.

Arin left the inn, shrugged the old coat he wore tighter around him, and made his way across the street, avoiding the icy patch Draven had slipped on. He handed over my coat. I shrugged it on, and we both stared into the well in silence.

"I have a plan," he finally said, looking up, squinting into the sun. "But it means we must all work together. We don't have to be... involved, if that's your wish, but I need your mind, I need your wit and your will. Are you with me, Lark?" He offered his hand for me to shake, like two strangers agreeing to a trade, not lovers whose hearts were entwined. I'd wanted him at a distance, but it hurt like no physical wound ever had.

"Will it stop Razak?" I asked.

"I hope so."

He always had hope enough for us all.

I grasped his hand and shook it, holding on longer than required. Or perhaps he held on to me. We half-smiled and let our hands drop. I opened my mouth to tell him I was sorry, that I loved him so much it made me crazy, that I was so damn afraid of hurting him, either by my own actions or by Razak's, that it was easier to push him away. But he turned and headed toward the inn, and the moment slipped through my fingers.

I watched him go—my prince bathed in winter sunshine—and I ached to love him in the way he wanted. But in what world would he and I ever be free to love? Certainly not this one.

Arin would say that perhaps, one day, we might make our own future. But only fools dreamed of happy endings.

THE COURT OF WAR'S huge gates hadn't gotten any less intimidating in our absence.

"All right, wait here." Draven started toward the gates.

Sand swept in wisps about his boots. The sun was beating down. Draven had suggested we arrive during the evening, not at the height of midday. Of course, Arin was of the mind that criminals and thieves arrived among shadows, so here we were, at midday, sweating in our boots, probably about to be arrested. Again.

My patient kareel snorted into my hand. We'd secured several of the odd animals at War's borders, and since we didn't encounter any sandworms, we made our way across the desert dunes in good time. Draven was home, but a long way from safe.

I shielded my eyes and watched Draven's figure grow smaller in front of the gates. "Do you trust him?" I asked Arin.

"Not in the least."

Noemi stood with Arin to my left. Their flimsy linen shirts rippled and flapped in the wind.

Gods, I hadn't missed the wind, or the heat.

Everything now hinged on Ogden not executing us the moment we stepped through those gates. Noemi would be fine; he didn't have any issue with her. Draven too, as these people were his kin. Arin and I, however, were on thin ice— or should that be shifting sands?

Arin stared at the gates, chin up, determined. His hair had turned into an unruly mop of golden locks, and the sun had summoned his freckles. He looked good, as though nothing would stand in his way, not even War's great gates.

A gust of wind caught Noemi's blue cloak and whipped it around her ankles. She swore and tried to kick it back. She'd insisted on keeping it. She carried Draven's folded under her arm. They'd struck up a bond these past few days. Perhaps, something more? The both of them could likely do with a vigorous tumble between the sheets.

War was our last hope.

If they refused to help, then the shatterlands would fall to my brother.

Still, Draven had a card up his sleeve to play. We just needed Ogden to listen and not swing his axe and take our heads without first granting us an audience.

"Can you see what's happening?" Noemi asked, squinting against flying sand.

"The gates are opening," Arin said. "He's being greeted." His eyes narrowed. "Hm."

Hm was not a good sound. I glared into the heat haze. Draven had been joined by three guards. They spoke a while, then Draven broke off and began to head back toward us.

"He still has his head," I said. As starts went, it was promising. But as he drew closer, Draven's face was not a happy one. The loose cuffs swinging from his fingers probably had something to do with that. "They'll take us in," he said, gruffly. "With Lark in cuffs."

With a sigh, I extended both arms. "It's as though they do not trust me."

"Did you explain Lark saved everyone from poisoning?" Arin asked. "He's done more for War than any of us." Arin's voice grumbled lower, gaining a threatening edge. "He almost died to st—"

"It's fine." I stepped forward. "I expected nothing less."

"No, I don't agree. This isn't right."

I nodded at Draven to go ahead but spoke to Arin. "And what do you suggest we do? Turn around and go where?"

Draven clipped the cuffs on and snicked the lock over. "I'll get you out of these just as soon as I've spoken with Ogden."

We all started forward along the sand-dusted road. Draven strode ahead again with Arin lagging behind him.

Noemi fell to the back with me, leading our two kareel. "You're doing the right thing," she told me.

"You speak as though I have a choice."

"You do not have to bow to anyone, do you realize that?" She stopped our march with her hand on my arm. "Lark, Razak admitted his mother was not of Pain's court. In Justice's courtroom, he said his mother was from the Court of Love. Do you understand what that means?"

"I've been a little preoccupied with surviving."

"*You* are the rightful heir to Pain's crown," Noemi said. "Razak is the half-prince, not you. Both your parents were from Pain's court. Razak's mother was from the Court of Love, and frankly, considering how quiet Pain have kept that piece of knowledge, I'd assume she wasn't noble. Whatever the history between them, you are a child of Pain and its king, not Razak."

My heart gave a little flip. That couldn't be right. "Does it matter?"

She nodded. "Yes. It matters to Razak. I'd guess it's always mattered a great deal to him. If he knew you were the heir, then it explains his..."

"Affections?" I suggested, and she gave me the pitying look of someone who knew my past and felt sorry for me.

"I thought you should know. With everything that's been happening, I wasn't sure if you'd understood the ramifications of the truth. He was so thrilled to have Arin there, I doubt he even realized the worth of the information he'd given away."

Then I was more a king than Razak? It was a fancy thought. I laughed her off and continued on, chasing Arin's shadow. "I'm no king, though."

"You could be. You'd make a better king than Razak. You have heart, you're brave, you understand Pain, and you're self-less." Noemi's speech quickened, her thoughts racing along with her pace. "I wonder, do you think your mother knew? Was that why Umair had her killed?"

"It does seem likely."

With Umair's love for his dead wife well-known, but her origins a secret, it would have been easier to erase the truth— and give me to Razak, to keep me close, keep the true heir controlled.

We were almost at the vast gate now. "Use the knowledge wisely."

I smiled back at her. "Freedom suits you."

"I never agreed with how much Justice controlled the shatterlands. But as an aide, I had no voice. I'm not sure I have much of a voice now, but I know what's right. And I'll fight for that."

"Knowing what's right puts you ahead of the courts— what remains of them."

"I've been thinking about that. I think the courts were designed to keep everyone fractured. Like the crowns, their people were forced apart. It seems... wrong, doesn't it? For our people to be isolated by a past we have no control over."

"It does." There was a great deal we still didn't know, thanks to Justice erasing that past.

A guard at the gate stepped aside and waved us on through. The wind swept sand into tiny vortexes as we entered War's gateway, and we emerged into the arena-like entranceway. When we'd fled, months ago, there had been a crowd present, and today was no different, including War's many warriors. They stared back at us and murmured among themselves.

What had they heard? What did they think they knew of Zayan? Was I Razak's accomplice or his victim, their enemy or friend? I'd been all those things. The cuffs had been sensible. It was a shame Ogden hadn't put them on Razak the first time we'd visited.

The Court of War's king marched from his warrior's ranks and approached Draven and Arin. His great axe gleamed on his back, and his thick braids had been gathered over one of his impressive shoulders.

Ogden's reputation was everything. If his people discovered Razak had stolen the crown out from under him, he'd be dethroned within hours.

We didn't want chaos. This was not the time for War to lose its king. We just wanted fairness, and for Ogden to listen.

The king stopped in front of us. His warriors stared, their faces stoic. Red banners flapped in the wind, and behind them all rose the grand pyramid—its interior artwork so like Justice's. Perhaps Noemi was right, and our fractured world hadn't always been so.

Could our Court of Misfits unite the shatterlands once more?

"Love's prince," Ogden boomed for the benefit of the crowd. "Back at my door again."

Arin bowed his head. "My king."

If Arin misspoke, Ogden would lock me up and throw away the key—if he was feeling kind. If the king were feeling unkind, he'd give me to the sands. And Arin had a history of never knowing when to remain quiet.

"Trouble follows you, Arin." Ogden dragged his heated, scornful glare over me, folded his muscular arms, and rumbled out a pensive sigh. "First Love falls, then Justice. Tell me, Arin, why does devastation follow in your wake? Perhaps, is it the company you keep?"

"May I remind you, Zayan saved your people from a grisly death by poisoning? At the potential cost of his own life? How many self-sacrifices have you made for your people?"

And there we had it. I was never getting out of these cuffs.

The king laughed. "Yes, but he didn't die, did he? There he stands." He swept a hand up and down. "And here you all are. Love, Justice, Pain, and War." His gaze snagged on Draven and narrowed. Draven knew enough about the missing crown to bring Ogden down. A few words from him in public, in front of War's warriors, and Ogden's reign would crumble.

A moment of understanding flickered between the warlord and king.

"My son is alive," Draven said, raising his voice so the court heard, and when he next spoke, he addressed everyone. "He was given to the sands, and he survived. He is a warrior by nature and worthy of War, but we cast him out. Pain took him in, and others we cast out. Razak has his strings in all of us, and we gave him those strings to pull." Discontented murmurs sailed through the crowd. Ogden's right eyebrow twitched. He glanced at the people, listening to their growing dissent.

"We are War," Draven bellowed. "And Pain is a threat! It's time we proved worthy of our name."

The winds carried his voice away, the flags went on fluttering, and nobody moved. Perhaps I imagined the change in the air and War's people. But if I did, then so did Ogden. The king bristled and unfolded his arms; he rolled his shoulders, making his huge axe shift against his back. "Come with me. Not that one——" He pointed at me. "Put that leech in a cell."

The guards came for me and grabbed my arms. My chains rattled. Freedom had been nice while I'd had it. But I never had possessed anything nice for long.

"Wait." The man who stepped from the crowd wore similar warlord clothes as Draven. "Ogden, my king." He knelt. "I was a guest that night, when the Prince of Pain attempted to assault our great court. If it were not for Zayan's sacrifice, I'd have been poisoned. I would not have seen my daughter's birth. I owe Zayan my voice. Whether it is heard or not, I must speak it."

"Aye," another man cried. "Let him go."

"Aye," a woman called.

"Silence!" Ogden boomed.

Remembering Noemi's words, I kept my chin up and fixed the king in my glare. His choices were limited. Go against his people and his instincts, or appear weak by keeping me chained? I was just a man, after all. What threat could a fool be to the King of War? He snatched the key from Draven, stomped over, and unlocked the cuffs. "Wrong me, boy, and I'll throw your bones to the sandworms."

"No fear," I said. "I have no designs on the Court of War. Your crown was a terrible fit."

He sneered and stomped away. "Bring them."

Whoever the man was who had petitioned for my freedom, I mouthed a thanks to him as we trailed by. He nodded. Strange, that feeling in my chest—a small tug of... pride? I'd done something good. I'd made a difference. And these people had noticed, they'd seen me. Not the fool, the magician, the entertainer—they'd seen *me*.

A stranger had cared enough to speak *for me*. And their voice had been heard.

CHAPTER 40

ark

SITTING at a council table as Zayan instead of providing the entertainment as Lark was a new experience.

Ogden had gathered his advisors—five of War's most respected men and women—and thrown us straight into the wolf's den without so much as time to clean up. I knew little of his council—nothing of who they were or where they came from—and I knew even less of the room we'd gathered in, with its vast arched windows, weapons on the walls, and bloodred banners.

Warlord Draven conducted official introductions, and then Arin took over, explaining everything that had happened since our quick exit that last time we'd been War's "guests"—leaving out the part where Draven had shipped War's crown to the enemy.

I watched, and I listened. This was not my place, nor were

these my people. I wasn't sure I had a people. But I *knew* people. I knew their tells, their twitches, their little gestures —and we were not trusted, nor were we welcome. Ogden's council had no idea why their king had granted us his time and leniency.

At least we were alive.

"I fail to see what any of this has to do with my court," Ogden declared, the moment Arin was done.

Arin's golden eyebrows pinched together in frustration. "Really? After everything I've just laid before you? You don't see Razak as a threat?"

"He cannot breach our walls. He'll soon grow tired of his games. Everything will return to the way it was."

Arin straightened, and I suspected my Prince of Flowers was about to reveal his thorns. "I hesitate to call this what it appears to be but are you afraid, my king?"

Well, that was one way to lose our heads.

Draven shot to his feet. "What Arin meant to say was—"

"You heard me," Arin snapped. "Well, Ogden? What other excuse is there?"

Ogden sat back in his throne-like chair, growing ever more quiet and dangerously scarlet.

Noemi glanced to me in desperation. But Ogden had no interest in listening to me. I could do nothing but watch.

"You will apologize at once!" one of Ogden's advisors yelled, slamming his fist on the table.

"May I speak?" Noemi interjected. "As the sole representative of Justice, it is my duty to placate disagreements."

"Justice?" Ogden blustered. "Your court was as corrupt as his!" The king threw a hand at Arin.

"My court was not corrupt!"

"Just inept," I said. The first words I'd spoken since taking my seat. My contribution silenced the entire assembly.

Ogden laughed and eyed me across the table. "So he does speak—*Zayan*. Must be quite the privilege sitting there, at my table. You're a long way from the gutter, boy."

I smiled and leaned forward. He'd clearly forgotten all I knew. A little reminder was in order. "Strange, don't you think, how Razak has three crowns, and we have Love's with us? So that must mean..." I counted down my fingers. "Hm, are you sure your crown is safe?"

"Perfectly safe. He has a fake. Costume jewelry, no more."

Noemi cleared her throat. "My king, princes, lords. The fact remains the shatterlands are already on their knees. We need War to fight for us all. And not all of Justice was corrupt. I certainly am not."

"You're an aide." Ogden huffed.

"I entered into Justice's service in my sixth year. I have trained, every day of my life, to become a serving member of Justice. I may not hold a title—Justice Ines was taken too soon to grant me that honor—or have noble blood, but I have the will, the knowledge, and the heart to stand here and represent Justice after our court was cruelly shattered."

"Due to your own incompetence."

I saw Draven clutch Arin's arm, holding him back. "Do nothing," Arin blurted anyway, "and you're not worthy of your own court."

A gag may have been useful about now. Four years behind a door had clearly stripped Arin of any political nuance.

This was likely why the shatterlands had always been separated and why the crowns were destined to remain apart. Arin was passionate, Noemi righteous but naïve, Draven— was Draven—and Ogden, in his stubbornness, would hear none of it.

They descended into bickering once more, and I pinched the bridge of my nose. This wasn't going to solve anything and if it continued, we'd be out in the sands by morning.

I shot to my feet, screeching the chair legs across the floor. "Enough! All of you. Bickering will see to it Razak wins. The fact remains there is no choice here. Ogden, you know you must act, which is why you're so adamant not to. You cannot sit on your ass and drink wine until Razak takes your kingdom from you—which trust me, he will. Two courts have fallen, yours is next. Act, or open the gates and let him walk in. Those are your options."

"Who are you to order me—"

"Nobody, I'm nothing, yet even I see you're on the losing side. If we do not combine our strengths, if we do not work together, we are all lost. *That* is the truth. Bicker all you like, it changes nothing."

Ogden glanced at the faces of his advisors; he had to act. Anything less looked weak. "Razak is no threat, but... I'll consider it."

A collective sigh of relief eased the tension in the room.

"Then, how do you suggest we stop Razak?" one of the advisors asked *me*.

I had a few ideas, but none of them involved anyone in this room. "That is for minds far greater than mine to wrestle with," I said. "However, two things will lure Razak from his court: threaten to kill me, or we parade our alliance in front of him until he can no longer resist tearing it all down. His ego will win out. It always does. As I'd rather stay alive, I vote for the second option."

I stepped from the table and turned my back on them all. Another moment among them, and I'd say all the things I shouldn't. They'd figure it out. As for me, I was not meant to sit around tables and argue the finer points of war.

What I needed was a bottle of War's finest wine, a sunset to admire, and perhaps a fiddle, if I could find one.

"Lark, wait," Arin called.

"You know what to do." I saluted and left War's chamber, slamming the door behind me.

CHAPTER 41

rin

OGDEN FREEING Lark had confirmed my suspicions: we had power in his court. And power meant everything at War's table. But power, without direction, was dangerous. Our discussions hadn't been moving forward until Lark had spoken up. His straightforward analysis struck like a slap to the face, sweeping away all the egos and bravado. We reached an agreement for Ogden to gather his forces and open the gates to all who sought shelter, including those arriving from Justice. We'd formed an alliance.

Albeit a fragile one, but an alliance nonetheless. Razak couldn't fail to notice.

"We should get cleaned up and celebrate!" Draven declared as we left the council chambers. The sun had set hours ago, leaving a chill in the shifting desert air.

He clapped me on the back. "Find Lark. Let's take the win and drink to the fact we still have our heads."

Tired, hungry, and filthy from the road, I might have preferred a soft bed to a bottle of wine, but Draven's and Noemi's grins wore me down. "All right. We'll meet you soon."

I veered off through the gardens and spotted an armed guard falling into step a few strides behind. We would, of course, be observed. I'd have been more surprised if we weren't.

I'd expected to find Lark in the gardens, not far from our meeting chambers, but he must have moved elsewhere after he'd walked out. The pyramid's dramatic tip gleamed under the moonlight, and that same moonlight draped the long viaduct bridge in cool light, and I knew exactly where he'd be.

The wind swept across the bridge like it had the day I'd joined with Draven. Another guard loitered outside the pyramid's main doors. "Is Zayan inside?" I asked.

The man nodded. "Been there a while."

"What's he doing?"

"Sitting."

Just sitting? I opened the door, told the guard to inform my tagalong I'd be inside, and entered, immediately spotting Lark sitting on the altar with a half-empty bottle of wine clutched in his right hand. He saw me and returned his gaze to the floor in front of the altar—the exact place where Razak had forced poison down his throat.

"We came to an agreement," I said. The vast space took my voice and bounced it off the sloped, painted walls. "As you said, Razak will not ignore an alliance of all three courts."

Lark lifted his gaze again, peering through his lashes, then took a swig from the wine bottle. He had the air about him that suggested trouble with a hint of wicked, the look he got when he was hurt and searching for something or someone to hurt too.

"You were impressive in the council." I leaned against the altar, next to him.

"Was I?" He laughed. "I was bored. There's no skill in that."

"Oh, believe me, there is. Council meetings often get bogged down by too much politics. We wouldn't have an alliance on the table without you."

His right eyebrow arched in query. "Truly?"

"Would I lie to you?"

"Yes, frequently." He took another swig from the bottle and offered it to me. "War is good for wine, at least."

I took the bottle and without ceremony, took several gulps—needing it. It was good, sweet, smooth, and reminded me of the sweltering nights Draven and I had spent discussing how best to stop Razak, when he'd known all along that he'd be the one to ensure Razak stole the crown and won.

The wine soured at those thoughts. "Draven has suggested we celebrate."

"You don't sound pleased."

I handed the bottle back. "Just tired, I think."

"Yes, it's been a long forever." He hopped off the altar and paced around the innocuous spot on the floor, taking the occasional swig of wine. "My brother doesn't love me, I know that, yet there's a part of me that wants to believe it, despite all he's done."

I watched Lark circle and turn over his memories, torturing himself anew. He didn't have to go through it alone, but he'd made it clear how he didn't want my help.

He stopped, planted his boots, and admired the art covering the pyramid's walls. "He's crawling around inside me now, and if we don't stop him, he'll be inside everyone, like a poison. That is not a world I want to live in."

"We *will* stop him."

He looked hard at me, almost sneering, and then a smile wiped all that away, leaving torchlight flickering in his dark eyes. "I sometimes dream it's just he and I left, ruling over a world of ashes. He saved me, and he'll do it again and again."

"He saved you from a death of his making."

"I tried to die..." Lark gestured at the floor. "He fuckin' saved me." He tore his sleeve up, exposing the vertical scar. "I cut myself, and he fucking saved me again. Is that love, Arin?"

"I'm not sure I'm the best person to ask, but it's not any love I know of," I admitted. "Love isn't kind, it's not fair either. So perhaps, yes, in Razak's own cruel way, it is his love."

It wasn't fair how I loved Lark but couldn't save him. It wasn't fair that his mother had been killed, when she'd loved Lark with all her heart. It wasn't fair that Umair's wife had been taken by sickness, and it wasn't fair how Umair had abandoned Razak, perhaps sparking this vicious chain of events into motion. Nothing about the love in our lives was fair.

He snorted, then chuckled. "Love is not fair," he echoed, savoring the words. "I think—" He stopped himself, studied the wall art, and sighed. "I *know* I can stop him."

"How?"

"Just me. Not you, or Draven, nobody else. Just me."

This was classic Lark. He'd do something dramatic, something foolish and outright suicidal, thinking it was the only option he had. "Lark?" I approached, careful not to force him away. This talk of killing himself and Razak bringing him back, of how only he could stop his brother? I didn't like the coldness in his eyes, or the chill in his voice. "You're drunk—"

"He's alone. Our father abandoned him; his heart is a fetid thing. But he has me. That's why he brings me back, that's why he cannot stand the thought of my dying. If I die, he's truly abandoned in this world. And *that* is what he fears the most." Lark's smile flashed, skirting bitterness.

"That may be so, but it's not down to you to stop him. It's gone beyond that now. With War, with Justice, we finally have the strength to prevent—"

He stepped close, so close that I lost a heartbeat somewhere in his glittering eyes. "I know what I have to do."

"And what is that?"

He set the bottle down and grasped both my hands, lifting them at my side. "Help me, Prince of Hearts."

"I don't—"

He stepped right and took his right hand from my grasp and pressed it to my lower back, clutching me close, as though to dance. Where was this coming from? "I was wrong to shut you out. I *need* you." He studied my face. Passion simmered in his eyes, but pain too. If he kissed me, I'd let him. *Wanted* him to. He'd pushed me away since he thought he'd been the one to propel Razak to godhood, and I'd let him, but now, he was pulling me close, letting me in. His hand tightened on mine. "You're the missing piece of me, like... a broken string in a fiddle, like..." He searched around for some more fancy words. "Wait, I have this... like the storm needs its lightning." Delight and wicked glee made his eyes shine.

"Really?" I spluttered a laugh, and Lark swept me around, dancing us to the music in his head. "Wait—"

"I need you as the thorn needs its rose."

"Oh by Dallin." I laughed, making us stumble, but he swept me along again. "Please stop."

He did stop, but he grasped my blushing face in cool hands. "You are my Prince of Flowers and I'm the Prince of Storms, and I've been a fool to ever doubt you, doubt *us*. The problem with us is me. I do not know how to be loved, but I'm willing to learn, if you'll teach me."

Tears glistened in his eyes now, sending another fracture through my heart. He blinked them away, unshed, but I'd seen them.

The need to have him, protect him, keep him safe, swept all my fears and doubts away. "Yes," I breathed, and flung my arms around him, crushing him close. "I have you, Lark. We'll save each other, I promise."

DRAVEN HAD SECURED several bottles of wine. We drank together, talked, laughed, and caroused in his chambers. Lark was in high spirits and managed to spin a raucous poem about a warlord and an aide from the court of ice. Its double entendre somehow sailed far over Draven's head, but not Noemi's, who blushed and laughed, clearly smitten.

I stumbled to my chambers near dawn, pulled Lark inside, and shoved him against the wall. I had his mouth under mine in a heartbeat, kissing him without a care. He always tasted sweetly delicious, like a drug I knew would carry me far away, where the woes of reality dared not touch us.

He gasped free with a laugh. "Why, Prince Arin, sex before marriage? How scandalous of you."

"Officially, I am married, just not to you."

His laughter cut off and his stare turned serious. My heart stuttered, tripped by anticipation of what was to come.

I knew he wouldn't hurt me, but his stare said otherwise. He pulled off my shirt and shoved me toward the bed, then swept in, attacking me with a kiss I had no chance of resisting. I fought with his clothes as his mouth swept in and claimed mine, then he was everywhere, hands and mouth, tongue sweeping, teasing up my chest, circling a nipple. He cupped my ass, hauled me off my feet, and dumped me on the bed, then lunged, claiming me under him in a storm of passion and heat that left my head spinning and my body alight.

"Wait," he panted, tearing off his shirt as he left the bed.

I squinted into the dawn-touched chamber, through the long shadows creeping from the windows, and there he was at the wardrobe, rummaging inside. Gods, what wicked thing did he have in mind now?

He snorted and donned my crown.

Shirtless, trousers hanging low on his slim hips, with Love's crown perched sideways on his dark hair, he sashayed toward the bed. I fought a laugh and failed, setting it carelessly free. He really was a fool, and I loved him for it.

"What?" He gasped, pretending to be hurt. "Am I so ill-suited to a crown?"

"Pearls and gold really aren't you."

He took the crown off and prowled up the bed, straddling my legs. "I have a devilish thought," he said, and planted the crown on my chest.

I could see that from his smirk. "Whatever it is, I'll do it."

He took the crown in both hands and propped it on my head, then knelt back and studied me. "It suits you. How does it feel, King of Love?"

I swallowed and righted its slide sideways. "This is the first time I've worn it."

"Oh, really?"

He moved to grab it, but I clutched it tight to my head. "I like it. Leave it."

"I was going to suggest we fuck while you wear it, but now I have my concerns come the morning. With the wine faded from your head, you might regret it."

"Excuse me, fool. Let's be clear, I'm not intoxicated enough to pass up such an opportunity. And this is Love's crown, after all. Surely, it's meant for fucking?"

He grinned and fell forward on both arms, trapping me under his warm chest. His silky black hair framed his grinning face, and I had that same heart-lurching sensation of falling. Was this why we fell in love? This was it, wasn't it? The freefall into the unknown, the thrill and fear of giving my heart away.

I tucked a lock of hair behind his ear, revealing more of his face, with its smooth cheekbones and fine, almost feminine jawline. "There's no other in all the shatterlands like you, Lark."

"Careful, or I may begin to believe you."

"I wish you would."

He turned his head and kissed my hand. "I am trying."

He skimmed his mouth down my wrist, then cradled my arm and sucked at the sensitive spot inside my elbow, lifting dark eyes to watch how I tried to resist moaning and failed. "Tell me what you want."

I didn't even know all the manners of lovemaking that were possible, but I saw the dark promises in his eyes. He'd bring any fantasy to life. There was more there now, a resilience, and a determination. He'd finally made his decision to fight for us, for himself.

"I want you," he said. "Just you, as you are—as we are, together." He laughed at himself. "I don't even know what I'm saying."

"I understand, I think."

His laughter ebbed away and he lay on me, placing his ear to my chest, over my heart. A heavy sigh fell out of him. "I realize I've built this up to be a thrilling night of lovemaking, but do you mind if we lay a while, like this?" He propped his chin on my chest and blinked. "I like the beat of your heart."

I wrapped my arms around him and he burrowed against my neck. Sometimes, Lark was at his most honest and vulnerable when he was quiet. No more acts, no more pretense. Just the beat of our hearts, together.

CHAPTER 42

rin

THE LETTER CAME two days later.

This hiss of paper shoved under the door drew my attention from my note-taking, but it was the purple seal that tore
me from the chair. I flung open the door. Multiple people
walked back and forth. Guards stood at both ends of the
corridor. But nobody hurried away. Nothing appeared out of
sorts.

The messenger likely wasn't as important as the message.

I closed the door, and for a few moments, I dared not
look. Purple meant only one thing. Pain.

A glance, and I had no choice but to read the swirling
script.

Arin, Prince of Love
Court of War

After picking it up, I stepped onto the balcony, where the

sun beat down and the sands blurred the jagged desert horizon.

Dear Arin, it began.

We are very different, you and I. Princes of Love and Pain. Yet, so very alike.

Acid burned my throat. The words on paper put his voice in my head: Razak. The elaborate *R* signing off confirmed it.

I razed your court, but I assure you, it was not personal. I respect you as a prince, never to be a king, of a court that no longer exists. You have nothing. But you are not powerless. You have in your hands a solution to end a terrible suffering.

Return Zayan to me, and I promise, I will not intervene should you wish to resurrect your court. Give me Zayan and save countless lives, including that of Draven's son. He's so like his father. So very ripe for picking. I know you understand. And you'll do the right thing, as the Prince of Love should.

I expect Zayan's return by the next full moon.

R.

Vicious hate burned its way up my throat. I gagged, grasped the balcony rail, and breathed the desert's hot, spiced air.

We'd known Razak had Draven's son. That wasn't the shock. The shock came from knowing the lengths Razak would go to for Lark's return. Killing a child.

Draven had known Razak capable all along, and now I had proof in my hands. But Razak wouldn't just kill the boy, he'd make him bleed, make him hurt, and the child would probably never know why.

By Dallin, Razak had to die.

I couldn't tell Draven of the letter and the threat to his boy. And if Lark knew, he'd race back to Pain, because despite thinking himself wicked, he was far from it.

Damn Razak's games.

But he'd made an error. He'd made the same error everyone always made when it came to me. He'd assumed the Prince of Love *would* do the right thing. He was wrong.

I scrunched the letter in my fist and pitched it over the balcony rail. The wind-tossed sand swallowed it. And now there was no letter, there never had been, and nobody need know. Razak was not dictating the rules of this war. Not anymore. And the world would have to end before I danced to his tune.

CHAPTER 43

ark

Something troubled Arin.

He'd been quiet since we'd rekindled the heat in our relationship almost a week ago. Oftentimes—when I glanced at him during council meetings, or when we visited the training warriors, or when Draven demonstrated yet another of War's vicious-looking polearms or axe—the hopeful glimmer had snuffed out of his silvery-blue eyes, leaving them colder, harder.

My Prince of Hearts was lying.

Of course, I was lying to him too. So we had that in common.

Although, not technically a lie—as there was no other place I'd have rather been than in his arms—more a misdirection. And I'd thought it had worked. When together, he and I were brilliant, like perfect notes in a symphony. He couldn't know I had ulterior motives for keeping him close, beside those of love. But he knew *something*, and he wasn't telling me.

Ogden had summoned us to a meeting in the pyramid, and as soon as we arrived it became clear this was no ordinary council meeting. Our Court of Misfits and King Ogden were the only ones present. Even his bulk seemed small in the temple's space. Its art spoke volumes, silently playing out scenes we still struggled to understand, while reminding me of my failure beneath Justice.

"I have disturbing news," Ogden said, wasting no time on lengthy greetings. "The Court of Pain has ceased all communication. It sits in silence across the borders. But we did receive one final report…"

Ogden had rarely appeared so grim. And Pain's silence didn't warrant this abrupt meeting outside his typical chambers.

"What has he done?" I asked.

Ogden huffed through his nose. "His council members are dead. All of them. He's slung their heads across the street outside his tower."

"By Dallin," Noemi breathed.

"Why?" Draven asked.

"Just their heads?" I asked. Because I knew why. And when Ogden leveled his glare on me for answers, so did the others. "They disagreed with him," I explained. "And it wouldn't have just been their heads he's hung." I raised my mangled hand. "He likely sent pieces of them to their kin, as a warning."

"I need to get my boy out of there," Draven mumbled. His hands clenched near his blades.

"Your boy is probably already dead," Arin said, in a startling display of heartlessness for the Prince of Hearts. "Draven is no longer of use to Razak, so the boy is no longer of use too. I'm sorry, but that's the way it is with him."

Draven staggered and paced away, then back. "He's not dead, Arin."

"We should assume the worst."

"No, Arin... I fuckin' won't assume he's dead. Until we know otherwise, I will fight for my boy. The same as I'd do for you. The same as you'd do for Lark. The same as we'd all do for each other. He deserves that."

I caught Arin's eye and tried to suggest with a look that he not rile Draven up. We needed him hopeful, not grieving. Although, Arin was probably right. The boy was likely already dead.

"Was there more?" I asked Ogden.

"All trade has ceased. The borders are closed. It sems clear he's learned of our intent to rally against him."

"Is he arming soldiers?" I asked. He had the funds, but with his council dead, he didn't have the knowledge to command an army. Could he finally have made a mistake?

"Our spies have seen no sign of preparations. However, we've also lost contact with the spies."

"Your spies are dead," I said. "And Razak will have people in *this* court. Root them out before they become a liability."

"How so?"

"The children you throw away, start with their parents. Look at grieving wives, husbands, and by the gods, I hope you've stopped that practice. Watch for letters. Razak likes to write letters." I dared not look at Draven, knowing a letter had been Razak's preferred method of contacting him.

"I can do all that, but soon I will need War's crown," Ogden said. "Our warriors will expect to see it."

"He'll never return it. You're going to have to lead your people without a crown."

Ogden scoffed, but there was fear in his eyes. He'd thought himself immune to Razak's scheming, but Razak had gotten to him, and he still didn't know how. That was how my brother worked, and what made him so dangerous. He knew all our weaknesses. Even mine. I glanced at Arin and saw him clench his jaw in frustration.

"There were reports of him killing dissenters," Ogden said.

"It will get worse." I sighed. "How long until your forces are ready?"

"Two weeks."

"The next full moon," Arin said, as though that had some meaning to him.

"Indeed." Ogden cleared his throat and reached inside his pocket. Of course the king had a letter, and of course the seal was purple. I chuckled, not needing to read it to know what it said.

Ogden handed it to Arin, who read aloud, *"Ogden, King of War, we can end this war, before it has begun. Give me,"* —Arin's voice faltered— *"Zayan. He is of no concern of yours. Return him to me by the next full moon and I'll return your crown. Your people will not follow a crownless king. R."*

Arin handed the letter back. "I assume we're not giving in to his demands." He didn't look at me—went to great pains to avoid looking at me.

And I knew what had been bothering him all this time. It was obvious. He'd known about the full moon deadline *before* reading that letter, because he'd received a letter of his own.

"He's trying to fracture you, tear you apart," I said.

"Us," Arin corrected. "Fracture *us*. You're a part of this alliance."

"Yes, of course, *us*."

"I considered it," Ogden admitted. "There is no love lost

between you and I, Zayan. But War does not bow to anyone and certainly not that rat prince and his demands."

"He can't be trusted. It's all lies," Arin said. "To give into his demands would invite more of them. Any letters should be destroyed."

Trust. It was in short supply lately. What had Arin's letter said? To return me for peace?

Ogden growled his disdain. "We will march on Pain and end this within days."

Except, Razak had a point. History dictated Ogden was not the king of War if he did not have its crown. His warriors would be reluctant to follow him without it. He had his fake, but he'd know the truth, and the fact his crown remained with Razak would weaken him.

"How ready are the warriors?" Arin asked Draven.

"They meet again in three days. They'll be ready."

I had to talk to Arin, ask him what was in his letter. Did Draven have one too? He hadn't mentioned it, and considering his past betrayals, it seemed as though the warlord would admit to being coerced a second time, if only to save what remained of his friendship with Arin. Perhaps that was why Arin had tried to convince him his son was already dead. Maybe forewarn Draven, because Razak had told him the boy would suffer if I wasn't returned?

We left the temple, and I followed Arin's brisk pace across the bridge, down the steps, and into the gardens. "He sent you a letter," I said, racing to catch up.

"Who?"

I laughed. "Come now, Arin. I know your lies."

He marched on, down the paths winding through lush undergrowth. He told me he used to come here with Draven, to sit and talk, drink wine and plot.

"Then you deny it? You haven't received a letter like the king's?"

"If Razak had sent me a letter, you'd be the first to know."

That didn't ring true, but he was striding too fast for me to see his face. I caught his hand, tugged him back, and stepped in front of him, blocking his escape. "Tell me, darling. Look me in the eyes and tell me the truth."

He looked me in the eyes. And his were beautiful.

"There's no letter, Lark," he lied. "You have my word."

It shouldn't have hurt. I knew him capable of smooth deception; it was a large part of why he so fascinated me. Arin was a formidable adversary. I'd hoped, however, our adversarial days were over, and he'd trust me enough to tell me the truth. The only reason he wouldn't, would be to protect me.

"Regardless, I suppose there will be one." He caught both my hands, turning my hold into his. "We should all be prepared. Razak will say and do anything to have you back. He'll bribe people in this court, like he did Draven. You need to be careful, Lark. Don't trust anyone."

I had more than enough mistrust to go around. "War's people appeared to have warmed to me." I'd even begun to entertain them some evenings, much to Ogden's dismay.

"Let's hope that welcome remains warm." He hooked his arm in mine. "Come, Draven has invited me to train. He says I'm a natural with a blade."

"Did he now?" I laughed.

"I can't juggle them, not like you can."

"I can handle many a dangerous thing."

I trusted Arin, more than I trusted myself. If he was keeping secrets, then the secret was worth keeping. Mine certainly was.

CHAPTER 44

rin

As PREPARATIONS for battle with Pain continued, I sword trained with Draven in the early hours of the day, while the air was still cool. Lark always slept late, usually having stayed up carousing in the feasting halls, telling raucous stories to the warriors, ignoring my concerns regarding Razak's spies.

This morning, however, when I reached the training yard, Draven wasn't there to greet me.

I gathered my hair back, picked a sword from the rack of weapons, and gave it an experimental swing, testing its weight. I didn't have Draven's muscles or his stamina, but we'd discovered I excelled at speed and lethal accuracy.

Razak would surely send soldiers out to meet War's warriors, and I had no intention of standing back and watching others fight for us. I needed to be able to hold my own. Besides, throwing a sword around was far easier than juggling.

I thrust the sword a few times, watching my footwork in the sand, then making sure to keep my stance balanced, and as I spun, I spotted Draven's familiar figure with another man, half hidden under an archway. I'd never seen the man before. He wasn't wearing War's colors, so he didn't belong at court. Pale linens wrapped around him, designed to keep out the sun and the sand. A desert dweller, not a noble.

Not unusual. Traders from outside the court came and went every day. Supplies were delivered. Not everyone at court was a lord.

Their meeting ended, and I returned to stretching and footwork practice. "Who was that?" I asked, as Draven made his way over.

"Huh?"

"Back there? The man you were with. I've not seen him before."

"Oh." He turned away and grasped a sword. "Just an aide organizing a few menial things."

Menial things that he couldn't discuss. He hadn't met my gaze. "Draven?"

He swung the sword, bunching impressive biceps, making the two-handed weapon appear featherlight. "Yes?"

This man had lied to me before, for weeks. He'd looked me in the eyes and convinced me to join with him, knowing he plotted with Razak against us. Would he betray me again? "Thank you for offering to train me."

Of course he would. For his son.

"As I said before, I'm happy to help. Are you warmed up? Let's begin."

If Draven had been sent a letter demanding Lark for the return of his son, he'd make that trade. And if such a letter had been anything like mine, the exchange would take place before the full moon. Whatever the means, whoever he used,

Razak would stop at nothing to get Lark. And Draven was an easy target.

We practiced parrying and footwork. I was not a natural dancer, and told him so, then suggested he should train Lark, who I suspected would be lethal with a blade. I'd seen him fling daggers with terrifying accuracy.

Draven chuckled. "Lark doesn't use anything as honorable as swords. Daggers, yes. Easier to conceal for the final blow. If Lark has a mind to kill a man, his victim won't see it coming."

They'd had their differences, him and Lark. Draven had reason to hate the Court of Pain, and he'd always blamed Lark for what happened in my court, but we'd moved on from that. Hadn't we? Would he really give him up instead of telling us?

Draven had been clear in the past; he'd do anything to save his son.

"No, you're right," I said. "Lark doesn't need swords." Draven had lied once, and he'd do it again. There was no use in questioning him, as he'd deny it.

We talked a little more, but with the sun rising and the heat beating down, Draven called off the rest of the training session, claiming he had a meeting with Noemi to go over who in the court might be vulnerable to coercion. He'd know all about that.

His meeting with the stranger was probably nothing. But if it wasn't, then I had to warn Lark. Draven had betrayed us once. And for his son, we all knew he'd do it again in a heartbeat.

LARK WAS PROVING ELUSIVE. I was one step behind him all day, always chasing his tail, until catching up with him in my chambers—our chambers, since he'd begun to join me in my bed every night.

The aides had drawn him a steaming bath, from which he'd stepped moments before I entered. His robe clung to his narrow hips and damp back, hinting at his lithe muscles.

"Been busy?" he asked.

"I've been looking for you for much of the day."

He scooped up a bowl of grapes and sauntered over. "Grape? They're delicious." His voice was a playful tease, suggesting he was either about to tell me of some scandalous gossip he'd heard during his nightly escapades, or he wanted me on my back between his legs. It could go either way. Perhaps both ways. Sparks of lust skittered low, catching my breath. But we needed to talk first.

I plucked a grape free from the rest. "Listen, I have some concerns about Draven."

"Oh? He said the same about you."

"He did?"

"I know, fancy that, the warlord casting aspersions on our sweet and innocent Prince of Hearts."

"What's he said?"

"Only that he thinks you received a letter."

I looked away, then back again, hoping Lark hadn't noticed. He was picking out the best grapes and popping them between his lips. "I suspect he's had a letter, and Razak wants you in exchange for his son. It's an obvious play."

Lark paused to consider it. "Rather too obvious, don't you think?" He grinned, tossed a grape into the air, and caught it in his mouth.

"This is serious. He's done it before." I stole his bowl and squared up to him. "Why aren't you more concerned?"

"I know Draven." Lark reached around behind me, trying to retrieve his grapes.

I switched the bowl to my other hand, and we danced in a circle. "You *knew* him before too."

"He's not the brightest, but he's also not stupid. He won't betray us again."

Lark reached the other way, and I switched the bowl again, then raised it above my head. "For his boy, he would."

Lark stepped back, cocked a hip, and arched an eyebrow. "You're playing a dangerous game, Arin. Give me the grapes."

I waggled them in the air. "Take my concerns seriously and you can have them back."

He glared, then swept in, all naked and hot, and laid both hands on my chest. "I do take you seriously, and I agree, he's vulnerable to Razak, but right now, in this moment, I have a great many things on my mind, and none of them feature Draven."

"Oh?" I blinked. His touch sizzled my skin, igniting little darts of lust. Lark's sultry gaze spoke of all the things he wanted to do. "What do they feature?"

"Mostly you, some grapes, that bath, and the bed, perhaps the wall, or the dresser there, or even the balcony, now the sun has set. I haven't decided. But rest assured, Draven can wait. And in a few moments, I'm going to take those grapes from you and make you beg me to feed them back to you. One. By. One."

I grinned and I lowered the bowl, if only to rest my arm. Lark looked down at the fruit, then at me, eyebrow arched.

"I'm not going to beg you to feed me." I gave him the bowl. "That's ridiculous."

He plucked a grape free, placed it between his teeth, and bit down inside a grin, and by the gods and all the powers, that single gesture had my cock responding like a puppet on his string.

"Get in the bath," he ordered.

I didn't move. Wanted to, but also... didn't. There would be a reward for obeying him, there always was, but a part of me resisted. Pride, perhaps. Soon, we both knew I'd do anything he asked. And he'd do the same for me. I almost moaned in anticipation.

"I'll make it worth your while." He fluttered dark lashes and set the bowl down on a sideboard.

When he turned again, he let his gown fall open, revealing his slim physique and hardening cock. I might have begged him to feed me the grapes right then, might also have realized he'd distracted me from whatever I'd been concerned with moments ago. He'd emptied my head of everything except him, and how droplets gleamed off his thighs and the dark patch of hair at his cock, how his chest had me imagining all the ways I could trace those muscles with my tongue. I imagined how I might lower myself over him, slick and ready, and how he'd stretch and fill me.

"Strip, Arin." He fluttered a hand. "There's my good prince."

I frowned and folded my arms.

"Oh, you want to play stubborn?" He tied his gown closed and folded his arms like mine, then jerked his chin. "Off."

The message was clear. I got nothing if I didn't play by his rules. I *loved* this, and he knew it. Muttering a few obscenities, I tugged at my shirt, unlacing the ties, and yanked it off, over my head.

He flicked his fingers again, gesturing at the trousers.

People dressed lightly in War, so it wasn't long before I stood naked, armed crossed, hips tilted, trying to ignore how his roaming gaze scorched my skin wherever it landed. Neither of us could ignore how my cock betrayed my increasing interest in his seduction. He smirked and turned away to collect the bowl of grapes once more.

"Get in the bath," he said.

There was no point in complaining when we both knew I'd do it. Besides, as I climbed in and sank below the water, I was glad for the warmth after a day sweating under the sun.

Lark knelt beside the tub and held out a grape, as though I were a child. "Well done."

I blinked at him, wondering whether and how to play along. "I get a grape?"

"What did you think you were getting?"

"You?"

"Patience."

I tried to take the grape, but he snatched it away and opened his mouth in demonstration. I huffed, then begrudgingly parted my lips. Lark poked a grape through, onto my tongue.

I'd rarely tasted a sweeter grape, or one as rewarding.

"Lie back."

I settled back against the side of the tub and laid my arms on its edges, anticipating whatever he had in mind. And he had such a wickedly brilliant mind.

"Close your eyes."

When Lark said these things, it made anything possible, as though his voice held magic, as though he could spin a whole world of fantasy with just a few words. I closed my eyes and listened to the swish of his gown and soft footfalls on the tiled floor.

"No peeking."

Damn.

He shuffled around, then came back to the bath; his gown swished again and the sweet smell of flowers rose from the water, bringing with it a thousand memories of the meadows of home.

Lark applied a sponge to my chest, gently rotating it. And

I half dreamed of better times, of a home that no longer existed, and of lying among the flowers with Lark, pulling petals and sending them flying into the air. Would we ever have that?

"Ah, I'm sorry, Arin, this was not meant to sadden you."

"No." I opened my eyes, finding them wet. "It's the scent, it reminds me of home. Did you know?"

He gave me the coy look, which meant he did, and wrung out the sponge. "Wet your hair."

I did, dropping all pretense of disobeying. His fingers massaged my scalp, then his thumbs rubbed down my neck. What kind of magic was this, that he was able to melt my bones with touch alone? He began to knead my shoulders and the moan that rolled from me was one of pure delight.

"Rinse off and climb out."

"I'm enjoying this."

"You'll enjoy more if you continue to behave."

I couldn't resist his promises. After climbing out, I stood wet, naked, already drying in the heat, body clearly eager for whatever he had planned. He sauntered forward and fed me another grape, making sure to stroke it across my lips before sliding it inside.

I caught his wrist, holding it steady. "Let me do something for you."

"Not yet." He pried my fingers off. "On the bed. Hurry, Prince of Flowers."

I almost ran, but that would have been undignified, so I walked, bare-assed, feeling his eyes on me the whole time, and flopped onto the bed. This was divine... It wouldn't last— tomorrow we'd be discussing war and Razak, and terrible things. But tonight? Tonight it was all about me and him.

"Face down, Arin, darling."

He poured oil on his hands from a bottle I'd never seen

before, clearly having planned for this earlier in the day. Rubbing oil over his hands several strides away, his cock was as interested as the hunger in his eyes.

I rolled onto my front, unsure if he wanted me ass-up or flat, or—

Warm, oiled hands swept over my ass, dipped into my waist, swept up my back, and then kneaded over my shoulders, applying firm pressure. I moaned again, already falling under his spell. Then his thumbs rolled in toward my spine and my moan lengthened.

"Gods, yes." I folded my arms under my chin and closed my eyes. The bed rocked, the mattress dipped, then his hands rode downward again. His fingers dug into my buttocks and kneaded hard, almost too hard. He pinched, and I bucked, tossing him a scowl.

Of course, he laughed. "Just testing your threshold."

I melted again the moment he returned to massaging my shoulders and back until my whole body buzzed, skin prickling hot and sensitive. I was so damned hard every tiny shift in pressure had me wishing he'd flip me over and swallow me to the balls. Or slide himself deep inside. Every time his fingers strayed to my ass and spread and squeezed, he teased a little closer, expertly building to what we both knew I wanted. I knew it was coming, and panted for it, so primed I lost all ability to think, becoming a creature of need.

Then he let go, leaving me writhing and desperate. *Now, let it be now.* But when the tight push of his cock didn't come, I glanced over my shoulder. He was there, kneeling over the backs of my knees, his cock willing but his expression distant. He looked... *through* me.

"What is it?" Had I done something wrong?

"Nothing, it's nothing." He tried to smile and failed—he never failed.

I twisted, quickly. Had he not enjoyed this? Should I have done something more, been more involved? I'd thought he'd wanted me compliant? "Lark, talk to me. Did you want me to do something?"

"No." He chuckled. "It's not you, I..." He trailed off again, appearing pained by his own thoughts.

"Ask it, anything."

He stroked my jaw, tilting my chin up, and I was unsure if I'd ever seen him so raw and vulnerable. "Will you take me, as I take you?" he asked.

Take him... how? "I don't—oh." Like *that*—our positions reversed. "I haven't ever... I don't know how." There were steps involved, like lubricant, steps he did so well. What if I fumbled things and made a fool of myself?

"It's really not difficult, once you've begun, and there are no mistakes you can make with me."

Not for him, perhaps, with his countless lovers. "I thought... We haven't and you seem to like me like that, so I didn't want to switch things around. All this time, have you wanted me to?"

"No, it's... complicated. And you weren't wrong, I do like to fuck you in the ass, Arin. I like it very much, in fact. And as you enjoy it, we'll continue in that manner. Forget I said anything."

I could not forget it when he wanted it, needed it even. He'd asked because it had meant more to him than a fleeting idea. I couldn't deny him after he'd been so generous with me. "If you want me to, I will. I may need some direction, but I want to."

The smile he'd lost earlier crept back to his lips. He really did want this. I'd wondered, sometimes, what it might be like to pleasure him as he pleasured me. But we'd fallen so easily into his taking charge that I hadn't cared to ask. But now the

idea might become reality, and I might have Lark under me...
My heart thumped harder, burning up my nerves with need.

"Ah, but there's more." He turned his face away.

"Tell me, please. Talk to me. Don't shut me out." I cupped his face and turned his head back.

"You are aware I need pain to finish? While you're inside me, I need it to hurt."

Wait, he *wanted* me to hurt him? I had in the past, in the throes of passion. He'd demanded it, and I hadn't hesitated, but this seemed different. What was he asking exactly? How much pain?

He licked his lips, gaze averted again. "It'll take more than a bite, Arin."

More like... the cuts on his chest? Or more like... choking him? That wasn't what lovemaking meant for me. I couldn't hurt him that way. "Lark, I don't think I can. I'm not Razak. I can't *be* him for you."

He tore himself away in a rush and stumbled from the bed. "That's not it. I shouldn't have asked. Forget it—"

"Wait, don't leave. Talk to me."

He stopped, head bowed, alone in the middle of the room, cold and naked in the moonlight. "I'm not asking you to be him, Arin. Quite the opposite. I want him gone, I want him out of my head and you in his place. I need you to take me, and own me, so I no longer think of him when we..." His throat clicked as he swallowed. "When we're together."

He swooped back to the bed and gathered my hands in his. "I need you in me, so you're in my dreams too. I need to see your face as you come inside me—not his smile. Gods, I know how it sounds. I'm sorry if it's wrong. I won't make you do it. But I never want you to be him." Breathless, he perched on the edge of the bed. "I should have stayed quiet. Have I ruined everything?"

I couldn't be Razak, I couldn't hurt Lark and love him at the same time. I could only be me. I straightened, still on my knees, and looked into his eyes. "I'll do it. But we do it my way. Will you trust me with that?"

He bit his lip. "Always."

How could one man be so strong and so vulnerable, in a single glance. I loved him, admired him. He was the bravest person I'd ever met. And, impossibly, he was mine.

"You have the oddest look on your face," he said, making light, because that was what he did—made light in the dark, made music in the quiet, made magic in the midst of hopelessness.

I captured his face in my hands and kissed him slowly, as though he were the most precious thing I'd ever held. His mouth opened, giving me permission, inviting me to take more. I savored him, loved him, kissed him with more than my lips, with my heart and my soul too.

He eased me back and knelt on the bed too, face-to-face, body to body, with the scented desert air sweeping in through the window and the quiet moon casting cool light over us. I stroked his shoulders, then kissed him on the neck, loving him with every touch. His fingers buried in my hair, and when I glanced up, he'd tilted his head back, surrendering in a way he never had before.

This was different. Something powerful was happening here, something important, a moment so simple but so profound. I loved him, and it wasn't just a word, or a feeling, it was *everything*. In every breath, every heartbeat, under my every touch of his warm, firm body, every fluttering kiss and quick sweep of my tongue.

He pulled me down with him, spreading his knees so his thighs bracketed my hips, and our breaths quickened together, our bodies so close the lines between us blurred.

Lark eased the bottle of oil into my hand, producing it from thin air, like magic.

I looked at it, then up at him. He nodded and spread his knees wider, trusting me to do this right. He'd said it wasn't difficult, and I ached to feel him on me, under me, however that would feel. I knelt back and stilled. He lay on his back, one arm flung overhead, the other at his side, his whole body a broadcast of gleaming skin and sculpted muscle. His beauty stole my breath and my wits.

"Arin?"

"Yes, yes..."

He chuckled, and so did I, and the tension disappeared, like his sleight of hand had magicked it away. I tried not to overthink it. It wasn't hard, he'd said, although I was. And so was he. He clutched a pillow and tucked it under his hips.

"Look at me."

"I am." His veined length twitched.

"My eyes are up here, prince."

I flicked my gaze up.

"Trust me," he said, dark eyes rich with cunning and delight. "You can do this."

I nodded, afraid my voice wouldn't hold, and clutched his thighs with oiled fingers, then stroked downward, seeking that part of him I knew would feel good, if I did this right.

I raised myself up on my knees, angled my cock, clutched his leg, and adjusted my position and his. The fact he stared at me, apparently not needing to blink, was both the most arousing and most terrifying part of all this. Tremors rippled through me, nerves and adrenaline conspiring to make me shake.

I eased my oiled cock to his hole. His gaze broke away when he dropped his head back, surrendering for a second time to my hands, my will, my cock. Gods, he was tight, but the oil saw to it he widened, taking me in. It seemed like a lot, like too much, and I withdrew, earning his challenging glare.

"Tease me and I'll soon switch this back around," he warned. "Stop worrying and fuck me, Arin. You won't—can't —hurt me."

I wanted to, but what if I did hurt him?

"You recall the time you struck me? A backhand to the face? You remember how I looked at you, how I smiled? I want the pain, I want it. So fucking give it to me, like I know you want to, like you've always wanted to. You have it in you to brutally fuck me, Arin."

I remembered that slap well. Remembered it like it was moments ago. I'd struck him to prove I hated him, and he'd liked it.

I hooked his thighs over my forearms and thrust my hips forward, sinking my cock deep into his tight grip. A bolt of pleasure snapped down my back, stuttering my breath and emptying my head of all thought. Lark threw his head back, mouth open, as though in a silent cry. He clutched the sheets, and his flushed, straining cock leaked. I thrust again, driving into him, fighting the friction and slick tightness to stay buried.

"Yes," he gasped, then threw me the most devastating smirk. "Fuck me harder, Prince of Flowers."

I lost all reason then, and thrust balls-deep, burying myself in firm, muscular heat. Gods, he was so hard, I wanted to clutch his dick, pump him, but I had both his legs high, my cock so damned deep, pumping in perfect rhythm. He was right, it was easy, natural even.

A shudder ran through him, so perfect I had to capture it. I dropped his legs and fell forward, shifting the angle danger-ously low, but somehow stayed buried inside. Then I scooped him up, sat him astride my lap, and clutched his ass, lifting him up and down my dick with his erection slick and rubbing between us.

He slumped close, hands on my shoulders, and let me set the pace. It was beautiful, *he* was beautiful. I bowed my head and bit his shoulder. He hissed; his fingers dug in. I tipped him back and lowered his shoulders to the bed, with his ass still on my thighs, my cock buried at the perfect angle, and I had him. He gasped aloud. I knew that electric sensation racing up his spine because he'd done the same to me.

I rocked my hips, pumping between tight muscle, then pulled him upright again and kissed his mouth, his neck. He gasped and nipped at my mouth, my chin, wherever he could reach, mad with lust. And when I looked up, he was watching, always watching, peering into my eyes and riding my dick. Something wild passed between us in those glances, some brilliant part of us scorched together to form a connection. He loved me. I didn't need to hear it, I saw it in his eyes, felt it in his quivering touch and trembling body.

He dropped his head back. "Oh gods, Arin, yes..."

He clutched my arm, gripping so hard it hurt. I tucked his ass back, angling my cock deeper, and watched as his mouth fell open, his body quivering like the strings of his violin. I had him now, he was mine. He panted; heat flushed his chest and neck, and threads of silken cum dribbled from his cock, slicking my belly and his. If I touched his cock, he'd come, but I had his ass propped up and my cock pumping, and it was all I could do quicken my pace and hammer hard into him, making him chase that brilliance.

"Touch me," he whimpered, his voice shattered. "Squeeze my cock."

I pulled my right hand out from under him and wrapped his dick in my fist.

"Arin, harder." I pumped him so hard my hand ached from the strain. "I think... I..."

I kissed him, bit his lip, and he stuttered, his whole body shuddering around me. His brilliant eyes blew wide and speared right through me as spasms of cum betrayed his climax at my hand. "Come in me," he growled. "Now."

I dropped his dick, shoved him down onto the bed, and lost myself to the feel of being inside him, chasing the high, feeling pleasure spool tighter and tighter. My thighs slapped his ass and the thick length of my cock slid in and out, then all at once, the pinnacle of ecstasy snapped and unraveled. I cried out, although I hardly heard it, since I was somewhere far away, burning up in a trance as my climax took me.

"Yes." He grabbed my hand and pulled me down on top of him, both of us slick with oil, sweat, and seed. His breaths sawed at my ear and his heart thumped against mine.

I turned my head, expecting to see his smile. A tear escaped the corner of his eye and slipped down the side of his face, disappearing into his hair. Another tried to follow it. I wiped it away and braced over him. "Lark?"

"Yes," he whispered, eyes shining in the moonlight. "Thank you."

"Gods, don't thank me." I kissed him messily and mumbled into his mouth, "It wasn't a chore."

I was still inside him and liked it, feeling connected and close, as close as two men, two souls could ever get.

"Do you think the bath is still warm?" he asked, after a moment of comfortable silence.

"Probably." I leaned sideways, propped on an elbow, with him still trapped under most of me. He gazed at the ceiling, his eyes dancing at some thought in his head. The tears were close, still there, in his eyes. Happy tears, I hoped. His smile seemed satisfied, as did his body. I skipped my fingers down his cock, making him hiss and laugh, then took advantage of the distraction to withdraw.

He gave a shudder, then looked over, sleepy-eyed and satisfied. "You liked it."

I shrugged. "It was passable."

"Passable?" he gasped. "You wound me."

"Ah, but I didn't wound you." I rested my head on my hand and skimmed my fingers in lazy circles on his chest, watching his face. I hadn't hurt him, not like he'd assumed he'd need. I didn't know what that meant, just that it was good, if his smile was any indication.

"No, I wasn't hurt. Yet I did come. Which was... a first, for me. You must be pleased."

"Naturally it takes the Prince of Love to make his lover come with a few strokes." I mimed pumping his cock in my fist.

"Naturally." He laughed, then sprang and wrestled me under him until there was nothing but laughter and his mouth on mine, the kiss so desperate it stole my breath. "I love you, Arin. Always. Never forget it."

"I know." I fought to keep from grinning like a fool even as my heart tried to deafen me.

He snorted and rolled away, then got to his feet and sauntered to the bath. "Of course you do, Love's Prince. Or are you a king now?"

"King of Flowers. I like it." I propped myself onto my elbows and watched him dip his hand in the water. "Would you be my King of Storms, if I asked?"

"Are you proposing?" He smirked over his shoulder, naked and temptation personified. Mine for the taking.

I'd meant the proposal as a jest, but we *could* join. Would he want that?

He laughed the idea off before I'd had a chance to reply.

"Come, bathe, and I'll tell you a tale of how the King of Flowers mends the King of Storm's broken heart. How does that sound?"

I might have told him yes, if the emotional knot hadn't choked off my voice. I didn't want this moment to end. It truly was special, like a dream come true—one of the good ones. And there were so few good dreams left. If I stayed awake and cherished every moment of this night, perhaps I could make it last forever.

He offered his hand. "The King of Storms was a powerful man, feared by all. He spent his days and nights in darkness and shadows of his own making, but few knew he sought the one thing he could not have. Love."

I climbed from the bed and made my way over. "Does this fantasy tale of yours have a happy ending?"

"Of course it does. It wouldn't be much of a story otherwise."

I tipped his chin up and peered into his fathomless eyes. "Does ours?"

"I have no doubt," he said. And lied.

CHAPTER 45

 ark

THERE HAD BEEN a time when betrayal was all I knew. *Traitor*. It was in my name and followed me like a shadow. I'd hoped those days were over. But there was one last thing I had to do, one last betrayal, and as I looked over at Arin, his expression content, lashes fluttering in his sleep, I hoped, one day, his hate would fade, and he might forgive my final act.

The desert's morning haze filtered through the shifting drapes. It was time. I crept from the bed, dressed without making a noise, and carrying my boots, I padded barefoot from the chamber. Outside, I tugged the boots on and hurried down empty corridors. War always seemed quiet in the mornings, likely due to their penchant for late-night drinking. Timing was everything.

I slipped by sleepy guards, passed through the training grounds, and spotted Draven's bulky outline near some of the less extravagant villas War's residents dwelt in. The buildings here spent half the day cast in the shadow of the palace's huge battlement walls.

Draven saw me approach and straightened. Beside his boot lay a traveling bag.

"Any trouble?" he whispered.

"None." I took the bag and slung it over my shoulder.

"Arin?" he asked.

"Asleep. He won't wake anytime soon." Pushing the bitter-sweet memories of mine and Arin's lovemaking aside, I adjusted the bag on my back and studied the wall's daunting facade. Draven had assured me it was scalable here, using the villa roofs to gain height first. He'd done it before, and if he could carry his bulk up that vertical climb, then I shouldn't have any problem—besides my lacking fingers.

"Lark, are you sure? Arin... He won't forgive this."

"I know," I said. Of course I knew. I'd burned too many bridges. There would be no going back.

He frowned and resigned himself to letting me go. "Friends are waiting on the other side for you," he said. "They'll take you to the border."

I nodded. I should thank him but found the words lacking. I couldn't have done this without him. He'd organized safe passage, and he'd given his word not to tell Arin. He wanted his son saved as much as I wanted all of this over. It was a lot.

I offered him my hand. "Thank you, Draven." We shook, and his smiled slipped sideways. "I know we've not always seen eye to eye—"

He yanked me into his arms, almost lifting me off my feet, then let go and clapped me hard enough on the back for me to almost choke on my tongue. "I know you don't believe it, but you're a good man, Lark."

Was I? I was righting some wrongs, that was all. And

saving War's people from what would be a pointless, bloody battle. "We'll see."

"Oh, almost forgot." He stepped back, collected a second, slimmer bag, and handed it over. "They're not common in these parts. I've been assured it's all tuned, whatever that means. I hope it's what you wanted."

I grabbed the bag and peeked inside. A glossy black violin was nestled in red silk. "It's perfect, thank you."

"Well then." He tucked his thumbs into his trouser belt and backed away. "I suppose this is goodbye. I hope this isn't the end, for Arin's sake."

A smile was all I could offer him, but even that fell short at the thought of leaving Arin in such a way. "He will not be pleased with you either."

Draven sighed, then took in a deep breath, filling his broad chest. "I know."

"Look after him." A new ache grew in my chest. "He won't want your help, but he'll need it."

"D'yah even have to say it? You know I will."

I shook his hand again and clasped his arm, meaning it. And this time, when our eyes met, there was no jest in it, no doubt either. This had to be done, and we both knew it.

"Save my son," he said.

I nodded. "Rest assured, if he's anything like his father, he'll be all right."

Draven blinked too fast, took himself back a few steps again, and peered up at the wall, trying to hide the emotion on his face. "You see how the roof leans away? Jump from there. There's a few blocks jutting out, you can't see them from down here, but once up there, the path is clear. There's a rope on the other side to help you down."

I shrugged the violin over my other shoulder and studied the route from the villa roof, up the wall. It seemed insurmountable. But all important journeys began with impossible goals.

Draven chuckled. "For your skinny ass, this'll be easy."

"Make sure to watch my skinny ass, Warlord. You know you want it."

He chuckled. "Get out of here, fool."

I headed for the side of the nearest house. Hopefully its occupants wouldn't hear my clambering along their rooftop.

"May the endless winds be at your back, Lark."

I threw the warlord a wave and started the climb. Once at the highest point, the footholds became obvious, and the jagged blocks making up the Court of War's exterior walls provided the way to its battlements at the top. I climbed steadily, one boot after the other, fingers dug into crevices, and made it to the top in quick time. At the top the wind buffeted from left and right, and beyond War's court, the dunes rippled like a red ocean.

Three people waited below, their faces hidden in head wrappings. Draven's people, the people of the sands. Good people. Pausing to catch my breath, I cast one final look over War's pyramid and its red-tinged world. Draven had vanished, back to his life, back to making battle preparations. And Arin lay sleeping. That ache in my heart grew. I grasped the rope and began the descent toward the sand.

The wind was no less harsh when I reached the ground. It howled like an omen. One of Draven's people nodded and slung a cloak around me, then handed me a wrap for my head, to keep the sand and sun at bay.

"Are you sure?" the man asked, his sand-encrusted eyes all I could see between the linen face-wraps. "Most want to leave Pain's borders, not get inside."

"I'm sure."

"We go east, collect the kareel. It'll be a steady ride from there." He handed over a pouch of water. "Ration it, and we'll get you there."

I fell into step behind them, kept my head down, and marched on.

Guilt burned like an open wound. Arin would wake soon, the bed empty beside him. He never would have agreed to this. Knowing the Prince of Love, he'd have bound my wrists and my heart to stop me from leaving.

"We have to hurry." Razak was right about one thing. It was time I went home.

"All right," my guide said. "Just so long as you keep up." He picked up the pace.

I glanced behind us and found War's court already blurred by windblown sands. Good. A little further, and the court would be gone altogether.

When Arin woke, he'd hate me with all his heart. As I deserved.

CHAPTER 46

rin

LARK WASN'T in bed when I woke, which was unusual for him. He'd probably be back soon.

I lay alone, thinking of last night, of his gentle touch, his many kisses, and his cool tears. I could still feel him, still hear his voice whispering in my ear, hear his demands to fuck him.

These were not the best of times to fall in love, or perhaps they were? I'd lost my home, my court, my family, but I had Lark. And with Lark, all at once, everything was worth fighting for.

I threw off the sheet, washed up, and dressed, then went in search of Lark. I'd slept late and stopped in the kitchens to raid the after-breakfast scraps. Lark hadn't been seen at breakfast, but he often skipped it. As I left, a few members of Ogden's council stopped me to tell me of a meeting planned for sundown to go over the strategy for getting the warriors to Pain's borders. I agreed to meet and sought Draven for our morning training sessions. He proved elusive too, probably with Lark, perhaps discussing any weakness in Razak's borders.

The day passed too quickly, stolen by menial tasks and interruptions by the nobles, asking after my old court and any future plans. By the time the sun had begun to set, and I was due at the council meeting, Lark still hadn't returned. It didn't matter, he'd be at the meeting. And later, I'd see if we could take our dinner in our chambers. We'd drink wine on the balcony and watch the sun set, just him and I, stretching out the time we had left before readying for battle, and maybe I'd pin him against the balcony rail and take him like I had last night. The thought trilled desire, setting butterflies loose inside me.

Draven was in the council chambers, Noemi too. They had their heads together. Ogden nodded at my arrival. "Let's begin."

Lark wasn't at the table. He'd be along in a little while. One of Ogden's generals explained how war's warriors would be split into three attacking fronts, like the prongs of a fork, and they'd breach Pain's borderlands in three key areas.

I glanced at Lark's empty seat. A small, unsettling slither of unease trickled down my spine. He'd probably got distracted somewhere, caught by someone wanting him to juggle or spin a quick yarn, as had happened since he'd been a regular at the evening feasts. Still, he'd have been informed of this meeting. And while he didn't think himself worthy of a seat at the table, he'd always made an appearance, if only to walk out again moments later.

"Has anyone seen Lark?" I asked, interrupting Ogden's general discussing the logistics of supplying a marching army.

Ogden grunted his impatience. "If we were to wait for Zayan, we'd never get anything done."

"I know that, it's just... has anyone seen him at all today?"

Nobody met my gaze, most uninterested. Draven tapped his fingers on the table in a restless rhythm. "He's probably in the training yard," he said. "I saw him there earlier. He said something about throwing knives, and I left him to it."

"Did he know about this meeting?"

Draven met my gaze. "I assume so."

"Are we done talking about the fool?" Ogden demanded.

The fool. I tilted my head and laid my gaze on Ogden. "He's a Prince of Pain, my king, and has as much right to sit at this table as any of us."

Ogden's smile was far from friendly. "Be grateful nobody has bundled him back to Pain where he belongs. I hear his brother has written enough letters to bribe half my court."

My heart thumped. I leaned forward. "There are more letters?"

"Wherever he is, I think it best your companion prince stays out of sight, don't you?" Ogden said.

I clamped my mouth shut and squeezed my hand into a fist instead of blurting a hundred reasons why Lark was the bravest man here. They knew, and they didn't like that Razak's own brother had saved the Court of War. I caught Draven's glance, expecting to see his fury too, but he faded away, cheek twitching.

"If you don't mind, and as we're nearly finished here, I have training to attend to," he said.

"By all means, go," Ogden dismissed him. "Have the warriors ready. We march in two days."

Draven nodded, stood. "My lords." And then he left, without so much as a glance or a good evening in my direction.

He'd met with that stranger in the training yard, he'd

admitted to seeing Lark earlier, and now Lark wasn't here. Nobody had seen Lark all day.

If Draven had received a letter like mine, asking for Lark in exchange for his son, he'd do it—he loved his son. Love made us all liabilities.

I motioned to stand.

"Arin," Ogden barked. "I need you here. We have a matter to discuss regarding the Court of Love—your court—and its future. Sit. You and I are not done."

I hovered, teetering on the edge of chasing after Draven, but my court and its people—many of whom were refugees in War—were important too. "Can it wait?"

Ogden's eyebrows lifted. "Sit, *King* of Love."

Reluctantly, I sat. "Go on."

CHAPTER 47

ark

RAIN POUNDED the ground in earnest, welcoming me home. Draven's people did as they'd been tasked and delivered me to Pain's borders. From there, I'd walked the back roads, keeping my head down and hood up. I'd waded through the river that coiled itself around Pain's cities to avoid the checkpoints preventing Pain's citizens from leaving.

Nobody guarded for people *entering* Pain, exactly as Draven had said.

Soaked through, chilled to the bone, I walked along somber streets and passed by increasingly grander towers, until entering the city proper. My feet ached, wet and sore in tight, soaked boots, but the cold no longer burned my skin— I'd grown numb. If I stopped walking, I wouldn't start again, and might even turn around.

I had to keep moving forward.

Black umbrellas bobbed over the heads of people streaming back and forth. Nobody paid me any mind.

And then I came to the first of Razak's warnings.

I stopped mid-flow among a stream of silent people and looked up at the string of severed heads slung across the street.

I didn't know their faces, nor their crimes. But the warning was clear. Razak had always been vicious, always cruel, but this was extreme, even for him. Power had tipped him over the edge, and now he was accountable to nobody.

It was time to face my brother, but first, I had my own message to send.

Shifting my traveling bag on my right shoulder, I pulled the black violin and its bow free of its own bag. Rain patted the shiny surface, then streamed like tears across its body. That same rain hissed on the street, the people, tapping on umbrellas, gurgling down gutters. Boots splashed through puddles. But the water could not wash away the acrid smell of fear. It clogged the city in a smog.

It hadn't always been like this, and it didn't need to be in future. Pain was necessary, it was a part of life, but its citizens had become Pain's prisoners.

I walked on, passing a second warning. This time the heads had been placed on spikes jutting from the bleak building facades. I slowed, then stopped, pushed back my hood, and studied their wrought faces, forever frozen in death. Razak's council, what had remained of them. He had no use for people who tried to reason with him. He had no use for reason itself.

Sighing, I swept my cloak back, raised the violin, and pinched it between my chin and shoulder. The bow rested on the strings, poised in anticipation. This was it, the moment everything changed. As soon as I played a single note, I'd be sealing my fate. Right now, I could still go back. All I had to do was turn around. Arin would welcome me, the war would begin, and thousands would die.

Fate rested on me, and my violin.

I was doing this *for* love. There was no going back.

I breathed in, listened to the rain, and pulled the bow across the strings in one thin, tight note. The sound pierced the hissing rain and march of the hundreds of people around me.

Someone bumped my shoulder.

I stumbled, regained my balance, and pulled the bow over the strings again, freeing three notes in quick succession, letting the city swallow those too.

Rain blurred my vision and clung to my lashes. The people marched on. Taking another breath, I tipped the violin and danced the bow across the strings. The music began slow, a tease of a few notes, and then grew, building, drifting, sweeping. People veered around me like water around a stubborn rock. I played faster, spilling notes from the strings now, coming alive, louder than the rain, than the thump of marching feet. The rain no longer drowned it out. The melody filled the street, rising high above our heads, and poured into every open window, every door, and all who listened.

Yes, see me, hear me. This is my song...
It doesn't have to be this way.

I walked on and played, making the music dance in the dismal gloom of Pain's streets. I was no longer a man playing a violin, I was magic. It beat through my heart, my veins, and it pushed me on. I played and exposed my soul.

The people slowed their relentless march. Some stopped, others joined them, until all around eyes watched, ears listened, and finally, they saw me. Lark, the player, the dancer, the boy who sang for coin, who'd only ever been free in music. And they heard that promise of freedom now.

Rain splashed from my bow's slashes, my arm burned from keeping the violin raised, and the cold tried to numb my fingers on the strings. But I played on and on, and it seemed as though the entire city stood and watched.

The music built and built, setting my soul ablaze like a beacon in the dark. I played as though my life and the lives of thousands depended on my every note. I played until I was lost.

A thick, heavy clapping rang out, landing like a hammer's blow, shattering the spell.

I tore the bow from the strings and stood, panting, in front of the tower, facing my brother atop the steps. He wore Pain's crown, and while the blood had gone, the crown's barbs remained fixed in his skull. Cruel madness gleamed in his eyes.

"Bravo, dear brother, bravo!" He went on clapping and descended the steps, dragging the hem of his purple cloak through wet puddles. "Quite the spectacle you make." He eyed the people gathered behind me, standing defiant in their motionless silence.

I saw them all, each and every one.

And they saw me.

Razak had a choice to make: kill me and hang my head above the streets, or welcome me home. The whole of Pain's world watched.

I lived, I breathed, I existed. I was Pain's prince too. And now the people had seen me, they'd heard me, and they *knew* me. I'd bared my soul to them.

Razak couldn't kill me, not without risking unrest. He was one man, king or no, and even with his stolen power, Pain's people were many. He studied them and me, then stretched out a hand. "Give me that violin."

Rain poured down my face, my neck. Rain dripped from his crown and beaded on his dark lashes.

Breathless, I met his gaze and handed over the violin.

His cruel smile ticked his lips. "You and your *games*," he purred, then slammed the violin over his knee, shattering it. He tossed its fragments into the gutter and snarled, "Welcome home, brother."

And so began the most important performance of my life. If I failed in this act, my audience wouldn't leave dissatisfied, they'd die. And so would I.

I dropped to one knee and bowed my head. "I come as a friend to your court, and as your brother who loves you, and as the traitor's son." I took Arin's crown from my bag and held it aloft, meeting his gaze. Gold and pearls sparkled. His eyes widened in disbelief. Now he had all four crowns, and all the power of a fallen god.

I'd given him the final piece of the puzzle. But his eyes narrowed on me.

It would take more than the crown of Love to convince my brother I loved him. It would take every trick, every misdirection, and every sleight of hand I knew. "All hail, the King of Pain, the King of all the shatterlands."

CHAPTER 48

rin

I'D STAYED AWAKE all night, waiting for Lark to walk through my chamber door with a tale of some misadventure he'd gotten tangled in. But as dawn approached, it was clear Lark was not coming back.

And Draven would pay for this betrayal.

The warlord had made himself scarce after the council meeting, and no matter where I'd searched, it had seemed as though he'd disappeared. I'd find him now.

I grasped a dagger from the training racks in the yard and with the court still sleeping, I hurried toward his room.

I should have cut his throat all the way the first time. None of this would have happened, and Lark would have been safe. I'd known then, how Draven was a liability. And he'd proven to be the worst of all my enemies. Razak hadn't lied while looking into my eyes; Razak hadn't bedded me while spilling my plans and secrets to our enemy.

If Draven had hurt Lark, Dallin help me, I'd cut him again from ear to ear.

I eased open Draven's chamber door and skipped my gaze to the bed, where a sheet outlined his sleeping figure. He didn't stir.

And to think I'd trusted him a second time? More the fool me. I crept in and stood over him. He slept at peace, knowing he'd traded Lark away. *How could he?* My fingers tightened on the dagger. *How could he do this to me, to us?!* I wanted him dead. I'd thought myself incapable of killing, but he'd driven me to this. I was not the same Prince of Love whose court had burned to ash. If Lark was gone, then I had nothing left.

I grasped his hair. His eyes snapped open. I pressed the blade to his neck. "Where is he?!"

Draven plunged a hand under his pillow, then brought out a knife and slashed it at my face. I lurched away, stumbling. *The bastard!*

"You think I sleep unprepared after last time?" he panted, snarling, and rising from the bed. "Gods damn you, Arin—"

"Where is he, Draven? What have you done?!" I lunged, thrusting the dagger. He brought his forearm up and my blade cut deep, zipping open his golden skin. Blood splashed up the wall. He howled and charged, slamming into me. His crushing embrace clamped my arms to my sides—trapped. I roared, thrashed, and sank my teeth into his shoulder. He flung me away, growling and gasping, then dabbed at the bloody bite mark. "Arin, stop. Listen—"

"To more of your lies? No. How could you!?"

"He wanted this."

My vision turned red. "No!" I marched forward. "That's the lie you tell yourself. Did you get a letter? Did Razak write you, demanding Lark's return?"

"Like he did *you?*"

I snarled. My letter was insignificant. "Answer the question!"

"Arin, just listen. I don't know what you think, but the letter had nothing to do with this."

"You *did* get a letter!" It was as I'd suspected. Razak had demanded Lark in exchange for Draven's son. I raged and lunged. Draven reeled, tumbled across his bed, and scrambled off the other side. I skirted the bed and charged after him, cornering him.

"I don't want to hurt you!" he snapped. "Arin, stop—"

I dove and thrust the dagger toward his throat. But his arm came up a second time, barring my strike, stopping it short. He grasped my wrist in his left hand, trying to lever me off. The tip of my blade hovered closer to his neck, so close that just a little more would see it pierce his skin. I surged, roared, and drove him against the bedside table. A lamp toppled off, smashing into pieces. He struggled, we wrestled, arms and hands, the knife poised between us. The blood from his bleeding arm greased his hold.

"I *hate* you." I threw the words like knives and watched them strike at his heart, making his face fall.

I was too late. Lark was gone. Draven had taken him. *Everything* had been taken from me. Lark was all I'd had left. I'd kill Draven, and savor it. The lying, selfish, bastard. "He's my everything. You took him!" I forced the words through clenched teeth.

Draven pushed back, muscles trembling, and began to inch me away.

"Damn you!" I'd kill him; he deserved to die, for Lark.

Fury lit my veins on fire. He wanted to live, I could see it in his eyes, but my desire for his death was far greater. He blamed himself for losing his son, he blamed himself for the fall of my court, that was why he'd faced the sandworm and almost let it devour him. He knew he was to blame for all of this. "It's all your fault, Draven."

His eyes widened. "Arin—"

"You *want* to die. So let it happen, let me finish what I began in my court. Just give up, it's all you're worth."

Hurt and knowing softened his snarl.

"You're a liar, a coward, and a traitor. A shame on the Court of War."

His wide eyes shone, wet with tears. *Yes, hurt, feel the pain, and know my agony.*

"You've ripped my heart out, Draven." The knife's point wavered near his whiskered skin. He'd weakened; just another push, and I'd thrust the dagger into his neck. *"Bleed for me."*

"Arin! Stop!" Noemi's cry stalled my descent.

Draven shoved, but I shoved down again. "This does not... concern you..."

In the corner of my eye, I caught her blue cloak rippling as she rushed forward. "Stop, Arin, this isn't you."

"It is now!"

"Please..." She swept in, grasped Draven's shoulder and filled my vison with pleading, green eyes. "Lark asked Draven to help him!"

What? Uneven tremors tore out my strength, trying to undermine me. "No, that's lies. Draven did this. He did it before, and he's done it now."

"I don't lie, you know this!" Noemi said, as fierce and true as any blade. "Draven *told* me. Lark made him swear to keep it a secret."

I blinked and peered deep into Draven's eyes, so deep I might find the truth buried there. Lark wouldn't lie to me again, not like this. He wouldn't carve out my heart, knowing how its every beat lived for him. He'd told me he loved me. He'd never betray me. "You're lying."

"No," Draven said, still holding me off. "It's the truth."

"No, he'd... He'd have told me."

"Arin." Noemi got to her feet and came closer still, her hands clasped together, pleading. "He knew you wouldn't allow him to go. You'd stop him, because it's who you are. You'd stop him, and War would march, and thousands of people would die. Lark believes he can prevent that. He thinks he can stop Razak alone."

My chest tightened, heart squeezing. "He would have told me." But saying the words aloud made the truth clear. If Lark believed he could save thousands of lives by sacrificing his, he would. Of course he would. I'd always known it. He believed he wasn't worth anything, thought he was a gutter whore, not meant for love or the likes of love. But he was my *everything*. And if I had to sacrifice the shatterlands to prove it to him, I would.

My heart stuttered, stealing my breath. A dreadful regret yanked on my wounded soul. Our last night together, the tears in his eyes... His body never lied, and his body had said goodbye. Lark had chosen to go.

I swallowed the sob trying to crawl up my throat. Tears slipped down my face. I wanted to rage and scream, but it wouldn't change anything. It wouldn't bring him back.

"Cut me, I deserve it," Draven snarled. "But if I die, who is going to help you save Lark?"

I dragged my glare back up to Draven's face. He hadn't betrayed me. Lark had, but the worst of it was, I understood why. I shoved Draven off, threw the knife down, and stumbled from them both.

Noemi rushed in to help Draven. I'd almost killed him. I'd been seconds away from killing a man for all the wrong reasons. And I would have killed him; I'd been mad with it, and still was.

The room tilted, or the world did. If I'd killed Draven, I'd have been the same as Razak. The letters...

Razak had gotten inside my head, made me doubt everyone, doubt myself. Even now, with him atop a throne in a faraway court, he'd dug his claws in and manipulated me.

He'd sent the letters to shatter us. And it had worked.

I swayed and stumbled onto the balcony, then clutched the rail. The moon had surrendered the night to the sun, turning into a ghost in hazy red skies, barely there at all. In a few days, it would be full, and we'd all be out of time. Because, if Razak had Lark, then the Prince of Pain had everything he wanted. When War marched, people would die. But Razak didn't care about that, or the lives of his own people. He didn't care about his court. He never had. He had Lark, and he had power. And in his mind, nobody could stop him.

Lark had known all this.

And he was right. He'd done the right thing.

I wouldn't have. But, now I had no choice. Exactly as Lark planned.

Gods, I hated him. And loved him. My fool, who was about to save the knight, and the world. And if I let him, he'd die for it. Because that was who he was. The most heroic of us all.

CHAPTER 49

ark

ECHOES OF A MASSACRE haunted Razak's tower. I passed a bloody handprint on the wall, a dried pool of blood on the floor. Death's smell hung in the air. The story had been left on display for all to see. A few terrified aides scurried out of our way like insignificant bugs. None of the other staff remained, having either fled or been killed.

The Court of Pain couldn't function this way. But Razak had never been interested in running the court, or its cities. He cared nothing for his people, only himself.

Razak's tower had become a tomb for those who had attempted to stand against him.

Was this what had happened in the buried palace beneath Justice? Did an ancient king fall within its halls? Dallin himself, perhaps? Was the same story painted on its walls doomed to repeat again here? I hoped, this time, to change its ending.

"I have a gift for you, dear brother," Razak said, sweeping down the corridors as though nothing about the sprays of blood on the walls were unusual. "I prepared it for your inevitable return."

Moments ago, he'd shattered my violin, and I'd knelt to him, claiming to bring him news of an imminent invasion. Since my display in the streets, he feared killing me, but Razak had worse weapons than death at his disposal. He wouldn't take my passion, like he had Queen Soleil's; he didn't want me docile and obedient. He never had. I'd likely be punished for my betrayal.

The gift would not be a kind one. He could fuck me, cut me—none of it mattered. Just so long as he *trusted* me. I was about to face the ultimate test, and my final act. All the lies, the acts, and the years of smiling and dancing and performing for the enjoyment of others—everything had led to this moment.

"I assume you have a plan? Your reason for being here?" He glanced over his shoulder. "As you have returned of your own free will. That sharp mind of yours will be plotting. Do you assume I'll welcome you with open arms after your stunt at Justice, hm, if you pretend to be docile?"

"I am always yours, dear brother. Even when it does not appear that way."

"I almost fell off that fuckin' bridge! If you truly wish to stand at my side, then your behavior says the opposite."

"All of that was necessary to fool Arin into believing I despise you and love him. Lies, I assure you, Razak. All lies."

He chuckled, then muttered, "To *fool* Arin... Such a shame you didn't bring Love's prince with you. I'd have you cut him from his balls to his chin, and then we'd see where your loyalty truly lies. No?"

"You will have him, Razak. They treated me as though I

were a prince. I attended every meeting. The information I have will guarantee you'll see him swing from the hanging tree."

He stopped, spun, and stared into my eyes. And I stared right back, calm, controlled, the truth in my eyes, on my face, hidden in my hint of a smile. Razak had the elusive power to yank out our will, he had Pain's crown hooked into his scalp, and now he had Love's crown too—my gift to him. But Razak wanted Arin writhing in his hands, wanted to breathe Arin's last gasp into his own lungs and watch the light snuff out of Arin's eyes. I peered into my brother's eyes now, and I knew how much he yearned for Arin's death, because that same yearning lived and breathed in me. He'd relish Arin's death, the same as I'd relish his. All that remained was to see whose story ended first.

"I want to believe you," he admitted. "But unfortunately for us both, I know you." He waved a finger. "We were always meant to be together, you and I." His glare softened, gaining shallow warmth. Above everything, Razak desperately wanted to be loved. I'd have to prove my love for him, in every despicable way.

He breathed faster, anticipating what was to come—nightmares in the making.

I was ready. This was all fantasy; none of it was real. Another dance, another lie. I was Zayan, and I loved my vicious, despicable brother.

He turned away and marched onward, cloak bellowing. "I admit, I may have wandered off the path somewhat. It's difficult to remain grounded with this gift of power in my hands." He looked down at Love's crown swinging from his fingers. "Knowing I can crush a soul with just a glance. You have no idea, Zayan. The power, the rush! It's as though their every death feeds me, makes me stronger." He laughed again. "I'm aroused just thinking it. I want to share it with you, share *everything* with you, but you must understand, Zayan, your lies are slippery things. I cannot merely trust you without proof. I'd be the fool, in that case. Not even with this gift of yours." He raised Love's crown. "Prove your love, convince me, and we will rule the shatterlands together as one." He stopped outside a door like any other we'd passed by and turned to focus on me. "But betray me, Zayan, and I will burn this world and everyone in it, starting with Arin."

"I am yours, Razak. I've been yours since the day you saved me from the hanging tree. Body, soul, and mind. Whatever it takes, I will prove it. We're brothers..." I dared reach for his face and found his cheek cool, soft, and damp under my fingers. "I love you."

"Such pretty words." He searched my eyes for the truth. All that power, a whole city and court on its knees around him, and he was just a man who wanted to be loved. "It remains to be seen if you stand by them."

He opened the door and a wave of coppery air washed over me, mixed with the sweet scent of sex and sweat. I blinked at the man suspended from the ceiling and slammed mental barriers down, keeping the horror far from my expression, but it twisted and lashed inside me. I smiled and stepped into the nightmare.

Theo hung naked by his bloody wrists from leather straps fixed to the ceiling. His flash of red hair matched at his crotch. His chest indicated he was breathing, so by some miracle the lacerations shredding his chest, back, and legs hadn't killed him—yet. Those cuts, they were so like the ones I bore.

"You see—" Razak strode over to him. "—you weren't here, and I needed someone. I knew of a girl in the court of Love who'd survived, a dear friend of yours. I had planned to find her, but then this one revealed how you'd been close during your time in Justice, and he was the far easier catch. So really, this display is your doing, Zayan." He gripped Theo's hair and lifted his head. Through the blood and bruises, recognition sparked in Theo's eyes.

I'll teach you to dance, I'd told him.

We'd met briefly, but in doing so, I'd sealed his fate. He'd saved Ellyn's life by admitting he knew me. So brave, so foolish.

Razak watched my face for any twitch, any sign that this was anything other than a wonderful gift. I laughed a sickening chuckle, approaching them both. "I'm almost jealous. He had all your attention, brother, while I had none."

"Oh, you had my mind. I penned many letters with you as their subject." Razak laughed too, and wasn't this just fucking fantastic, the two of us, two brothers, bonded in love and sex over the torture of an innocent man. My stomach churned, trying to eject the sight because my eyes could not. By pure strength of will, I kept a smile pinned to my face, playing the beloved, devoted brother, the villain in this tale—Razak's favorite fucking toy.

I peered into Theo's dull eyes. The single blessing in all of this was that he appeared to be without his will. Hopefully, Razak had stolen that first. Without it, Theo wouldn't have cared about any of this. But with his passion, his will, he'd have begged Razak to kill him. Perhaps to have your will stripped from you was a blessing in disguise in this case.

Theo was a shell, emptied and spent, hanging from Razak's ceiling.

The sweet man I'd met, the man who abhorred lying and had never been outside Justice's walls, would never learn to dance.

Bitter rage clogged my throat. I pushed it down, pushed it

all down, trapping it so deeply inside that I made myself soulless, just so Razak didn't see the disgust and horror when I straightened, smiled, and stepped intimately close to my brother. Inside, I screamed.

"I'm here now," I purred, close enough to see lust sparkling in his eyes. "String me up," I whispered. "Hurt me as you hurt him." I brushed the words over his lips. I'd thought I was the weak one, but it was clear how I was his weakness. He'd bound me, fucked me, cut me, used me for his pleasure, but I'd always had power over him because during the years he'd kept me chained, he'd loved me. Arin had said I was stronger than Razak, and I was beginning to believe it.

No wonder he'd struck the Court of Love first. Love was a force unlike any other.

I cupped my brother's face, as I had so many lovers, countless times, and I stroked my thumb across his cheek. "I love you." Tears swelled in his eyes—the first I'd ever seen from him. "Truly. I love your sharp mind, Razak. I love your brilliance. And I love how you feel when you fuck me."

Love was how this ended. Our father had sought a forbidden power to resurrect his lost love and failed, but Razak had claimed it. Razak wanted love. Each of us coveted love, relished it, went to war for it. Justice upheld laws to protect it; we feared love, hated it, and burned worlds for it. Love had begun this, and it would end it. *Love was the key.*

Razak slammed his mouth over mine. I heard Arin's crown clatter to the floor as Razak's arm encircled me, crushing me close. This had to happen, I was ready, I'd do anything to convince my brother I loved him, that all of my lies had been *for* him. It was the only way to save lives, to stop him and save the shatterlands from his madness.

The power to tear out souls made him a god, but *his* soul was mortal, and it pined for love.

The kiss was bitter and sharp, worse than any he'd forced on me before, but I gave it back to him, mirrored his passion with the lies of my own.

He pulled back and clutched my face. "Cut him with me, like we used to. Cut him, bleed him, and fuck him. Do this and prove you're mine."

"Yes." I grasped the back of my brother's neck. Oh, to choke him now, to wrap my hands around his neck and squeeze the life out of him—but if I failed, all would be lost. I had to go further, I had to make him believe the lie, make him think his story had a happy ending, even if it cost me my soul.

Razak peeled away and skimmed his fingertips along Theo's bruised shoulders. Theo didn't respond, and I didn't expect him to. The worst of his pain was over. He breathed, his heart beat, but he was an empty vessel. Razak grasped Theo's shoulders and licked up his neck. "Hm, delicious. Such a shame you missed this one when he still had his fight," my brother said, full of glee. "I remember how you prefer it when they fight. You were always the one to hold them."

I had liked it, because I'd been in control, hurting someone else, just as I was now. But this control was balanced on a knife's edge. One wrong glance, a single misstep or misspoken word, and Razak would know my lies for the pantomime they were.

I tipped Theo's chin up and looked into his vacant green eyes. If any part of him remained inside, I hoped wherever he went next was good to him, and maybe there he'd learn to dance. Leaning in, cheek to cheek, I caught sight of Razak's enraptured face behind him. He had his hands on the man's hips, his mind far away, and as Theo's whole body jerked to the thumping rhythm of Razak's cock, Theo's lifeless shell no longer felt any of it. It would be easy to condemn Razak for his actions, but I'd played my part in similar trios before. I was no innocent in this.

"I'm sorry," I whispered over Theo's listless lips, then kissed him.

It would have been easier had Razak taken my soul, then guilt wouldn't have burned all the way through it. But this *should* hurt, it should burn and rip me apart. If it hadn't, I'd have been no different from Razak.

While Razak fucked Theo, I crept my hand up to smother Theo's mouth and nose, cutting off his breath. *I cannot teach you to dance, but I can free you from this nightmare.* Maybe, when my time in this life was done, we'd meet again, and there, we'd dance in fields of flowers.

Theo didn't struggle, and within moments, his breath no longer came, and when I placed my hand on his chest, nothing beat back.

I met my brother's lust-flooded eyes.

Razak knew I'd killed him but didn't know why. To spite him? Or because I liked it? A cruel smile twisted my lips. "Imagine it," I said. "Me as your prince, you my king, and how we'll shatter the world and remake it anew. With us, together, nobody will defy you."

Razak laughed, threw his head back, fucked Theo's cooling body, and with a cry, he spilled his seed into a dead man.

And all I had to do was lie with my body and soul while clinging to the hope that both survived what came next.

CHAPTER 50

rin

WE'D BEEN MARCHING for two days across desert sands and into cooler climes, until rain began to fall and never let up. Now, at Pain's city border, our warriors lined the wide river's edge, preparing to pass over one of several bridges into the city itself.

War's black and red banners clung to their poles, weighed down by rain. Clouds of purple and black churned above Pain's towering buildings, each peak as jagged as a thorn, or as sharp as Pain's crown's jagged barbs.

This time when I'd approached Pain's borders, it hadn't been in a carriage drawn by one of War's awful trains, but atop a horse, as the King of Love. Albeit without my crown. Draven had taken Love's crown and given it to Lark. *All part of their plan.* A plan of which the details given to me were scarce. I was supposed to trust Draven had Lark's well-being in mind, and trust that Lark would prevail. *Trust them.*

I did trust Lark. I trusted he believed this was the only way. I trusted he'd slit his own wrists if he believed it would do some good. And that was the problem. By Dallin, both Lark and Draven were testing my loyalty and my patience.

A commotion broke out at the front of the line, stirring the troops. So far, we'd met no resistance from Pain, no soldiers, no people. But I wasn't as naïve as to think Razak would let War march into his city unchallenged.

I kicked my horse forward. The ground beneath its hooves had turned to sloppy mud. War's warriors looked up at my passing, falling quiet. Ogden's huge outline dominated the large, lumbering kareel he rode. He'd stopped at the bridge, at the center of the commotion.

There were no soldiers on the bridge, and the checkpoints had been abandoned. However, across the other side, blocking our entry into the city, stood lines of what appeared to be unarmed civilians.

I trotted my horse alongside Ogden's kareel. "What's the issue?"

"Children," the king said.

"What?" I stood in the saddle and peered across the mirky bridge, through the rain.

Hoods hid their small faces. They stood defiantly, each one clasping the hand of the next. "By Dallin... they're children?!"

They'd been dressed in red and black, to make it clear whose children they were. War's rejects, given to the sands and taken by Pain. Pain's *benefits*. And leverage against War's warriors, against its king.

The message was obvious. To get to Razak, Ogden's warriors had to cut down their own kin.

Fucking Razak, he had a counter to our every move.

"Children," the king fumed. "He has children fight his battles! He is no warrior, no king! He's a coward!"

My horse shied at the king's gusto. "Your mistake is assuming he'd fight fair," I replied, trying to calm my flighty steed. "Send a messenger, ask him to meet us on the bridge. Make it clear I'll be there. He'll come."

"I'll go," Noemi offered, geeing her horse up alongside us. Draven rode in behind her. Rain soaked Noemi's red bangs, gluing them to her face, and turned her blue gown almost black. But her expression was as fierce as ever. "They won't strike down a member of Justice."

Draven grumbled his dissent. "You don't know that," he said. "Razak does not care for any court but his own. And you've already wounded him once. He'll likely kill you on sight."

"I'll go," she repeated. "I can do this. It's why I'm here. Justice is balance. I will mediate."

Ogden huffed. Wearing only his gleaming circlet around his neck, rain streamed down his barrel chest. He had amor but had opted not to wear it. Lark would have laughed at him and made some quip about a king without armor. But Ogden still lacked his crown, and all of this was an act, a performance of his own. He didn't need armor; no arrow or lance could pierce his skin. "My warriors will not cut down children," he said.

"Why not?" I snapped. "You threw them out!"

"How dare you?! Those reprobates are nothing to do with us."

"Can't you see? Look at them! They wear your colors. They are the sons and daughters of War—"

Ogden muscled his kareel against my mount. "Silence, Arin!"

"Silence me, Ogden, if you wish, but your ugly truth is just across the water and Razak is using it against you now."

"Enough!" Noemi scolded. "By Dallin's sake, those children are waiting for us to save them. Stop bickering. Ogden, arrange an escort to accompany me over there."

I nodded at Noemi. She dipped her chin in return. I owed her much, not least for saving me from making the mistake of killing Draven in a rage. But she'd also saved Lark in telling me his truth. If anyone could save those children, it was her.

Ogden harrumphed and grumbled, then gee'd his wet, shaggy kareel alongside Noemi's horse. "Come then, Justice Noemi, let's get this done."

I tore my glare from them as they went in search of a guard and peered across the bridge to the lines of children. There were so many—of all ages it seemed. Draven had said something about the endless winds coming back around as punishment. This was surely War's reckoning.

"He's a blustering fool," Draven drawled.

"Yes, he is." He was more than that; he was a coward. He'd found every excuse not to challenge Pain, until there was no other option. "He'll get the warriors and those children killed."

Draven peered across the water too. "Lark is our best hope. He will come through."

"Come through with what exactly?" I asked, not for the first time during our march. And every time I'd asked, Draven had claimed he did not know. Exactly as he would now.

"If I knew, I'd tell you."

I folded the reins in my grip and arched an eyebrow. "These lies are tiresome."

"It's not a lie, it's the truth, Arin. Lark feared I'd be a

liability, as did you. He told me only the minimum. Just that he knows he can stop Razak."

"I don't know what's true with either of you anymore." Lark's final betrayal stung my heart every time I thought of it, and on the march here I'd had too many hours, too much silence, to reimagine our last night together. Every time I recalled it, the pain grew. Loving Lark had hurt me like nothing else.

We fell quiet, with just the sound of pounding rain.

"Do you think my boy is among them?" Draven asked quietly. "To see his face..."

It was possible. But unlikely. "If Razak knows you're here, which we have to assume he does, then your boy is valuable leverage." Draven gave a low growl. "Prepare yourself, Draven. When Razak was relatively sane, he'd have killed your son. Now, reasonable minds cannot fathom what Razak will do."

"I'm going to gut the prick and hang him from his insides."

"I'd pay good coin to see that."

"For you, I'll make it free."

I smiled, despite the grim surroundings. "Frankly, you'd better hope I don't get to him first. I've designs on that neck of his."

Draven rubbed *his* neck. "A quick death is too good for Razak."

"Yes, but we are not monsters." I caught Draven's eye. "Yet."

A blue-clad rider and guard broke from our line and crossed the bridge. Neomi dismounted on the other side of the river. Although the rain drowned out her voice, I had no doubt she'd make a convincing case to meet with us. Razak would come. He wouldn't be able to resist. Would he have

Lark with him? What if he'd already taken Lark's soul, what if Lark was an empty shell? I squeezed my horse's reins.

"He'll be all right."

"You had better pray to the endless winds he is, Draven. If he's so much as lost another finger, I will make you pay with yours."

"He *will* be all right, Arin. Trust him. He knows Razak like no other soul on the shatterlands. If anyone can play that bastard like a fiddle, it's Lark."

"That's what I'm afraid of."

Draven glanced over. I sighed and shifted in my saddle. "Lark fears he and Razak are the same. He fears what he's capable of, and Razak will do everything in his power to turn Lark into his shadow. They are each their worst enemies."

"I'm surprised to hear you claim they're alike. I thought so, at first, but Lark is nothing like his brother."

"I *know* Lark. He'll do anything to bring down Razak, to save the rest of us, even at the expense of his own soul. He's more than capable of terrible things. I just hope the price isn't too great. And I hope he succeeds, because if he gets hurt, no amount of warriors, children, or honor will stop me from riding over there to save him. War, Justice, and the rest of you be damned. I'll burn the shatterlands to ash for Lark, and I hope Razak damn well knows it."

Draven absorbed the words awhile, then smiled. "Woe will befall anyone who dares cross the King of Love."

We waited in the rain, staring at the lines of silent children staring back. Razak knew we wouldn't cut them down. We'd have to find another way into his city, another way to root him out. I couldn't rely on faith that Lark would save us. We needed a plan to get to Razak. Everything else was secondary. Killing Razak was the only goal.

But how to kill a man with the godlike ability to extract every warrior's will to fight?

Carefully, Lark would say. I wished he was here, riding a horse alongside me. He'd have laughed at all of us, then ridden on out there and pulled a magic card from his boot, changing the course of fate.

Noemi returned. "Razak will meet with us on this bridge. Look for the purple banner. He'll be there."

"Can we kill him during this meeting, or must we negotiate with a mad man?" Draven asked.

Noemi appeared less than impressed with the idea. "We are meeting in the spirit of discussion. I doubt he'll leave himself exposed to attack. He'll have protection of some kind."

I stared at the vacant spot on the bridge where the checkpoint had been abandoned. Razak had stabbed me, tried to kill me, taken my life, my court, my everything from me. But he would not take Lark. I'd kill him with my bare hands if it came to it.

"We must negotiate, for the sake of the children," Noemi said.

"You cannot negotiate with madness," I whispered. Whatever happened, it ended here. It had to. There was no going back, no surrendering. War had discarded their less-than-perfect children, giving Razak the weapons to beat them with. This was their own doing. I'd give the order to march through those lines, and if nobody followed, I'd do it alone.

"May the endless winds be at our backs," Draven said softly.

I lifted my face to the rain and sent a silent wish to Lark to stay strong. I was coming for him. "We wait for the purple banner."

LATER, with our campfires burning along the river's edge, we got word of a purple banner fluttering from the abandoned checkpoint's wire barricade. I, alongside Draven and Ogden, mounted up and rode out to meet the three waiting figures.

Lark stood beside his brother.

I dismounted my horse and tried to sort everything I'd seen riding to meet them. Lark had his will intact, which was good, but that was the only good thing about any of this. Razak's crown was still embedded in Razak's head, and in front of him, he clutched a young boy. But not just *any* boy.

A glance at Draven confirmed it. He stared at that boy with eyes so wide, there was no use in hiding his love.

Draven stomped forward. "You vicious weasel—"

Razak lashed out with a hand, and Draven crumpled to his knees.

"Don't!" I took a step, then caught Razak's warning gaze and froze. The remnants of his bitterly cold power rattled around inside me, like broken glass. I had no wish to feel his grasp on me again. "Razak, stop!"

Draven writhed, teeth gritted against the onslaught of having his essence torn from him.

"Stop!" Ogden boomed. "Or we march on your city!"

"We come with peace in mind!" Noemi's cry cut through them all. "Those were the terms!"

Lark yanked the boy from his brother's arms, applied a blade to the child's throat, and smiled.

Everyone froze. Razak glanced sideways at his brother.

Lark's smile was as sharp as the dagger he held. A dribble of blood ran down the boy's neck.

Razak dropped his hand and Draven slumped forward, gasping and choking, freed of Razak's grasp for now.

Razak's smile for his brother spoke of familial pride, and by Dallin, they were so alike in their dashing purple and black attire. If it weren't for the crown, there would be little to tell them apart. Lark's eyes shared his brother's touch of madness.

This had to be part of Lark's plan, because if it was anything else, then he was already lost, and none of this mattered. I stared, trying to make him look at me, make him see what he'd done to me, to *us*. Make him see how he'd hurt me, and how I loved him, loved him so much that I'd forgive him anything, even this. But he stared instead at Draven while keeping the young boy pinned to his legs.

"My, my, what an audience," Lark said, his voice as smooth and soft as oil. "It appears, brother, we have them concerned."

Ogden took it upon himself to step forward. "Prince Razak—"

"King," Razak interrupted, lifting his chin. "Do you not see my fucking crown?" He laughed. "Oh look, none of you are crowned, none of you are my equal. You are so far below me, you're all ants, scurrying around my feet."

"*King* Razak," Ogden said, making it sound as though he'd had to wring the word out of his bones. "Surrender and we'll leave your city and your citizens intact. Defy us, and we will destroy everything in our path. War never loses."

Razak blinked. "Is that so?" He sighed. "How disappointing. I had hoped you'd at least prove entertaining." His gaze scoured us all and came to rest on me. "My dear Prince of Love."

"King," I said. "I'd like my crown back."

Razak's eyebrows lifted. "Say *please*?"

"Fuck you."

461

He laughed and clapped his hands together. "Yes, now you are always so brilliantly entertaining. Isn't he, Zayan."

"He is," Lark purred.

"Was he as fiery when you had him on his back and fucked him, dear brother?"

"Always." Lark smirked.

Heat climbed my face. "End this before more people die. Sit on your throne and make your court dance, but leave the shatterlands as they are. There is no need for bloodshed."

Razak tapped his finger against his chin. "You clearly do not know how power works, having never had any true of your own. And what little power you did have, I took from you." He spread his hands. "You're offering me nothing. I've already destroyed Love and Justice, and War will destroy itself, as is inevitable, considering its blundering king. But rest assured, we will welcome you into our new world."

"'We'?" Noemi asked.

"Oh yes, Zayan and I. You see, we've come to an understanding. Did you know he's played you all along?"

"You scheming rat!" Ogden surged. Draven lurched to his feet and blocked the king from making a mistake.

"Is this true?" Noemi asked Lark.

"I was never one of you, and we all knew it. You each wanted to save me, thinking me lost. I was always exactly where I needed to be." Finally, his gaze came to rest on me. "You especially, Arin. So adamant I could be saved, making you my hero. I told you time and time again, I am not who you think me to be."

It wasn't true. It couldn't be. We'd been here before, with Lark's lies tangled around us. And it *was* lies. I knew him, his kiss, his body, his breathless gasps when he came undone in my hands. I knew his soul, his heart. I knew every piece of him, and I knew this was a lie.

"I loved you." The tears weren't hard to summon. I only had to stop holding back the heartache.

"That's your mistake."

Razak watched, appraising, determining, scouring every word and glance for the truth.

"Razak, you have the power to prevent further bloodshed." Noemi stepped forward. "You have everything you wanted. Let the children go."

"Says the bitch who stabbed me. Justice let my father rot beneath its foundations and hid the truth from the shatterlands. You are the worst of all the courts, with your corrupt laws that we all must follow, all except *you*. The courts—" He snorted. "—the shatterlands, it's a cruel joke. Dallin knew it. He tried to regain his power, and you all buried him for it, trapping the source of each of our passions, our will, beneath your foundations. The shatterlands are mine. Your people are mine! The air you *fucking breathe is mine! You live because I tolerate you! Now get out of my sight before I harvest your souls!*"

The air around him warped and twisted, rippling as though thick, like water.

"Go!" I yelled. "Retreat now!"

We clambered onto our horses, but as the others galloped to the relative safety of the riverside, I hesitated. My horse shied again, dancing. Razak laughed, but the sound of it carried far and wide, across the river, into the city, and beyond. Beside him, Lark looked at me and brought the bloody knife to his lips. He licked the blood from its surface and when Razak turned and swept away, Lark followed, throwing his own wicked laugh at us for believing in him.

I trusted him.

I loved him.

I knew how strong he was, but also how vulnerable. Razak was his weakness.

What if he'd lost himself in the dark? A storm never ended if the sun did not break through.

He'd need me to light his path back.

I turned my horse and galloped toward War's front lines.

The shatterlands could not wait on Lark's plan. We needed our own.

I dismounted outside our hastily erected tents and strode toward the king's. While Razak's attention was on the west side of the city, on our front and the warriors and the line of children, we'd send in a band of smaller, less obvious warriors, unnoticed. Draven would be among them. He'd lead them. He'd find Razak and kill him. Diplomacy, peace talks—none of this would work.

I stomped through mud, veering around the outside of the camp, where it was less crowded. We had to fight like Razak, not like Ogden wanted. Underhanded, scheming. It was the only language he knew.

A shadow shifted in the gloom to my left. A blur shot out of the dark. I barked a startled cry, but a hand muffled my voice. Something hard struck the back of my head, ripping my balance away. The ground rushed up, someone caught me. Too fast—too much. I opened my mouth to call for help but a rag was thrust between my teeth, almost shoved down my throat.

No, no! I kicked, dug my heels in, and the second blow swooped in and stole my consciousness away.

CHAPTER 51

ark

"The night is cold, and my heart is heavy with sorrow, but I know that someday we'll be together, and I'll wait for that tomorrow."

I stood at my old chamber window but imagined I stood on a cliff with the broken fragments of my violin in the dirt, all around me. I couldn't play. All I had left was my voice. And so I sang.

I hadn't been cuffed, not this time. I'd laughed and kissed Razak and come in his hand, let him spill down my throat. *It had been so much easier to fuck him before I knew what freedom tasted like...* I'd surrendered pieces of my soul to cement the lie, but now, as I stood at the window of my old chamber, peering through bars that forever followed me, the bruises burned and my skin crawled, and inside my head the screams never ended.

I had so little of my soul left to give.

My hands shook, fingers trembling. I took a drag on the pipe and let the pennywort lead me away to that distant meadow, where the sun forever shone, the ocean thundered, and Arin stood on the beach, juggling pebbles—or trying to.

Fuck. I was too deep into the dance to trip now.

Something Razak had said during the meeting on the bridge, about the crowns... about Dallin. Sonya had told me Dallin himself may have once lived in that ancient castle, and Razak had implied Justice had buried him there. The clues had been in those wall paintings. The crowns, the kneeling, hollow-eyed people. It all came down to the crowns. Crowns that had always been kept apart, and when brought together, they'd unleashed Razak's chaotic power to sap a man of his will to live. The crowns were the key. I had to get them together again, all of them, *close* together—like I'd seen in the wall art. *"And I'll wait for that tomorrow,"* I whispered, needing to hear the words, using them to ground me.

The door opened behind me.

"Zayan, my dearest..."

Ice touched my spine and my stomach flipped, trying to eject itself. I hadn't eaten since arriving, couldn't...

I forced a smile onto my lips, pushed away the wretched burn of Razak's touch, and made sure my eyes gave nothing of my turmoil away. "Is it done?"

"The warlord's boy is secure. Such a fighter, that one. He tried to bite me. Can you imagine it? Such a shame he'll likely have to die."

Draven's son wasn't dead, not yet, and that was all I needed to know. I'd save him. If I could save only one soul, let it be his.

Razak swooped in and nuzzled my neck. "You smell like sex. And pennywort."

I'll wait for that tomorrow...

Tomorrow was a lifetime away. As distant as the horizon.

I handed over the pennywort pipe to Razak. He took a long drag, filling his lungs, and blew smoke toward the ceiling.

"Kidnap Arin," I said, when his eyes turned glassy. "He is the King of Hearts. He's their strength. Kidnap him and it will all fall apart." It was a logical step, to extricate Arin. And the idea would cement any notion that I didn't care for him.

Razak eyed me with curious glee. He chuckled and sauntered to the bed, where the sheets lay tousled and reeked of sweat. "Tell me how."

"Draven leans on Arin, his every word; he loves him. Ogden is a fool. Take Arin, and Draven will lash out. He's strong but will rush in without preparation. Noemi wants to be seen as the one to balance them out, to bring order to chaos. But she doubts herself. She was not born a noble, she has no right to wear a crown, and she needs the support of others, like Arin, to step up. Ogden's only here because of Arin's insistence and because he cannot be seen to back down when, in his mind, the weakest of the courts, the Court of Love, steps up. Remove Arin and the dominoes fall."

"Hm," Razak folded his legs and bounced his foot, still smoking his pipe. "And what shall I do with Arin, once we have him? Do you have a plan for that too?"

My Prince of Flowers... My true love. The reason my heart beat. The sunshine to my storm. "Kill him, of course."

"Of course." Razak leaned back and braced his arms on the bed. "Your mind is a razor's edge. We should hurt him first, no? Do to him what we did to that flaccid aide from Justice?"

"String him up like you did Theo? Yes." My heart thudded so loud it drowned out my voice. Someone else said these terrible things because it couldn't be me. "Cut him, fuck him, make him writhe in blood and choke on cum."

Razak's smile grew. "You are a true Prince of Pain."

I was more worthy of that crown on his head than he was, more Pain's son than him, more my father's rightful heir. My heart pounded, trying to break out of its cage. I turned away and fought to level my breathing. If he heard me struggling, saw me falling, he'd know my lies. *Someone help me... Arin, help me... I'll wait for that tomorrow... Help me do what needs to be done... A beautiful lie... I am all things, and none. A boy who sings for coin. A lark on the wind...*

"It is a good thought, a solid idea. Remarkable really, how alike we are sometimes," Razak said. "Arin is truly the crutch they all lean on. But last night, while you slept, I secured our victory."

"Oh?" I asked, swallowing my thudding heart. What had he done? When I turned, all was well on my face while pieces of my heart and soul shattered and rained around me.

"Come, my beloved." He stood and presented his hand. "Allow me to introduce to you our victory."

I took his hand and walked through desolate blood-stained corridors, down to the foyer, and outside, to a waiting black carriage. Razak led me inside. The hairs on the back of my neck prickled. Whatever this was, wherever we were headed, I'd endure it—but as the horses lurched and the carriage jolted into motion, the tingling continued down my spine.

I'll wait for that tomorrow...

I spotted the dagger I'd used to threaten Draven's boy hooked into a sheath at Razak's hip. If I were to snatch it and attack now, he'd yank out my soul long before I could open a vein.

"I thought you'd have the crowns with you," I said, making conversation. "After going to such great effort to secure them."

"They're safe." He folded his legs and tapped his boot to the rhythmic clip-clop of horses' hooves.

I had to know where, and once I did, I'd make him take me there, steal that dagger, line the crowns up like in the wall art images, and what would be, would be. As plans went, it was damned flimsy. But I needed to make it so Razak wouldn't see the dagger coming until it was already buried in his heart. I'd gotten this close; he believed my lies. It was almost over.

The somber, rain-drenched city blurred by the windows. A niggling itch began at the back of my thoughts, like the pluck of an out of tune violin string—a beginning, a warning.

"I'll wait for that tomorrow."

"What?" Razak said.

I'd spoken aloud. Fool. "Nothing, a song, that's all..."

"A song?" He bounced his boot. "The crowns."

"What about them?"

"Do you want to know where they are?"

"It's of no concern."

He leaned forward. "Are you sure? You seem very concerned."

The slight change in his body language tingled that sense of unease down my back. Since we'd climbed into the carriage, the change in him had been growing, becoming a loosening, as though only now he'd begun to relax. Why was he so comfortable? Where *were* we going?

"Bendrik's chambers. I have them there," he said. "One in each corner of the room. Except this one." He tapped the crown on his head. Perhaps I imagined it, but it seemed as though the barbs dug a little deeper into his skull and his eyes gleamed brighter. "We can't have everyone knowing where they are and leave them together, now can we?"

"Certainly not."

469

"Do you know why? Did you decipher the past, clever Zayan? Did you see what has been in front of your eyes all along? In front of everyone, if they'd only looked up from their closeted courts?"

Something was wrong. His smirk was the bitter kind.

If I leaped from the carriage, it would be over. If he even allowed me to get that far. If I snatched the dagger, he'd rip out my soul. I turned my gaze away, sent it out of the window onto rows of blurred trees. We'd left the city far behind.

This felt familiar. How he sat, the road we rattled along, the galloping horses. And that persistent out of tune violin note at the back of my mind, growing louder and louder.

"The crowns are the key," I said, because he looked at me as though I had to say something.

"It's best if you don't think of them as crowns at all. Four corners, four courts, four plates on the scales of balance. Dallin made them not as a way to bring peace to the lands, he made them to ruin peace. He made them as weapons."

The carriage driver slowed the horses, and the carriage rocked to a halt. Razak grasped the door, flung it open, and dropped down into puddles.

A track continued up the hill, winding its way through the forest.

Fear yanked my heart from my chest. I knew where we were, and why I was here. A lifetime of horror and agony piled on, freezing me rigid.

"Come now, Zayan." He grabbed my arm and hauled me from the carriage. "Aren't you pleased to be back again? So many wonderful memories here."

I stumbled on wet stones and rain-filled divots. I'd walked this track before with our father beside me. I'd walked it before and seen Justice Ines swing from a branch at its end.

Only one question remained—who swung from the hanging tree now?

It wasn't over. He might yet still believe me. I could get to the crowns. I knew where they were, if he just believed me.

We climbed the hill, to the dreaded tree with its gnarled, reaching branches. I stopped, frozen in place. This couldn't be happening. Not yet. I wasn't ready. This wasn't the plan. Not here, not yet. Not Arin, swinging there.

"Move!" Razak shoved me in the back. I stumbled forward, and Arin lifted his head.

Not dead, not yet.

The rope lay loose around his neck.

"So you see, Zayan, we think alike. I'd reached the same conclusion as you. Taking Arin was the perfect play. Extract Arin, and it all falls." Razak rested his boot on Arin's stool and tipped it back. Arin's boots slipped, the rope creaked, his chin jerked upright. No, not again, not like my mother, not like this, not Arin, my sunshine and honey prince, not him, *never him*.

I lurched. "No!"

The toes of Arin's boots skimmed the tipped stool as he tried to hold himself aloft. He gurgled, choking.

Razak smirked over his shoulder and brought the stool back down. Arin stumbled but stayed upright, gasping.

"And there we have the truth of it," my brother said. "The fucking truth of it all."

My breath came in jagged gulps. Rain hammered, soaking me through, blurring my sight. "Arin?"

"Don't let him ruin you," Arin croaked and panted, tears of rain wetting his face. "Whatever becomes of me, don't let this define you. You're so much better than him."

"Shut up!" Razak snapped. "Or I'll kick the stool away now. Did you truly think I'd fall for your lies, Zayan? I know

471

you. I know your mind like I know my own. Are you so blinded by love that you could not see how obvious you were? Lies are the only weapon you have, dear brother."

"Razak, you fiend!" Arin snarled. "Leave him. Rip my will away and be done with it."

"No, that would be too quiet a death for you, Prince of Hearts. I'm going to watch you thrash on the end of that rope and watch Zayan's love die with you."

"Please..." I staggered forward, splashing through mud and puddles. "Razak, no, don't do this. I'll do anything."

"It's a little late for that." Razak's backhanded slap whipped my head around. I reeled and dropped to my knees in the mud. Fire rushed up my face. "You are nothing compared to me! This is my court, my crown, my fucking reign, and you are a whore, bought with coin, a nothing boy I dug out of the dirt. How dare you think to fool me!" His cold hands locked around my throat and rattled me to my core. *"How dare you. I will fucking kill you here, like I promised. Kill you and fuck you and cut you to pieces!"*

"Razak, stop! Damn you, stop!" Arin cried. "Leave him, please. Lark, no..."

Razak twitched at the name and struck me again. White spots floated between us and the thudding in my chest filled my head. Blood swam in my mouth. His fingers clamped on again and squeezed, turning all the air in my lungs to fire. I gasped, heaving, and dug my nails into his hand.

"No, Lark, no!"

Razak leaned in, his snarling, hideous face my whole world. "You will never be free of me. Do you understand? Pain is all you will know. You will beg me for death, and I will never relent. You will never leave that room."

"Stop!"

I'll wait for that tomorrow...

472

"Do you understand me, brother?!"

I managed a small nod, and he tore his hand away. Air poured down my throat, into my lungs, and immediately spluttered back up again. Choking, I coughed and heaved on my hands and knees in the mud.

"Dearest Arin." Razak turned toward the tree. "It was always going to come to this."

Arin spat, striking Razak's cheek. "You're not even a true blood Prince of Pain. Your mother was from my court, and you're half Love. Zayan has more claim to that crown than you!"

My brother wiped his cheek clean. "Such fire. I see why Zayan is fascinated by you. Truly. But my father was weak, and whoever he chose to fuck is of no concern of mine. It ends here, as it was always going to. Because we all know, when it comes to love, there are no happy endings."

Horror turned Arin's face white. "Wait, no—wait!"

Razak propped his boot on the edge of the stool. "Goodbye, Arin. And rest assured knowing Zayan's life will be torture, since he's known love and had it torn away. The worst pain of all."

On my hands and knees, I croaked out the words to my mother's song under the same tree she'd died hanging from. *"The night is cold, and my heart is heavy with sorrow, but I know that someday we'll be together, and I'll wait for that tomorrow."*

Razak frowned, lowered the stool, and spun to glare at me. "What is it with that song? Is it supposed to mean something? What?"

Arin's shocked, haunted, and terrified eyes fixed on me too.

I spluttered. "My mother's song..." Was she here now in spirit, if we had such things?

"So dramatic," Razak growled. "But I'm bored, and Arin needs to die."

I saw it happen as though in a dream, or a nightmare. But when nightmares end in horror, you wake up. Razak kicked the stool, Arin dropped, and there was no waking from this nightmare.

rin

*"The night is cold, **and my heart is heavy with sorrow, but I know that someday we'll be together, and I'll wait for that tomorrow.**"*

I didn't know what it meant when Lark sang, only that this couldn't be our end. I hooked my fingers into the rope in a desperate attempt to stop the inevitable.

I hadn't felt the drop, just a vicious tug crushing my fingers to my throat.

I dangled, kicked, spun. *Help, no...* No, this couldn't be my end. It wasn't supposed to end like this. *Please, anyone, someone...*

Through blurred tears, I saw Lark rise.

He produced a dagger as though from thin air, like magic, and flung it toward me—the rope jolted, I dropped, but still dangled, still spun, still choked and cried and wheezed.

Razak whirled toward Lark. He missed Draven emerging from the trees behind him. I blinked, throat ablaze, tears streaming. Draven was here... *Help, please... I can't... hold... on...*

Please... save me.

CHAPTER 53

ark

THE DAGGER I'd stolen from Razak flew through the air, and its wicked edge sliced Arin's rope—but not through it. It frayed, unwinding, and Arin dangled, boots thrashing, face a shocking purple and blue.

Draven was here—as we'd planned it, the song his trigger to emerge from hiding. And as I lunged for Arin, Razak turned on me. He raised his hand, fingers splayed, intent on tugging on my will, so sure in his powers, so blinded by his belief he was an unstoppable god.

Draven thrust a blade into Razak's back, hooked an arm around Razak's neck from behind, and squeezed.

The rest I didn't see—only Arin, as his writhing slowed. I righted the stool under Arin's boots, propping him up, but the rope had locked around his neck. I yanked on it, trying to pry it free, then stumbled on the stool, losing my footing. It happened so fast yet took a lifetime. He was dying, right in front of me, life fading from his bloodshot eyes. I stepped up again, clutched Arin to me with one arm, and tugged on the rope, easing its chokehold. "I've got you." The rope's corded length eased, and Arin gasped. "I've got you."

He choked and wheezed, slumping into my arms.

"Breathe. I've got you." I said it over and over, and once the noose had loosened enough, I looped it up over his head, freeing him. He flung his arms around me, toppling us off the stool and almost to the ground. But I had him and breathed him in, holding him close, steadying him on his feet. He panted and coughed, folded in my arms.

"What should I do with this piece of kareel shit?" Draven asked.

I almost didn't care. I stroked Arin's hair, snagging on dried blood where he'd been struck. *Kill Razak.* Draven had my brother pinned to the ground, under his knee. Razak spluttered, half-drowning in the bloody mud.

"Don't kill him. We can't kill him." But I wanted to, for almost killing Arin. I wanted it so much I could taste it. But we needed the crown, we needed to know the other crowns were where he'd told me. His death would come, but not yet.

Draven grabbed Razak by the neck and yanked him backwards. *"Where's my son?!"*

"Lark." Arin scrunched my jacket in his fists, pulling my focus back to him.

"I'm here." *I'll never leave you again.*

He leaned back, still clutching me, and his face was pale, his freckles stark. And it was all I could do not to crush him close and never let go.

"You wretched, lying, vicious bastard!"

Only three words would come. "I love you." I kissed him quickly. "I'm sorry."

A strangled sob tumbled from his lips. "I was dying, I was dying—"

"I know." I pulled him to my chest again and his tremors tumbled through me. "I know, I've got you. I'm never letting you go."

His fist thumped my chest, with no strength behind it. "I hate you, Lark!"

"I thought you might."

He sniffed and shuddered a sigh. "You planned this—Draven is here, so you planned all of this together—and you didn't say!"

I looked at Draven, at his forlorn face, and struggled to speak the truth. "Yes."

Arin pushed away, stumbled some, then righted himself and his clothes, regaining some composure. "I hate the both of you." His glare fell to Razak still thrashing and gurgling in the mud, then he strode over and kicked Razak in the side, once, twice.

I flung my arms round him and pulled him back. "Stop."

"Why isn't he dead?!" Arin screamed. "Kill him! Kill him now!"

"The boy..." Razak spluttered, lifting his cheek from the mud. "The boy... Kill me and he'll die..."

Draven clamped his hand down on the back of Razak's head. "You mean my son?"

"Kill me, and he dies!"

Draven's expression turned desperate.

"It's true," I said. "He has him somewhere."

Draven let out a soul-weary growl. "If we let him up, if he gets either of us in his sights, he'll rip out our souls."

"I won't," he gasped. "You have my word. Let me up and I'll help you."

"Your word is the most worthless thing in all the shatterlands." Draven looked to me again; I was still holding Arin back. "Where's my son?"

"He's safe!" Razak choked. "Let me up, and I'll tell you."

Draven eased his hold but leaned in and snarled in Razak's ear, "When I am done with you, you'll wish for death."

Arin bucked me off and stumbled free, catching his breath. "We can't trust him. He'll say anything to get what he wants," Arin said.

I knew that. But we *needed* Razak. There had to be a way to cripple him *and* make him compliant. This power had been wielded and defeated before. I'd seen it, hadn't I? In the art all over War's pyramid temple and the art below Justice... a clue to how this ended. I searched my memory of each scene, and then knew. "Let him up, but cover his eyes," I said, turning away to search under the tree for the dagger I'd thrown.

The images on Justice's walls of the kneeling figures with empty eyes... I knew what it meant.

Draven grasped Razak's arms behind his back and hauled him out of the mud to his feet. He bucked and struggled. "I'll kill you all!" Razak kicked, thrashing, but Draven had him.

Razak stilled as I approached. The power he wielded tried to slither its way inside. I slammed my hand over his eyes, forcing his crowned head back against Draven's chest.

"Zayan, you love me," Razak said, his voice turning soft and vulnerable. "I know it's true, I saw it in you. Please, brother, don't do this to me. We're family. We only have each other. Nobody understands us."

I spread my fingers, forcing his left eye open. Mud caked his lashes. His eye swiveled and locked on me. The dark pupil swelled, and within it, madness squirmed like a pool of eels. I raised the dagger.

"Wait! No, no!"

"For my fingers, *beloved brother.*" I thrust the dagger into his eye. His screams filled my ears, like the sweetest music I'd ever heard. He bucked, writhed, and twisted. He screamed and screamed, and I carved his eye from its socket. The orb came away and dropped into my hand. Razak slumped, now silent.

The art on the walls, the people with hollow eyes... I backed away, admiring my masterpiece, and handed the eye to Arin. "Now he can't focus on us, so he can't direct the power."

Arin snatched Razak's eye from my fingers, dropped it in the mud, and crushed it like a grape under his heel.

Draven gave Razak an experimental shake. "He's out cold. I stabbed him in the back, only shallow, but there's a chance he might bleed out."

"We're not that lucky," Arin said.

"We need him alive. There's a carriage waiting down the hill. Let's get him inside." I had to get the crown unlatched from his head somehow and take it to the others. With the crowns together, we'd know if we had a chance of ending this nightmare. We also needed Razak to reveal the whereabouts of Draven's son.

Draven threw Razak over his shoulder, carried him down the track, then we unceremoniously shoved him into the carriage. I instructed the driver to take us back to the tower. He didn't say a word about our royal cargo.

Arin sat beside me, glowering. I'd betrayed him and then set him up. Although having him hang from the tree had been Razak's plan, mine had been the same. Kidnap Arin, bring him to the tree, and in the last moment, with Razak's guard down, Draven would save us. He'd been more than willing to prove his loyalty. It had worked but may have cost me Arin's love.

"You both knew?" Arin asked so quietly, I wasn't sure if I'd dreamed it.

Draven glanced at me, seeking answers too. I closed my eyes and sighed. "I told Draven to watch for your disappearance. And when it happened, to visit the tree. He didn't know why, or that you'd be... hanged."

Arin turned his face away. "Damn you."

"I don't expect forgiveness." There could be no forgiveness for the things I'd done.

Nobody replied, not with words. Draven gave me his sorry-eyes while Arin stared out of the window and dabbed at his red, raw neck, occasionally glancing down at Razak.

When we arrived back at the tower, Draven and I carried Razak up the steps. In the rain and darkness, nobody noticed. "The basement. Take the stairs, that way. He told me the crowns are there."

Bendrik's chambers hadn't changed. The fireplaces were cold, which meant the room was cold too, and the pool had been emptied, with no sign of the bloody water or the man's body I'd left behind. Arin didn't know what I'd done here, and now was not the time to remind him of how vicious I could be.

Perhaps Arin's cold shoulder was for the best. We were close to finishing this. We'd had our moment, our happy ending, and now it was time for him to prevail, survive, and make a new life.

Razak groaned, and Draven dropped his head, smacking it on the floor. "Gods damn," the warlord grunted. "He startled me."

I set my brother's boots down and crouched beside his head, ignoring his groans. When Draven had dropped Razak, the crown had struck the tiled floor first and rung a note, almost as though the sound were deliberate. The musical note was familiar; I'd heard it before. In Justice.

The other crowns were here, placed on each corner of the empty pool—the black and red of War, the sapphire and silver of Justice, and the gold and pearl of Love. And Razak's crown of Pain, fixed to his head like a stubborn limpet to a rock.

Arin approached behind me. "How do we get it off?" he said. "How do we unattach it?"

"Unattach his head?" Draven suggested.

"Not yet, we need him alive."

I hovered my hands on either side of the crown, not yet grasping it. As soon as I did, its razor-like edges would cut into my hands. I could feel its thrum, the same as the note it had chimed, the same as the reverberating humming in Justice, when the crowns had been close.

"What happens after we have it?" Draven asked, circling around behind me too.

"We place them close together, touching, I think. Something like that."

"You don't know?" Arin asked.

"I saw some things below Justice—images, like those in War's pyramid. The crowns, when they come together, unlock something. Their proximity opened the seal, and here, now, I think if we place them even closer, they may undo the damage, somehow. Perhaps?"

"That's a great deal of unknowns, Lark," Arin said. "What if it does the opposite? What if it makes him stronger?"

"That's why I have to get it off him."

My brother's remaining eye twitched.

"He's waking up," Draven warned.

We didn't have time to debate what may or may not

happen. I clamped my hands onto the crown. Sharp barbs of pain shot through my palms and up my arm. I hissed but dared not let go. The damn thing was coming off my brother's head if I had to sever it from his neck myself.

"Lark?"

"It's fine." Blood dripped onto Razak's face—my blood. He twitched under each new drop, stirring back to wakefulness.

"Hurry."

Draven placed a boot on Razak's chest and brandished the short sword he'd stabbed Razak in the back with. "I have him. When he wakes up, my handsome face will be the first thing he sees."

The crown's cool metal burrowed into my skin and its barbs retreated from my brother's skull, turning instead on me. What if the damned thing wouldn't let go?

I tugged, and it tore free of Razak's scalp, taking scabbed hair and skin with it. Now I had it in my grasp, where I supposed it belonged. The resonating hum filled my head and trembled through my bones. What if I wore it? What if that was why I was here? Would the power of the crowns then be mine?

"Lark?" Arin stepped in front of me. "Lark... We need to put the crowns together, remember? You said they have to be close for this to work—whatever it is."

Razak's dark, liquid chuckle bounced off the tiled walls. "He wants it, the power. He likes it. Always has. I took it from him, did you know, Arin? He had it, briefly, and I took it. But he's tasted it. It was his. I knew, I've always known. He is Pain's prince, and now he has its crown. Go on, brother, wear it. Own it. Let it take you. You've always wanted to—"

Draven's right hook slammed Razak back to the floor. "One more word and Arin will cut out your tongue."

Razak glared one-eyed at Draven. "He's too weak."

Arin shot my brother a look that made it clear he was not the same prince Razak had stabbed in Love's court many moons ago.

"Lark, wear it, if you like," Arin said, turning back to me. "But the pursuit of this power destroyed your father, and your brother. Your mother wouldn't want this. Danyal wouldn't want this."

"What about you?" I asked, my voice echoing, untethered inside my own mind. "What do you want?"

His soft smile was a ray of sunlight through black clouds. "You," he said. "Just you, the *real* you, not a prince. I want the you in there—" He placed his hand on my chest. "—in your heart."

His touch hauled me back from the crown's allure. "Of course, no... I don't want the crown. I never have." I shot Razak a snarl. "I'm not you!"

He snorted. "You're too pathetic a creature to take up your birthright."

I turned toward the pool in the middle of the room. The crowns had to go together; they had to touch. I knew this much from the warnings on the walls. Put them alongside each other, and we had a key—either to the end of all this, or something worse. There was only one way of knowing.

I climbed the pool's steps, then stepped down into its empty basin and crouched. I tried to set the crown down, but its barbs had hooked into my skin. Panic fluttered my heart. "Arin, it's stuck."

Arin dashed to my side and attempted to pry it off too, but the barbs sliced his fingers.

Razak's laugh echoed. "You're wasting time. Draven's son has precious moments to live."

"What did you say?" I heard Draven strike Razak but was

too focused on my own situation to care. "If you've touched my son, I swear I will take you apart piece by piece," Draven warned.

Arin teased the crown's barbs from my skin, but as the blood smeared over both our hands, it became harder and harder to see if we'd made any progress. "Gods, your hands... Is this working?" he asked.

"It's letting go. I think."

"Where you both stand, Zayan killed a man," Razak announced. "Seduced him with lies, then cut his wrists open and watched him bleed out. Of course, he pumped him to climax first. He does like to kill them as they come."

I glanced up. Arin's frown shadowed his face. He pulled at my fingers, prying them off the crown, one by one, but didn't look up at me.

"He's killed countless, and he fucked them as they died," Razak continued. "Is that the butcher you wish to spend the rest of your days with, Love's Prince?"

"Draven," Arin growled. "Shut him up."

"He'll forever be broken," Razak went on. "I broke him. He'll never be yours. He's mine, he'll always be mine! I'm in his head, *forever*."

Draven's punch silenced him. Razak knew he was on borrowed time; he'd say and do anything to save himself and hurt me. The problem was, it was all true.

Arin pulled my right hand free. It trembled, dribbling blood onto the pool's shiny tiles. This was all I deserved. I should hurt; pain was my birthright.

I pried the crown's barbs from my flesh and abandoned Pain's crown in the middle of the empty pool.

Standing, a wave of dizziness blurred the room. *So much blood on my hands... Has it always been there?*

Arin hurried off and collected his crown, then set it

beside Pain's—the pair so very different, one vicious and barbed, the other regal and beautiful. They were not meant to be together, just like us.

As Arin collected Justice's crown and brought it closer, the background hum grew louder still, thumping against my ears and chest.

Razak stirred.

"Is it working?" Draven asked.

"Something is happening." Arin hurried to collect the last crown: War's. Its rubies gleamed bloodred and as he approached, the resonating waves of sound grew heavier still, pushing down and down, hammering into my skull.

Arin stumbled into the pool. "Gods, it's almost unbearable."

"Place them closer together, quickly!" I slumped against the pool's edge and the audible assault stretched needle-thin, jabbing into my skull. This had to be it, the final piece, the end of it all. *By Dallin, please let this be right, please end this nightmare.*

Arin fell to a knee, almost dropping War's crown. Teeth gritted, he shoved it across the pool's floor, slotting it into the remaining corner. The moment all four crowns touched, the sound slammed in like a physical force. Tears streamed from my eyes, and the pounding tried to shatter my mind. Four crowns, touching. Their gems shone, filling the chamber with brittle, colorful light.

But as horrifying as the sound was, and as beautiful the display, nothing else appeared to happen. The crowns discharged their hideous scream and gleamed as though lit from within, but there was no display of power, no sign that we'd been successful in sealing off Razak's ability to yank out souls.

Razak's laughter rolled through the noise.

I lunged from the pool's edge and yanked Love's crown away. The screaming song collapsed back to its irritating but less debilitating state, and the three of us stumbled, panting.

"Your faces?" Razak chuckled. "So desperate, and so pathetic. Is that all you came here with, hopes and guesses? Did you think the power would unbind itself from me and return to those crowns? Is that what all this is about?"

Draven grabbed Razak by the neck and rattled him. "You piece of shit. Where's my son?!" He punched Razak in the gut, doubling him over, then grasped his hair and flung him to the floor. "Where is he!" Draven slammed a kick into Razak's side, curling Razak around his boot.

No, he'll kill him!

I dashed from the pool, grabbed Draven, and pulled him away, but he twisted free. "Stop." Draven lunged, I danced in front of him, shoved, and we wrestled, and Razak laughed as though this was the best night of his life. "He has the answers!" I shouted. "We need him."

Draven roared and threw himself away, then paced the far side of the room. "My boy, where is he? Just tell me that. I've done everything you've asked of me, betrayed the people I love. Just tell me where he is. Let me save him, Razak. Damn you, where is he, please?"

Razak snorted. "Gasping his final breath, I expect."

I backhanded Razak so hard he sprawled to the floor. Blood dribbled from between his lips, but his stunned silence didn't last. He grinned. "I'll take you to the boy, but we must hurry. He does not have long."

Draven caught my eye. He didn't trust Razak. None of us did. Any time he made demands, he was thinking of himself. If he wanted us to go somewhere, then it was likely a trap. But what choice did we have?

"I'll tell you how to destroy the crowns," he added. "Isn't that what you want?"

Arin climbed from the pool. "Why should we believe you?"

"Because I want to live." He licked blood from his lips. "I know I've lost. You'll kill me, I see it, even with one fucking eye." His one eye swiveled to me. "I cannot wield the power without direction. I've tried—it churns within me, furious and chaotic. It knows its trapped. Let me live, and I'll help you."

"Tell us how to fix this," I said. "Tell me how to destroy the crowns and we'll let you live."

He snorted. "Says the man who lies with his every heartbeat. No, not you, brother. Arin, give me your word. I'll take you to the boy, and I'll tell you how to destroy the crowns, but you must give me your word, Prince of Love, that you'll let me live."

Arin peered down his nose at the ragged mess that was my brother. Beaten, bloody, bruised, missing an eye, stabbed in the back. All he had left was the power, now churning and trapped within him, if he was to be believed. Taking his eye had hobbled his ability to lash out, but all of this still felt like a ruse. He said he'd lost, but we'd be fools to believe him. He was a mess, but he wasn't behaving like a man who'd lost.

"Quickly now, Draven's son's life hangs in the balance," he said. "Delay a moment longer and his young life will be over. His death will be on your hands, Arin."

"Fine, all right," Arin snarled. "We'll let you live. But tell us, how do we destroy the crowns and the power they unleashed?"

"Your word?"

"You have it. I swear, Razak, you'll live."

Razak swallowed and looked at each of us in turn, perhaps finally understanding his place. "Bring the crowns together, as you have here, but with someone from each court alongside them, together and in agreement. Once you have that, the crowns, and their power, will shatter. Dallin made the courts to oppose each other—we were each made to forever be opposites—thus the crowns would never meet and the power would remain subdued. Justice learned of his ways and imprisoned him, all the courts came together to see it done, and that was how it's been, until my father learned of the truth, and so did I. The crowns and the courts must be in alignment, or nothing changes. Believe me or not, that is the truth, and now you owe me—"

Draven swooped in, hauled Razak to his feet, and pressed his blade to his throat. "Nobody believes a word of this kareel-shit. Take me to my boy."

"Yes, yes." Razak panted. "The river— I'll take you there. Arin, your word, remember? Call Draven off." His single-eyed glare fixed on Arin, pleading with him to keep Draven controlled. "You will not go back on your word. I am to live. We agreed. You and I."

Arin snarled. "I won't forget."

I handed Arin his crown. "You'd better take it. We can't leave the four crowns here. It's too dangerous."

He propped the crown lopsided on his head. "Let's be done with this."

Draven supported Razak's limping, bleeding body and led the way from the chamber. I followed. Blood soaked Razak's back from Draven's earlier attack by the hanging tree. With any luck, he'd die slowly, in agony. Arin had vowed not to kill Razak, but I hadn't. And my brother was right about me, I was a killer.

It was almost over. Razak sensed it. So did I. The final act was here, playing out around us.

He knew I'd stop at nothing to see him dead.

He'd have one trick left to play; he always did. Whatever it was, I'd be ready.

rin

WE PASSED beneath the foyer's dramatic chandelier and pushed through the main doors onto the tower's steps. And stopped.

People filled the streets, and all of them stood in silence, their faces tipped up, wet with rain. Hundreds of them, all dressed in greys and blacks. Pain's people.

Lark slowed beside me. "They came..." Was this his doing?

"What is this?" Razak snarled.

"They came," Lark said again with a smile. "They heard my music, and they came."

"All of you!" Razak boomed. "Traitors! He's not your prince—*I am!*" He shoved from Draven's hold, taking advantage of Draven's surprise, and with rain mixing with the blood on his face, he raised his hands. "All traitors must be punished."

"Stop him." Lark dashed toward Razak. Draven lunged for him too.

Razak's snarl made it clear, it was all or nothing.

But he couldn't control the power, he'd said as much.

He raised both hands to the rain. Lightning forked, and a blast of chaotic, heart-rending power rolled outward, slamming into Lark first, then Draven. I only knew I'd been struck when I blinked at the wet marble steps beneath my hands, my thoughts silent and heart hollow. Something terrible had happened, but I didn't know or care why. There was... nothing in me. I was empty. Cold. Like stone.

The vicious wave wasn't done. Its ripples went on, diving deeper and deeper, washing more and more warmth away.

I lifted my head and blinked through the rain to Lark.

He stood with his hand on his brother's shoulder, his head thrown back, and the majority of whatever Razak had unleashed poured *into* him, shielding me behind him. Whatever was happening to me, rolled over and through him, wave after wave. A hundred times worse. I was dying inside, my will, my passion, all of it wilting on the stem. Then Lark's light would die like this too, and I couldn't bear it, not him.

A defiant spark sizzled to life inside me, burning in the cold and the dark.

Nobody hurt Lark and lived.

I swayed to my feet, numb, merely existing. The weight of my own lifeless flesh tried to hold me still, but the fire to save Lark burned strong and grew ever brighter, pushing the numbness away. Waves of power beat out from Razak's body, channeled into Lark, and washed over the crowd, beating them down. Somewhere distant, I knew this was devastating, knew it would be our end—mine, theirs, all of us—and if it wasn't for Lark absorbing half of his brother's onslaught, we'd already be vacant shells.

Torn between surrendering and letting the spark burn me up, I heaved my heavy limbs forward. The spark, I had to follow the hopeful spark as all around the masses toppled like dominoes.

Lark, hold on, I'm coming for you...

Then Lark tore his hand from his brother's shoulder and kicked Razak in the back.

Razak pitched forward. The pulsing, lashing power cut off. He let out a cry and tumbled down the steps, sprawling into the motionless half-numbed crowd.

Lark buckled, clutched his head, bent double, and staggered backward. *"Someday... we'll be together... I'll wait for that tomorrow... Someday... be together... wait... tomorrow... Someday... together, tomorrow."*

Heat began to thaw out my limbs as Razak's vampiric pull retreated. "Lark?" I touched his shoulder.

"Get away!" He tried to run and fell. "Stay back. I can't..." His chest heaved. He thrust out a hand, holding me off. "I can't control it. Arin—" He gasped, then clutched his head again. *"I'll wait for that tomorrow—Arin, kill me, kill me now... Please. I can't—it's too bright, too much, gods, help me."*

My thoughts moved through molasses, slow to catch up. He'd taken Razak's power. A power he'd never wanted, but desired. It would tear him apart, and he'd let it. Because in his mind, he deserved to die so that others lived.

I pulled him into my arms. He fought, thumped at my chest, my face, tried to writhe free, lashed and bucked. My crown toppled off. But I had him—*I had him.*

"No, Arin, hurt you, stop, let go... I can't... Tomorrow... together... some daytomorrowtogethersomeday."

I grasped his face in my hands. He'd squeezed his eyes closed. His lips moved, as though in prayer, repeating the same song words over and over. My Lark, my Prince of

Storms. He clung to those words, clinging to the pieces of himself as he broke apart in my arms.

"Lark, listen, I'm here, hold on, hold on to me."

"It's terrible and brilliant and I want it... I'll hurt you, everyone... I'm worse than him. I like it, I want it—"

I pulled his head against my shoulder. "I've got you. You're nothing like him. You're stronger than he is. He made it terrible, but you can make it right. I love you, Lark. You're not alone. I have you." I had to help him, to stop his agony. Somehow.

Draven knelt. "What can I do?"

I didn't know. I didn't know how to help him. "Draven, Razak... Get Razak..." I searched the bottom of the steps, but Razak's body was gone. It didn't matter. Only Lark mattered. "Help me, Draven. Help me save him."

"How?"

There was a way. There was always a way.

"It's madness," Lark hissed. "It desires..."

My gaze snagged on my crown nearby, sparkling in sunlight.

Sunlight.

The clouds that always smothered Pain's city had broken open, letting in a waterfall of sunlight. The rain had stopped. Light warmed the steps and bathed Pain's citizens in its warm glow, stirred them from Razak's onslaught.

There was hope, there was *always* hope.

"You saved them, Lark. You saved them. You are the best of us. You have to believe me." I cupped his distraught, pale face in my hands. "You can do this. Hold on, please hold on..." I silently pleaded with Draven. We'd struggled and fought, the three of us, but we were here, together. That had to mean something. War, Love, Pain.

Draven glanced at my glittering crown. "Shatter them," he said. "All of them."

Yes, with the crowns gone, Razak had said the power would unravel.

Shatterlands.

Shatter the crowns.

But we needed all four courts. We needed Justice.

"Find Noemi, Draven, go—find her. We need her now."

He ran, and it was all I could do to hug Lark close and rock him as he sang his song in a broken voice, clinging to the shredded pieces of his mind.

"The rain has stopped," I told him. "You did that." He rocked and hummed and mumbled. I stroked his hair and tucked him close. "You are my everything. You're my heart. I hope you know it. I hate you sometimes too, I'll not lie, but I love you more. You're brilliant. Your heart is bright, and you are not what he made you, Lark. You're a shining star in his darkness. Please, hold on." I grasped his mutilated right hand and clutched it to my chest. It wouldn't be right, if he died for this, for us. Despite him wanting it to end that way. But I could see him, standing on the edge of that cliff, wanting to step off.

"I'm sorry," he whispered. "I've hurt you, lied, betrayed, traitor..."

"No, no." I threaded my fingers into his hair, still holding him close, rocking him, wishing Draven would hurry. "None of that was you. I see you. You're the man who tried to teach me to juggle, you sang to me in the prison cell, you saved War's people, you've saved me over and over. I see you, Lark, and I wish—" My voice caught. "—I wish you'd love yourself as I love you, then you'd know how remarkable you are."

Gods, Draven, hurry... I'm losing him.

Tears wet my face, and I couldn't even claim they were rain.

"We're going to shatter the crowns," I told him. "We'll make it end." He didn't move, didn't reply. "Lark?" I eased him back. His head lolled, eyes closed. "Gods, no—Lark?" I touched his face. So cold. Why was he cold? His heart... I pressed a hand to his damp shirt and waited to feel his warmth, feel its beat. Nothing. "No." I laid him down, blinked tears away, and grasped his wrist, feeling for a pulse. "Please?"

There, the *thump-thump*, but it was weak, so weak.

"What use am I if I cannot save love?"

What kind of world was this if good men like him died while those like Razak escaped? It wasn't right, it had never been right. "We'll change it, you and I. We'll change it, Lark, I promise." My heart ached, choking me. "You'll teach me to juggle, won't you? I'll try harder, and you'll laugh, then tell me all the ways I'm a terrible prince. Please... please hold on." I couldn't do this without him. I couldn't be the Prince of Love with a broken heart. We hadn't yet danced in the rain, we hadn't made love on the beach, we hadn't counted flower petals in the meadows, and he'd never be free if he died here.

"Damn this world," I snarled. If Lark died, then the shatterlands weren't worth saving.

"Arin!" Noemi cried, running up the steps. "Oh, Lark, no."

"Help me, please," I sobbed. "Help me."

"Yes, I'm here, Arin. How? Tell me how."

Draven knelt and scooped Lark's lifeless body into his arms. "The crowns, let's go," he ordered, taking charge.

I plucked my crown up from the step and raced after them. They were here, I wasn't alone, *we* weren't alone. Our Court of Misfits was together. I had to believe it, I had to hope.

As we descended the stairs down to the dungeon pool-room, Love's crown began to tingle in my fingers. We had all four courts present, all four crowns. Once shattered, Lark would be saved. No more courts, no more crowns, and whatever happened after would happen with Lark beside me.

Noemi and I ran into the room ahead of Draven carrying Lark.

"Stop there," Razak snarled. He stood at the pool, Draven's son against his legs and a knife at the terrified boy's throat. "Take one more step and the boy dies."

Fury and desperation boiled my thoughts.

"Razak!" Draven roared. He took a step forward, still carrying Lark, but Razak tugged the blade and blood wept from the boy's neck. He hadn't cut him much, but it was enough to stop Draven.

Razak jerked his chin. "We're all here, I see, all the courts. Well done."

He barely looked like a man, and certainly not like the elegant Prince of Pain he'd once been. Blood and mud coated his clothes, face, and hair. Half his face was a mess of blood and weeping pus. He was a mad thing, held together by hatred.

"Give me Zayan, and you get the boy."

"No." I moved but stopped again under Razak's warning glare. The boy sniffled in his grip. He didn't know us, didn't know why any of this was happening. He wore black and red, like his father, but he likely didn't even know what that meant. He was innocent.

Lark would make such a trade. He'd give himself up for a boy he didn't know.

But I wasn't Lark. "You're beaten, Razak. Look at you. You're nothing but rags and spite."

"Lay Zayan down at your feet, warlord, and your son gets

to live a long, prosperous life with his father. Your wife named him as a babe, did you know? Would you like to know that name?"

Draven gulped a sob. "Don't do this. Don't make me do this."

"It's easy, all you have to do is give me my brother. He's mine. *He belongs to me!*"

"Razak, be rational," Noemi said, still hoping for the impossible. "We can help you. Let the boy go, surrender yourself, and Justice will consider your surrender when it comes to sentencing."

"'Sentencing'?" He laughed. "You have no right to judge me."

If Lark were conscious, he'd have a plan, a trick up his sleeve, a knife to throw, but he lay in Draven's arms, out cold, consumed by an unleashed, ancient power. Dying.

"You love him," I blurted. "You love Zayan."

Razak stilled and studied me, studied my face, looking for the trick. There was none.

"He's dying, Razak. Whatever he took from you, it's eating him up from the inside. He'd rather let it consume him than turn into you. He'll save everyone, save us all, just not himself. You love him. You don't want him to die any more than I do." I raised my hands, Love's crown hanging from my fingers. "Let us end this. Help us save Zayan's life."

"You can't have him, Arin, you and your perfect ways. Your court is the worst of them all—weak, worthless, *nothing.*"

I hadn't realized how personal this had been for Razak, but now I knew his mother was of Love's court, and he was half Love, his mad reasoning made strange sense, at least to him. He'd said it wasn't personal, and it wasn't, not between us. But between him and my court it was. All his life, he'd thought he'd been abandoned, thought himself lesser, been desperate to prove he was strong, better, while keeping Lark —the true heir to Pain—trapped in his shadow, unable to shine.

"He's dying, Razak. Let Draven's boy go. Let's end this." *Do one good thing in your wretched, selfish life.*

Razak's one-eyed glare snapped from me to Draven to Noemi, seeking the trap, but we didn't have anything left to fight with. This wasn't about us; it was about saving Lark.

"You promised him. Nobody can kill Zayan. Just you."

Razak's weeping eye widened. "But I didn't mean to do it. Zayan took it back. He took the gift back. I didn't mean to do this. I don't... I don't want to be alone."

I stepped forward. "Help us destroy the crowns."

He looked at Draven and Lark, then down at the boy clutched against his legs.

He had a heart, somewhere beneath all that pain. To be able to love like he did, he had to have a heart. Lark was his weakness. Lark had been right, he really was the only one that could stop Razak, but not in the way he'd thought. Lark's death would be Razak's undoing.

Razak shoved Draven's boy toward us.

Draven sobbed and knelt, laying Lark down. He rocked back on a heel, his face crumbling in tears, and held his arms out. The boy hesitated a step, then threw himself into Draven's embrace.

"The crowns," Noemi said. "Now, Arin."

Razak stayed in the empty pool and stared at the hateful crown of Pain in its place alongside the others. Just so long as he stayed there and didn't move or attack, we could do this.

Noemi climbed the steps up and over, taking her place behind Justice's crown.

"Draven," I urged.

He let his boy go and stumbled into the pool to stand beside his crown.

And now all that was left was me.

The crowns already thrummed, and when together, they'd scream again. And with the courts alongside them, they'd shatter. Saving Lark, saving the shatterlands, saving us all, even Razak.

I approached, and the crowns resonated, whining aloud like dying creatures. Lark writhed but I walked on; I couldn't stop for him. This had to happen.

Razak looked up, past me, at Lark.

When Lark's howling began, it took everything I had not to break, turn around, and rush to him. This *would* save him. Razak glowered at me, at all of us, but he remained, and then grasped Draven's hand beside him, and Noemi's to his right.

I stepped down, pushing through the cacophony as though pushing through thick oil. Lark screamed, the crowns wailed, and by the gods, the noise tore through my head, my mind, my soul, and my heart. I knelt, placed Love's crown beside its kin, and straightening, I grasped Draven's and Noemi's hands.

The connection between us all, and between the crowns, sparked a cascade of light. Power breathed in, flooded the room, surged and rolled, pouring as though the ocean had been funneled down the tower, into its basement, and into us. I couldn't let go if I'd wanted to. Bitter pain, violent war, sharp justice, and obsessive love—all four slammed down, landing like hammer blows, and the crowns shattered, throwing us back.

I struck the side of the pool and dropped to my knees, landing hard and gasping.

The ringing in my ears made my head spin. Something

wet and warm ran down my neck. Blood, from my ears, my face. But I survived, I was alive.

Razak ran from the pool—filthy purple cloak bellowing—toward Lark.

A dagger, he had a dagger. He couldn't mean to hurt Lark after everything we'd just been through.

"Stop him!"

CHAPTER 55

ark

I'D BEEN DROWNING in agony, swallowing it, breathing it, coated in its poisonous barbs—I'd invited the power in, I knew that much. I'd *wanted* it. But holding it took everything I had. Arin had been with me, for a while, his voice and his warmth soothing, and there, in his arms, I'd drifted.

But then the pain had surged, and the screaming began. The whole of the shatterlands screamed, and so did I.

It came and went like a firework through my mind, leaving silence and numbness behind.

Arin...

I blinked at the tiled walls, walls I remembered, but I couldn't place how I'd gotten here.

"Lark!"

Arin!

I turned.

Not Arin. Razak straddled me, dropped, and his fist struck me low in the gut. "Razak?"

He leaned forward, filling my vision with his scarred and bloody face. "Brother. It can only be you and I. He can't have you. Nobody can have you. We die together, and in death, we'll be together, forever." He pressed a dagger to his own neck.

"No." I grabbed his arm. "No, don't. Not like this." He fought my hold, tried to drag the blade across skin, but it couldn't end here, not for him. I held his stare, held his hand, and the dagger.

Draven loomed, and his face told me to let go, to let my brother die here, on his knees, straddling me. Let him cut his own throat and bleed out.

"You're mine." Razak sneered. "In life and death."

I shook my head. "I'm not dying for you. And you're not dying here. Draven, hold him."

Draven grabbed a fistful of Razak's hair, holding him still. I pulled his hand gripping the dagger away from his throat, then pried it from his fingers. We had him. *Finally*—we had him. Draven hauled him off me, and he went, stumbling while dangling from Draven's fist.

"You rat bastard, you're ours now."

"No!" Razak howled. "You can't do this."

"No? The only thing keeping you alive is Lark. Once he gives the word, I'll break your thin spine over my knee."

Arin flew in, wrapping me in his arms. He hauled me upright. "Lark... Lark, gods, you're all right?" He grasped my face. "You are all right? Did he hurt you? The dagger, I saw the dagger—"

"It's all right." I smiled, almost laughed at his outpouring of affection. "I'm all right." I wasn't, but it didn't matter. "Is it done? Did you do it?" Cuts marred his face, and blood had dried a path from his ear, but he seemed to be well enough.

"It's done. It's over," he said. "We did it, we broke them. It's truly over."

Almost. It was *almost* over.

Arin sobbed a smile. "Are you sure you're all right?"

Tired, cold, aching, but alive. Which was the most I could hope for. I gripped his shoulder. "You saved me, didn't you? Even though I told you not to."

He smiled. "When have I ever listened?"

He helped me up, saying something about thinking me gone and how he'd never forgive me if I died, as though I had a choice in the matter. He mentioned Razak—about helping Razak destroy the crowns. His smile was all I needed, which was a good thing, because his voice was growing ever distant. He turned away, briefly checking on Draven and Razak, and I dabbed at my side, where Razak had punched me—and my hand came away soaked in blood.

Not a punch then.

The knife he'd held, he'd stabbed me with it.

Strange, how I couldn't feel the wound, just tired, and cold... I looked up and found Draven glaring past Arin, right at me. He'd seen my hand, the blood. I shook my head. It was nothing. I wiped my hand clean on my already bloody coat.

It wasn't over.

Not yet.

"Bring Razak," I told Draven. "I have a gift for him."

Draven asked Noemi to stay with his son, and we left the room and stepped out of the tower into startling sunshine. Pain's streets steamed under its rays, and above, the endless storms had passed. It didn't seem possible. I'd never seen the city in sunlight. So beautiful and fitting for a goodbye.

"That carriage—" I nodded toward the black carriage, the same one we'd commandeered earlier. Unsurprisingly, the driver was missing. But I knew the way.

"No." Razak squirmed in Draven's grip. "Zayan, what are you doing? Where are we going? Release me. Arin, you gave your word."

"Did I?" Arin shrugged. "I don't recall."

Razak's chest heaved. "You *lied*?"

"Fuck me." Draven laughed. "He actually believed you."

"How dare you laugh, warlord," Razak snarled. "I'll have your tongue!"

"And who is going to follow your orders, prince?" Draven asked, sweeping a hand at the crowd milling around the baking streets. "None here seem to care." Draven dragged Razak into the carriage, yanked the red sash from around his waist, and tied Razak's wrists behind him. Draven nodded, ready.

I took up the reins in the driver's seat, and Arin climbed alongside me.

"Where *are* you taking him?" Arin held my gaze, and he knew. He nodded.

I snapped the reins and trotted the horses toward the city outskirts. It wasn't far. My side throbbed, beating hot and heavy with the motion of the carriage. I had to do this one final thing, and then I could rest. Maybe forever.

The rain clouds returned as we left the city for the forest. And soon, the rain began again. The roads narrowed, turning into a muddy track, and eventually we came to a familiar hill.

Arin climbed down first. With him focused on Draven and Razak, I dropped from the seat, gasped at the bolt of pain, and slumped against the carriage, clutching my side. But my brother hadn't killed me yet... I just had to do this, just this one final thing... The resolution, the end. And then, the tale would be over, its story told.

Draven hauled Razak out. My brother's eye blew wide. "No. No, you can't. You can't do this. You love me, you know you do. Zayan, no..." He tried to dig his heels in, but Draven muscled him on, up the hill, through the same mud-thick puddles we'd splashed through earlier.

"No!" he yelled. "Arin, if you let him do this, it'll ruin him."

Arin wasn't listening. He looked up at the hanging tree, the tree Razak had almost hung him from, and there was nothing left to say.

Draven growled at Razak's attempts to writhe free, then clamped Razak's neck in his thick fingers and swung him around beneath the oak's main branch.

"Do you have rope?"

Arin scooped his frayed rope from the mud, and without a word, fashioned a noose from its remaining length. He flung it over the branch and tied it off. The noose dangled, its threat clear.

Razak stared at it, no longer fighting. "Justice will imprison you all for this."

"This is justice." I nodded at Draven, and together with Arin, he righted the stool, held Razak on it, and slung the noose around Razak's neck. Once the rope touched his skin, he froze.

"You can't," he begged me. "Zayan, you can't. I'm your brother."

"You say *brother* as though it means something."

Arin moved to my side, instantly chasing away some of the cold trying to fill my veins.

"It does... to me." Emotion clogged Razak's voice. "You were always mine, my whole world. I did all of this *for you* —for us!"

All the times he'd chained me, made me dance until my feet bled, choked me to within a gasp of life, the times he'd cut me, used me, fucked me... And this wasn't even about me.

His father had hung my mother from this tree. And on that day, I'd vowed to do the same to Umair. But he'd died, far away, never knowing me, never facing justice. This was justice.

"Please..." Razak begged. "I don't want to die."

In the past, when I'd hurt people, when I'd killed, I'd felt nothing. But I felt something now, seeing my brother slung up in the hanging tree.

Satisfaction. Peace. Relief.

"Please," he begged. "I love you." Tears fell from his remaining eye, but as he searched each of our faces for a shred of empathy and found none, his tears stopped and his snarl returned. "So be it, but I have killed you too. I have killed you, Zayan! Just like I said I would!"

I placed my boot on the stool. "Dance for me, Razak." And kicked it away.

He dropped, the rope snicked taut, and he danced, choking, writhing. I absorbed the sight of his every twitch into my memory, soaked up his every splutter, and reveled in every single one of his final heartbeats.

Until there he hung, limp. Dead.

And it was done. The story told. The nightmare over. And I was done too.

I let out a sob and dropped to numb knees in the mud.

Arin's arm came around me. He said something about peace, asked about Razak's final words, claiming I was dead too—then Arin noticed the blood on his hands, my blood, and he called my name. *Lark*, he said. Lark, like the bird. And I heard my mother tell me that one day, I'd be as free as a lark. Today was that day.

I closed my eyes. It was finally over.

I was free.

rin

"THERE IS NOTHING TO SMILE ABOUT."

Lark's sleepy smile grew while his eyes remained glassy from sleep. "You're mad." He tried to sit up and winced as his abdominal muscles bunched beneath the bandage.

"Mad?" I asked. "Not at all." I shoved him back down into his pillow, perhaps using a little too much force since he hissed and blinked wide eyes at me. "You didn't think to tell me you were stabbed? It didn't cross your mind?" All right, I was mad—furious, in fact.

He arched an eyebrow. "If I had, you'd have whisked me away, and Razak would have writhed off the hook again." He relented and sighed, staring at the ceiling, likely thinking of his brother swinging from the rope, then peered at me from the corner of his eye. "If I said I was sorry, would you believe it?"

"Some." He believed his actions had been right. But by

Dallin, in those final moments, as Razak swung and I saw the blood on the ground, Lark's blood... It was only by luck we'd been able to bundle him back into the carriage and get him to War's healers before he'd bled out. Razak *had* almost taken him to his death.

"I am, you know? Sorry."

"I know."

"Where are we?" he croaked, looking about the room with its sandstone walls and rippling drapes. "Is this War?"

"Sort of."

"Sort of?"

"It's no longer War. Ogden abdicated and surrendered ruling powers to his elected council. The Court of War changed its name to Bozra, by the vote of its people. The formalities are still being processed. Many meetings, lots of documents. It's a good thing you slept through it. You'd have hated every moment."

"Sounds horrifying. How long was I out?"

"Two days."

"Two days and War is no more? What else did I miss? What of Justice?"

"All the courts are disbanded. There was nothing left of Justice and Love, regardless. And all the courtly origins were problematic, now we know we were destined to fight, forever keeping the people and its crowns apart. You have woken in a new shatterlands, Lark. One with no courts, and no borders. One you helped bring about." There was a great deal more to it than that, but he didn't yet need to know how War's warriors had demanded Ogden step down or they'd revolt. At least the days of giving children to the sand were gone.

"All I did was play my part, and the violin."

He struggled upright, and this time I let him. Stopping him from doing anything he had his heart and mind set on was a pointless task. He'd always find a way. And playing the violin while lying wasn't all he'd done. To get close again to Razak, he'd have done far more. I didn't want to think on the parts of him he must have surrendered to Razak, but none of them would have been good. Perhaps, one day, he'd tell me. But not today.

"You did so much more, and you know it."

He rubbed the base of his missing fingers, as he often did when thinking of Razak. "Just so I know if I have to run, am I likely to be arrested?"

"No. Draven and I explained your behavior had been part of a great plan."

"And Razak's death?" he asked carefully.

"Ogden and Noemi enquired. I told them he'd been dealt with. Nobody has asked for details."

His dark eyes widened. "Did you cut him down?" He swallowed.

"No."

Razak still hung in that tree, and he would until his flesh had rotted from its bones. As he deserved.

"The power's gone." He bowed his head, then lifted his gaze, his eyes full of hope. "I don't feel it. And you shattered the crowns. It's truly over?"

"I think so, yes. There are logistical issues with the collapse of the courts—"

"Such as?"

"They're not your concern right now." I pinched his chin and made him look into my eyes. His lashes fluttered, but those eyes of his were as brilliant as always. When I thought of him writhing moments before we'd destroyed the crowns, it hurt as though that pain were my own. And all the terrible things he'd done— He'd blame himself for it all. If only he'd listen if I told him he was brilliant and that he was my hero and the hero of the shatterlands. If I said the words, he'd laugh and tell me no fool could be a hero.

He lunged and planted a quick kiss on my lips, then hissed and pulled back. "Ouch."

"Rest." I laughed.

"I've been stuck with enough knives over the years to know this was a mere scratch."

Razak had tried to gut him, to ensure they'd die together. "It's rather more than a scratch, my beautiful lie." Standing, I sighed and watched him try to hide how much he hurt. "If you get out of this bed, I'll send your favorite nurse in—dour woman, terribly bossy. She remembers you."

"Gods, not her. She's worse than Razak."

"Then stay. I'll be back later. If I discover you've left this bed, I will make you pay."

"Really?" He fluttered his lashes. "In what way, exactly? So I can look forward to it."

I laughed and left the room, clicking the door closed behind me. He was going to be all right. He'd survived; he was damn good at it. Hopefully now, he'd focus on living.

"How is he?" Draven leaned against a nearby wall and straightened as I approached. War's tropical gardens spread below the terrace, where huge palms swayed, and the people of War—Bozra—bustled about, preparing for a new life without a court. Some said it was without a purpose, but they'd find one. We all would.

"He's awake." I leaned against the low rail and gazed over the gardens, not seeing a damn thing. I saw in my mind how Lark had collapsed after his brother's hanging, how his blood had turned the puddles red. And my heart raced now, like it had then.

Draven puffed out a sigh. "That's good."

"I almost lost him," I whispered.

"He's tougher than he looks."

"That's an act, and you know it."

Draven leaned on the rail beside me, admiring the same view I did and probably seeing none of it "You should take him home, to Love."

"It's not Love anymore, and I have nothing there—no home, no family. Nothing to offer him."

"I doubt you're short on friends, though? You and Lark? You'll find a way. Together, you make a force not to be reckoned with."

Perhaps. But he needed to heal, and so did I. "Do you think he'll come, if I ask him?"

"I think he'd be a fool not to."

I wanted him to come with me, to be with me, but Lark belonged in Pain. The people there needed a leader, someone to unite them, even if it wasn't a court. Pain was in crisis—no council, no court. Its finances were in turmoil, which meant all the shatterlands was on the brink of chaos. The councils from each new district would try and balance our new existence, but there was much work to be done. Change was perhaps inevitable, but overnight change was a shock that could collapse it all. That was what happened when a world was built on lies. The truth shattered it. Now the truth had to rebuild a new world from the wreckage.

Lark wouldn't want to rule; he hated councils, and he couldn't sit still long enough to tolerate long, drawn out discussions. If he didn't want to go back, I'd support him.

I looked over at the warlord and saw my friend, a man who had loved me, and perhaps still did. And I loved him too. "You could come with us?"

He chuckled at the idea. "And be your third wheel? No, my place is here. My son is finally home. He's learning what freedom means, and I have so much I want to teach him. A whole lifetime..."

"I'm glad you found your boy, Draven. He'll make a remarkable man, and you an incredible father."

Draven flicked a lock of hair from my cheek. "Take Lark home, rest, make room for love for a while. You both deserve it."

I caught his hand and gave a gentle squeeze. "Thank you, and I'm sorry for... the almost stabbing you incident. Again. I have some issues with trust."

"It's all right. I should have known not to cross you."

"Yet you did, for Lark."

"He has a way of persuading people to do what he wants."

"I can hear you talking about me." Lark stood propped against the doorframe as though it were the only thing holding him up. He wore a loose shirt and linen trousers, and both hung off him, as though he'd struggled to throw them on.

"Didn't I tell you to stay?"

"I took your threat as a challenge." He limped over, clutching his side, and offered his hand to Draven. "Warlord, in the past, I may not have been kind to you but you always had my respect. I owe you my heartfelt thanks. I couldn't have saved Arin without your help."

"No need." Draven hauled him into a gentle hug. "I'm glad you're all right, Lark."

"I almost killed Draven because of your plotting," I told Lark as they separated.

"Well, I did warn him you'd be displeased."

Draven laughed. "Arin was extremely *displeased*. I almost lost my head a second time. It's only Noemi's arrival that saved me."

"I meant to ask," I wondered aloud. "Why was she coming to your chamber at that hour, Draven?"

He gave a snort. "Not for the reasons you think."

"Uh huh."

"Then those puppy-dog eyes you give her are purely platonic?" Lark added.

"You're both wrong." Draven folded his arms. "She's a friend, and she's not interested. I'll say no more."

Not interested in Draven? Then her tastes surely lay elsewhere, and not in the male form. It was said the people of Justice's first love was always justice itself. Perhaps she had no need for romantic companionship.

"Don't give me that pitying look, Lark. Or do you lament the loss of my cock?"

Lark spluttered a laugh, then clutched his side and wheezed through his pain.

"I'm fine alone," Draven made clear. "I have my son. I'm in a good place. My only regret is how I helped Razak, in those early days."

"Razak got to us all."

We fell silent and gazed over the gardens, thoughts lost in the past.

Lark slumped against the rail, then shifted close and rested his head on my shoulder. "I an beginning to suspect I should have stayed in bed."

I chuckled. He was impossible. "Shall I take you back?"

"Not yet. I'm enjoying the view. And being with you both."

He didn't want to be alone. I knew that feeling well and squeezed his hand. If it was truly over, then we were both free to do as we pleased. He could go anywhere he wished, be with anyone. And while I loved him more than my heart could hold, I also knew he was too bright and brilliant a thing to keep to myself.

"I'll go with you," he said, clearly having heard my earlier concerns. "I can't go back to Pain, not yet. Take me to your home, Arin. I want to see the flowers."

I wrapped my arm around him and tucked him close. "All right."

ark

THE WAGON RATTLED so much that I had to lie under its canopy and try to keep the movement from unpicking the vicious stab wound Razak had left me with. I was a long way from healed, but I'd get there. We all would.

The wagon I rode in wound its way along the roads from War, toward Love, and I watched the fluffy clouds build and felt the air cool, then fill with the light scent of flowers after the rain. *Home*, my heart told me. Since the moment I'd first seen Arin's court and knelt before him as a nineteen-year-old young man, I'd dreamed of being a part of Arin's world, and now that dream was coming true.

We passed people on the roads, returning home with what few belongings they had. With the threat of Razak gone, they'd begun to rebuild without fear.

Noemi came with us. She wanted to help build a new shatterlands, and to do that, she had to see all of it. I suspected she would ask Arin and I to join her in this hopeful venture, but I wasn't ready to do any more for others. Whatever happened next would be for me.

We arrived at the Overlook Inn on a bright, sunlit morning to find the inn teeming with life, inside and out. There appeared to be a traders' market taking place in the street outside. Arin helped me climb down from the wagon, and the smile on his face made everything worth it. He was home, and these were his people.

"Is that you, Lark?"

I turned at a voice I recognized. Ellyn stood outside the inn's front entrance. Her eyes widened, then brimmed with tears.

"Hello, Ellyn."

She set the plates aside on a trader's stall without looking and flung herself into me, wrapping her arms tight. "Ah, easy... I'm fragile."

She pulled back, glowered, and stepped away. "You asshole."

"I missed you too."

"I have a mind to slap you, but as you're all messed up and scruffy, I clearly can't do that, so just understand I'm mad at you, but... I did miss you." She chewed on her bottom lip. "And I'm glad you're all right. Even though you lied—*a lot*. I'm still mad. When you're feeling better, I'll slap you then. Just know you have a lot of making up to do—"

"Hello." Noemi appeared beside me. She'd traded her blue cloak on the road and wore a pair of green pants and a brown waistcoat, with her red hair bundled high. "I'm Noemi, Lark's friend."

"Oh." Ellyn blinked at Noemi, then at me. Her face flushed some more. "Hello." She wiped her hands on her apron and smiled. "I suppose you're Lark's latest conquest?"

I coughed a laugh at Noemi's puzzled face. "Actually, Noemi meet Ellyn, a dear friend, despite hating me for much of our friendship, as you can see."

Noemi smiled politely. "I've learned those who love Lark often dislike him too."

Ellyn gasped. "Did he lie to you too?"

"Well, yes, but not without reason. Many of them justified."

Ellyn swept forward. "Would you like a drink? We have some marvelous lemonade. And you can tell me all about how Lark is a terrible friend."

"I'd like that, but he's really not that terrible."

I spotted Arin watching all this unfold while leaning against the back of our wagon and making no attempt to rescue me. "You two bond over mutual dislike. I'll be with Arin, over here..." They'd already paired off, chatting animatedly.

Arin spun a flower between his fingers, and as soon as I was within reach, he tucked it behind my ear and kissed me on the lips, lighting a spark only for him to stoke it hotter with a hungry look.

He came alive here, under brilliant sunlight, golden hair gleaming. The new beard he'd gained on the road did wonders to rough him up, and frankly, I couldn't wait to drag my nails through it later. There had been no privacy on the road, but now we'd arrived, I hoped we might have some time to reacquaint ourselves with each other. It had been too long. Any longer, and our bodies would become strangers again.

He twined his fingers with mine and nodded at the bustling market. "Isn't this wonderful? They're all coming back."

"An open wound eventually heals itself."

"That's a very *you* observation."

"Well, I am me, so—"

He swooped in and trapped me to the side of the wagon. "I'll rent us a room. I paid the innkeeper handsomely the last time I was here, with the gold you gave me. He'll let us stay as long as we like. We may perhaps even... make a life here? I can wait tables and you can..."

"Pick pockets?" I chuckled. It was a fancy dream, and one I might just make real.

Blue eyes searched my soul. They were bright with happiness and then softened with hope. "Stay with me? *Heal* with me?"

Heal? What did that even mean? "I don't know how," I admitted, feeling foolish. "I've been Pain's prisoner my whole life. I don't even know where to begin healing."

"I do." He smiled and nudged my mouth with his. "I know exactly where to begin. Will you trust me to help you?"

I let his hand go and clasped his whiskered face instead. "I trust you with my heart and soul. But more than even that, I trust you with my love. There's no other in the shatterlands I trust more."

"Gods, I love you," he breathed against my lips. "In all my dreams about us, I never dared dream I'd return home with you."

"Probably because I don't deserve it."

He slammed his mouth over mine and thrust a kiss on me, its touch so devastating it left me breathless and reeling. "You're my hero, Lark," he said.

I almost laughed, but the look in his eyes left no room for humor. He meant it.

"And if you tell me fools can never be heroes, then I'm going to drag you into a room at that inn and worship your every inch, so you'll never doubt yourself or my love again."

"Is that a threat, because it sounds delightful."

"Gods, Lark, you drive me crazy, and I love you for it."

I kissed him in a slow, teasing way. His body thrummed so tightly, it wouldn't take much to tip him over the edge and drive him wild. It felt good, knowing he wanted me with the same desperation I felt for him. As though he were my sun, and I his flower. I needed Arin. Without him, all was lost.

"Arin, Ellyn has offered to— Oh my." Noemi stopped talking.

"Pfft," Ellyn said. "This is nothing. I once discovered Lark in the palace gardens with a very handsome pair of noble-man's legs around his neck and his mouth on... well... you know."

Arin gently broke the kiss and bumped his forehead against mine. "Let's come back to this after I've arranged a room."

I brushed my cheek against his and whispered, "Oh, I'll come for you." Then stepped out of his embrace, leaving him propped against the wagon with his back to us, fighting hard to will his body back under control. Although, the glance he threw over his shoulder suggested he may have lost that fight.

To Ellyn, I said, "If I recall correctly, I invited you to join us in the gardens that night in what would have been a spectacular threesome."

Ellyn rolled her eyes all the way to Noemi. "Lark knows men are far too troublesome to love."

"Oh?" Noemi's blush deepened. "Then your heart finds comfort with women?"

Ellyn fell silent, a minor miracle in itself. "Yes, I... Does yours?"

Draven's words regarding his and Noemi's friendly relationship came back to me, and with the manner in which Ellyn smiled at her, it appeared as though I'd found my next pair to match.

Arin rented a room, organized our scant belongings be brought in later, and key in-hand, he invited me inside, then locked the door behind us. I didn't make it another step. Arin's arms came around me, dragging me into his embrace. He nuzzled my neck from behind. "Tell me what you want, I'll do anything... just so long as it involves loving you."

"Love me then, Love's prince. Tell me a story with your body, and take me away," I said.

"I will." He laced his fingers with mine. "I'll take you to wherever you wish to go. Although, I'm not the most skilled of storytellers here."

"You're a better liar than juggler."

"I've been practicing."

"Hm, then will you show me how you juggle balls?" I asked, and with a smirk, Arin dropped to his knees. Yes, I'd found my happy ever after with the Prince of Flowers, the Prince of Hearts, the Prince of Honey and Sunshine. And perhaps, with his help, I truly did deserve it.

CHAPTER 58

rin

I MADE sure to treat Lark as though he were the most precious thing in all the shatterlands. More precious than any gem or jewel in Pain's vaults, more precious than all the flowers in my meadows. His every shudder rippled through me, and every moan was a delight to hear. I laid him on the bed, ordered him to stay, and undid his clothes, taking off each layer to reveal the prize beneath.

His eyes tracked my every move.

It didn't seem real, he and I, here with no threat hanging over our heads. Love was a heady drug lifting my heart and soul, entwining both with Lark. He laced his right hand with mine, fingers missing, and I drew it to my lips for a kiss. Of all his stories, his poems, and fantasy tales, ours was the most amazing of all.

I straddled his hips, the both of us now naked. He stroked my thighs and skimmed my navel, making my breath catch.

With a laugh, I leaned forward, trapping him under me, and reveled in the feel of hot skin and firm muscles. "Did you ever dream people like us would get a happy ending?"

"No," he admitted. "All my dreams were nightmares, until you showed me hope was a real thing."

I rose up and clutched his erection in my grip, caressing his slick length. His eyes turned to dark pools of lust.

"Are you still mad at me?" he asked, biting his bottom lip.

"Perhaps." I gave his cock a squeeze and he bucked, then laughed breathlessly.

"I was about to ask if you'd punish me, but I see you have that covered."

"Oh, I'm going to punish you, Prince of Storms." I smiled, dropped his cock, climbed off him, gripped his thighs, and shifted him higher, placing his ass onto my lap. His legs spread, bracketed around me, and now I had him where I wanted him. "And you'll beg for more."

Pleasure danced in his beautiful eyes. "Prince of Contradictions."

We were slick enough to begin with, and as I stroked my cock over his hole, his cock jumped, eager for touch. I'd give it—give him—everything and anything he desired. I was wholly his, in every way. I'd die for him, live for him, and as I stroked in and out, lighting a spark to the tinder of passion, I knew he'd do the same for me.

"Marry me," I said, gasping, thrusting. I clasped his cock again, making him arch and moan. His lips parted and his tongue swept over them. "Join with me, be mine, and I'll be yours." I scooped him up, clutched him close, chest to chest, breathless and dizzy. My cock throbbed within him, while his leaked against my abs.

His smile danced. He draped his arms over my shoulders.

"You could have a thousand others, any man or woman you desire."

I brushed my thumb along his bottom lip, then dragged it down and kissed him. Our tongues teased. I nipped and blinked away. "You are worth a thousand of them. More. I want only you. So will you?"

He lifted a shoulder in a weak shrug. "I'll think about it," he lied. He'd already made his choice. The yes was in his eyes, in his body and how he quivered around mine. His body never lied.

"Yes, of course yes, a thousand times yes, fool." He laughed.

I laughed too and kissed him harder, then there was no more laughter, just taste and touch, tremors and hisses, until we moved as one, colliding in love. I was his fool, and he my prince, and nothing had ever been more real in my life than this moment.

This true love.

CHAPTER 59

$\mathcal{L}$ark

THAT NIGHT, the inn overflowed with customers. Ellyn worked the tables, with Noemi not-so-discreetly watching her. She made sure to top our drinks up, and we learned of how the inn had helped keep the town alive, and word had spread that not all was lost in Love. Even before Razak's defeat, Love's people had begun to return. There were a few whispers too, of how Prince Arin had returned, although if he had, he surely couldn't look anything like the bearded, golden-haired, scruffy traveler I couldn't tear my gaze from.

"Arin." Ellyn reappeared with a bag and handed it out to Arin. "I'd have had it earlier but there were a few last adjustments. I hope it's right."

"Thank you." He took the bag, its contents bulky enough to take up our small table. "I'm sure it's perfect."

Ellyn's gaze caught mine in a peculiar way before she went

back to working tables. The pair of them had conspired without my knowing.

Arin set the bag down against his leg and went back to discussing how to form a council with Noemi, and how, as an ambassador for peace, she might travel each realm, helping unite them.

And I was supposed to *not* ask about the bag?

I pretended to listen to Noemi's fascinating insights on fair governing and snuck a few glances at the bag. We hadn't been in town a day, so whatever was in that bag had been organized long before we'd arrived.

"It's killing you, isn't it?" Arin said, catching me trying to peer inside it.

"I have no idea what you mean."

"Just ask."

I laughed. "I don't care what's in the bag."

"Oh, then you don't want it?"

"No, it's none of my business."

"It's not as though it's been crafted especially for you, taking many weeks. Since you woke up in War, in fact. I sent a rider ahead. Are you sure you're not interested?"

"Weeks?" It *was* killing me.

Arin laughed and handed over the bag. "For you, my love."

My love. Noemi watched, smiling, and then Ellyn made an appearance, all flustered and messy but her eyes alight with glee. If I didn't open the bag soon, she'd blurt out its secret.

I yanked open the drawstring top to find the most glorious black and purple violin resting inside.

"Draven said your eyes lit up when he had one made for you in War," Arin explained.

I'd lost Draven's violin when Razak had smashed it, and it had been a marvelous instrument, but I could already tell this one was special. Because Arin had commissioned it. Its body was a glossy black with dark purple highlights. I freed it from its bag, bringing it into the light, and balanced it in both hands. It was the perfect weight—heavy enough to hint at a sturdy quality, but light enough to dance with me.

"It's yours," Arin said. "You deserve so much more. Maybe one day you'll believe me?"

My heart galloped. Tears gathered in my eyes, but I blinked those away before anyone noticed. "Perhaps." I tucked the violin under my chin and plucked a few notes; the sound was true and fine, perfectly tuned. This violin and I were going to get along. I picked up the bow and trilled a few notes, filling the inn with music. Yes, this would do nicely.

Arin and Noemi gazed over the table, as though expecting more. I'd collected a few observers nearby too. I couldn't play here, could I? The inn was packed, wall to wall, and I ached from our journey and the wound in my middle. But the music called to me, and as the instrument was already in my hand... What effort was a little tune?

The last time I'd played, I'd walked through the streets of Pain and woken a people from their slumbering agony. I'd played for them. I always played for others, or for coin. But now, with Arin's gift, I played for me.

Bow to strings, I set the music free. It flowed through me and the violin, into the hearts and minds of everyone here. Already bespelled, I stood and played as though I were alone, for the love of it and nothing else, nobody else. I played a light, joyous, uplifting tune—lighter and brighter than any I'd played before. And I played it for me.

And then, when it ended, I stood breathless, stunned back into a room full of people, all staring. For a little while, I'd been somewhere else, I'd been free. Arin had given this to me. Somehow, after so much pain and strife, against all the odds and despite my best efforts to sabotage us, Arin remained, and impossibly, so did his love.

He stood and clapped. "For Lark!" Others joined him—until the whole inn roared with applause. For Lark, for me, the boy who played for coin, and for hope.

Arin wiped the tears from his face, then swooped in and wiped away tears I hadn't known I'd cried. "Now do you see? You deserve to be happy, Lark."

I crushed him close and buried my wet face against his neck. Perhaps, in our story, the villain did get a happy ending after all?

Or, perhaps, I'd never been the villain of this story.

Maybe the fool had always been the hero.

THERE ONCE WAS A COURT JESTER,
Whose heart was light and gay,
He made the kingdom laugh and smile,
With every trick and play.

BUT AS HE danced and sang one day,
He saw the Prince of Love,
And in an instant, his heart did stop,
As though touched by Dallin above.

FOR THOUGH THE jester played his part,
And kept the court in mirth,
His heart was captured by the prince,
Who ruled all hearts on earth.

. . .

HE DREAMED of holding hands with him,
    And sharing breathless sparks,
    Of feeling love's sweet caress,
    And soaring with the larks.

BUT HOW COULD SUCH a thing be real,
    When he was just a clown,
    And the prince, so regal and refined,
    Was higher in renown?

HE TRIED to hide his love away,
    And keep it locked inside,
    But every time he saw the prince,
    His heartbeats did collide.

AND THEN ONE DAY, the prince came close,
    And whispered in his ear,
    "My treasured jester, you are my heart,
    And I've forever loved you, dear."

AND WITH THOSE WORDS, the jester knew,
    That all his dreams came true,
    For he had found his true love,
    And his heart was fixed anew.

AND SO THEY danced beneath the moon,
    And laughed the night away,
    For love had conquered all their fears,

And made them free to play.

AND EVERY TIME the jester joked,
He'd look to Prince Arin,
And know that they would dance forever,
To the music of his violin.

~ Lark

If you enjoyed Lark and Arin's adventure, please leave a review for the series.

If you want more epic gay fantasy filled with anti-heroes, and all the angst you didn't know you needed, try the Prince's Assassin series. Simply search for Ariana Nash at your favorite book store.

ABOUT THE AUTHOR

Born to wolves, Ariana Nash only ventures from the Cornish moors when the moon is fat and the night alive with myths and legends. She captures those myths in glass jars and returning home, weaves them into stories filled with forbidden desires, fantasy realms, and wicked delights.

Sign up to her newsletter here: https://www.subscribepage.com/silk-steel

Printed in Great Britain
by Amazon